CAUGHT IN THE MIDDLE

a romantic suspense

CAUGHT IN THE MIDDLE

CASSIE M. SHIELS

COVENANT

To Great Aunt Ina Rae, who dropped off a box of romantic suspense books for me to read and opened my eyes to the genre.

Cover image: *Romantic City Walk - A couple walking hand-in-hand in an urban setting* - AI Generated, by Arthur ©stock.adobe.com

Cover design by Julie Olson

Published by Covenant Communications, Inc.
American Fork, Utah

Library of Congress Cataloging-in-Publication Data

Name: Cassie Shiels
Title: Caught in the Middle / Cassie Shiels
Description: American Fork, UT : Covenant Communications, Inc. [2025]
Identifiers: 2024939253 | 978-1-52442-799-3
LC record available at https://lccn.loc.gov/2024939253

Printed in the United States of America
First Printing: May 2025

31 30 29 28 27 26 25 10 9 8 7 6 5 4 3 2 1

ACKNOWLEDGMENTS

THERE ARE SO MANY PEOPLE who believed in me and this book, even in times when I doubted I could write such a story. This was one of those books where a small spark of an idea started the hope, but I felt like I lacked the know-how. I braved up, though, and attempted it, and after that first draft, I knew I had something special, and at the same time, I knew I had written the whole thing wrong. So, I put it away and practiced writing other stories until I felt like I had enough skill to try writing it again. During that time, my family wouldn't let me forget this story and how much I wanted to write it. Thank you for not giving up on me and this dream. I want to thank all of you who said I could do it.

Special thanks to my mom, Alice Miller, who let me read an early draft to her during a car ride and encouraged me to keep writing it because she knew it was worth it. To my dad, who always encouraged me and is excited about my writing dreams. To my brother Joseph Miller, who kept asking about this book even when I put it on the shelf to perhaps one day write. I promised him I'd finish it, and I'm glad I could keep that promise. To my other brothers, Jeremy and John, who happily talked to me about aspects of this book. To my sisters, Chalice and Clarissa, who never doubted me and happily listened to my story's ups and downs. To my husband, John, who gave me the writing time when I needed it and who puts up with me and the stories in my head. To my kids, who are just as excited about my stories as I am and who sit down to listen to me read a paragraph or two or more or tell me if something sounds okay. You all are a part of this dream come true.

I'd like to express my gratitude to Paige Edwards for being the best beta reader and accountability partner. I couldn't have done this without her and her encouragement. Thanks for Morgan Wilson for your editing skills. Thanks also to Kiri Patterson for your support and positivity. The same goes for Janelle Amundsen, who let me do daily check-ins while I was rewriting. You all are the best writing friends.

Special thanks to Kami Hancock, who encouraged me to submit this book to Covenant after I got to show her the first chapter at a writing conference.

I want to thank Covenant for choosing to publish this book and letting it be part of your book family. I have dreamed for a long time of being one of your authors and having one of my stories be part of your list of published books. This truly is a dream that has come true, and it's all because of you. Thanks to your art department for the amazing cover, the publishing department for all of their hard work, and the editing department who made this book shine.

Thanks to my wonderful editor, Ashley Gebert, who knows the right questions to ask to improve my book even more. I appreciate your efforts. I couldn't have done this without the whole team at Covenant, who worked with my book during the editing and publishing process. You all are the best!

Lastly, I want to thank my amazing readers. Thank you for choosing my book and spending time with Annie, Sam, Jeremy, and my favorite crew of criminals.

CHAPTER 1

Annie bolted down the busy city street. Her left hand clutched her purse strap while her right curled around her keychain-size pepper spray. She hoped never to wield her bottle, but the city miscreants might force her hand at any time.

Before arriving in the city, she imagined the hustle and bustle wouldn't affect her, but she was wrong. The longer she lived in LA, the more differences she noted from her hometown in rural Idaho.

A car horn honked, and her heart leaped into her throat like a pinball launched into a new game. Pinpricks of adrenaline raced up her arms, and she pressed a hand to her pounding heart. More cars zoomed past, causing the hot air to move in an artificial wind.

The Walk sign glowed brightly on the opposite side of the street. She focused on the luminous figure of a person on the Walk sign while ignoring the danger rushing around her. Biting her lip, she wrapped her fingers tighter around the pepper spray just for something to hold onto and prayed no one ran the red light.

A crosswalk was something ordinary—simple white paint applied on a blacktop road. At least to everyone else, but not to Annie. A crosswalk had become an unreliable bridge between life and death. Before moving to Los Angeles, she never worried about busy streets.

With more than one double look left and right, she sucked in a deep breath and darted across the street. On the other side, she lurched to a stop and leaned against the red brick building on the corner. Relief filled her heaving chest. The uneven gruff texture scuffed the skin under her fingers and grounded her while her heartbeat slowed to a regular pace. Her long blonde hair curtained her face. Hopefully, no onlookers had noticed her near panic. Once she calmed, she pushed her hair back and turned to face the next part of her excursion.

The restaurant at the end of the street caught her eye, and she straightened. A low "Oh" escaped her lips when she saw the outside dining area. One day she'd work in a place like this. A flowy linen canopy wove in and out of twisted steel to create a spectacular roof. Swinging light bulbs interlaced between the fabric added a cheery twinkle. The lights reminded her of the starry sky at home. Annie had spent countless summer nights outside in Idaho, wrapped in her granny's old quilts while she enjoyed the sky.

Shaking off the nostalgia, Annie quickened her pace down the sidewalk. If she kept this "meeting" short, she could return to her apartment before darkness overtook the sky. The enormous city made nighttime feel nefarious.

Annie straightened her simple button-down shirt and approached the chest-high, wrought-iron fence that surrounded the outside eating area. White rock and minuscule desert plants encompassed the bottom of the wall. Crisp, white linen covered the tables and fluttered in the breeze. Somehow that only added to the restaurant's allure. She eyed the guests enjoying dinner and hoped she could avoid searching inside for Dillan, her ex-boyfriend.

Dillan waved lazily from the center of the tables under the canopy. His blond hair stood in short, gelled spikes, and he wore a plain, black hoodie. His outfit was not appropriate for a restaurant of this caliber; he'd never paid much attention to things like proper apparel. Annie let a slow breath escape her lips.

This was his final second chance.

With the best forced smile she could summon, she made her way to the metal gate in the fence. "Lord, help me stay strong," she pleaded as she wound her way through the tables to Dillan.

"You made it!" Dillan leaned back in his chair, putting his hands behind his head. His eyes indicated she should pull out the chair across from him.

"I said I'd come." She lowered herself into the soft chair, unsure if he thought she was irresponsible.

"That's one thing I like about you, Annie-Franny. You're always true to your promises." He smiled again, and for a moment, Annie caught a brief glimpse of her best guy friend since the ninth grade. Annie cautiously smiled back. He'd also broken her heart more than once. She'd hear him out as agreed, for old time's sake. As he said, he could trust *her* word.

"I ordered us some steak fries as an appetizer while I waited. I hope you don't mind, but I am starving." He looked around to see if his order of fries would arrive from that simple statement. When they didn't appear, his gaze moved to the basket with rolls in the center of the table.

"Steak fries sound fantastic." She checked her watch before she put her elbows on the table and rested her chin on her hands. "I'm here, so what did you desperately need to discuss with me in person?"

Dillan shuffled his feet under the table and leaned closer, an excited luster in his eyes. "Annie, I've meant to ask you something for a while now."

Her breath stilled while her heart hammered hard against her ribs. Oh, no. This opening to a conversation never concluded well. Last time, he'd convinced her to sell alarm systems out of state. The first time, he'd proposed, an experience she'd rather avoid repeating at all costs.

"Annie Grey." He leaned closer, his smile spreading broader, and his dimple sprouted on his cheek. "I know things have been . . . challenging for us since we arrived here this summer."

That was a significant understatement. After spending months convincing her to come with him this year and sell alarm systems, he'd abandoned her. Instead of showing her the ropes and sharing tips from his two years of experience, he'd ignored her. He spent all his time with guys who acted like they belonged behind bars.

Dillan reached across the table, but Annie put her hands on the edges of her chair. Perhaps he'd take that as a sign. Instead, he smirked. "You were my best friend in high school and my girlfriend the year we graduated. I know I can trust you. You never lied or ratted on me when I made mistakes, and you risked everything when you came to work in California. I never thought you'd leave your granny's house." His nose wrinkled as if he caught a sudden whiff of something rancid.

Annie didn't appreciate the direction of this conversation. She shouldn't have agreed to meet him tonight.

"I can see my influence paid off." He winked and chuckled to himself as if he were laughing at an inside joke. Dillan's hand darted forward, and he tucked a strand of Annie's light-blonde hair behind her ear. In the movies, girls would sigh at such a moment.

She waited for that reaction. It didn't come. All she did was shudder at his touch. Annie pushed her chair back. "Dillan, please, it's . . ."

"Wait," he said, again attempting to grab her hands. "I need to say this first."

She slumped in her chair but waited for him to spit it out. The sooner he talked, the faster she could leave.

"Annie, it's because I trust you that I want to ask you something important." He looked over his shoulder, checking that no one could overhear them.

Her pulse quickened in her wrists without her permission. Good gravy. She didn't want this. She'd already lived through refusing his proposal once.

His gaze shifted to the nearest tables before he leaned even closer. "I wanted to ask if . . . if you'll come with me and act as my lookout tonight." He smiled like he'd offered her the whole world on a diamond-encrusted platter.

Annie stared at him, unblinking. Every word he said ran through her head, twisting and turning until she realized precisely what he'd meant. "Y-your lookout?" She blundered the words so badly they hardly sounded like words.

"Yeah." He brightened even more, pulled off a hunk of roll, and buttered it as if he had no idea what had gone on in her head. He tossed the bit of roll into his mouth with such relaxed ease that Annie could hardly believe it. How dare he ask her to become part of his illegal crew?

He must have read her expression, because he set down his roll and dusted the crumbs off his fingers. "Only this once, Annie-Franny, I promise. Arnold stumbled onto a phenomenal opportunity that was too good to be true. If we pull this off, baby, it could set us up for life."

Dillan leaned forward, his hands wide as if imagining something incredible. "Think about it. Everything you've ever wanted will be yours." His eyes gleamed like a dog staring at a Thanksgiving turkey. "I'm serious; it's that good. Pull out your phone and put whatever you want in your Amazon cart. We will achieve all our dreams in one night." His greedy look faded, and a bit of fire burned in his eyes instead. "You'll see after this score that I'm worth it, and I'll show you what our new life will look like together. That's right—I'm asking you to take me back, give me another chance, and trust me as much as I depend on you. After we do this job together, you can forget about saving for dumb culinary school. Who cares about all the hogwash of working a regular nine-to-five job? We're going straight to stinking rich."

Annie sunk deeper into her chair. Her chest felt like it did when she walked outside on a negative-eight-degree winter morning and breathed in the frigid air too deeply. But somehow, this felt worse . . . so much worse. She shouldn't have come here tonight.

"You want me to commit a crime?" she whispered, her hands wadding up the corner of the tablecloth into a snarled ball.

He shook his head. "You're looking at it all wrong. It's not exactly a crime. Think of it more as a favor for a friend. Our target won't miss what we're taking. Believe me; they don't remember everything they own. We'll probably nick a few more things as we go. They won't realize anything is missing, at least not for a looong time." He pumped his fist into the air. A warning bell rang through her mind, and she trembled. Her ex-boyfriend had morphed into a hardened criminal.

Dillan picked up his roll and slathered on more butter. "Besides, as the lookout, you're hardly involved. You're a minuscule part of the team. My crew and I will handle the challenging aspects of our plan."

Hardly involved . . . but still entwined . . . in a crime.

Annie scrutinized him munching cheerfully on his dinner roll as if he hadn't said the most ludicrous thing ever. It was like he lost all his faith in God, in humanity, in what most people called real life. His bright-hazel eyes used to hold comfort and friendship. Now, they held something bleak, like an undetectable disease. He wasn't the man she had known. He'd changed over the past few years. A pang of hurt grew in her chest until it consumed her.

She swallowed hard and looked away from him. Where had her charming Idaho boy gone? It was good she hadn't agreed to marry him the summer after they graduated high school. If she had, she would have fallen victim to whatever pestilence lurked within him.

She counted to three to get up her nerve, forced back her chair, stood, and looped her purse over her shoulder. "I can't help you."

"You can't?" His eyes darkened instantly, and all friendliness evaporated.

She swallowed hard but backed up another step. "I refuse to help you." She spun on her heel and darted away from the table to the small gate in the surrounding fence.

"What do you mean you won't help?" he shouted after her, his voice hard and ugly.

Tears pricked at her eyes, but she didn't slow down. She'd given up everything for this summer job that Dillan swore would make her enough money to pay for admission to culinary school. She'd left her small-town home, everything she knew, and abandoned her granny. The way things had gone, she didn't have enough money saved for even the tiny technical college in Idaho Falls, let alone a school with a cooking degree. Her hopes for a better future had evaporated in the summer heat because of him.

A new emotion rose inside her chest. It was red, grisly, and vicious, and it gave her speed. Annie raced down the sidewalk, the constant LA traffic a zooming, honking blur while she ran. The noises that caused her anxiety were out of focus, and she dashed forward with a determined step she hardly recognized.

"Annie, wait up," Dillan called from behind her, a sharp edge to his voice.

He'd followed her.

Darn.

She picked up her speed. "No, Dillan. I'm saying no!"

Nothing but the red hand on the Don't Walk sign by the crosswalk could have slowed her down. Annie halted, panting from her run, and glared at the signal that stopped her escape.

"Come on, Annie. This is not a big deal." Dillan huffed, his breath coming out in gasps from chasing her. He grabbed her hand.

She yanked it out of his reach, stuffed it into her purse, and pulled out her tiny can of pepper spray. She waved it like she held a bomb with a dead man's switch.

He rolled his eyes. "We both know you aren't going to use that. What I need you to do is so simple that a child could do it. You stand where we tell you, keep an eye out, and you make a fifth of the cut. It's effortless money. I don't understand why you'd refuse."

He didn't understand. Wow, he'd changed even more than she thought. They'd grown up together. She knew the Christian values that they were both raised with. "I refuse, Dillan, because I don't want to sell my soul. I'm not going to do something wrong because you want me to. God wouldn't like it, and I don't like it. Get that through your head."

He waved her comment away. "God doesn't care what we do."

Annie's jaw fell open. "He does too."

Dillan sneered. "You're outside of His reach, darlin'."

"How could you say that?" Annie snapped.

Dillan rolled his eyes. "Doesn't matter. I don't have time to argue with you. Look, you obviously have a problem with my plan, so don't think of this as a crime. Reframe it, and we won't have an issue." He put his thumbs and pointer fingers together to make a rectangle in front of her face.

Annie glanced up at his dark eyes that used to look so bright. A new pang of hurt surged through her to the center of her chest. "I'm sorry, but you can't reframe a selfish crime into something good."

He made a growling sound and clenched his fists. "It's not selfish if it's my destiny. I refuse to return to my friends with the news that I informed you about our plan and that you declined to assist us. I assured them you'd agree to help. I bet my life on it."

"Why would you do that?" How dare he try to guilt-trip her. "You know how I felt when you got arrested last year. You know how much I detest what you're doing here in LA. Instead of us selling alarm systems together, as you promised, you returned to illegal activities. You're a criminal. You've chosen a different path, a path I will not walk with you."

A warm feeling filled her chest. She'd made the right choice to walk away, and nothing he said would change that for her, not even their past relationship.

Dillan scoffed. "You won't survive long without me."

Annie swallowed hard. That wasn't true. She'd already lasted two months without him. "Leave me alone, Dillan Collins. I don't want what you're offering. I will finish my time here and then return home to Granny and beg her forgiveness for ignoring her advice."

The crosswalk sign finally turned bright white with the Walk signal. Annie pivoted to race across, but he grasped her hand. "Forget your qualms; do something spontaneous for once in your life."

"I'm sorry." She yanked, but he didn't release her. His grip caused her finger bones to bash painfully together.

"I'm not taking no for an answer," he said, his voice severe.

"Yes, you are." She aimed the pepper spray and hit the button on pure instinct. The jet hit Dillan right in the face. With a howl of pain, he let go of her arm.

She didn't wait to see what happened and darted across the street. Heart pounding, she ran as fast as she could, dodging people and praying for the next crosswalks to have Walk signals. Rushing into her apartment building, she avoided the elevator and hurried up the stairs to the second floor. Her fingers shook as she pulled out her silver key and rammed it into the lock before she scooted inside and secured her door tight. Breathing hard, she fell on her knees and clutched her sides.

"Lord, don't let him come after me," she prayed. Once she caught her breath, she leaned against the door and fought the tears building in her eyes.

She should call the police. Annie twirled her cheap phone around in her fingers. Dillan and his friends could hurt someone. They were planning to do something illegal. She pressed her thumbprint to the bottom of her phone and unlocked it but paused before she hit the phone app. What could she tell the police anyway? Dillan and his friends wanted to rob someone, but she didn't know who, what they wanted, or how the police could find Dillan. All she could give the police was a tip that they wanted to rob someone and get rich. That wasn't enough for them to go on.

Frustrated, she tossed her phone on the couch and trudged into the kitchen. Luckily, she'd left a tiny bit of mint chocolate chip ice cream in the freezer, and tonight she'd finish it. With no AC, Annie pushed her peeling windows halfway open to let in some air. Drinking in the slight breeze, she slumped on her love seat that barely fit in her petite living room.

She turned on her thrift-store television to the cooking channel. Free cable was the only perk to this tiny place. Picking up her spoon and the carton of ice cream, she settled in for the night. It might take several episodes, but she hoped to forget all about Dillan and his plan.

CHAPTER 2

Bang!

Annie's eyelids flew open, and her heartbeat raced at full throttle. Another bang sounded through the darkness, and she jumped. Her ears strained. Her body tensed. Loud laughter followed, proving the noise that woke her was nothing distressing. Her neighbor's car doors slammed again, explaining the first two bangs. She sucked in a few deep breaths and forced her heart to relax. She still wasn't used to all the nighttime noise.

Annie picked up her empty ice cream container and spoon from the floor, stretched, and turned off the TV quietly playing her cooking shows. With a long yawn, she checked the clock on the kitchen oven. 1:47 a.m. Groaning, she walked through her motorhome-sized kitchen and into her tiny bedroom. Her eyes darted to her lumpy thrift-store mattress. It wasn't much more comfortable than the small couch.

Annie pulled on a comfy oversized gray T-shirt and light-pink shorts. She crawled under her covers but tossed and turned for the next quarter of an hour. Balling her thin blanket on her stomach, she turned to face the window, begging for a breeze. Unfortunately, the night air didn't feel like giving her a break from the heat.

Her eyes found the photo of Granny, Pa, and herself sitting on the edge of the Snake River with their toes in the swirling water. "Help her forgive me, Lord," Annie prayed. Granny loved her enough to forgive her . . . right? With only four weeks left to work summer sales, Annie hoped she could make this whole mess of a job worth it. She would have left California already if she hadn't needed every penny to go home.

Stupid Dillan and his ridiculous plan. She rolled over and stared at the dark ceiling. Granny would tell her this mistake was part of God's plan somehow, though right now Annie didn't understand why. Her dreams of attending culinary school weren't any closer. Annie rolled over and looked out the small window at the lights across the street. Most of her friends were already halfway through college, and she hadn't even started her education. Dillan had sold her on this job, claiming that she'd make more money in four months than working at the crummy diner as she'd done for the last two years since graduating high school.

Guilt wormed its way around her stomach. She'd chosen not to call the cops on Dillan, but perhaps she chose wrong. Her eyes flicked to look at the clock—2:02 a.m. She may never know. Groaning, she fidgeted in bed for a minute or two more but couldn't get comfortable. She grumbled, tossed her blanket aside, and stomped back into the kitchen.

With a yawn, she opened the fridge and found the empty milk carton she'd unceremoniously shoved inside yesterday morning. She unscrewed the lid and peeked inside. There were a few droplets left in the bottom of the carton. Not enough to warm up in the microwave.

Darn.

Sleep would continue to elude her without a warm cup of cinnamon milk. A squeak from the hallway made her pause. She stood still and forced her ears to listen for the distinctive noise. Only silence pounded against her eardrums. Had she imagined the sound?

Another squeak followed the first. Her gaze slid slowly toward the direction of the noise. She recognized those creaks; they came from the floorboards outside her front door. Her breath halted in a tight wad in her throat. She fumbled for some kind of weapon and came up with her bright-pink spatula.

What would that do to anyone?

With a huff, she dropped it and picked up her frying pan. She listened for the telltale third squeak. If it came, whoever crept through the hallway would end up directly outside her front door.

The creaking-board sound could have come from one of her neighbors . . . attempting not to rouse anyone. A considerable number of them got in late. No burglar would dare break in now . . . not that she had anything for them to steal. She didn't live in a high-class neighborhood. If anyone did break in, they'd take one look around before rushing out, yelling that they'd wasted their time.

Her heart rammed against her ribs when the distinct third squeak came. It sounded more like a foghorn to her attuned ears. The doorknob wiggled. She blinked. It looked still. Had she imagined it? She scrutinized the bronze, round knob, her eyes never straying from it. She'd locked it appropriately—she always did—but she itched to run forward and double-check it.

A knock sounded on her front door. Annie jumped and slammed her knee into the kitchen cupboards. Clenching her teeth, she bit back a yelp at the same time her phone rang. She picked up and saw Dillan's name and photo. "Hello?" she said, rubbing her knee, her eyes still on her front door. She didn't trust him, but if anyone with a diabolical nature waited on the other side of the door, at least she could tell someone.

"Annie, I'm outside your door. We need to talk right now."

Seriously?!

Massaging her knee, she leaned against the counter. The fear dissipated. Of course her ex-boyfriend walked calculated through the halls like a practiced thief.

"It's two in the morning, Dillan, and I recall I said to leave me alone. I don't want to get caught up in your illegal escapades."

He snorted. "Escapades? Nice. Listen, I need a place to hide until . . . something blows over."

Annie closed her eyes and prayed she had enough patience for this encounter. "Dillan, if you got in trouble with your little caper, you must go to the police. If you're here trying to hide from the cops, I refuse to harbor a fugitive."

His voice took on a pleading tone. "The cops aren't on my trail . . . someone else is. Come on, Annie. I need your help. I'll leave before you return home from work, I swear."

Annie knew how much his promises were worth—nothing. She'd fallen for that tactic more than once. He obviously thought she'd crack and bend to his wishes and let him back into her life. Not this time, Dillan Collins. She would not fold. She would not willingly open her door for him. The sooner he accepted that, the better.

"I'm sorry. I can't help you."

He knocked sharply on the door. "I'm desperate. Help me one last time, and I'll go, and you'll never hear from me again."

Annie clutched her frying pan tighter, her hands shaking. "I'm not dumb enough to fall for that line. I'm sorry that you're in trouble. If you need a hideout, go to the cops. I am certain they'd love to help you with your situation. Leave now, or I'll call them myself."

She hit End on her phone and held her breath. Would he go? She held firm this time, but she didn't know how long she could continue to do so. If he kept chipping away at her resolve, would she falter? Could she keep saying no, repeatedly, forever? She had cared a lot about him a long time ago.

"Stop acting so stubborn. I helped you when you needed it in high school," he shouted, his voice coming through her thin front door. "I taught you how to drive when your granny couldn't stomach it. I'm the one who saved your heinie from that hole in the wall you dared to call a restaurant."

Annie muttered to herself and picked up her phone. It rang only once before he answered. "Changed your mind?" he asked, his voice all chipper again.

Faker.

Which emotion was the real one? None. "Dillan, you broke my heart. You lost my trust when you deceived me. I'm sorry. I can't let you keep harming me because you helped me in the past."

"Who hurt who? You pepper-sprayed me in the face tonight," he shouted, a fist pounding on her door. "That messed with my vision on the job. You could have gotten me killed."

Annie's whole body shuddered, but she forced a shaky breath through her lips and attempted to calm her shaking limbs. "That should have sent a clear message to you that our friendship is over."

He barked one loud laugh. "I seriously doubt that, Annie-Franny. You need me." With that, he hung up.

Straining her ears, she listened for the three squeaks on the floorboards that would signal he'd left. "One," she counted, tapping her fingers against her arm.

"Two." At least he moved away from her door.

"Three."

Wait. Dillan hadn't agreed with her that their friendship was over. He hadn't said he'd back off. He hadn't stated anything about leaving at all. A prickling sensation crawled its way up her arms. All three squeaks came in quick succession, and with a loud bang, her door burst open, wood splinters flying in every direction.

On instinct, Annie dove to the kitchen floor; her frying pan crashed to the ground with an earsplitting clang.

"Sorry, Annie, I can't accept no for an answer, not after you ditched my crew and me."

Annie looked up from the floor. Dillan closed her broken door and slid her cheap couch in front of it. A shiver ran up her arms and settled in her chest. "What . . . what do you mean?" she asked, getting to her feet, her hands empty. She held no weapon this time to defend herself, and he'd blocked the only entrance or exit.

"I mean that I promised them a lookout. You know what happened because you refused to help me? We got caught." He stuffed his hands in his oversized vest pockets and chucked handfuls of items in the corner of the living room.

Wrappers, crumpled-up paper, a couple of thumb drives, a ring of keys, and a banana peel bounced off the wall and landed behind her tiny TV. He extracted from the same pockets a crumpled paper with what looked like a floor plan for an expensive house.

"You see this?" He slammed it on the counter. "We hit this place last night to get some lame information for a rich guy who refused to pay up when we couldn't get it, and you know what? This job wasn't my big blue-whale-sized score like Arnold claimed. The job wasn't worth it." With a swing, he slapped the page off her counter, and it fluttered to the floor. "We didn't even breach the house." His voice cracked before he cleared it and straightened up. "Now we're all destined to die, including you."

Annie gasped. "Why? I wasn't a part of this. I said no. I didn't go."

"You knew our plans, and since I promised my crew you'd help, I don't think the hitman cares if you ditched us." He jabbed his finger in the direction of the house plans.

Annie shook her head. This wasn't happening. "Hitman? I don't want this trouble. Dillan, you have to inform the police." She pointed to her blocked door.

He rolled his eyes. "I can't go to the police. They won't understand. I'm a suspect in more than one of their investigations. I can't walk in and tell them I attempted to rob a mansion last night. They'd lock me up before I got another word out of my mouth."

"Lord, help us." Annie rubbed her temples.

"Sure, pray," Dillan said, swiping a cookie off her counter. "It's not going to help."

"It might," Annie said quietly.

With a mighty swallow, he choked down the cookie. "Got any milk?"

"No."

He shook his head and went to pick up the house plans from the floor.

Annie rubbed her arms. "Why did you do it? Why take the risk?"

A wicked grin spread across his face. With the house plans in hand, he straightened up and puffed out his chest. "The thrill." He shrugged. "There's more opportunity in thieving. A glass ceiling does not squash us. We're free to do what we want. You wouldn't understand." He waved his hand as if dismissing her. "Listen, there is a small chance you're not in danger. Lloyd and his men might not know where you live, so I chose to hide here. You were only a random name on a piece of paper. He saw my face. I'm the one who has to clear out of here. He might not find you if you lay low."

Annie didn't know how to respond, so she changed the subject. "What did you try to take?"

A twisted smile spread across his face. "I told you I was going to steal my future, our dreams, a way to set us up good and pretty." He rolled his eyes. "Not lame info."

Annie curled her fingers around the bottom of her T-shirt. "Dillan, there is never going to be an *us*. I don't think we even believe in the same things anymore."

"You're wrong," he scoffed.

A tiny red dot appeared on his shoulder. It slowly moved down toward his chest. Annie's heart rate shot up, and she turned to her living room window. Her blinds were only halfway down to allow the breeze to penetrate her room. Someone could easily see inside.

"Dillan." Her eyes grew wide as she realized what that dot might mean.

His hands curled into fists. "Forget it. It's better if you don't know what you could have had. I have to hide for the next few hours before I hit LAX. I'm staying here."

"Dillan!" Annie shouted, pointing to the tiny red dot that settled on the center of his chest. "Look out."

Dillan looked down. He sucked in a sharp breath, his eyes widened, and he took a single step forward. Then Dillan sputtered and stumbled toward her; a circle of red blossomed on his hoodie. His knees buckled a couple of feet from her, and he fell face down. No bang or crack accompanied the shot.

Annie jumped back, her eyes widened, her mouth open in a silent scream, and every muscle in her body seized up. Her heart beat so erratically it drowned out all other noise. Blinking rapidly, she shook her head. No, she must have imagined it. Though her imagination had never conjured up something so horrible before.

The small red dot moved across the floor. On instinct, Annie dropped to her stomach behind the counter. She counted to five to calm her nerves before she peeked. Dillan was still unmoving, but the dot zigzagged across the floor as if searching for her. Arms shaking, she army crawled into her bedroom. Her ragged breath moved through her chattering teeth. Her ears strained for sounds.

There were none.

Call 911, she thought over and over. She crawled to her bedside table for her phone, but it wasn't there. *911*, she thought. She had to call 911.

CHAPTER 3

Annie wanted nothing more than to curl into the fetal position and sob. Dillan had claimed there was a hitman after them. Then he'd gotten shot. She couldn't roll over and let them shoot her too. "911," she said under her breath, her eyes searching for her phone. She saw it on the chair by her bedroom window. Her eyes darted to the window; this, too, she'd left slightly ajar to let in some air. She didn't dare approach it.

What if the red dot found her?

Voices carried through her thin walls. Annie flinched at the unmistakable sound of her front door opening and the scrape of a couch shoved out of the way. Her hand clutched at her chest. She tapped her bedroom door with her toe, closing it the last few inches. She reached up and pushed the knob in to lock it. *Don't make a sound*, she thought, clasping her hand over her mouth to muffle her breathing.

"Looks like you shot Dillan," a man with a gruff voice said. "What about the girl?"

Annie clenched her teeth, her breath coming in short huffs. *Don't faint. Don't faint,* she thought to herself. With trembling arms, she crawled to the chair and grabbed her phone. She had to call 911 immediately.

Her phone was off. Annie pushed the power button. She grabbed her light-green Converse shoes and stuffed her feet into them just in case she had a chance to run.

"I didn't think you wanted her dead yet," said a second man casually as if commenting on the weather. "I only aimed for him and swept the room with my scope."

A third voice sounded loud and clear through her thin bedroom door. "If she's here, I'll find her."

"She'd better be, or I'm holding you responsible," the first man grumbled.

"You instructed me to snipe the guy, and I did. Even with the blinds halfway closed on that minuscule window, I hit my target," grouched the second voice.

"You hit one of your targets. Get back downstairs and watch the alley. We'll take care of this," commanded the first man.

Their footsteps sounded closer. There was nowhere to hide. Her phone finally turned on, but an update popped up instead of her regular screen. Annie shuddered, and hit accept on the bottom of her phone. The last thing she needed was an update right now, but it left her no choice. Her eyes darted all over her room for any sign of hope. Her bed sat three inches off the floor. Her closet had no doors. The mini bathroom felt wrong too. She had no escape from this deadly situation. She needed help.

"Let's find her." The gruff voice sounded from her living room. "Watch my back."

"And if we locate her?"

"We shoot on sight."

It would take only a few minutes to search her tiny apartment. They'd find her and kill her just like Dillan. Tears pricked her eyes, but she blinked them back. She crawled behind the old stuffed chair next to her window. If they were in her apartment, she didn't need to worry about the tiny red sniper dot finding her now that the danger was only a few feet away.

The chair wasn't much protection, but it was better than nothing. Using the chair as a shield, she looked at her phone, hoping the update had disappeared. The phone had gone to sleep. Biting back a groan, she fumbled with her password, her hands shaking so badly she could hardly hit the numbers.

The door handle to her room jiggled. Annie's tonsils seemed to cut off her air supply. Whoever stood outside her bedroom door swore. "It's locked."

"I said to watch my back. Move out of the way," barked the guy with the gruff voice.

Annie finally entered her phone password correctly. She dialed 911 and sank as low to the floor as she could. Maybe if they didn't look in this direction, she could pass for a pile of laundry in the dark corner. She held her phone to her ear as her door handle turned again.

Come on. Come on. Why wasn't her phone ringing?

With a loud crack, the door splintered. Shards of cheap wood flew in every direction as the door fell off the old hinges and crashed to the ground. Annie froze, her eyes bulging, unable to move, unable to do anything. *Don't scream*, she thought repeatedly, pressing her lips firmly together.

A bulky man stood in her doorway. He wore a black ski mask over his face and a tight short-sleeved black shirt to match. A gold chain thumped against his chest. She watched him remove a black pistol with a silencer from behind his back. His bulky hand curled around it, making a thick, jagged scar on the back of his hand stand out. Annie clenched her teeth as he walked toward her closet.

Her phone wasn't ringing. She moved enough to look at the screen on her phone. Her eyes locked on the gray screen. Call failed. With a shaky finger, Annie tapped the green call button on her phone, praying it would connect.

The black-clad hitman walked into her tiny bathroom. Now was her only chance to escape him. Annie glanced between her tiny, half-open second-story window and her smashed door. Running out the broken door would lead her into the path of another man with a gun. That wasn't an option.

She heard her shower curtain whip aside.

She trembled too much to pass for a pile of dirty laundry. She needed to escape. *Help*, she prayed. She had little brain power beyond that one word, yet she hoped God would understand all the meaning packed in that small word.

"911, what is your emergency?"

Footsteps sounded in her bathroom. She had mere seconds. She couldn't wait for help, divine or otherwise.

With trembling fingers, Annie set her phone on the chair and shoved open her second-story window the rest of the way. Below in the light of a streetlamp, an old dumpster stacked full of smelly garbage leaned against her building. She had no choice. Before she thought about it, she squeezed out of the window and hung onto the rough brick with her fingers.

"She's going out the window," yelled the man.

Annie let go.

She landed hard in the slimy dumpster. Pain shot through her body from the fall, and she gasped for breath, her eyes bulging. One of Dillan's murderers tried to stuff himself out of the small window at an odd angle. Gasping, Annie slid to the edge of the rancid dumpster. The gun went off. The bullet ricocheted off the metal lip of the dumpster, inches from her. The sound of metal hitting metal dug into Annie's ears with new, sharp pain. Annie's eyes zeroed in on the lump the bullet made in the metal of the dumpster.

The man swore and adjusted his abnormal shoulder position in the window to take better aim. Annie pressed into the garbage against the taller metal edge and let the rubbish fall around her. It was her only hope for protection.

The sound of gunfire pounded in her eardrums for a few seconds before she realized no bullets were hitting the dumpster. She chanced a glance up to see the bulky arm firing into the alleyway instead. Annie turned to look but couldn't see who returned fire through the darkness. Who would shoot at an assassin?

A curse rent the air, and the hitman disappeared from the window. A crash of a door sounded from above, meaning he was on his way. It wouldn't take long for him to rush down the stairs. Annie had a choice to make. She could stay in the smelly garbage and see what happened or risk running for it. Whoever had shot at the assassin must not have her slotted as a target. She'd much rather risk running into them and escape.

With no time to lose, she scrambled to the shorter edge of the dumpster; her garbage-covered fingers slid across the rust-coated edge as she attempted to hoist herself out. Adrenaline pumped through her, but her arms shook too much to lift her body weight.

Hurried footsteps sounded on the pavement, and she dropped back into the waste. Something burst under her heel and splattered up her leg. Annie closed her eyes, her entire being praying for help. A hand holding a sliver gun appeared, followed by a second empty hand. This one reached out to her, palm open.

"Quick, we have seconds," a man's voice said.

Annie raised her gaze a couple more inches and found herself looking at the face of a young man, maybe only a couple years older than her, with slight stubble on his chin. His dark hair was expertly styled, and he wore a suit worthy of a James Bond movie. His icy blue eyes darted between her and the alleyway before he reached his hand farther into the dumpster.

"You have to run right now. Grab my hand."

Annie raised her grimy hand, and he wrapped his around her wrist. Standing up, she glanced at his hand, unsure how he'd help her like that. With a small huff, he holstered his gun in a shoulder holster under his coat and reached for her with both arms. Annie hesitated for half a second before she put her hands around his neck while he slid his hands to her ribs. He lifted, and she leaned against his shoulders while pulling up her feet to avoid the lip of the dumpster.

He set her on her feet and immediately pulled out his gun again. Annie winced until she saw that he had his eyes on the alleyway. "Run as fast as you can," he pointed in the opposite direction before crossing the alley and ducking behind a different dumpster.

She stumbled a couple of feet down the alleyway. Her whole body resisted the movement, and she fell to one knee. She'd never outrun the hitmen like this, even with the strange guy's help. She was done for, just like Dillan. Her breath came in heaves.

She couldn't get enough air. Her back hurt from her fall, which made it hard for her to think. Annie shook her head in an attempt to clear it and forced a few slow breaths. She had to move now. The guy in the suit was right. The assassin would not hesitate to shoot again if he reached the alleyway before she escaped.

"Come on, Annie. You can do this. You can run," she convinced herself.

Sounds of yelling started at the front of the alley. Time had run out.

She grabbed a rain-rumpled newspaper from the ground and held it over her head. Maybe if she looked homeless in the dark, she'd have a fighting chance to escape the gunmen.

Maybe.

Ignoring the pain coursing through her body, she raced to the end of the alleyway. She didn't dare look back to see if anyone followed her. She made it onto the sidewalk before the shouting and gunshots started up again behind her.

Annie turned the corner and took off, running as fast as she could. She imagined the brutish men jumping into their cars, guns pointed in her direction like in her favorite action movies. Cringing at the thought, she jaywalked across the street, which was thankfully empty of vehicles in the middle of the night, and ran for another alleyway. She didn't stop there; it was far too close to the danger. She emerged on the other side of the next block and ran left instead of right.

This street had more cars rushing by, and that meant more people who might ask questions about her garbage accessories. Annie needed a safe place to hide—a place where the gunmen couldn't find her. She needed half a moment to think about what to do without worrying they'd shoot her.

Holding her burning sides, she jogged down the road and darted off the sidewalk to a small cluster of palm trees by a parking lot. Crouching between the trees and a black SUV, she caught her breath. She couldn't keep running like this in the middle of the night. She needed to contact the police.

Annie glanced at the surrounding shadowed buildings and spotted a brightly lit hotel across the parking lot—finally, a bit of luck. Hotels had showers, rooms to hide in, and phones. They might take pity on her. A glob of something green fell to the ground. Or maybe she'd sneak in and pay them back later. A black car came racing onto the street two blocks behind her. Her heart skipped a beat, and she flattened herself into the gravel-covered ground behind the SUV in the parking lot. She had no idea if the car was the hitmen's car searching for her, or if the car simply needed to slow down. Regardless, she had to keep moving.

On high alert, she scampered around the cars to a large bush on the other side of the hotel parking lot. Her eyes darted between the back entrance in the shadows and the brightly lit front entrance. Which did she dare use? It must be getting close to 3:00 a.m. Neither looked safe, but *safe* was relative right then. Sucking in a deep breath, Annie glanced left and right, darted across the street to the hotel, and dove into another scratchy bush.

"Please, I need a way to get help. Let someone compassionate sit at the desk tonight," she pleaded, half in prayer, half to herself. Her heart pounded so hard in her ears that it made it hard to listen for anyone following her.

Gathering up every brave cell in her body, Annie stood and scurried to the front lobby. The doors opened automatically, and she skidded to a stop in the middle of the tile floor. A man in a red jacket looked up, and his jaw fell open. He shot to his feet. "No, no, no, we don't take in strays off the street. Especially ones that smell like a dump," he said with a bit of a Spanish accent. He waved his fingers at her as if shooing her out the door.

Her lungs burned, and she wrapped an arm around her ribs. She bent in half to catch her breath but kept an eye on the glass door. "I'm not—" Gasp. "A homeless person—" Gasp. "I need to call the police."

The man squinted at her before narrowing his eyes. "What for?"

Straightening, Annie approached the desk. "Someone broke into my house, and I had to jump out the window to escape. Can I borrow a phone, please? This is an emergency."

He raised an eyebrow, murmured something in Spanish under his breath, and placed a landline phone and a box of tissues on the counter. "Don't leave a mark on it." His eyes scrutinized her for another second before he added a bottle of hand sanitizer to the counter.

Annie couldn't care less if she was forced to bathe before he allowed her the call; she needed that phone. She grabbed a couple of tissues and quickly cleaned her hands with the sanitizer, then picked up the phone and hit 911. The man behind the desk rolled his eyes and yanked the phone toward him. He hit the nine button, then 911, before handing it back to her.

Annie attempted a grin, but she doubted the expression on her face looked like one. The blessed sound of the phone ringing filled her ears. Annie sagged against the counter with relief.

"911, what is your emergency?"

Annie started talking at top-notch speed, beginning with Dillan and what he asked her to do this evening. She didn't stop for breath or to let the person on the other side of the line get a word in. "Then I found this hotel and called you." Her eyes darted to the man behind the desk to see his jaw open again. Ignoring him, she focused on her call.

"We already have officers dispatched to your apartment. Are you safe where you are?"

Annie looked out at the darkness behind the glass doors. "I honestly don't know. I'm not even sure where I'm at."

"The Red Barron Hotel, ma'am," the guy behind the desk said.

"Okay, remain there. I'll send someone over to get you. We have some questions, and we need a statement from you. Can you do that?"

She looked at the guy behind the desk. "Can I stay until the officer comes to get me?"

The man nodded, murmured in Spanish, and started busying himself behind the desk.

"He says I can stay."

"Okay. An officer will be there soon."

Annie hung up and looked around the room. There were a few couches and a couple of chairs in the lobby. Unintendedly, her eyes darted down to look at her soiled clothes and shoes. No matter where she sat, she'd ruin the furniture.

"Don't you dare," said the guy behind the desk. He tapped her shoulder with a white key card and pointed to a hallway. "Second floor, the sixth door on the left, room 206. Do what you can to"—he gestured to her—"make yourself somewhat presentable." He yanked the phone off the counter and rubbed it with hand sanitizer.

The last thing Annie wanted to do was argue. Instead, she strode through the lobby and down the hall to the elevator. She'd take a moment to clean up before she spent the rest of the night in the police station. She looked left and right down the hallway. So far, no murderous thugs followed her. Maybe she didn't have to keep running.

Armed with a plan, Annie reached the elevators and mashed the Up button. *Please let no one come out*, she begged silently, plucking at her nasty clothes.

The second the doors opened, Annie shot into the elevator and hit the Door Close button. Wheezing from all the running, she pressed the level 2 button and prayed no one was waiting to come down when she reached that floor.

With a ding, the elevator doors slid open. No one stood in the hall—her luck continued. Unwilling to risk it for longer than she had to, she raced out of the elevator. The hallway appeared empty, but just because no one stood in the hall now, didn't mean those men weren't still looking for her.

She found her room and placed the keycard on the reader until it flashed green. She bolted inside and flipped the light switch closest to the door. Two simple queen beds, a desk, and a TV lined the walls. Annie pulled off the Do Not Disturb sign and placed it on the hallway door handle before she closed and locked the door. She pulled the extra hinged door lock into place and looked for something to block the door. A small armchair glowed in the light from a floor lamp. She pushed it across the room and settled it against the door. It wasn't much but it was better than nothing.

One look in the mirror confirmed her worst fears. Stinking muck from the dumpster coated her entire body. Something white had splattered up her leg, and red smudged her shoes. Was it ketchup? Was it blood? His blood?

Horrified, she ripped them off, turned on the hot water in the shower/tub combo, and threw her shoes and clothes into the bottom. Fighting tears, she climbed in. The water scorched her skin, but she didn't care. She needed it to singe off every trace of this night from her body and her clothes. But no matter how much the water stung, it couldn't burn the images from her mind.

Fingers shaking, she tore open the new soap bar set out on the side of the tub and rubbed it on a fresh white washcloth until she got a good lather. She began wiping all the muck off herself. Next, she dumped the whole bottle of shampoo on her head and violently scrubbed.

She didn't want to think about what had happened, not one little bit, so she kept mumbling about what she had to do next while scrubbing herself over and over. After the bottom of the tub filled with bubbles from all the soap, she started kicking the suds around to help wash her clothes. A few tears slipped out of her eyes as she scrubbed. Her tears mixed with the soap and water swirling around her feet.

As much as she wanted to stand in the hot water and sob until she eventually got into a fit of hiccups, the second worst thing that could happen to her—other than Dillan's murderers finding her—would be the police showing up with her still in this shower.

Annie scrubbed her clothes as best she could, even rubbing the hard soap against the red stains on her shoes. She worked until she got all signs of dumpster grossness off her clothes and called it good enough. She turned off the hot water and wrapped up in the fluffy hotel towels from the metal shelf. It took forever to squeeze all the water she could out of her clothes. If only hotel bathrooms came with clothes dryers. The hair dryer on the wall caught her eye. It was better than nothing.

She turned it on and dried her underwear, T-shirt, and shorts into a slightly less damp state. Annie glanced at her hair, which had started drying into a fuzzy mess, and sighed. Unfortunately, once it dried to this point, it was a lost cause. Now at least she only looked disheveled and not like a walking garbage can. She dressed, making a mental note to thank the front-desk guy for helping her. It was the least she could do after borrowing the hotel room.

Feeling slightly better, she opened the bathroom door. After a disastrous night like tonight, she needed to return home to Idaho. Who cared if it cost her and her granny every cent they owned to get her there? She'd walk all the way home if she had to, but one thing she knew for sure: she'd never return to that apartment again. It didn't matter that she had a couple weeks left with her summer sales job. She didn't care about her thrift-store furniture or clothes. She hadn't brought anything of worth with her to LA anyway. She'd give her statement to the police, ask them if they could deliver her phone and purse, and then she'd leave.

She raked her hands through her fluffy hair. Things had gone from bad to worse to dreadful in only an hour. Pinpricks raced up her arms. Hopefully the police would believe her and wouldn't blame her for what happened to Dillan. With one last look in the mirror, she frowned at her abhorrent appearance, moved the chair blocking the door and reached for the hotel room door handle, but it was already turning.

CHAPTER 4

Annie backed up a step as a new tremble rushed through her body. Was it housekeeping twisting the knob? The hitmen? It couldn't be the police. They would have knocked. The door caught on the precautionary hinged door lock. She clapped her hands over her mouth, stopping a scream. The door closed, and Annie watched as what looked like the corner of the Do Not Disturb sign slipped between the door and the lock. It wiggled back and forth, and to her horror, the lock moved out of the way, and the door burst open.

Annie jumped and stumbled backward, landing hard on the edge of the queen bed. Eyes wide, she stared at the door. A man slipped into the room—the man who'd helped her out of the dumpster in the alley.

His blue eyes darted around the room, taking everything in quickly. "Are you alone?" he asked. Another man, who was dressed all in black and looked like he worked out for a living, checked out the room but stayed in the hallway.

Annie opened her mouth but then closed it again. How could she answer that question? If she said yes, would he shoot her because they had no witnesses? If she said no, would he search the room and then shoot her after he found out she lied? Either way, his icy eyes told her what her heart already knew.

She was caught.

"Never mind," he said. "Reaper, keep an eye out."

The man in the hall nodded and blocked the doorway with his bulk, his arms folded. The handsome guy in the fancy suit closed the door and reached behind him to lock it, keeping his eyes on Annie the whole time. He was here to kill her. She was almost certain, except for one thing. If he'd wanted to end her, he would have shot her in the alleyway. Unless he had to do things on his terms. He couldn't want anything good with the way he slunk into her room.

Annie gulped and looked around for a weapon, something, anything. All she had within reach was a TV remote. "H-how did you . . . find me?" she stammered, inching her hand toward the remote. It was better than nothing.

A slight smile appeared on the man's mouth. "It's what I do. We need to talk." His eyes darted toward the chair by the desk, then back to her, giving her a hint. Did she dare obey his silent request? She wrapped her hand tightly around the remote and weighed her options. She had none. If he chose to kill her, she was dead. Like a lobster living in a restaurant tank, it was only a matter of time.

The young James Bond look-alike didn't turn away from her. She had no idea what to do in this situation. Red color spread up her cheeks, and she rubbed the buttons on the remote with her thumb, trying to think of anything to get out of this situation.

He leaned forward, fixing her with an intense stare. "You're in a lot of trouble."

I'll say, she thought. Annie looked toward the door instead of the chair he'd indicated.

"I wouldn't," he said, his voice calm and steady. Again, he nodded to the chair. "This will go smoother if you cooperate." He folded his arms across his chest.

Annie pressed her trembling lips together and numbly walked to the chair. She sank into it. How could God let this happen to her? She wasn't prepared to die; there had to be a way out of this mess or at least something she could say to free herself.

He strode to the bed, sat on the end across from her, and unfolded his arms. He leaned forward until his elbows rested on his knees and his chin lay on his hands. His blue eyes narrowed a bit. "I'm going to ask you some questions. You are going to answer them *honestly*. Do you understand?" He talked slowly to ensure each word lodged in her brain.

She shivered at his words and prayed that an escape plan would appear in her head. That and some excellent ninja skills she knew she didn't have. She never dreamed she'd find herself mixed up in anything like this, or she would have taken karate classes instead of cooking classes.

When she didn't respond, he straightened up. His suit jacket moved enough that she could see the gun in his shoulder holster. All rational thought left her. She jumped to her feet and chucked the remote at his head. With a smooth swerve, he dodged, and the remote shattered against the wall. His eyes narrowed at her, and Annie fell back into the chair. All the fight drained out of her.

"Please don't kill me. I had nothing to do with whatever this was all about. You have to believe me. I told Dillan no. I told him no." Her voice cracked, and her words got softer. "I told him no." Annie clasped her hands in front of her chest like a small child. If she looked harmless, perhaps he'd let her go.

The man held up his hand to stop her scattered mumbling. "I'm not here to kill you. If you remember right, I saved you."

Saved her for what? He could have a heart of stone, just like the guys who shot Dillan.

He stood, walked to the window, parted the curtains, and glanced down at the street. Annie looked toward the door. Should she make a break for it? Then she remembered the other guy he'd left to keep watch in the hallway. She had nowhere to run.

"I need you to explain to me what happened tonight," he asked, his eyes focused on the street below.

Annie blinked and cranked her neck in his direction. She had no idea why he'd ask her. He'd counter fired at those hitmen in the alleyway. If anyone had an idea of what happened, it was probably him. Unless she got into the middle of some kind of turf war. That or he wanted to trick her into talking.

"Um . . . I'm not sure what to say."

He turned and gave her a sharp look.

"You told me to answer honestly," she said, quickly tossing her hands up.

His stern look softened, and she felt the tightness in her stomach release the slightest smidge. He couldn't be completely heartless if he could mellow at her comment. Maybe she could beg her way out of this. She'd say charm her way out, but she'd never been much of a charmer.

"Fine, I will let you have that one for now," he said, his voice still firm. He folded his arms across his chest. "Why did you jump into the garbage in the alley?"

She let her gaze fall to the floor and said barely above a whisper, "I had no choice."

When he didn't respond, she glanced up. His eyes narrowed in her direction, but not in confusion.

She groaned and pressed her back deeper into the chair, hoping it would give her some support. "I jumped into the dumpster because of the assassins."

He rubbed his chin again. "Does this have anything to do with the job Dillan Collins and his crew pulled tonight?"

Annie's stomach twisted into a tighter knot, and she swallowed hard. "Yes," she breathed barely loud enough for her ears to hear. "Well, no. I'm innocent."

His hand curled into a fist at his side. "Do you know what he was up to or why he pulled that particular job?"

Annie took in a slow deep breath. "No. He claimed it would set him up for life, but that's all."

The man nodded and let the curtains fall back into place. He walked over to the bed and sat down in the spot he'd vacated, but this time, he looked slightly less rigid. His eyes scanned her, taking in her fuzzy blonde hair and stained shoes. Annie didn't look like much. Her whole outfit probably cost less than twenty dollars. She had hardly any savings and few skills to recommend her. She was an ordinary girl who didn't deserve this kind of situation. He must have come to a similar conclusion, because his lips curled.

"So, you weren't involved in his failed heist?"

"I told you I'm innocent. I refused to help him."

He studied her a little more. "How much would it take for you to go away? To disappear and forget this whole thing ever happened?" His eyes stayed on hers as if he could find her answer written on her irises.

She grimaced against his tone, but a tiny bit of hope wriggled to life in her chest. Maybe a higher being was still watching over her. "That's all I want. I want to go home and forget everything that happened this summer, especially the last twenty-four hours. But I don't have a way to make that happen." She lowered her eyes to the floor. How pathetic did she look? She thought failing at Dillan's guaranteed summer job was her lowest low, but this moment beat that.

The man stood and paced the length of the room but didn't say anything to her. Finally, he pulled out his thin silver cell phone and punched in a number before he turned to face her. Did he feel like he had to keep an eye on her? She wasn't a villain or thief, but she, unfortunately, wore the victim's badge.

"Midnight, I need you to drop what you're doing."

Midnight? What kind of person went by the name of Midnight? She'd heard a lot of different names while working as a waitress, but never a name like that.

"Yes. Shut it, will you? I need a ticket—" He snapped his fingers at her.

"To Idaho Falls, Idaho," Annie stammered, her eyes wide. She could hardly believe her ears. Could he send her home? She imagined the feel of her granny's arms around her, comforting and protecting. Maybe today didn't have to end with a bullet in her head.

"One-way to Idaho Falls, Idaho." He shook his head at whatever Midnight said on the other side of the phone call. "Next available flight. Stop asking questions and just book it." He hung up the phone and went back to the curtains.

He parted them again, his gaze darting around. Annie thought it odd that he kept looking outside, but she knew nothing about this strange man who could grant her wish like a magical genie and send her home. She'd deal with his oddities if he held that kind of power.

His phone rang a moment later, and he answered it after the second ring. "When? Fine. We'll have to make that work. The name—"

He turned back to Annie and raised his eyebrows, hinting that he needed her to fill in the information.

"Annie Grey," she provided, her eyes wide. This was happening. She could call a car to take her to the airport and return home. Thoughts of Dillan wormed their way into her head, and some of her elation faded. What would everyone at home think about his murder?

It's possible they'd blame her.

"Annie Grey. Yes, I know it's a girl's name." He rolled his eyes. "Email me the tickets. I'll worry about this; you do what we discussed tonight. Bye." He dropped his phone on the bed and stormed past her to the door.

He opened it a crack. "We'll need a car," he said to the man outside before promptly closing and locking the door again.

A new shiver ran down her spine. If this guy tracked her down, it's possible the hitmen could do the same. Had luck or, better yet, God sent this man to save her? Maybe prayers really were answered. "Thank you," Annie said, barely above a whisper.

"Don't mention it." He walked past her to the window. "I mean it. You cannot mention our meeting to anyone. Ever. I don't exist, and it is essential that you remember that. If anyone comes asking questions about how you got home or anything else that might seem innocent, you ignore them. I was never here; you were never here. None of this ever happened. Is that clear?" His eyes bored into her with an intenseness she'd never seen before.

"Yes," she said, feeling the tension between them return in full force. What kind of person made requests like that? It was strange to think that he could claim he didn't exist. She had no idea what kind of man she had stumbled upon. Not your average Joe. That was abundantly clear.

She swallowed her questions. She wouldn't start bugging him with her worries if he was willing to pay for a plane ticket home. She'd let it all go—him and the haunting sight of Dillan on her living room floor, Dillan's betrayal of their friendship, the job she wouldn't finish, and the life she'd dreamed up that would never come true. She'd attend Dillan's funeral if they had one. He might have chosen a different path, but they once were good friends.

The spy-like guy took his gun out of the shoulder holster, and Annie winced. But he didn't point it at her. Instead, he ejected the magazine to check the bullets. Without glancing at her, he pushed it back into the gun.

A tiny silver gun followed the first, this one from his pant leg. He did the same thing with it. She knew she should probably act like she didn't see either of them, but that was impossible. Her gaze was glued to the guns, and she couldn't turn away. She gulped over and over instead of breathing normally, and shivers ran up and down her arms.

He walked over to Annie and gently pushed her chin until her gaping mouth closed. "Not a word," he said calmly. His icy eyes connected with hers, and she couldn't look away.

His touch sent a shiver down her throat, and she doubted she could speak at that moment even if she wanted to. He dropped his hand and his gaze. Annie wrapped her suddenly goose-bumped arms around herself.

"Your flight doesn't leave for six hours. I promise I will keep you alive until you board the plane, but I don't like babysitting."

"I am not a baby," Annie mumbled under her breath.

He must have heard her because his forehead furrowed, and he sat across from her again. "Since you're new to this, let me explain something about the guys chasing you. It doesn't matter if you witnessed a crime, are an accessory to one, or even if they think you heard something. If they find you, they will kill you. There is nothing you can do about that."

What about the police? They were coming for her. She could talk to them, and they could catch the men after her.

"What about the police?"

"What about them?" he asked.

"They want my statement. They're on their way here right now to talk to me. They can stop those guys from hunting me down . . . right?"

His jaw tightened, and a shadow entered his eyes. "You called them . . ." He rubbed his forehead with three fingers. "Of course you called the police. We don't have a ton of time. I need some answers. The faster you cooperate, the sooner this whole nightmare can end."

Annie trembled at the look on his face and curled her fingers under the edge of her shorts, needing to hold on to something.

"How long ago did you call them?"

She shrugged. "I don't know. Maybe an hour ago. I had to call them from the hotel's front desk."

His eyes narrowed. "Let me guess, you dropped your cell phone in that dumpster and now have zero connection to your normal life." One eyebrow shot up as if challenging her to contradict him. When she said nothing, he nodded, a glower forming on his face, and walked back to the windows, shaking his head as if she were dull-witted.

Annie shifted in her chair. "Excuse me, my life doesn't reside on my phone, and I didn't leave it in the dumpster. I accidentally forgot it in my room after I tried to call 911."

His head snapped up. "Why did you do that?"

She let out a slow breath and twirled her chair further away from him. She didn't owe this strange man any more answers. "I shouldn't say anything—fifth amendment and all." He might have chosen to send her home, but that didn't mean she could trust him. He'd proven that by allowing her to see him hide guns on his person.

He stormed over to her, swung her chair around, put his hands on the armrests, and leaned down until their faces were only a foot apart. "I need to know everything about this whole mess. You have to tell me every detail. Your so-called friend Dillan got mixed up in something way over his head, something I'm trying to stop." His icy eyes claimed control of hers. If he thought a stare-down would wrangle the information out of her, he thought wrong. Annie clenched her teeth and returned his stare with one of her own. She knew her rights.

Annie focused on his eyes until her own started to water. A twitch of a smile appeared on his face, and he straightened. "I respect anyone who can hold their ground. I won't force you to tell me, but any details you do choose to share will help." He held up his hands and stepped closer to the queen bed. "I'm not going to hurt you. I proved that in the alleyway, and I swear I want to help."

He waited, his eyes on her. Annie squirmed a little under his continued scrutiny. Two choices lay before her. She could shut up and wait for the police to arrive and risk losing his help, or she could give him more details. He might help keep her safe until she reached the airport if she talked.

Annie didn't feel like she had much of a choice. She needed help. It was possible God had sent him to save her. She'd prayed for his intervening power in her apartment, and only minutes later, this man helped her out of the dumpster. Unbidden, Dillan's words echoed in her head. *God doesn't care what we do.* A shiver ran down her spine, and she shook off the feeling and those haunting words. She knew He cared; He had to.

Looking up, she saw the attractive, albeit dangerous, man watching her. She needed to believe in someone, and he was willing to help her. All the police might do is take her statement and release her, or with the way the last twenty-four hours had shaped up, they'd arrest her. She could tell him one thing to keep herself safe.

"I . . . didn't have time to wait for the police. Those guys who shot Dillan were coming to get me, and I had to jump out my window, or they would have shot me dead. I set my phone down to open the window."

"How involved were you? Did you recognize the men?" he asked, his eyebrows pinched together. "I need to know."

The image of the black-masked gunmen filled her head, and she shivered. "I don't know them at all. When I refused Dillan, I didn't spend time asking more questions." She put her face in her hands and tried to forget the moment the little red dot found the center of Dillan's chest. Tears pricked in the corners of her eyes, and she bit her lips to keep them from trembling.

He walked to her chair and leaned in close. Annie's breath hitched at his nearness. He reached forward and put a hand on either side of her on the chair arms. Slowly he pulled her chair across the room until he could sit back down on the queen bed with their knees touching. He looked Annie right in the eye.

"Start talking; the smallest details matter." He folded his arms and looked pointedly at her.

"You first. Why should I tell *you* anything more? I don't know anything about you or why you're here," Annie pressed, uncomfortable with how close he was. She could smell the danger oozing off him, mixed with his cologne. Add to that the guns she'd witnessed, and she had no idea if trusting him was a remote option.

His face softened a little bit. "You should tell me because if I'm blindsided by something you're hiding, I cannot guarantee your safety."

Annie looked him over. Sincerity showed in his eyes, something she hadn't expected to see. He acted like he honestly wanted to help her return home. However, he wasn't a cop or part of the FBI or CIA or he would have identified himself as such. Annie shook her head and scooted her chair back with her toes.

He sighed. "Haven't I shown you that I'm a nice guy? More than that, I am absolutely capable of making good on my promises. You can trust me."

"You might not have hurt me, but that doesn't mean I can trust you. If you want me to trust you, then tell me who you are and who you work for," she snapped.

He gritted his teeth for a moment. "If you must know, my name is Samuel Erickson."

He paused as if gathering his thoughts. Annie compared the name he gave her to his face. He looked like he could pass for a Samuel.

He steepled his fingers. "I do a lot of different things for a lot of different people. Some of them are bad. Some of them are good. I only do the bad things because it will lead to a better outcome for more people. I twist the truth for a living if the occasion calls for it, and yes," he said, patting the gun under his jacket, "I am exceptional with a gun."

That explanation didn't make her feel any better. "I can't pay you for helping me," she blurted out.

His eyes twitched like he found her comment amusing. "I'm not asking for payment. As I said, I am a decent guy. Currently, I'm involved in an . . . undercover operation, which has turned more complicated than I planned. You need to get out of here before you get caught in the middle of something you don't want to become involved in. So, if I were you, I'd start talking."

He leaned back and looked at her as if she were about to tell him some fantastic story worthy of crime novels. The truth was that she wasn't anyone special, and she was caught up in something she didn't understand.

CHAPTER 5

Annie gulped, and her eyes darted between the door and the window. Any chance he only wanted to trick her into talking, then shoot her in the back and toss her into a dumpster? She rolled the end of her oversized T-shirt in her hands, mentally calculating how long it would take the police to arrive at the hotel. According to her math, they should have already arrived. He was her only hope.

She looked down at her hands to avoid his eyes. "All right . . . I think they wanted to shoot us both. Please don't ask me why, because I don't know anything." She relayed what happened between her and Dillan last night and in her apartment that morning, how she'd dropped her phone in her room to open the window before she jumped out of that second-story window into the dumpster to save herself. She closed her eyes in a feeble attempt to forget the feelings she'd felt during those horrible moments. Once finished, she looked back at him, unsure what she hoped she'd see in his eyes.

Samuel pinched the skin between his two eyebrows, a bit of a guttural sound escaping him. "This isn't good. I can't simply send you home." He pulled out his phone and began texting someone.

"What? But you bought the plane tickets." Panic seized her. He'd prepared for her to go home already. He couldn't back out now. She'd have no way to get home after she finished with the police. "I can't stay here. I need to get out of LA. Those guys are after me." She knew she shouldn't have believed him. The phone call to the so-called Midnight person was probably a farce. A lie to get her to trust him enough to talk, and she'd fallen for it.

He turned his eyes back to her, his mouth tight. "For one, you're a suspect in a homicide—something I could have dealt with, but if you leave the city, that action will only convince the police of your guilt. Two, the gunmen have your phone, Annie."

She shook her head, unsure what that had to do with anything. "It's replaceable. It wasn't even expensive."

He sighed, giving her an annoyed look. "They'll have all your information. Everything. Where you live, your friends, your family, your bank info. Everything. If I put you on a plane this evening, you'll end up dead within two days. Sending you home now is worse than keeping you here. Do I like it? No."

He dragged his hands across his cheeks as if trying to massage out pain in his jaw. A haunted look flashed in his eyes before he shook his head, as if trying to shake off whatever thoughts had crept into his mind.

This didn't look good for her. She needed to take action and run away from this guy, no matter if God had sent him to help her or not. Annie clutched her ruined shirt in both hands and begged her feet to move. Her heart raced again. She hadn't done anything to deserve this. Dillan, God rest his soul, had chosen to do illegal things and had somehow gotten her mixed up in it. She wanted to leave, to feel safe. She wanted to go home. She wanted to forget.

Samuel looked over at her, the corners of his mouth twitching as if he wanted to smile. "Don't worry, Annie. I won't send you to your death. I'm not that kind of person. We'll figure out where to put you until it's safe." He gently pushed her chair back until it tapped against the hotel desk. With her out of his way, he stood and moved to the window again. It was a curious habit of his. One Annie didn't dare ask about.

His words, "where to put you," echoed in her mind. The image of a cold, dank, leaky pipe under the street filled her mind: her hands were bound, her hair ratted, her throat sore from screaming for help. He wasn't the kind of person to leave an innocent girl in a horrible place like that . . . was he? She looked him over again. Right now, she couldn't tell. He gave off a hero-like young James Bond vibe, but was he a hero or a villain? He'd helped her out of the dumpster, but he hadn't acted much like a hero since.

Annie let her gaze fall back to him. "I'm sorry, but what do you mean—'where to put me'?"

He kept his eyes on the street. "I told you, Annie. I'm in the middle of something you don't want to get involved in. I promise you'll thank me later for stashing you somewhere safe."

"Stash me *where* until you're done with *what*?" Did later mean hours, weeks, or years? Annie appreciated that he acted like he wanted to help her, but she didn't want his help if it led to a drippy pipe prisoner situation.

He didn't look at her when he spoke. "Until I figure out what to do about you and your situation, you'll have to hide."

Okay, she'd had enough of his cryptic words. He wasn't a policeman or an officer or agent of the law, meaning she didn't have to do anything he said. "Let me guess; you want me to simply accept that?" she shouted, jumping to her feet.

"Yes," he said matter-of-factly, his eyes still on the street.

That's it. She didn't care if he booked her a flight home or if she had to fight her way out of this. She was done. The hotel binder on the desk caught her eye, and she grabbed it before she changed her mind. "No, I won't allow you to kidnap me," she spat. Emotion bubbled and boiled in her chest, and she lobbed the binder at him. It missed him completely, hit a lamp, and both items fell to the floor—the binder with a thud and the lamp with a crash.

He spun toward the noise, his hand automatically reaching for his gun.

She blinked off her surprise and rushed for the door. "I'm going to the police station right now." It didn't matter if the officer on the phone told her to stay put. They obviously weren't coming for her.

Samuel moved like a cheetah and jumped in front of the door before she could wrench it open.

"Stop. It isn't safe." He leaned against the door, his arms folded in his expensive jacket, his breath contrasting with his relaxed stance. "I've seen this kind of situation before, and it didn't end well. The police can only do so much. You aren't safe on your own. The streets and your home are both dangerous. You have to trust me."

There was no way to get around him. Annie pushed and shoved. He'd somehow turned into a granite statue in the last two seconds. "I can't trust you."

"Try," he said, unmoving.

Annie threw up her hands. "What about my granny?"

"What about her?" Samuel asked, gesturing for her to retake her seat.

Annie held her ground inches from his face and folded her arms to match his stance. Raising her chin, she fixed him with a stern glare. "I live with my granny. I'm only here because I'm dumb enough to have trusted Dillan." She swallowed hard at his name. "Idaho is my home. If I'm in danger, then so is she."

Samuel didn't move an inch from the door. "You're the target, Annie. They won't harm your grandmother unless we give them a reason to. Which we won't."

There was that *we* word again. They were not a *we* at all. She moved left and right, but she couldn't get past him. Finally, Annie stumbled away from the door. Her back hit the small wall across from the door, and she slid down the smooth surface into a heap on the floor. "How did I become a target? I don't know what Dillan did to get himself shot."

She pulled her knees to her chest, wrapping her arms around them. Defeat crept into her heart. If she hadn't grown up a good Christian girl who learned at age two that swearing was distasteful, she would have let out a string of cuss words, with every single one directed at Dillan Collins. This was all his fault; may he rest in peace. Annie buried her head in her hands, her fuzzy hair falling across her face, unshed tears stinging her eyes. She didn't dare close them for fear of seeing Dillan's death replayed over and over again in her mind.

Samuel moved away from the door and slowly crouched in front of her. "Annie, I'm sorry you're in this situation. I know the kind of people you're running from; most targets don't survive things like this. At least they don't if they try to go it alone. You are a loose end. A lot of these criminals have a no-loose-ends policy, therefore . . . you are a recipient of their vengeance, even if you did nothing."

He lifted his hand as if he wanted to reach for hers but checked his hand before he touched her. "You shouldn't have to pay for someone else's choices, but we can't change what happened. We can only move forward."

Annie held onto herself but nodded. She had no more energy to argue anymore. Samuel let out one short breath and moved away to the window. He twitched the curtains aside, and Annie chose to ignore him. Maybe she'd stay glued to this spot until her world settled down.

"Not now!" Samuel groaned from the other side of the room. He snapped the curtains shut. "We have to go."

"What? Why?" Annie asked, glancing around the room for a reason that would make them jump up and leave. Weren't they safe behind a locked door with a guard in the hallway? "Is it the cops?" Part of her hoped so.

"No." He darted across the room, grabbed her by the elbow, yanked her up, and pulled her along with him. "It's much worse than that."

"Ouch! What's going on?" Annie asked as he flung open the door to the room.

The man in the hallway jumped to attention. Samuel didn't answer her.

"I can walk by myself." Annie yanked her arm out of his grip.

Samuel looked doubtful but didn't grab her arm again. "We have a problem," he said, turning toward the elevators. The other man must have accepted that as enough explanation because he fell into step behind them. Samuel turned to the man. "Reaper, this is Annie. Annie, Reaper."

He grunted at her.

A soft ding sounded, alerting them to the elevator doors opening. Samuel shoved Annie into the housekeeping closet to the left of the elevators. Annie stumbled against the shelves, holding extra shampoo and soap. She had to grab wildly onto the shelf to keep from toppling to the ground.

"Hey, I'm a person, you know," she snapped at Samuel, who held out a hand to help her up. Annie ignored his hand and used the shelf to pull herself straight. He shrugged and moved closer to the door.

Reaper cracked a smile so brief she barely saw it before he pulled the door closed, leaving only a tiny gap where she could see into the hallway.

Samuel shot her a stern look and held his finger against his lips, effectively silencing her. Annie stood, her breath sharp and uneven. Samuel kept a finger to his lips and peered through the small gap in the doorway. Annie copied him.

A thin, young-looking man in a cream linen suit and with wild brown hair backed out of the elevator. He looked a little younger than Samuel, probably close to her age. Two enormous men followed him out of the elevator. The lanky guy raised his arms wide, almost as if he were attempting to block the two enormous men from following him.

"Look's like Midnight's up to the task," Reaper mused under his breath.

The two men pushed past the skinny guy who rushed after them. "Fellas, I told you Mr. Erickson isn't here. Even if he was, it's 4:45 in the morning." He darted past them in an attempt to block their path again. "How about I make you an appointment after the sun's up, aye?"

The two brutish men pushed past him again and stomped down the hallway. "*Capo* wants us to see him. He doesn't care what time it is—"

The men disappeared from view. Annie leaned forward to see through the small crack in time to spot Midnight giving them a quick thumbs-up behind his back as he raced after the two men.

Samuel let out a short laugh. "Never subtle, that one," he said, pulling the door open. "Reaper, he might need a hand."

"On it," Reaper said in a deep-toned voice. "What do we tell the Warden?"

"I'll deal with him later," Samuel said. "If he asks, tell him something pressing came up and not to worry. We are still on schedule."

Warden? Annie glanced from Samuel, to Reaper, to the closet they were hiding in. A warden was the person in charge of a prison. Reaper and Midnight sounded like code names, not everyday names written on a birth certificate. What were these men, criminals?

Without another word, Reaper pushed past them and raced down the hall. Samuel grabbed Annie's hand this time, and they darted into the elevator right before the doors closed. She studied Samuel. He didn't look like a criminal, not that she'd met many. He looked and acted more like a super spy than someone who belonged in jail.

"Let me guess, those guys are associated with *your* problem, since they don't look like the ones chasing me," Annie said, yanking her hand from his. She twisted her stained shirt in her hands, unsure what to do with them now. Unsure if she could even trust this man who had saved her. Samuel grinned but didn't say anything while the elevator descended.

He put out an arm to prevent her from moving forward when the elevator stopped. Annie watched him move his other hand to the inside of his jacket before he stood in front of the silver door. Annie could imagine his fingers curling around the handle of his gun.

Why did everyone have a gun today? His head moved left and right as if checking out the hallway. Seemingly satisfied, he motioned her forward. They moved out of the elevator and into the hall that opened to the ample lobby space.

Together they turned the corner, and Annie spotted the large glass entry doors. A burly man entered the hotel. His hand brushed back his dirty-blond hair—a hand with a thick, jagged scar right down the middle. Instantly she froze, and her arms shook. She recognized his scar. It was a scar she hoped to forget, but deep down, she knew that image would be burned into her mind forever, ready to haunt her dreams.

Annie gasped and turned back to the elevator. Samuel followed her without question. Once in the safety of the metal box, Annie fell to her knees on the hard elevator floor and tried to breathe. The doors closed, and Samuel crouched beside her.

"Yours, I presume. This is interesting. He's smarter than he looks," he said casually, as if notorious evil men were nothing to him.

"How did—How could—" Annie mumbled, her head fuzzy. She didn't know how much more of this she could take.

"It doesn't matter how they found you. Just that they did." Samuel tapped his chin. "Are you sure that you called the police?"

Annie nodded; she'd bet her life on it. The 911 number wasn't easy to mess up.

"Interesting." Samuel hit the number two button in the elevator. "If he spotted you, he'll think you got off the elevator on this floor. The front desk will confirm you were staying on the second floor, but his trail will end there."

Once the elevator stopped, he looped his arm around her back and pulled her out of the elevator into the stairwell. She felt a little weak in the knees, so his arm became a blessing. What a pair they must have made. Opposite in every way.

With his arm around her for support, they raced down the stairs and slipped out a door leading to the parking lot. An airport bus waited on the road next to the hotel. Samuel pulled her into the bus and walked her to the back. He pushed her low in a seat, but he sat up tall in his. She assumed he wanted to hide her with his broad shoulders.

Other people piled in after them, chatting about their early fights out of LAX as if everything in the world was hunky dory. For them, it probably seemed like a regular day with nothing untoward. They'd probably spent the last several days soaking up the sun at the beach or Disneyland and were ready to fly home with cheerful stories and souvenirs. Only her world seemed to be collapsing right in front of her face.

"What are we doing?" Annie asked as the bus pulled away from the curb.

"The stakes are too high for us to sit around and wait. That man is the one who tried to kill you, and he seems to have some good resources. I'm sending you away on the first available flight. New York, Chicago, Atlanta, England. It doesn't matter."

"Are you kidding me?" Annie didn't like this turn of events one bit.

"You can't go home, and you most definitely can't stay here. We all tracked you down in less than two hours." Samuel put a finger to his lips and shot her a look that clearly said, "Keep quiet." She didn't want to keep quiet. She wanted to yell, scream, and shake Samuel until he understood what it was like to be in her shoes right now.

"You can't dump me at the airport," she hissed. "The police want to talk to me, and I need to get home."

He covered her mouth with his hand and looked around at everyone else on the shuttle. Nobody seemed to be paying them any attention. "Listen to me. I don't think the police plan to show up at that hotel. Someone must have redirected them, or they would have arrived by now."

Annie's hated to admit he was right. They weren't coming for her.

"I'm sorry this is inconvenient, but I'm near the end of something big, six months in the making. You're in as much danger with me as you'll be on your own. Maybe Claw could help, especially with the problem of you being tied to a homicide, but there's no guarantee that she can keep you safe. Not if your assassin has a man on the inside, a dirty cop." He paused as if thinking that through but then shook his head. “If you stay here, your ‘guys’ will kill you. I’m sorry to tell it to you straight, but it’s the truth of the matter. I’ve seen this scenario before. I know what will happen to you. You have little choice left but to flee.”

Annie groaned. She knew he spoke the truth; she could feel it. “I don’t have money, clothes, ID, or a phone. How am I supposed to get help? How am I supposed to know when it’s clear to go home?”

Samuel straightened in his seat. “You aren’t going home, not for a while.”

Annie suddenly felt small and weak and exposed. She couldn’t believe this was happening to her. That one choice, one mistake, led to this mess. Had God abandoned her, leaving her to face this burden alone? Dillan claimed places like LA were outside of His reach. Annie didn’t want to believe he spoke the truth. It went against everything she knew.

Samuel lightly tapped her arm. “I swear to you that I will fix your situation, track you down, and take you home when things are safe again. You have my word.”

Annie couldn’t believe this. She wouldn’t stand for it. “I’m sorry. How do you expect me to simply trust your word? Trust that you, a complete stranger, will find me? Trust I’ll do fine alone with nothing and no one to help me?”

Samuel gave her a sympathetic look. “Because I always keep my word,” he said, pulling out his phone and opening the airport’s website. “This is the best way. The only way.”

He was serious. Annie looked over his shoulder as he scanned the flights, her heartbeat hammering hard in her chest. She couldn’t let this happen or let him choose what she did next. She looked out the bus window at the city rushing past her and prayed harder than ever for divine intervention.

“Do you know anyone in Texas?” he asked in the same tone as if he had commented on the weather.

Annie sat back in her seat and folded her arms. “No.”

“Perfect.”

“How is that perfect?” Annie mumbled, a new nervousness twisting in her gut.

He smirked as if he’d won a baking competition. “Because no one will know you there. You have no connections. It’s perfect.” He slipped his phone into his pocket, his smile falling into a scowl when he caught sight of her less than grateful expression. “If you’d rather try to face this on your own, fine. I won’t force you into this plan. At least my conscience will be clear if you wind up dead in the gutter.”

She would have slapped him across the face if she knew him better. Instead, she turned away from him and stared out the window, fighting the tears that welled in her eyes. They exchanged no more words until the bus pulled up to the curb at the airport.

"Are we doing this?" Samuel asked under his breath, his gaze following the other passengers exiting the airport shuttle.

Lord, help me, she silently prayed, hoping that He did care what happened to her. Everything felt confusing and messed up; she desperately needed a God who cared. She looked around for an angel or a sign . . . anything . . . but all she had was Samuel and her hope that he was the answer to her prayers.

"I don't think I have another option," Annie said, her voice breaking on the last word. She swallowed hard, her arms trembled, and she folded them to keep them steady. "Unless hitchhiking home is an option."

Samuel made a face. "It's not."

CHAPTER 6

They exited the bus, and Annie followed behind him like a stained gray cloud. He walked fast, and she had to jog to keep up. She didn't mind flying, but flying to an unknown city without any means to care for herself wasn't her idea of a good plan. Samuel's sharp intake of breath made her look up at him. He grabbed her arm and pulled her out of the line to the escalators. Annie groaned. She was tired of getting towed around.

"Can you quit doing that?" she asked, attempting to pull her arm away, but Samuel only tightened his grip.

"I was afraid of this. Stupid. I shouldn't make these kinds of mistakes. The Warden will have more than one harsh word for me," he mumbled as he dragged her toward the baggage claim. Annie had no idea what he was talking about. He'd stopped making sense a long time ago.

"Don't say anything. I'll deal with this," Samuel said. "They are my problem, not yours."

Two burly yet nicely dressed men came stalking up behind them and started shouting in a language Annie didn't understand. Samuel spun around to face them. He shifted her behind him in one smooth movement, shielding her from the men. A new fear rushed through her like a waterfall. Were they after her, too? Did she have more people to fear than the man with the scar?

The men gestured to her and Samuel, shouting in that same language. Samuel shouted back at them in whatever language they'd all decided to speak. Annie looked around. Everyone in the airport stared at them. If only she could disintegrate into dust and blow away. More than one person pointed out her less-than-nice appearance. Compared to Samuel and these other men, she looked homeless.

One of the burly men reached for Annie's arm, but Samuel whacked his hand away and put his arm protectively around her shoulders instead. Annie had no idea what was happening, and from the looks on their faces, she didn't want to know. Samuel wrapped his arm tighter around her shoulders, strangely giving her the first feeling of security she'd felt all day.

After Samuel pointed to the airport security team that stormed their way, the men stopped shouting. "We're going with them," Samuel whispered quickly to her out of the side of his mouth. "We don't have a choice in the matter."

The men grabbed Samuel's and Annie's arms and escorted them outside as if they were prisoners, directly into a waiting dark-blue sedan with tinted windows.

Their newfound guards squished her and Samuel in the middle of the back seat. With a brute on either side blocking the doors as if they needed to ensure no one could open them and escape. Annie ended up smashed tightly against Samuel, her body half turned toward him, her face practically pressed into his neck. Normally she wouldn't have allowed such closeness, especially with an attractive guy, but these unfeeling men had left them few options. Annie assumed Samuel had tried to talk them out of kicking them from the airport and failed in his negotiations.

She glanced left and right at their ruthless guards. Her breath hitched, her throat tightened, but she bit down her emotions. Now wasn't the time to lose it. Instead, she focused on the bright sunrise chasing away the last of the night.

Several tense minutes later, Annie peeked at Samuel. How had their situation gotten worse? They drove silently, except for the man sitting up front with the driver. He talked on his phone the whole time in the same foreign language. They drove directly to the hotel Annie had chosen that morning and pushed them out of the car onto the sidewalk more forcefully than necessary.

Letting out a long breath, Samuel looped his arm around hers and dragged her into the lobby. The men in the sedan watched through their tinted windows until Annie and Samuel walked through the hotel doors. Annie doubted those harsh men would drive far. If she had to guess, this situation was why Samuel kept spying out the windows.

Stone-faced Samuel moved her on his left side so he blocked her from the man sitting at the front desk. For the second time that day he led her to the elevators. She itched to know why he'd resorted to shouting with those guys at the airport but kept her peace. She'd ask once they stopped long enough to breathe.

Samuel hit the button for the fourth floor, and they moved up a couple levels. He didn't waste time and darted out of the elevator the moment the doors opened. Annie followed behind him. A cleaning cart sat against the wall halfway down the hall. Samuel sped toward it while Annie followed along until they saw a room with the door propped open. A housekeeper walked out of it with a bag full of garbage in hand.

"Thank you for working so fast. We checked in early," he said, kicking out the door stopper. He fixed the maid with a dazzling smile.

The woman blushed, reached into the room, and dragged her vacuum into the hall. Annie and Samuel slipped inside, and Samuel closed the door behind them. Annie looked around with a strange sense of déjà vu filling her.

Samuel's phone buzzed before they had a moment to process what had occurred. He gestured to the small stuffed chair in the corner before he yanked his phone out of his pocket. Annie glanced at the screen on her way past him. It was a text from Midnight and only two letters, *DD.* Annie looked up at him, puzzled.

"It means our 'friends' are done searching every inch of the hotel and are coming back down."

Done and down. A code. If he communicated in codes, then maybe this was another clue as to who Samuel was. "Oh," Annie said, falling onto the chair.

Samuel sat across from her on the queen bed, texting.

Annie had so many questions that it proved hard to pick which one she should start shouting first. Calmly, she tried to sort through them. About five minutes later, a knock sounded on the door. Samuel went to open it with a hand on his gun in the shoulder holster. He knocked once, and two knocks sounded in return. He nodded and opened the door.

In stormed the young guy she'd glimpsed earlier—Midnight. His brown hair looked more disheveled. He wore electric-blue glasses and a winning smile. "What was this whole thing about? A test? I swear it was a test. I insist the Warden still doesn't trust me. Me, after all I've done to prove myself these last few years. When Mr. Benicci's men showed up here, and I knew I had to face them on my own, my heart pounded so hard that I knew if I died of a heart attack, the Warden would see to it that *untrustworthy* was engraved on my headstone," he said, drawing his finger through the air with a flourish. "I didn't think you'd pull a stunt like that on me unless there was a purpose, so don't leave me waiting. Tell me, did I pass?"

Samuel shook his head with a bit of an eye roll. "You passed," he said dryly.

"Yes," Midnight said, pumping his fist in the air. He noticed Annie sitting there staring at him.

He stuck his thumb out at her. "We commandeered her room?"

"No," Annie and Samuel said together.

Now that she'd sat quietly for several minutes everything started to hurt. Annie pulled her knees up to her chest as the pain from the abuse her body had taken that night radiated through her.

"Any chance you're going to explain?" Midnight asked, looking between her and Samuel.

"We're in trouble." Irritation laced each of Samuel's words while he filled Midnight in on her disastrous morning and the elaborate mess they now found themselves in.

Midnight smacked himself on the forehead. "So, it wasn't a test. I didn't pass anything? The ticket was for her." He jabbed his finger in the air at her. "Oh man, Sam, how could you have made such a mistake? That's what had brute and brainless worried. They thought you were trying to skip town on the job with the money. A one-way ticket at the last minute . . ." He tossed his hands up and fell backward on the queen-size bed. "If the Warden gets wind of this, you're in worse than a pickle." Midnight stage whispered to Annie. "The Warden is our boss."

Samual folded his arms. "The Warden already wants to see me. I made our situation worse when I showed up at the airport, where more of Benicci's men were waiting for me. We have to figure out what we need to do to salvage this job before we're fired." Samuel scratched his chin briefly before taking out his phone and walking into the far corner of the room. He spoke low enough that Annie couldn't hear him. He leaned against the wall, looking out the curtains like before. Midnight rolled over and studied Annie. A huge smile spread across his face.

"Midnight." He raised his eyebrows as if such a thing should impress her and wiggled to the headboard. When she didn't respond, his grin faltered. "Though if it makes you feel better, you can call me Jeremy."

It did make her feel better. Jeremy sounded like an actual name. "Annie Grey."

"Nice to meet you, Ann." Jeremy unwrapped a mini-size chocolate bar.

Annie sighed. "It's Annie. There's an *i* and an *e* in my name for a reason."

"Sorry. Nice to meet you, Ann*ie*," he said, emphasizing the last sound in her name. "Bad luck on the circumstances, though." He stuck out his lip, looking like an overgrown first grader.

The corner of her mouth quirked up. "Thanks. I've hardly had a second to process it."

He waved her comment away. "Don't worry. It will hit you like a truck later on. It always does."

Great. That's exactly what she needed.

Annie's eyes darted to Samuel. It didn't look like his conversation was going well. "Have you and Samuel worked together for a long time?" Annie asked, mostly to distract her swirling thoughts.

He shrugged. "About four years." He laughed suddenly and lightly slapped her on the arm. "If Sam were a superhero, I guess I'd be his sidekick. A sidekick. Me. Now that's a laugh." He chuckled silently to himself.

Annie looked down at her stained shoes. "So, I'm—what—the damsel in distress?"

"At least we all know our roles," he said, pulling out a second candy bar and taking a huge bite. He offered it to her, a string of caramel connecting his chocolate to the corner of his mouth. She shook her head. Annie hadn't eaten today but doubted anything would have stayed down if she'd tried.

Samuel started yelling into his phone in the same language he'd spoken at the airport. Jeremy swallowed the rest of his candy bar.

"Italian," he said, pulling out another chocolate bar. He nodded at Samuel.

"Wow, he speaks it exceedingly well." Annie kept her eyes on Samuel by the window

Jeremy shrugged as if speaking Italian like a local wasn't a big deal. "Sam speaks seven languages."

Annie's eyes widened, and she hugged her knees tighter to her chest. It felt strange sitting in a room with someone smart enough to speak so many languages. They watched Samuel pace, yell in Italian, and check the windows. Finally, after about a half hour, which felt more like twelve, he hung up.

"So?" Jeremy asked.

Samuel pinched the skin between his eyes. "Our client is threatening me, the Warden is not pleased, and Annie's life is on the hook."

Jeremy swallowed his third chocolate bar. "Accurate summation," Jeremy dusted off his fingers. "This is a mess you've gotten us into. That isn't like you. You're slipping."

"To be fair, her ex started this mess, not me," Sam said, falling into the rolling chair by the hotel desk.

Jeremy snickered. "I hope you didn't tell the Warden that. He doesn't like excuses."

"I'm not senseless. I, however, have more chances left than you and our old buddy Crank combined." Samuel massaged his jaw.

"Not once you add our damsel in distress and the impromptu trip to the airport to your tally," Jeremy countered. "What are you going to do? If experience has taught me anything, you have two hours to fix it or . . ." Jeremy drew a line across his throat.

"I'm working on it," Samuel snapped.

Jeremy laughed and tapped his watch. "Tick tock."

Annie looked from one man to the other. "Good grief, you guys have more drama than the bridezillas at the bridal store I used to work at," Annie mumbled, tightening her arms around herself.

Samuel and Jeremy both turned slowly to face her.

"Or not," she said quickly. The last thing she wanted was a problem with these men. She had enough problems with people who wanted her dead.

"What did you say?" Jeremy asked, turning to look directly at her, his fourth candy bar forgotten.

Samuel scooted his chair closer to her, his eyes shining with interest. "You worked at a bridal store?"

"Yes," Annie answered hesitantly. Working in a dress shop wasn't a crime. They wouldn't shoot her and leave her for dead because she used to iron formal wear after school. Annie cringed at the thought.

Samuel scooted the desk chair forward until he was knee-to-knee with her. Annie groaned. "Not this again."

Samuel ignored her. "What did you do there?"

Jeremy nodded encouragingly, curiosity written all over his face. This seemed more than a little weird. They were guys, macho guys. Why would they care about an old job that had to do with dresses?

"I'm sorry. I didn't mean to interrupt your argument. Pretend I didn't say anything." Annie tried to shrink away, but there was nowhere for her to go. The chair didn't have enough give to let her back up an inch.

Jeremy huffed and ripped open the bag at his feet. He pulled out a laptop and opened it.

"You don't have to apologize." Samuel leaned forward and put a hand on her knee. She knew he meant the gesture to feel comforting, but it only unnerved her more. Her eyes narrowed on his hand. Samuel cleared his throat and removed it, clasping both of his hands together instead. "Annie, you're not in trouble."

Annie snorted. "That's the understatement of the millennium. I'm in more trouble than I have ever been in my entire life."

Samuel's lips twitched. "Just tell me what you did there."

Jeremy pushed his bright-blue glasses back up his nose. "She was hired as a bridal press girl at a shop called *Hearts Bound Forever* when she was sixteen. She worked there until she graduated high school, and then she worked at a diner in her hometown."

Annie whipped around to look at Jeremy. "How did you figure that out?"

He popped his fingers and leaned back, looking satisfied with himself. "That's what I do. I'm a hacker." He beamed as if admitting he bottle-fed puppies.

Annie's jaw slowly dropped open. "A hacker?" So they were criminals. She turned to look at Samuel. "Then what are you exactly?"

"I already told you what I am," he said, leaning back in his chair. "We're talking about you right now."

"No, you told me that you do good and bad things. That doesn't tell me what you are." Annie wasn't going to let him get away with not telling her. She needed some kind of answer if she were to continue trusting him with her life.

He took a deep breath and leaned toward her after a moment of thought. "Some people label me a gentleman thief. I feel a tad young for that title, so I prefer a grifter, but I'm employed most often as a fixer. But we"—he pointed to Jeremy and himself—"are not bad guys. I promise to explain more later. I need you to tell me what you did at that job."

A fixer? A hacker? "Holy country gravy," she whispered to herself, sliding deeper into the crack of the chair. God hadn't sent good people to save her. He'd sent criminals.

"Annie?" Samuel pressed.

Annie kneaded her forehead with her fists. "Why do you care about a job I finished three years ago?"

"It says she was a press girl, Sam," Jeremy cut in. "I'd assume she ironed dresses." Jeremy pulled a bag of peanuts from his bag and tossed a few nuts into his mouth.

Samuel looked at her, his eyebrow raised. Annie clenched her fists. "Yes, and I fixed buttons, bustled dresses, repaired beading. You know, I made sure the dresses looked good for the bride's big day. But I don't know what that has to do with anything."

Samuel jumped up, a smile spreading across his face. He snapped his fingers and slid the chair back to the desk. "The Warden is going to love me. Annie, you are our lifesaver." Without another word, he pulled his cell phone out of his pocket and strode back to the window.

Annie looked at Jeremy. "Are you as confused as I am?"

Jeremy shrugged. "That's his 'I know how to save everything' face."

Annie had no idea why talking about one of her past jobs would give him that look. She hadn't said much.

Samuel talked excitedly in what sounded like French—at least someone's day had brightened. Annie wiggled in an attempt to get more comfortable on the stuffed chair but every angle ached. Right then, she wished she were alone in the hotel room. Then she could have turned on the cooking channel, rolled up in the fluffy bed, and stayed there for as long as she wanted.

Samuel suddenly switched to English. "Oh and tell Crank to meet you there. I'll catch Claw up. Thanks. Bye."

Within a breath, his phone returned to his ear. "Claw, I need to meet up with you. We can join you at location B." Sam checked his silver watch. "I can make that. See you there."

Sam clapped his hands together, drawing Annie's and Jeremy's attention. A bright smile lit up his face. Annie blinked; his smile changed his whole demeanor. It made him look more like a regular, handsome guy instead of a world-famous dangerous spy. "Jeremy, meet us at location seven at seventeen hundred hours. Annie will need a full ID profile. I'll text you the details. Annie, you and I are going out."

"Why? Where? It's not safe," she said, tightness forming in her shoulders.

"Trust me, Annie. This venture is going to help all of us." He smirked, standing in what she could only describe as a superhero pose, straight back, chin raised, hands on his hips. It looked natural on him, like he owned the stance.

Unwilling to make a mistake that would land her in the gutter, she shook her head. "What about those men who are looking for us?" She didn't want to risk it. She'd done enough running for one day.

"They left about ten minutes ago. Come on. We have a lot to do, and we don't have a lot of time." He walked past her to the door and opened it before turning to her with his eyebrows raised.

"Not till you tell me why." She sat back and folded her arms.

"Ah, snap!" Jeremy laughed. "You're not a pushover. That's for sure."

Samuel shot him a dark look. "We are going to meet up with my detective friend to find out what's going on with your situation and set a plan in motion to keep you safe and finish our contract, okay?" He raised his eyebrows as if challenging her to ask more impertinent questions.

Annie let out a long, slow breath. She'd chosen to trust him when he saved her at the airport. He'd already proven he could keep her safe more than once. She had to believe that whatever they were about to do would help them. She dragged her sore body up and followed Samuel out of the room. Jeremy finished his sixth mini candy bar as they left. Annie supposed he wasn't in a hurry like they were. She had to run to keep up with Samuel's quick pace and longer stride.

"How good are your acting skills?" he asked as they entered the elevator.

"As great as anyone's, I suppose. I'm no professional, if that's what you're asking."

"Okay," he said, with what looked like a worry line on his forehead. "We can work with that. How fast can you shop?"

Annie's eyebrows shot up. "Shop?"

"Look, I'll explain more later when we are in a secure place, but suffice it to say you will have to look like you belong in my story and the excuses I made up on the spot at the airport if you are to remain safe." He eyed Annie's stained clothes and fuzzy hair. "Right now, you don't look the part."

Annie couldn't argue with him about that. "I can shop fast." She'd had some practice at her local thrift store, which often closed early. Thank goodness she didn't have to stay in these stained clothes.

"Good. Keep your head down and don't do anything to draw attention to yourself. You must remember that those men are still looking for you."

She nodded but didn't need the reminder. She'd never forget how she trembled when the hitmen busted her bedroom door open. Mentally shaking herself, she pushed that thought out of her mind. She wouldn't dwell on it.

He walked her through the lobby and led her outside to a new, shiny, black convertible Ferrari. "Is this real?" she asked, eyeing the car.

He chuckled. "Get in."

She pulled open the door and tried not to let her mouth hang open. *This is ridiculous.* "Not to tell you how to do your job or anything, but undercover grifter, fixer, or whatever you are and Ferrari don't mesh well."

He pulled a pair of posh, black sunglasses from his jacket and flipped them open. "Depends on who you're trying to impress. They call me in for jobs where the target needs to feel impressed." Flashing her a million-dollar smile, he started the car.

Seriously, who is this guy?

If her life wasn't on the line and her so-called friend hadn't been murdered last night, she would have turned to mush at the smile he gave her. She found Samuel handsome. That much, she'd admit. Who wouldn't?

He pulled the fancy car out of the parking lot, flashed her another dazzling smile, and hit the gas pedal.

CHAPTER 7

Annie kept her eyes on the road outside the window while they drove just above the speed limit. She absentmindedly plucked at her slightly damp clothes. Her comfort clothes were proving more uncomfortable by the minute; at least they were on the way to find some replacements.

Even if she could return to her apartment, she wouldn't step a foot through the door. Dillan's still form lying on her living room floor would haunt her for the rest of her life. She shivered. She'd ignored all of Granny's warnings and advice in pursuit of money to go to school. Look where that got her.

Annie clasped and unclasped her hands together while they drove. One worry after another hit her hard. She shook each of them off, but the events of the last twelve hours proved hard to shake. She could attempt a conversation with Samuel to free herself from the tumult in her mind, but it was easier to remain quiet. She had only seen situations like this on TV and had no idea how to act in real life. With a sideways glance at Samuel, she chose to stay silent. He focused on the road, his jaw tense.

Annie glanced out the window and watched the city rush past her. She shifted uncomfortably. Her body ached, her mind spun, and her emotions swirled, all while the blood in her veins rushed fast. When she left home, she'd fully expected this city to grant her every wish, that this job opportunity would fix all her problems. Instead, she'd botched it. Dillan had failed to mention that not everyone was successful.

Like a fool, Annie thought she could change her fate by breaking out of her predestined life. All of her school mates and neighbors expected her to work as a waitress forever in the crummy diner. Everyone she knew claimed she'd never attend culinary school. Everyone but her granny thought that her dreams would only ever remain dreams. Even when she'd landed a job at the bridal store in the next town over as a press girl during high school, kids at school had said the same. Because she came from a low-income family and grew up with her grandparents, her future was engraved in the stars—unchangeable, foreordained, and guaranteed, no matter how hard she worked or how valiantly she prayed.

Fate ruled, and she belonged in a lower-class job that would barely pay the bills. People like her didn't have a "dreams do come true" moment. As much as she wanted to go home, she knew her failure proved them right, and that pain hurt. She would return home and end up exactly where she'd left—at that crummy diner.

Why had she tried?

Dillan's face swam in front of her mind. *He* was why she'd tried. She'd trusted him and believed with her whole heart that this plan was a gift from God, not a curse.

After about a half hour, the car slowed and stopped. The tall, crowded buildings faded into the background as they entered what looked like a regular family-centered neighborhood.

Samuel unbuckled his seatbelt. "Let me do most of the talking. Detective Price is a friend, and she can help us ensure that things haven't gotten out of hand and that my plan can move forward. Come on," he said, opening his door.

Annie swallowed hard. If God had abandoned her into the custody of thieves, she had to do what she could to get out of this situation and back on track. She shivered and followed Samuel out of the fancy car. The small park they arrived at looked like an afterthought, like the city planner had no idea what to do with the random triangle of space and filled it with grass, a tree or two, and a swing set.

A woman sat on one side of the lone picnic table, a soda and a bagel smeared with cream cheese in front of her. She had medium-length, thick blonde hair woven into a braid. Her khaki-colored light-weight jacket and maroon blouse looked tasteful but not nearly as expensive as Samuel's clothes. Samuel picked up his pace, and Annie had to rush forward to keep up.

Once they were closer, Annie spied the detective badge hooked onto the woman's belt. She looked between Annie and Samuel, her eyebrows raised. Yes, she'd noticed the stark difference between the two of them. Who wouldn't?

"Annie, I'd like you to meet Detective Price, but we call her Claw. Claw, this is Annie Grey. The woman who lives at the apartment on Main with the homicide last night."

Detective Price's—Claw's—gaze narrowed, and her hand went to a pair of handcuffs hooked to the back of her belt, but she dropped her hand without pulling them out. "Let me guess, you were there too."

Samuel held up his hands. "Perhaps. What if I told you she didn't shoot the guy?"

Annie's gut clenched. She would never do something so horrible. The worst thing she'd done was attempt to walk away from Dillan and his whole plan.

"And you'd know this because . . ."

"I'm a witness."

Claw shook her head, but a brightness remained in her eyes. "Darn it, Kraken. Remind me why I put up with you?"

"Because I make up for the trouble." Samuel slid onto the bench across from Detective Price, so Annie followed suit. Her relief and worry teeter-tottered in her head. Why had the detective called Samuel . . . Kraken? Then it hit her. Kraken was his code name.

A smile formed on the detective's face, and she rolled her eyes. "We're finished at the crime scene."

"Is she a suspect?" he asked, nodding at Annie.

Claw stared at them both for a moment before she shook her head. "No."

Sam leaned against the picnic bench as if settling in for a great tale told by a professional storyteller.

With a smirk, Claw picked up her bagel. "First of all, she has no priors or motive that we can find. Second, the apartment building security cameras caught her unsavory friends entering the building about three minutes after the sound of the first gunshot. Your girl"—her eyes darted to Annie and back to Samuel—"placed a 911 phone call about two minutes later. The recording of the call has sounds of gunfire and men shouting a lot of incriminating things. Her second 911 phone call she made about twenty minutes later filled in a lot of blanks. Thanks for that, Annie," Claw said, raising her soda.

Claw took a drink and put the can on the picnic table before she continued. "The medical examiner says the guy was shot with a long rifle from a distance that matched the roof of the apartment building next door."

Samuel whistled. "Where I bet you found the bullet casing."

Claw snapped her fingers to acknowledge his statement. "And a fair few in the alley. Speaking of which, I'll need a statement from you both. Even though she is off the hook for the murder, she is still a person of interest and shouldn't leave the city." The detective took a large bite of her bagel, the cream cheese squishing out over the edge. She swiped the excess cream cheese off with one long finger and popped it into her mouth.

Samuel rubbed his forehead. "Shouldn't leave the city. What if she's in neighboring cities with a friend?"

Claw licked the cream cheese off her lips before she spoke. "Don't push your luck, Kraken. Seeing as she could identify the shooters, I could try for witness protection for her if—"

Samuel started shaking his head.

"But I know how you feel about that." Claw rolled her eyes behind her bagel. She acted like she thought Samuel was a fool. With a one-shoulder shrug, Claw took another bite of her bagel. "She can return to her apartment after the crime scene cleanup guys are finished, and we can have the police keep an eye on her."

Annie felt her shoulders drop. The only good thing that registered in this entire conversation was that she wasn't wanted for murder. She couldn't return to that apartment. She couldn't. They had to understand that.

Samuel tapped his fingers on the top of the picnic table. "I wanted to know if the police would release her into my custody."

Detective Price shot to her feet. "Have you gone insane, Kraken? I might have the ability to explain away why you were at that apartment and white lie a bit about how I got Miss Grey's statement, but I can't entrust her safety to you."

"Hear me out," Samuel said. "When Annie called 911 hours ago, she was promised an officer would come talk to her and no one has shown up. That means someone stopped the cops from coming, but guess who did show up? Her hitmen."

Claw's eyes narrowed. "What are you saying?"

Samuel shrugged. "You work with me. Who's to say our target Mr. Lichens doesn't have an inside man on the force?"

Our target? That meant Claw was helping Samuel with his job. What kind of cop did that make her? Annie shuddered and folded her arms against the sudden goosebumps that burst up her arms.

Claw knocked her knuckles against the table. "Okay. I'll look into that, but Miss Grey—"

Samuel held out a hand to stop her. "Needs to stay with me. You know what I have to accomplish, the information I need to retrieve for Mr. Benicci, and our goal for Mr. Lichens. I can't do that without her."

Annie's head whipped around, and she stared directly at Samuel, but he kept his eyes on the detective. Claw held his gaze in what looked like either a staring contest or some kind of silent conversation.

"You also know that she's far safer with me than with a police detail because you know who we're dealing with."

Finally, the detective turned to Annie for the first time during this entire conversation. "I won't allow you to feel bullied into helping Kraken with his scheme. You don't have to become involved. I can stop this right now before you get caught up in it."

"She's already part of this, Claw. She's a loose end. Her friend Dillan tried to break into the Lichenses' house last night, which is what got him shot."

Claw's head whipped back to Samuel so fast it looked almost unnatural. "You're serious."

He nodded slowly. "My contact told me about a newbie crew and an inside man who were hired to break into the same vault we got hired to crack. I arrived on the scene in time to see a masked man take out several members of this hodgepodge team. One guy, Dillan, got away, but with the hitmen hot on his trail. I followed him to find out who hired him. I kept my distance when I saw him enter an apartment. I had my phone out and was on the verge of calling you when I heard gunshots. I returned fire when they attempted to shoot Annie, and I helped her escape. That's what happened."

He looked down at his hands, his jaw tense. "Someone wants inside that vault before me. Our time is up."

Claw shook her head. "We can't risk someone ruining this job."

"Exactly. If Annie comes with me, I promise to protect her, and we can get this done."

Claw worried her lip and took another drink while she thought this over. Annie's head swirled. She hated the idea that Samuel wanted her to help him. She didn't see how she could, yet she disliked the idea of returning to her apartment alone.

Finally, Claw turned to Annie. "You can come with me if you'd like, Miss Grey. I will set you up with the protection I promised, but if you want to go with Kraken, I won't stop you. It's your choice."

Annie swallowed hard. If she wanted? Honestly, right now, Annie had no idea what she wanted. They kept talking about her like she was a five-year-old instead of a grown woman. Annie wrung her hands, her mind spinning. Did she want to stick around while Samuel, Jeremy, and Detective Price went after this Lichens person? No, definitely not. She'd had enough guns in her life already.

Claw tapped her fingers against her soda can. "If you choose to come with me but don't want to return to your apartment, I can set you up in a hotel or something until you're cleared to leave the city."

Samuel shot to his feet. "And what, gift wrap her for the assassins? You do that, and you might as well call them and tell them what time to expect her."

"It's all I can do," Claw snapped.

A sharp pang hit Annie in the stomach. She hated to agree with Samuel. As much as she didn't know him, she could feel the sincerity of his words. He understood the danger she found herself in. The last thing she wanted was for those hitmen to find her. She did know that if she had to stay in California, she would not survive alone.

Claw picked up the rest of her bagel and soda. "That's the best I can do without putting her in witness protection. You know how it works." She raised her eyebrows at Samuel as if trying to emphasize her point. Annie looked from one to the other.

"You know that's why I'd rather do things my way," Samuel said, straightening his jacket and returning to his perfect gentleman mode.

Claw chuckled. "This is why we work together, Kraken." Her gaze sliced over to Annie. "So, what will it be? I think we all agree that your options are limited. Either I can help you, or Kraken can." She looked at her watch. "But I need an answer right now. My lunch break is over."

Annie's insides squirmed. Biting her lip, her gaze darted between the two of them. Her head screamed that trusting the police made more sense, but her gut didn't agree. What kind of person earned the nickname Claw? What kind of detective associated with people like Samuel? He'd promised more than once that he'd get her home alive. Claw had made no such claim.

"I'll stick with . . . him for now," she said, hardly believing those words escaped her lips. A warm feeling filled her chest, confirming her choice.

A slow grin spread across Claw's face. "Great. I think that's wise. Especially if we have a mole in our ranks somewhere. I'll keep in touch." With a wink, she walked off toward a maroon four-door car, leaving Annie and Samuel alone in the tiny park.

Samuel immediately pulled out his phone and started a new text message.

Lord, if you still care about me, she prayed silently. *Help him help me. Please. Let this be the right choice.*

After a few more minutes, Samuel nodded toward his car. "Let's go. We need to get our shopping done."

Right, shopping. She looked down at her clothes and felt the smallest smile tug at the corner of her lips. At least she could look forward to changing into something better.

Annie rode silently but studied Samuel. His perfect dark hair and suit were hardly wrinkled from the crazy night. Worry lines appeared at the corner of his eyes, but the rest of his face remained emotionless. He wasn't James Bond, per se, if he didn't work for the government. Samuel was more an asset than anything else; an asset Claw called Kraken. It all felt so confusing.

Annie knew that a kraken was a mythological sea monster. The thought made her stomach tighten into a wad. For the first time that day, she wished she had her phone to look the creature up. Maybe the nickname held clues about the man sitting next to her. Would it hurt to ask? A tremor ran up her spine at the thought of asking him anything, but sitting silently didn't help her nerves either.

Annie tapped her fingers against her leg to drum up some courage. "Why did Detective Price call you Kraken?" she said a little too fast.

A corner of his mouth lifted. "I work with a bunch of different people who prefer to use code names instead of real names. When I stepped into this . . . line of work, I was given that name."

"Because?" Annie pressed, hoping that he'd give her a little more information.

He shrugged. "Code names are sometimes earned, and sometimes they are simply given. Claw is sharp and to the point. Jeremy is Midnight because of the late hours he usually keeps." He glanced at her. "Kraken is mine because I'm happy working quietly in the shadows until I'm needed front and center, and when I strike, I strike true and take down the whole ship."

His grip tightened on the steering wheel. "That's what I do, Annie. I take down people who hurt others. I stop groups of thugs and gangs of men who think they can hurt innocent people with no consequences because the police can't touch them. I make it so the police can arrest them. I pull down their empires. I sink their ships."

"So, you're a spy?" she asked, trying to piece together his explanation.

Samuel scoffed. "Sometimes I wish I were simply a spy. I'm a fixer, remember? I go in and fix problems no one else can."

Annie stared at him, eyes wide. "Why help me?"

He sighed. "Just because you got in their way doesn't mean you deserve to die."

A bit of warmth lit inside her chest. Did she dare hope he spoke the truth? Annie tried to examine the warmth but couldn't reasonably determine what it was. The lightness was a relief compared to all her other crushing feelings that morning.

She let a small amount of hope grow in her chest. Hope that Detective Price, or Claw, was right in leaving her in Samuel's care. Hope that Samuel wouldn't regret helping her. Hope that soon she'd finally have a story worth telling other people, because that is what she wanted this day to become—simply a story.

CHAPTER 8

ANNIE HONESTLY EXPECTED HIM TO take her to a secondhand thrift store or a department store, not a high-class boutique like La Fontaine. She couldn't help but stare at the window display, her eyes wider than a giant-sized pizza. Everything looked sleek, modern, and fancy, from the white pouf chairs to the black mannequins wearing designer clothes to the large crystal chandelier that shimmered in the light. Then there stood Samuel in his suit. He looked like he fit in here perfectly, unlike Annie, who looked like a hobo who had wandered in, lost and confused.

He opened the door to the shop and fixed her with a no-nonsense look. "Annie, I need you to trust me and go with whatever I say, okay?" he whispered out of the corner of his mouth. "For right now, I'm your brother, and we'll keep our story simple." He put a hand on the small of her back and gave her a small shove into the store. Now she knew why he asked her about her acting skills. If he wanted her to act like him, all rich and fancy, they were done for.

"Don't say a word unless you have to." He tapped his finger against his lips and rang the bell on the counter.

"Mr. Erickson," said a woman with black, slicked-back, chin-length hair. She wore all black, and her wrapped shirt, which ended with a large bow on her hip, screamed of fashion. "What a pleasure to see you again." Her eyes turned to Annie, and she balked. She looked like she had swallowed her tongue. Annie hid her snicker with a cough. In confusion, the woman turned slowly back to Samuel for an explanation. Annie shifted uncomfortably and looked down at her shoes.

This wasn't a good idea.

"Farica, it is a pleasure," Samuel said, taking her hand and bowing over it like men used to do in the Regency era. "But it hasn't been a good morning for us. This," he said, gesturing to Annie, "is my half sister, Annie. As you can see, she's had the worst morning."

Farica's nose wrinkled. "That I can. Tell me," she said, linking her arm through his, her doe eyes growing wider. Her red lipstick caught the light from the chandelier as she smiled, giving her lips a model-shine appearance.

Samuel looked over his shoulder as if to ensure no one could overhear him. "Poor Annie arrived this morning to stay with me after her boyfriend dumped her. Her luggage was lost on the airplane and a baby spit up all over her during the flight. One of the flight attendants gave Annie her workout clothes. A nice gesture, but sadly, she had no style."

Annie gawked at him. He'd lied to Farica with so much ease.

"How horrible," Farica said, floating over to Annie. "You poor, poor dear. We'll have you put to rights in no time, Miss Erickson. What are we looking for?"

"Everything," Samuel answered. "The airport has no idea what happened to her bags."

"Say no more," Farica said, her hands over her ears. She linked her arm through Annie's and whisked her to the back room without another word and pushed Annie behind a curtain. She and a team of three consultants started showing Annie clothes with price tags Annie had only seen on tags for formal wear. Annie tried to choose one simple outfit out of the bunch, but Farica gave her a hard look.

"Don't feel guilty about spending your brother's money, sweet girl. It wasn't your fault your clothes were lost and ruined. Besides, after a dumping, a girl needs an outfit that makes her feel like a million bucks."

Annie agreed with the feeling-like-a-million-bucks part, but that didn't mean she needed to spend a million bucks.

"I'm sure the airport will find them soon," Annie said, touching the soft fabric of a navy-blue skirt.

Farica snickered and handed Annie the skirt. "I'm sure they will. Until then, your brother is generously trying to help you. Don't disappoint him."

Swallowing her doubts, she let Farica and her team pick out several outfits. She started ignoring the price tags. Annie found it easier not to know how much they cost. Once in new underthings, Annie tried on outfit after outfit for Farica's approval. It took a while to please the woman, but finally, Farica declared they had everything Annie needed.

Farica turned to Annie, her nose crinkled. "You'd better change into a new outfit before you leave the store. I can't have you walking out in your old . . . things." Farica picked up Annie's stained shoes, T-shirt, and shorts and whisked them away, leaving her with no choice.

Finally finding herself alone in the dressing room, Annie took a slow, deep breath in an attempt to keep her sanity. New clothes were hung up all around her, each of them begging to be worn. She picked a light-pink flowy blouse with tiny white flowers, and cute white shorts. Gritting her teeth, she looked at the tags. She about swallowed her tonsils whole. Annie sank to the floor, hugged her knees to her chest, and took a few more deep breaths. Never in her life would she spend such a sum on a shirt and a pair of shorts. Her prom dress cost a grand total of seventy-five dollars, for crying out loud.

"Knock, knock, I thought you'd appreciate this until you see your stylist." Farica slipped a bedazzled hair tie through the curtained door.

"Thanks," Annie stated quietly. She had to pull herself together. Samuel wanted her to match his story, and a homeless-looking woman would only get her killed. The men hunting her would never expect to see her in designer clothes.

Wait a second. It finally hit her. This was a disguise. An expensive disguise, but still a disguise. Samuel was protecting her with this getup.

"This makes so much more sense," she whispered. These weren't her clothes to keep. They were clothes with the specific purpose of hiding her from the people who wanted her dead. Once the danger cleared, Samuel would probably return them.

Feeling much better about this situation, she quickly dressed in the new clothes. Annie walked out to find one of Farica's assistants outside her door. She came forward and helped Annie tie her hair into a soft bun so the frizz looked less pronounced. She handed Annie a pair of gold dangly earrings, brown strappy sandals, white sunglasses, and a turquoise bag. Now the disguise felt complete, Annie thought. Turning slowly, she looked in the mirror and clenched her jaw so it didn't fall open. She never would have recognized herself.

Smart move, Samuel.

Farica came around the corner and clapped. "You look fantastic! I've already included a makeup kit with the basics, more accessories, and a few sample perfumes, so you're all set." She took charge of packing up the rest of the items in the dressing room. Farica's team wrapped the clothes in pink-and-gray-striped tissue paper before they slipped them into shiny black bags with pink lettering on the front.

"We'll wait for you up front, miss," one of the assistants said, leaving Annie alone. Still considering herself in the mirror, she slid on the sunglasses to complete her look, and a shiver ran down her arms. She didn't look like herself. Not one bit. "Thanks, Samuel," she whispered.

Feeling for the first time like she might survive this nightmare, she walked through the curtain into the waiting room and waved at Samuel, who was paying for the clothes.

His eyes widened a bit, but otherwise, he hid his reaction. "Looking good, sis," he called, retrieving a jet-black card from Farica.

He glanced at his expensive-looking silver watch and feigned urgency. "We have to go. We're already late. Thank you, ladies," he said, flashing Farica and her assistants his brilliant smile.

They turned into warm, sappy goo at the sight of his shiny white teeth. Together he and Annie loaded the car, got in his Ferrari, and drove away from what Annie couldn't call a store.

"Thanks for the disguise," Annie said. She gazed at her new white shorts and strappy sandals. "I don't even recognize myself."

"No problem. It's a kill-two-birds-with-one-stone situation. The people watching us—my people," he clarified, "wouldn't have bought that you are my half sister if we hadn't done something. And hopefully, this will keep your people off our tail for now. I'm working for a win-win situation here."

So was she. Annie peered in the car's side mirror. "I didn't realize your people were still watching us."

He nodded slowly, his eyes on the busy road. "Every second of the day. Mr. Benicci likes to keep tabs on his investment. It took all my convincing power to make them think I had picked you up from the airport and they had missed that somehow. But they bought it, for the moment. We don't need to worry as long as we act our parts."

Annie's eyebrows scrunched together. "You told the men at the airport I was your half sister?"

He nodded again. "They would have shot us both if I hadn't."

Annie's mouth went dry. There were far too many threats on her life in the last twenty-four hours.

Samuel glanced at her quickly. "I must stress that they will shoot us if we give them any reason to see it differently. It wasn't part of the plan, but you've found yourself on not only one hit list but two."

She nodded slowly. Honestly, she didn't want any part of his undercover business, but they were strangers who had to trust each other to survive. It made her wish she had snuck away from him at the hotel. A nasty thought itched its way up to the surface of her brain and she knew that if he hadn't taken her in, she would have already caught a bullet.

CHAPTER 9

Samuel stayed quiet during the drive, but Annie kept her eyes on him. He baffled her. Somehow, he simultaneously balanced the tough-guy and the handsome-rich-guy vibes. Annie had never met anyone like him. She bit her lip, considering how she felt about him. Part of her heart screamed to run away while another part worried about how good he was with a gun. It felt strange to admit that even a small part of her trusted him, but she did. Hopefully, that wouldn't come to hurt her later.

Samuel drove them to a restaurant near the beach an hour away. From the driftwood window frames and the large crab sign on the front, she assumed it was a seafood place.

"Let's go," he said, getting out.

He tossed his keys to the valet. Annie stumbled out of the car and followed him inside. She smirked when she saw Jeremy sitting in a crab-red vinyl booth, talking to the waiter. Now, Jeremy she liked. He was easy to like and figure out, unlike Samuel.

Jeremy grinned when he saw them approach. The restaurant was so loud she barely heard his hello. They slid into the circular booth next to Jeremy. Annie didn't like that she ended up sandwiched between the men, but what could she do? They were her only hope of survival.

"Hey, Annie. Looking sharp."

She offered Jeremy a weak smile.

"How did it go?" Samuel asked, thumbing the edge of the menu.

"I got it covered," Jeremy said, munching on a large dinner roll from a basket in the middle of the table.

Samuel fixed Jeremy with an inquisitive look. "You backtracked everything? Got it all done?"

"Oh yeah, it was cinchy. I might have overdone it a little." Jeremy turned to Annie and nudged her elbow. "You are now officially Annie Erickson, Samuel's younger half sister." He knocked something into her knee under the table, and she looked down to see a white leather wallet. Annie picked it up and opened it. Inside, she found a new phone in a pink sparkly case, a fake ID, what looked like five hundred dollars in cash, and some credit cards.

She gasped at Jeremy, who winked and started on another roll. For a skinny guy, he could sure eat. Annie glanced back at Samuel, who perused the menu. They both seemed so at ease . . . as if this exchange was a typical kind of thing. She slipped the wallet into her new purse. Her fingers trembled a little bit. Being raised a good Christian girl, all this lying felt wrong. Wasn't a fake ID breaking the law? Hadn't she told Dillan yesterday that she wouldn't take part in a crime?

"Are you sure all of this is necessary?" she said loud enough for them to hear.

"Oh, you bet," said Jeremy with a wave of his hands. "It's nothing, so don't worry about it. This is the kind of stuff I started to do in third grade. It's the only right way to keep you hidden and safe."

Annie blinked at that comment. She doubted a fake name was the only right way to keep her from ending up like Dillan.

Jeremy winked and grabbed the last roll in the basket. They'd better order quickly before Jeremy decided to eat the table.

Annie turned to look at Samuel. She felt like she needed to say something, but words failed her completely. How did she sort through the tangled mess of her emotions? If someone had told her yesterday that she would be sitting right here in her current situation, she would have laughed in their face. Days like today didn't happen to ordinary people.

"Thanks," she finally managed to say. That, at least, felt appropriate. They were both doing a lot to help her.

Samuel didn't respond.

"May I take your order?" a waiter asked a moment later.

Annie quickly picked up the menu while Jeremy asked about the three different kinds of shrimp. Everything in her mind started spinning, trying to process the events of the night and this odd day and her new identity. She didn't think she could stand staring at all the choices in front of her.

"And for you, miss?"

"Salmon," she said, picking the first thing she saw. "With rice and asparagus."

He nodded and turned to Samuel, who ordered the halibut, loaded baked potato, and a mixed-greens salad. After the waiter left, Samuel turned to her. "It's a good thing I already had a half sister in my fake identity for this assignment. We don't need any real deaths on our hands, so let's talk about the details."

Jeremy nodded, focused entirely on the last of his bread.

"For the time being: You surprised me with a visit. Had a rough morning, but you're back to yourself by now. We're from a rich family with houses in New York, Las Vegas, Miami, and Tahiti. You live in New York with my stepmom—your mom, Leilani. If anyone asks you about my business dealings, you know nothing. You've traveled the last year, keeping up with your studies online. You don't pay attention to what I'm doing anyway."

"You're studying English," Jeremy added. "I thought that no matter what, you've at least read some of the classics, so an English major made the most sense."

"Thanks for the vote of confidence," she mumbled, a new worry building in her chest. She had read some classics, like *Pride and Prejudice* and *Great Expectations*, but wasn't an expert on them.

Jeremy turned to her. "Hey, I had to work fast, and honestly, we don't know you. I considered fashion design because of your job experience at the bridal store but decided that knowing how to iron dresses didn't mean you'd know how to design them."

Annie nodded as her crazy day finally caught up to her. They were right; she somehow decided to trust two strangers with her life, letting them control it. Her lips trembled, and the room suddenly felt hot. She needed to get out of there. "Excuse me," she said to Jeremy, nodding toward the restrooms.

She didn't know if Samuel would move for her. Jeremy shrugged and moved out of the way. She didn't look at either of them as she ran to the ladies' room. The tears started to fall the moment she opened the door. She darted into a stall and buried her face in her knees. Body shaking, the tears came fast and furious, turning into sobs before she could stop it.

They honestly didn't know who she was or if she could keep up with their story. What if she messed up their plans? They trusted her to act the part. She didn't even know if she could do it. She was a simple Idaho girl. A girl whose ex-boyfriend had been murdered only last night. A girl who didn't want to end up the same way. How could she act like some rich girl so their covers weren't blown? What if she got them killed? Maybe she should leave. Sneak out that back door. Cut her losses and chance going home without their help. The shooters certainly wouldn't think she'd hitchhike.

She'd decided to trust Samuel in the first place because he pulled her out of the garbage and told her to run while he charged the hitmen. What would happen to her if she went along with this deceptive plan? It's possible she would fall further away from what she knew about right and wrong. Annie wiped the tears away and took out her new wallet. Could she do it? She had no idea if she had the capability to lie to everyone around her to save her own skin.

The door opened, and she pulled some toilet paper off the roll and wiped at her eyes. She expected to see a high heel walk past. Instead, shiny black shoes and dark navy-blue pants stopped on the other side of the stall.

Samuel.

"Good gravy, Sam!"

"Good what?" he asked, a hint of laughter in his voice.

"You're in the ladies' room."

He sighed. "Yeah, I am. Apparently, my sister is having a hard breakup, and the ladies in the restaurant thought it was so sensitive of me to try to talk you into coming back out to dinner."

"I'm sorry," Annie said, leaning her head against the cold metal stall wall.

"You don't need to apologize. Jeremy and I are used to accomplishing things quickly. I didn't think about how hard this day has been on you. I'm sorry I didn't consider it. I don't want to add to your worries, but I must be honest with you."

Honesty. That she could handle.

"The men watching me know you exist. We're both in trouble if we don't play it right with them. Your experience working at the bridal store is something we need to take down an abominable man. We need you, Annie. I'm sorry, but I need you to unlock the door and come out. For just a few days, I need you to become Annie Erickson, a woman who got dumped, is good at English, and has one awesome brother.

"Do this, and I promise I will return you home safe. I will remove the threat against you. This won't last long; it's already almost over. There is little more we'll ask you to do, but Jeremy and I promise to walk you through it. You're not in this alone. We will keep you safe."

"I don't understand why you're helping me," she said so quietly she didn't know if he'd hear her.

He sighed, and it sounded like he leaned his head against the door. "Several years ago, my real sister was murdered. She told me she was in trouble, and I didn't take her seriously. I was young and dumb, in my junior year of college, and caught up in my own life. I could have stopped it, Annie. I could have helped her. Instead . . ." He paused, and Annie waited with bated breath. Samuel let out a long sigh full of emotion.

"I didn't lie when I said I knew someone in your situation. If I don't help you, you'll join Hazel—my sister—and your friend on the other side. I couldn't live with your blood on my hands too, not when I know I can help. Let me help you. I know faking your identity is new, hard, and not what you want to do right now, but it will also save your life. If you are Annie Erickson, then we can help each other. I'll save you from the men hunting you while we take down a horrible, corrupt man. If you stay Annie Grey, however, we can't help you at all."

Annie looked at her fake ID and took a deep breath. A tremble ran up and down her spine. She needed their help, and if she could help them in return, why shouldn't she try? She owed Samuel for saving her life. With a long, deep breath, she straightened her shirt and unlocked the door.

"Leave it to my *brother* to explain away my splotchy face before I even have to think about it." Annie rubbed her arms, still trying to get a grip.

The corner of his mouth lifted and put his arm around her, pulling her into a side hug. Annie got a strong whiff of what smelled like shaving cream and a citrusy soap mixed with gunpowder. Strangely, his arm also eased the hurt. She leaned into the hug, soaking up the comforting feeling she desperately needed. "That's what big brothers are for." He flashed his brilliant white teeth and steered her out of the ladies' room.

A few older women gave Annie a sad smile as they returned to their table. Jeremy gestured to all the food that had arrived and unrolled his napkin with a flourish. Annie couldn't explain it, but that small action alone lifted her spirits. She scooted into her spot and quietly ate her meal while Jeremy and Samuel discussed their plans in a code she didn't understand. For the first time all day, she was glad she didn't have to speak or even understand them. What happened next was in their hands.

CHAPTER 10

Jeremy left the restaurant first to run errands after swallowing his food in record time. Annie couldn't help but wonder where he kept all that food. He was a beanpole of a guy, so where did it all go?

Once they finished, Annie silently followed Samuel to his car. He drove them to the same hotel. "Jeremy officially got us rooms," he said in response to her questioning glance.

He seemed calm, as if on a relaxing vacation, until they pulled into the parking lot. Annie noticed his jaw muscles tense. His gaze lingered on a black van parked across the street, its windows half rolled down.

"Don't make it easy for them to recognize you. Act the part," he said before throwing his car into park and getting out as if he hadn't noticed the suspicious vehicle. Annie's hands curled into fists, her breath short. He opened her door, and she pried her fingers open to give him her hand. "Smile," he said through his teeth, his lips not moving.

She flashed a tight smile that probably looked more like a grimace. She did not possess the skills to mimic his brilliant one. Nonetheless, she urged the corners of her mouth up more. Annie's muscles clenched, but she forced herself to move. He put his arm around her shoulders, and they walked quickly into the hotel. His arm didn't bother her as much as it did earlier in the day. She saw the gesture for what it really was—a shield.

Samuel winked at the ladies at the front desk in the hotel lobby. One turned slightly pink before he pulled Annie around the corner toward the elevators. Nothing bad happened this time as the elevator rose slowly to the fourth floor. They found the hallway empty. Samuel picked up the pace, and they jogged to her room. He opened the door with a key card Jeremy must have given him, but held out his hand to stop her from entering. He flipped on the light and looked around. With a satisfied nod, he waved her to follow him in.

Annie immediately fell onto the couch, tired to her bones. It had been a long day, the kind that belonged in a record book. Samuel went directly to the window and split the curtains enough to spy outside. "I got you your own room, but with those men keeping watch outside"—he nodded out the window—"I think it's best not to split up. Jeremy will arrive soon." He looked around the room. "With the two beds and the couch, we should be fine. Are you comfortable with that?"

She shrugged, too tired to care anymore. "I've trusted you this far."

"I'm going to get our things from the car. You come to this window and call me on your phone if anyone so much as moves in that car."

Annie didn't like the sound of either of those things happening right now. She needed a calm evening with no trouble at all. With the sun setting outside, wasn't there some kind of nighttime truce? Probably not. Villains, thugs, and thieves thrived at night. With a groan fit for the stage, she moved to his spot by the window. "Okay, but I don't have your number."

"Yes, you do. I'm listed as 'big brother' in your new phone," he said tapping her turquoise purse as he walked past her to the door. "No one but me or Jeremy comes through this door. Got that? Not hotel staff or someone claiming to be on the 'team.'"

Annie nodded. Seemingly satisfied, he left. Annie gently parted the curtains exactly as she had watched him do multiple times that day and stared down at the black van. A few minutes later, Samuel and a bellboy appeared with a trolley. They laughed about something as he unlocked his car. No one in the black van moved.

Annie watched as Samuel and the bellboy piled packages onto the cart. Still, no one moved. She let out a slow breath as she watched them disappear back into the building with all their packages. Maybe there was a nighttime truce after all.

A loud knock sounded on the door. Annie's heart rate went from normal to turbo in one second flat. She looked back outside the window. Nothing had changed. Heart beating so hard she could feel it in her throat, she tiptoed toward the door. She had no weapons or training of any kind. What should she do? Hide? The knock came again, and she swallowed hard before she stood on tiptoe and looked out the peephole in the door. Knocks on doors were now officially scarier than sidewalks.

Jeremy stood there, a broad smile on his face. Annie let out a sigh of relief, her arms wrapped around her chest in an attempt to help slow her heart rate. She sucked in a few breaths before she threw the door open.

"Hey there, Annie. You forgot the secret knock."

"I didn't know we had one." She stepped out of his way and held the door open for him.

He laughed, pulling two rolling luggage bags, one of them white and the other black. On the other hand, he balanced a pizza. "I'll have to tell Sam. He's slipping. He should have briefed you on that before he left you alone. Don't worry. I'll hold it over his head for a loooong time."

Annie brightened at the comment. Jeremy parked the suitcases against the wall and slid his pizza onto the desk. "Sam let me know about the situation. I'd ask if you want one of the queen beds or the couch, but I'm more of a couch kind of guy, so I'll selfishly take that. I hope you don't mind." He slid off his bag, which had been strapped across his chest and pulled out a laptop.

"Are you sure?'" she asked, looking longingly toward one of the beds with white, fluffy pillows.

"Positive." Jeremy settled on the couch and started typing away on his laptop. The prospect of the soft bed proved far too tempting. Without hesitation, Annie pulled the covers down and slid, fully dressed, into the first queen bed. It felt heavenly. Her sore body melted into the mattress. The pillows were unbelievingly fluffy, and the sheets felt so good she could cry. A girl needed sheets like this after a day like today.

A minute later, two knocks sounded on the door. Jeremy stood and knocked once before another knock answered. With a nod, he pulled open the door and helped Samuel tug the trolley into the room. They whispered while stacking all her bags against the wall. If they saw no need to include her, then she wouldn't worry about listening. With their things in the room, they both sat down on the couch. Samuel began scrolling through his phone, and Jeremy checked his computer. If they were going to ignore her, the danger must have passed for the day. Smiling at that thought, Annie let her heavy eyes fall closed.

Maybe she would wake up at home in Idaho, kind of like Dorothy. She never would have come to work summer sales, never would have learned what danger looked and felt like, and never would have met Samuel or Jeremy. Her crazy Oz adventure would never have happened and could remain a colorful dream. Dillan would have been disappointed, but in that scenario, he wouldn't have died.

A tear slipped out of her eye. Dillan might have lost her friendship several weeks ago, but he had been a good friend for a long time and a boyfriend for a short time. Another tear followed. Now he was gone. She hadn't one spare moment to mourn his loss all day, but now his death hit her full force. A third tear rolled down her cheek, and she sniffed. Once the police released his body, they'd hold a funeral in Idaho. She'd go, depending on how long it took for her to return home.

Annie sniffed back the tears again. She didn't want to cry. She'd already cried over losing Dillan after he'd refused to change. A hand touched her shoulder. She jumped and looked past her covers to see Samuel. He handed her a couple of tissues, his eyes soft as if he understood. She took them, and without a word, he moved back to the couch and resumed his work with Jeremy. Annie dabbed at her eyes and nose and clutched a pillow to her chest. Mashing her eyes closed, she thought about her home until she fell into that oblivion only granted by sleep.

Annie woke sometime later to a conversation she didn't want to overhear.

"I know it's difficult, so why did you decide to assist her at a time like this?" Jeremy said.

"I knew I had to," Samuel's voice answered.

"You always 'have to,' Sam. You can't help it. All I've seen you do the last few years is try to lend a hand over and over again." There was enough frustration in Jeremy's voice that Annie couldn't help but wonder if Jeremy wished he worked with someone else.

"I know, but I can't ignore people who need me. I can't leave someone to suffer or even die when I know I can do something about it. Why do you think I got into this game in the first place? I never signed up to become a fixer. Growing up, I never wrote down *grifter* on my school papers. I never dreamed that I'd find myself here right now. It wasn't in my five-year plan."

Annie shifted as silently as she could. She hadn't wanted to overhear their conversation, but now she found that she couldn't stop listening. It provided more clues to the puzzle of Samuel.

Jeremy snorted. "None of us planned on this life. It's the kind that finds you, except for Steel. I think she was born for this kind of thing. Annie wasn't born for this life; you and I both know that, and if we're not careful, she'll get sucked in too."

Samuel huffed. "I won't allow that. I'll protect her from that fate."

"How can you prevent it? This is how it starts, Sam, with one enemy or one job. We were going to make it work somehow without her. Sure, it added a lot more risk, but we could try—"

"No," Samuel interrupted. "The Warden's only allowing her to stay because she has a spot on the team. A spot he felt we should have filled months ago. We both know he didn't like feeling one man short."

"I could still book a flight to Idaho," Jeremy said in a low tone.

"You and I both know that isn't a good idea. It wasn't earlier this morning, and it still isn't. She's now a part of our plans. Mr. Benicci barely accepted my cover story. Like it or not, she's the key to making our heist work, and we all know it. There's no turning back for us. We will carry on. We have to. She has to. Afterward, I'll take her home, and she'll forget all about it. She can return to her regular safe life. It's that simple."

"Is it?" Jeremy asked.

"Yes. And—"

"I knew there was an *and*," Jeremy teased.

"She might know more than she thinks. If I've considered that option, her so-called hitmen have as well."

"Whatever you say, boss."

"I say it's late. Let's go to bed."

"Now that I can agree to." Jeremy yawned.

Annie closed her eyes as they moved about for the next few minutes. She heard a loud sigh and cracked one eye open. Jeremy stretched out on the couch, a wide smile on his face. He settled into his pillows, relaxation overtaking his expression. She envied him. How could he look so calm at a time like this?

Samuel walked out of the bathroom, and she closed her eye. She heard him walk past her and flop onto the other bed beside his beloved window. She kept her eyes closed until both of their breathing steadied. Her mind spun with their conversation, her emotions twirling, mixing, and crashing into a ball of confusion.

Granny's sweet face swam into her mind. Granny always knew what to do. Unfortunately, Granny had no idea of the danger Annie was in. A new worry churned in her gut, and before it drove her crazy, she decided to do something about it.

Annie eased out of bed, knowing that sudden movements would have both men reaching for guns. She snatched her new pink, sparkly phone off the bedside table and snuck into the bathroom. It's a good thing she knew her grandmother's number by heart. Annie dialed it, knowing full well that Granny was up this late. Granny slept from seven to eleven but woke up at eleven to cook their real dinner before she did a project. While Annie grew up, Granny always claimed that the middle of the night was magic for grownups, not kids. She'd serve Annie a bowl of chili or a casserole before she sent her back to bed. Annie listened to the phone ring, her pulse racing. Granny had to answer.

"Hello?"

"Granny, it's Annie." She let out a long sigh.

"Annie dear, please tell me you finally quit that dreadful job and are on a layover in Salt Lake City on your way home. I got a nice pot of our favorite chili on the stove and some cheese rolls in the freezer. All I need is forty-five minutes, and we'd have the perfect hot midnight meal."

Annie clutched her phone to her chest for a moment. She needed Granny's voice so much. "No, I'm sorry I can't come home for—at least a few more days."

"Annie honey, you know how I feel about you following Dillan's strange plans to make money. There are other ways to save for culinary school. You belong here, honeybee."

"I know . . ." Annie bit her lip and blinked to keep the tears at bay.

"Dillan used to be such a sweet boy, but I'm afraid he's become more of a troublemaker. I could see it in his eyes. Honeybee, we will find a way to pay for your schooling. I promise. Just come home, love."

Annie laughed. Granny was fine. They had this argument every other phone call. "I wanted to check on you and make sure you aren't going crazy without me. Is everything all right? Everything normal?"

"Yes, dear. Same old boring life on an old boring street. Our town isn't big enough for mischief or mayhem unless you count Mr. Drews yelling at anyone who puts a toe into his yard."

Annie breathed a sigh of relief, feeling lighter than she had all day. Granny's soothing voice was an extremely needed solvent.

"Where are you, Annie dear? You sound all echoey."

"Still in California."

"I didn't realize California was so echoey."

Annie snorted. "Very funny."

"No, seriously."

Annie honestly had no idea if she could give her location over the phone. Jeremy probably safeguarded her phone, but what if Granny's phone was tapped? She shouldn't give out any pertinent information—just in case.

"I'm in a bathroom, so that explains the echo."

Granny laughed lightly. "Sure does."

"Look, Granny, just call me if anything seems odd or feels a little off. I want to make sure you're okay. This is my new number. I lost my old phone."

"Certainly, dear, but aren't you coming home soon? I doubt much will happen between then and now except the usual."

Annie hoped not. She'd had enough excitement today to last her for years—strike that, forever. Yes, she'd had enough excitement for forever. Jeremy hit it on the head; she wasn't born for this kind of thing, and the universe or God wasn't about to choose this kind of life for her simply because she tried to change her fate. She'd become the best homebody ever, maybe take up some crazy craft and get a bunch of cats. That would fix things. "I love you, Granny."

"I love you too. Book your flight, love. I worry about you and Dillan. He's still in his own place, right? He didn't convince you to live in sin?" Her tone reminded Annie of when she was sixteen and started dating boys.

"Gross, Granny." She'd never wanted that kind of relationship with Dillan. Even dating him had felt a little weird. She bit her lip, her gut churning with the memory of his death, but if Granny knew about what happened, she'd only worry about Annie more. "Granny . . . I made a huge mistake. You were right. I want to come home. I have to finish a few things first, and then I'm coming home to stay."

"Well, if that's the outcome of this trip, I'm glad."

Annie felt a pang in her heart. Granny had never liked Dillan or this plan.

"I mean . . . I'm sorry, sweet girl. Do you want to talk about it?" she asked, but Annie could hear the smile in her voice.

"Not really."

"Come on, what did he do to lose you?" There was far too much joy in her voice for Annie's liking, but she knew Granny meant well.

"It wasn't much. He started to do things I disagreed with, and when I spoke to him about it, he got mad and told me I was a nitwit. So I told him to leave me alone. He . . . won't bother me anymore." Annie gulped.

"Good girl. He wasn't worth your time, honeybee. I've said that again and again all through your high school years."

Granny may have never liked him, but in high school, he'd taken the place of a best friend and boyfriend all rolled into one. It was that version of Dillan Annie missed and mourned. "I know." Her voice cracked despite her best effort.

A long sigh came over the phone. "I'm sorry you're hurt about losing his friendship, love. Say your prayers. Jesus can take away your pain if you let Him."

Tears rushed to her eyes. "He hasn't answered many of my prayers of late," Annie admitted, thinking about her horrible day. She didn't want to confess it to Granny, but she felt abandoned by God.

"Oh, honeybee, just because you don't recognize the answers doesn't mean they aren't there."

Annie nodded. She knew Granny believed that, but Annie didn't know if she did right then. "I've got to go, Granny. It's late. But I sure love you."

"I love you too, honeybee. Be safe."

She wanted to say, "I'm trying," but she knew that would only prompt Granny to ask more questions. That wasn't something she wanted. She settled for a simple "Bye."

That conversation had not eased her mind as much as she'd hoped, but at least she knew Granny was okay, for now.

Annie turned to look in the mirror. Her hair had become a mess again. Groaning, she yanked the crazy-looking bun out the rest of the way and let her light-blonde hair fall free. She had no idea if she had PJs in her bags, so sleeping in the clothes Samuel had bought her earlier seemed like her best choice. She left the bathroom and crawled under the fluffy covers.

"You know your granny's phone is probably tapped," Jeremy said sleepily after Annie settled under her covers.

She guessed she shouldn't feel surprised he'd woken up. "Yeah, I do."

"The shorter the conversation, the better, for your sake," he said, burying his face into his pillow.

"Noted," Annie said, rolling the other way. She couldn't help but wonder if the hitmen could put a tap on Granny's phone in less than twenty-four hours. If they could, she might be in more danger than she realized.

CHAPTER 11

Annie woke to the sound of cereal crunching. Her stomach immediately grumbled. Rolling over, she spotted Jeremy sitting on the couch, balancing a bowl of cereal in one hand and his laptop on his knees. He looked so ridiculous that she didn't even try to stop a small giggle.

"I brought up more cereal from the hotel breakfast bar if you want some," he said, pointing to a stack of mini cereal boxes, paper bowls, and unopened milk bottles.

"I'm starving." Annie looked over at Sam's bed to find it neatly made and empty. The sound of water came through the bathroom wall. At least she wasn't stuck with slobs. She poured her cereal into a paper bowl.

"Mind if I turn on the TV?" she asked tentatively.

Jeremy shook his head, not even looking up from his computer. Annie settled back on her bed with her food and turned the TV to the cooking channel. It took a couple minutes, but once her favorite chefs started chopping and frying, her nerves settled a bit, and her muscles relaxed enough that she didn't feel like her whole body was clenching, ready to spring.

The bathroom door opened, and Samuel came out in a nice blue button-down shirt and slacks that weren't even close to casual. He looked incredibly handsome and still gave off that super-spy vibe without the tux-like suit. His hair looked wet but combed. He gave her a brief smile that made her heart leap in her chest before he moved to the breakfast food on the desk.

Annie turned away and focused on her show. She ignored Sam's discussion with Jeremy. Since her day yesterday hadn't turned into an Oz-like dream, she needed all the relaxation she could get. Breathing in and out slowly, she watched the chefs on the TV struggle through an eggs Benedict challenge.

A few minutes later, right after they sauced the eggs Benedicts with the perfect hollandaise sauce, Samuel sat next to Annie on the edge of her bed and placed a box of brown hair dye in front of her. "Any chance you ever wanted to become a brunette?"

"What?" Annie said, her gaze darting from his face to the box. "No, no, no, I like my blonde hair."

"So do we," said Jeremy through a bagel and cream cheese he procured from seemingly nowhere.

Samuel put a hand on her shoulder. Goosebumps and a zinging thrill rushed through her at his gentle touch and the kindness in his eyes. She had to swallow hard to reverse the feeling. "This will help keep your guys off our trail. Believe me, today we need them unable to track us down. Besides, I have brown hair, and we'll sell our cover better if my sister does as well."

"I'm only your half sister," Annie spat.

Jeremy laughed. "Now you're getting into the role."

Annie glanced down at the box of hair dye. Her stomach squirmed at the idea of putting that stuff in her hair. "I have no idea how to use this. I've never dyed my hair before. What if I mess up and turn my hair green?" They'd never had extra money for hair experiments. Granny always insisted they could use their money for better purposes and trimmed Annie's hair with the kitchen scissors.

"Don't worry," said Jeremy, licking his fingers to clean up any stray cream cheese. "Sam is a pro. He worked at a hair salon for about four months a year or so ago. Great cover."

Samuel checked his fancy silver watch. "It's 7:00 a.m. If we are going to do this, we need to get started."

He picked up the box and held out his hand. "Come on, Annie. Trust me. You can do this. I guarantee it's not a big deal."

Annie blew out a long breath. "I've trusted you with my life."

He quirked an eyebrow. "But not with your hair?"

Annie groaned as Samuel and Jeremy laughed. Annie twisted a lock of her hair around her finger. "Fine, but if I hate it, you fix it before I go home."

"Deal." He offered her his hand again.

Annie swallowed her last bite of cereal and set her empty bowl on the nightstand. Jeremy leaped up and twirled the desk chair around. He pushed it past them and settled the chair into the bathroom in front of the sink.

Annie numbly sat down. She wrung her hands as Samuel moved her long hair out of the way and wrapped a towel around her shoulders. "Relax," Samuel said, giving her shoulder a slight squeeze. He rolled up his sleeves, revealing his toned forearms. His smile felt warmer than usual, softer. Maybe this was his genuine smile? It looked nothing like his million-dollar smile from yesterday. Being a grifter meant he often acted differently to match the circumstances. The question was if he was playing a part now or if this was him just being him.

"This cream will protect your skin." He applied a small amount of the white cream onto his fingers and lightly brushed it on her forehead next to her hairline. A warm, delightful tremor shot down her skin when he removed his hand, making a genuine smile of her own appear on her lips. Annie looked at her light-blonde hair in the mirror and let out a slow breath. She couldn't fret over this. Hair dye wasn't even close to what she faced yesterday.

Samuel pulled on purple gloves and mixed some creamy light-brown stuff with something from a large purple bottle. Annie looked away, not wanting to watch as he worked with a small, black brush with tiny, short bristles. If she discounted the fancy clothes, he did look a lot like a hairdresser.

When he began brushing the concoction onto small sections of her hair, Annie closed her eyes and tried to think of something else, anything else. She thought about Granny and how much culinary school cost. She thought about Dillan and wondered what would have happened to him if he hadn't gotten killed. She thought about anything besides what Samuel was doing to her hair and how nice it felt to feel his fingers moving softly through it. No one had ever run their fingers through her hair.

"Annie, are you okay?" he asked. "You're trembling."

"Yes," she lied. *Okay* was a relative word. Right now, she felt a lot of things, and she wasn't sure *okay* made the list. "I hope I don't look terrible."

Samuel laughed. "I doubt that's possible."

"Come on, Sam," she snapped, opening her eyes. She shot him a hard glare. "You saw me with garbage-stained clothes and hair so frizzy I must have looked like I electrocuted myself."

He snuck a quick look at her, a soft grin on his lips. "Yet I stand by my statement."

Heat rushed to Annie's face. He hadn't said the word *beautiful*, but the fact that he'd even implied the idea astounded her. She glanced back at his face, but it had become businesslike again. She caught sight of the brown goo all over her head and closed her eyes again. It looked worse than the garbage sludge.

She groaned, and Sam gave her a soft nudge before lifting her hair away from her ear. She liked the idea of calling him Sam. It made him feel more like a regular human. Working with a super spy might seem cool, but Sam wasn't a spy. He dressed like James Bond, but he wasn't Bond himself. Besides, as his "sister," the nickname fit her cover.

This time she focused on the slight flutters in her stomach when he touched her hair or when his fingers brushed her ear. It helped more than her earlier racing thoughts. She knew she shouldn't feel any attraction to a man like Sam. She shouldn't let his touch affect her in any way. But if focusing on the flutters got her through the hair-dyeing process, she'd allow it for this moment only.

"Right, that step is all done." He clapped an ungloved hand on her shoulder, raising one eyebrow in amusement. A flutter of delight flew down her arms, and she found for a moment that she could hardly breathe. He set the timer on her phone and walked out, leaving her alone with her thoughts. Annie took a long, cleansing breath, shook off the confusing feelings, and peeked at the mirror.

She winced. It looked worse than she thought. Annie stared at her hair, all wet with brown goop. Her hair was piled on her head and all stuck together. If Dillan weren't already dead, she would have killed him for getting her into all of this. If not for him, she would be at home with Granny. She could have been learning how to bake Granny's famous pies and delivering burgers at that crummy restaurant—not running for her life with two strangers and becoming a brunette. Her anger fled as quickly as it came. She shouldn't think such things. "I'm sorry, Dillan," she whispered.

When the timer rang, Sam came back in and checked her hair. "That will do." He handed her a pair of gloves. "Rinse it out." He nodded to the shower. "We'll see how it turned out." He left, pulling the door all the way closed. Annie walked forward and locked it. It's not that she didn't trust them. Sam had been nothing but a gentleman toward her. However, she needed to feel like she had some control over something when it came to her privacy.

Annie leaned over the tub and rinsed her lengthy hair, grumbling the whole time as the goo turned the water an ugly brown. She avoided the mirror after she finished and walked straight into the room. Samuel came over and lightly pulled his fingers through her wet hair, making goosebumps shoot up her arms.

"I think this will work. Will you allow me to dry it?"

Annie nodded. She'd rather he did it. She wasn't sure if she could face her hair yet. Sam took her hand and dragged her back into the bathroom. He froze for a moment, looking at her hair.

"Oh no, did the color not stick?" Annie didn't want to relive that process.

He laughed. "No, nothing like that. When was the last time you cut your hair?"

Annie shuffled her feet. "I don't know. A year? Maybe closer to two years?"

"You ready yet?" Jeremy asked as he knocked on the bathroom door. "We don't have much time left."

"Almost," Sam replied. He took out a pair of hair scissors from his bag on the counter.

Annie backed up toward the tub. "Oh no, you put those things away."

"Annie, bangs and a little trim will make your hair look nicer and more expensive. You do come from a wealthy family, remember?"

Yeah, right. Unless he was talking about her cover. Of course he was talking about her cover. That is why they'd done all of this in the first place. "Right . . . fine . . . do it quickly."

Annie hid her eyes behind her hands while Sam trimmed and layered her hair and cut curtain bangs. "Perfect. You ready to see it?"

She shook her head.

"I'll dry it first. You'll like it better dry anyway."

He pulled the hair dryer off the wall and got started. Annie never thought she would enjoy a man drying her hair, but after a while, she relaxed. The soft fluttering feeling returned to her chest, making this experience worth it.

Sam turned off the hair dryer and hung it back on its frame. "All done. Ready?"

Annie shook her head. "No."

"Come on. It's not like I dyed it neon green or anything."

"I guess that's true." Annie spun around and quickly opened her eyes before she chickened out. Her hair was a soft brown color. Still light, but definitely brown. The bangs that Sam cut framed her face softly, changing her look completely. Her face shape even looked different. It all suddenly fit—the clothes, her hair, their cover, and everything else.

"Wow." She couldn't take her eyes off her reflection.

"Is that a good wow or a bad wow?" Sam asked, a tinge of worry in his tone.

"A good one," she said, elbowing him in the side as she imagined a sister would. "It's shocking that my voice is coming from that person in the mirror."

Sam laughed.

"Are you two finished yet?" groaned Jeremy.

"Yep," Sam said with an extra smile at Annie. "She's good to go."

"Good, because we've got to leave right now."

"Can I change first?" Annie asked, eyeing her rumpled clothes.

Sam nodded, and they walked to her pile of black bags. "You can put all of your things in here." He wheeled the white suitcase over to her.

Annie nodded and started packing. Sam and Jeremy followed suit. A few minutes later, Annie had all her new things in her suitcase except the outfit she wanted to wear.

Jeremy taped his watch when she raced into the bathroom to change. "You know what, I'll call a ride and meet you there."

Annie kept her eyes away from the mirror while she changed into a yellow eyelet sundress and camel-colored boots with flowery cut-outs to keep her feet from overheating.

She added a pair of gold earrings that Farica chose for her and put her white sunglasses in her hair and added a little makeup. With her lips pressed tightly together, she spun around and looked in the mirror. Her new style didn't look bad, but it was so not her. "But I'm not me," she told herself in the mirror. "I am Annie Erickson, Samuel's half sister. I can do this." With an encouraging nod to herself, she left the bathroom.

Sam's eyes widened when she emerged, but he blinked and assumed a casual look. Together they left the hotel room, pulling their rolling bags.

"Here," Sam said once they were in the elevator. He pulled a gold necklace with a small heart-shaped locket from his pocket. A fancy letter *A* was engraved on the front. "It completes the look."

Annie pushed her hair out of the way as he clasped it on. A warm shiver ran down her spine as his fingers brushed the back of her neck. She looked down at the necklace. It did complete the look. She tipped her sunglasses so they fell over her eyes and gave him her best impression of a dazzling smile.

"You're getting there," he said as the doors opened. "Keep it up, and we'll be golden."

Sam handed the key card to the woman at the front desk, giving her his knee-weakening grin. The woman turned a lovely shade of pink as they left. Annie couldn't blame her. Sam did have quite an effect on people, herself included. Annie needed to remember that no matter how much her heart fluttered or her skin tingled at his touch, it was all fake. Sam acted, tricked, and grifted his way through life. He acted the part twenty-four seven, and she honestly had no idea who the real Samuel was, and she may never know the true him.

CHAPTER 12

Samuel drove casually as if he had no cares in the world. How did he keep all that stress bottled up inside? Annie felt like she'd fall apart if anyone startled her the slightest bit. She tried to look at ease, but her muscles only tensed worse. This only further proved that she was a regular human in this situation.

Twenty minutes into their drive, the salty smell of the coast assaulted her nose. "Where are we going?"

He tapped his fingers against the wheel before he answered. "We are going to meet the team. This situation required a lot of prep work, and now that it's done, the Warden is bringing everyone else in for the main event. I won't lie to you; what we are doing now is risky, not just for you but for all of us. If the Warden and I didn't feel like you could help the team, you wouldn't meet them at all."

Annie clasped her hands together to keep them from shaking. Meet the team? The last thing she wanted was to get *more* involved. She trembled at the idea that he'd trust her with more information. She doubted she could handle more people like Samuel.

"Every member of this team has a special skill, something that we need to pull off this job. They are professionals. For your sake, they need to think you're one of us: a newbie, a new recruit. If you need training, that's fine, but you cannot be a regular citizen. As my sister, it makes sense that I would bring you in if I needed your help. You must make sure they believe that story. Got it, Annie Erickson?"

He peeked at her, taking his eyes off the road for a second. "None of them can know the truth. They'll test you. Not with dates, numbers, and things you can memorize off a dossier, but they may try to trip you up." He turned away from her, his eyes focused on the road. "Don't worry about getting them to trust you. They won't. Trust in this business only goes so far and is only tied to the job. Only Jeremy, the Warden, and I will know your true identity. Let's keep it that way, okay?"

His request honestly felt like a tall order. Annie prayed she could do as he asked. Although she doubted she could fool professionals. She looked down at her designer clothes and her new brown hair whipping in the wind. Sam had spent a lot of time and money on her disguise. He'd protected her so far. She must trust him. "I'll try, Sam."

His eyebrow raised, and he glanced at her out of the corner of his eye.

Annie groaned. "Fine. I'll do it. Happy?"

His lips upturned into a slight smile. Shifting gears, he changed lanes and took an exit. "A couple more things: Don't speak to them unless you have to. Don't share stories or girl talk or let them corner you. They're masters at extracting information. I trust them to finish this job, but I wouldn't trust them with your life. Remember, you're not alone, and Jeremy and I will help you. You'll do fine."

Her throat felt dry. How could everything be okay after a speech like that? If he meant to put her at ease while also warning her, he'd missed his mark entirely. She did not feel at ease.

They drove along the coast for a little while before he pulled into what looked like a long line of abandoned white-walled warehouses. There were thirty of them at least. The area had a broken metal fence surrounding it. Weeds grew out of the cracked cement, and rough, disproportionate gravel crunched under Sam's tires.

He drove through a dilapidated gate and through the maze of warehouses, zigzagging enough that she had no idea how to return to the entrance. After a couple minutes, he turned his car toward a garage-style door near the back of the warehouses behind a large, overgrown, scraggly-looking, ocean-wind-bent bush. Instead of stopping in front near the large dirt-spattered door, he drove through the small space between the warehouses. Behind, they found a hill that rose sharply from the earth. A ramshackle-looking carport blocked their way, half leaning against the hill. Sam pulled inside, obviously unconcerned that the carport might cave in and ruin his fancy car.

In one smooth move, he took off his sunglasses and tossed them on the dash. "Are you ready?"

"No." She bit her lip. "But I'm going anyway."

He nodded his approval before he got out of the car.

Annie took a fortifying breath, put a shaky hand on the door handle, and counted down. "One, two, three." She pushed the door open to find Sam waiting for her, his softer smile on his face. The one she suspected was his real one. He held out his hand. With a small gulp, she let him help her out of the car. He didn't let go of her as she expected. Instead, he wrapped her arm around his and escorted her like an old-time noble lady.

Together they walked to the side of the warehouse opposite where they had driven past it. The twisted trees and bushes that were smaller versions of the one up front blocked this side of the warehouse. Together, they completely obscured the plain white door. Sam lifted a small, white plastic flap to reveal a high-tech-looking keypad. His fingers paused, hovering over the buttons.

"There's one more thing I should mention. Inside this place, we use our code names. I'm not Samuel; I'm Kraken. And Jeremy isn't Jeremy; he's Midnight. Code names are important in this business. A slip could carry dangerous consequences. Got it?"

She nodded. "I'm still Annie, right?"

He smirked, a bit of warmth entering his eyes. "Yes, you are still Annie, for now."

He punched in a ten-digit code, and what sounded like bolts unlocked from behind the door. Annie wrung her hands and sucked in a deep breath as quietly as possible. The door clicked and then swung open. A large guy emerged from the black depths and eyed them up and down.

Annie stepped back, a tremor racing up and down her spine. She knew this man. He'd stood outside in the hallway when she met Sam. He wore a dark suit but much more casually than Sam. It was unbuttoned, revealing a thin T-shirt that left little to the imagination. Rippling muscles made the shirt poke out. He must emphasize his muscles on purpose as if he had some kind of statement to make. His jacket fit well, but Annie could see the way the fabric stretched over his bulging biceps. He wiggled a toothpick in his mouth before he gave them a short nod.

"Nice to see you, Kraken."

"Reaper."

Reaper turned to her and raised an eyebrow, his eyes sweeping over her, looking for something—although Annie couldn't fathom what he hoped to find.

Sam took a step in front of her. "The Warden expects my sister."

Reaper's thick, dark eyebrows shot up before he stepped out of their way. "I didn't know you had a sister. I assumed Krakens worked alone." He eyed Annie as if trying to see through her disguise. Would he? He'd met her at the hotel before. He could figure her out if she made one wrong move.

"Not this time," Sam said.

Annie's face pinked as a new kind of warmth flooded her. Sam hadn't ignored or belittled her presence. Dillan always had. Her respect for Sam went up a notch.

Sam shot Reaper an award-winning smile and pulled Annie into the room after him. How many smiles did this guy have? Did he come up with them on his own, or was there some training he and all these people went through? A question with no answers. At least not during a time like this.

They walked into the dim warehouse. A sick dread entered her stomach, like the time Dillan had convinced her to try a new roller coaster. That roller coaster had led to her swearing off all roller coasters for the rest of her life.

Annie's gaze darted about in an attempt to take it in. Only a couple of lights lit the center of the enormous warehouse. In the dim edges, all sorts of large crates and storage containers stood, appearing innocent, like they weren't blocking the lit center of the room.

Sam led her around one of the longest storage containers. A sizeable U-shaped couch sat at the edge of the circle of light. Whiteboards and computer equipment took up the top half of the lit area. A large executive table with black rolling office chairs surrounding it rested in between.

Jeremy sat at a long desk in front of four huge computer screens, each showing him working on something different. His fingers flew across a keyboard next to the computer. His laptop sat at his elbow, running yet another program. It must have made sense to him because he was working studiously.

"Hey there, Annie." Jeremy raised his eyebrow as if challenging her. He didn't need to worry; Sam had made the rules clear.

"Midnight," she said, returning his raised brow with one of her own.

He snapped his fingers and twisted his hands to give her two thumbs up. He chuckled and stuffed a chip into his mouth before he continued working. From the dark, almost like ghosts, other people materialized from different angles. Only one woman glanced in her direction. The rest of them made their way to the U-shaped couch.

Annie trembled. She couldn't help it. She needed to act brave, like this wasn't the scarcest thing she'd ever agreed to do, but acting brave proved harder than she thought. Annie assumed it best that she didn't say anything at all.

Sam escorted her to the couch and motioned for her to sit at the top of the U. She obeyed, and he stood beside her. Two women and three men turned to look at her, all of them sizing her up. Annie couldn't help but wonder what they'd see in her. Would they see who Samuel wanted them to see, or would they see the real Annie underneath the disguise?

"Reaper, you already met my sister. Sneak, Ink, Crank, and Steel; this is Annie." He pointed them out so she knew who they were. "Annie, meet the team."

Annie's eyes immediately went to the woman with big Hollywood-style blonde hair—the one called Steel. If Annie didn't know any better, she would have pegged the woman as a supermodel. She flashed Annie a grin that matched Samuel's brilliant one. They must have received the same training.

Annie's eyes skipped over Reaper, since he'd met them at the door, and landed next on Ink. He had a sketchbook in hand and dark, smudged fingers. He wore a black leather cap over his curly blonde hair, and he gave her a sly grin before turning a page of his notebook and sketching furiously. She let her gaze move on quickly to Crank.

He sat with his bulky arms folded across his chest, looking like a cross between a brutish biker and Mr. Clean. He wore a tight gray T-shirt, jeans, and what looked like an old-fashioned cowboy six-shooter and a scowl. Annie doubted her safety while hanging out with this crew. How did she know none of them would simply choose to take her out?

Sneak sat on the couch's armrest on the opposite side of Annie. Sneak grinned at her as if they were already best friends. Appearing thrilled to see her must have been another required skill. Sneak wore her dark, black hair in a way that reminded Annie of Cleopatra. Add the olive-toned skin, and Annie did not doubt that this woman had Egyptian blood in her veins.

Annie gave them all a fleeting smile. She gripped her own hands tightly to keep them still. Thank goodness none of them jumped right in to question her about who she was and what she was doing there.

"She's shorter than I expected," Steel said, staring Annie down.

"I think she's adorable. Welcome, Annie," Sneak said, shooting Steel a hard look.

Steel held up her hands and rolled her eyes. Ink sniggered but kept drawing.

"I'm sorry, Kraken, but is a newbie necessary?" Steel asked, eyeing Annie from her boots to her light eyeshadow.

"What do you have against newbies?" Crank growled before Samuel could respond.

"Nothing," Steel said, turning away. "Unless they ruin the job and lower my cut," she mumbled loud enough for them to hear. A pang of new worry settled in Annie's chest. What if they didn't accept her or voted her out?

Crank whipped around to look at Sam. "You're lowering our cut?"

"Not by a single penny," Sam said, his gaze slicing into Steel and Crank. "Annie is here because we need her, same as the rest of you."

Steel snorted and folded her arms across her ample chest. "If you say so."

"I do." Sam fixed her with a hard stare.

Steel held up her hands. "Excuse me for worrying over my cut. I have . . . things to pay off."

"Like your hair bill?" Reaper said, a wide grin on his face.

Crank and Sneak chuckled, one a low deep sound, the other light and tinkly like a bell. Steel rolled her eyes. Ink snorted and flipped a page of his sketchbook before he started another drawing. Annie briefly caught sight of what he'd sketched. It looked like a quick rendition of her and Samuel. Annie didn't know how she felt about him having a sketch of her. Not when he could use it for a nefarious reason.

The sound of a cane clanking on the cement drew their attention. An older man who looked like he was in his early sixties emerged from the dim surroundings. His salt-and-pepper hair was swept back stylishly, and he wore a maroon velvet jacket. He leaned on the chrome handle of his red-and-white marbled cane. A slow smile grew on his face, showing off perfect white teeth. His gaze swept the room, landing on each of them individually for a second before moving on until he got to Annie. He turned and faced her, evaluating her more than anyone else.

"Our newest recruit." He gave her a deep nod that honestly felt more like a bow. "I'm pleased to finally meet you. I'm the Warden." He pursed his lips as if his code name alone should impress her.

Annie glanced at each member of the team in turn. They lived and worked in a completely different world than she did, and it showed. Slowly, so she didn't draw anyone's notice, she pinched her arm hard. It hurt . . . a lot. This was real.

The Warden tossed Samuel his cane. Samuel caught it easily. The Warden took one more look at his crew before he nodded what looked like his approval. With a few steps forward he sat down at the head of the table. "Let's get to work."

CHAPTER 13

As one, everyone stood and moved toward the table. Sam squeezed Annie's shoulder before she stood and followed him to a seat. Jeremy stayed where he was, still typing away and snacking on chips.

The Warden scooted forward, placing the tips of his fingers together. "You are all here because of your skills. As with all my master plans, I assemble a team of individuals whom I feel are most suited for the—let's call it an adventure." Everyone in the room chuckled, but Annie could only get her lips to twitch. Gah. She felt like a dumb monkey who understood something was funny but didn't get the joke.

Please, Lord, don't let this make things worse, she silently prayed, hoping God would hear her plea.

"My advance team"—the Warden nodded to Sam, Jeremy, and Reaper in turn—"have painstakingly laid the groundwork and left you all the fun."

Ink and Crank whooped like they were at a football game and their team had scored a touchdown.

"Thanks, Kraken, for doing all the hard work," Ink said, stretching. "I love it when I can join in for the end bit."

"Come off it, Ink. You know it was Midnight who did the heavy lifting," Crank said, tossing a rolled-up ball of paper at Jeremy's head.

"Excuse me," Reaper said, bulging out his muscles and causing everyone around the room to laugh.

The Warden shook his head, clasped his fingers together, and settled himself back in his chair. He looked at Sam, and everyone else followed suit. "We're ready for you."

Sam nodded to Jeremy, who turned to his computer monitors. He started typing until one image of a man's face lit up all four screens, making it one giant picture.

Sam stood and walked to the space between the table and Jeremy. Annie's arm hairs stood up in anticipation. "This is Roger Lichens."

Crank snorted while Sneak nodded her approval. Ink, however, kept sketching, his face not revealing what he thought.

"Lichens is the most notorious blackmailer we know. He's daring. He doesn't care if his customers are rich, poor, professional, or unskilled. His prices are high, and no one can back out of their contract. The majority of his contracts, however, are with the most-wanted criminals on the FBI watch list."

The picture changed to an extravagant house, the kind that was protected by a large gate and a guard house. Annie had approached a couple of those guard houses when she first came to California because the addresses were on her sales route, but after two or three, she stopped trying. The guards only glared at her until she rushed away.

Sam turned enough to point to the screens. "This is the Lichenses' mansion, or one of them." He turned to beam at everyone. "It's nice, yeah?"

Sneak leaned forward, her fingers fluttering on the table. "I can't wait to see the floor plan." Her eyes narrowed in Jeremy's direction. He snapped his fingers and pulled up a complex-looking floor plan.

"Lichens is exceptionally careful," Sam continued. The police have never been able to get close to the guy. The blackmail he holds for his patrons is so secure that no one has ever attempted to break into his lovely home." Sam's gaze darted to Annie briefly, and she knew what he wasn't saying. No one had attempted it except for Dillan and his crew. "Our clients need their documents removed from Lichens's vault before we hand him over to the police on a silver platter. Our clients are extremely insistent upon it."

His eyes darted to hers. Annie knew firsthand how staunch their "clients" were about them succeeding. That's what got her into this position in the first place.

Sam returned his attention to the screens. "The Lichenses' mansion has top-notch security. Six guards walk the premises along with two in the guard house at the front gate." The screens changed to show where the guards were stationed with little black dots. "Security cameras cover every angle of the yard and garage, as well as the house's main rooms on the first two floors and along the roof." Jeremy highlighted the cameras with tiny orange dots. There were a ton of them. This looked impossible.

"Inside, there are at least five guards on rotation twenty-four seven. For those of you counting, that makes thirteen guards at all times. The vault we need to break into for our clients is not only brilliant, but it's the newest on the market and has never been cracked. He updates the code regularly. He doesn't trust that code to anyone else on his payroll."

Jeremy changed the photo to a giant safe, and Steel scooted forward, her eyes intent on the screen. "The safe is located on floor zero under the walkout basement. Meaning there are no windows. It's in a room, within a room, within a room, each one with a different security passcode and fingerprint scanner. The only way to get to ground zero, that we could find, is an elevator requiring a key belonging to Lichens himself or his head of security, Tyson Savage."

A photo of a beefy man popped up on the screen. "This guy is no joke." Samuel turned to Reaper. "He earned his head-of-security job because of skill. I have it on good authority that he's the only one trusted to watch floor zero on the day we infiltrate."

Reaper scooted forward his fists curling on the table. Annie couldn't see why they acted so calm. Sam painted a picture that screamed all bets were off. It seemed better to cut their losses and run for it. She glanced around the room and saw that everyone's faces still held interest. Was she the only one who felt like this couldn't be done? Either they were all crazy, or Annie had missed something important.

"It sounds impossible." Sam raised one eyebrow high. "Of course, it is daunting if you look at it like this, but with the groundwork that Midnight, Reaper, and I have spent the last six months on, we will succeed."

Sam tapped the table twice with his hands, a new energy filling him. How he could feel excitement now, Annie had no idea—not when he'd spent the last quarter hour explaining how this "job" had almost no chance of succeeding.

"Midnight, let's show them the plan." Sam nodded at Jeremy, who put a copy of what looked like a wedding invitation on the screens. "Security is always heightened and yet weakened when a large event happens. Lucky for us, Lichens's daughter, McKay, is getting married to her Prince Charming. His name is Ron."

A photo of a young couple popped up on the screen. A young guy, a little older than Annie, with strawberry-blond hair and a winning smile, held a girl with dark-blonde hair and a rock the size of California on her finger. Sam gave the team a knowing look. "In three days, they're holding their rehearsal dinner. This is when we'll pull off our heist, steal Mr. Benicci's information, and gift wrap Lichens for Claw."

Steel clapped her hands, a bright expression on her face for the first time. "Perfect. Are we attending the dinner as a couple, Kraken?" She wiggled her eyebrows suggestively.

A couple? Annie didn't like the way her stomach soured at the thought. She eyed Sam and glamorous Steel. They probably made an attractive couple, the kind that turned heads at events. They wouldn't appear subtle, but maybe that was the point.

"Sorry, Steel. This time none of us can attend as dinner guests."

Everyone looked shocked before they started talking in raised voices at once.

"Wait a minute—"

"See here—"

"I don't do low profile."

Samuel clapped his hands to calm them. "It's unfeasible to infiltrate an intimate rehearsal dinner when the bride and groom handpicked their guests. However, we have found each of you a specific job to get into the house that night. We'll go over details later, but the quick gist is simple. The Warden will hang out in the van calling the shots. Midnight will also be in his favorite van doing what he does best."

Midnight paused typing to give the team a thumbs-up. Ink and Crank chuckled.

"Reaper got hired as extra security for the event a couple of weeks ago. Not the kind that is granted real access, but we know he always finds a way in. Ink, it took some convincing, but Linda, the bride's mother, has agreed that an oil painting of the day is not only necessary but vital. You will create the masterpiece over the next several days on-site."

"Yes!" Ink set down his sketchbook for the first time and gave a slow clap. "Finally. I told you I could pull off the dramatic painter."

"Yes, we know," Reaper groaned. Everyone laughed at that, including Annie.

Sam waved his hands to calm everyone. "Crank will put his driving skills to use as one of the limo drivers, and Sneak is the new wedding photographer. Their usual photographer had an unfortunate accident last week."

Sneak brightened and clasped her hands in front of her face. "Sounds fun. Ink, I'll need to borrow your camera—the good one."

Ink rolled his eyes and kept sketching.

"Steel, you'll work with Sneak as her photography assistant."

Steel's jaw dropped, her eyes displaying a mixture of emotions. "Is this a joke?"

Sam's eyes narrowed a bit. "That way, if you need to leave to grab a new lens, photography bounce, or whatever the photographer 'forgot,' this cover gives you a built-in excuse to leave the room and find the safe. Got it?"

Steel leaned back in her chair, looking unhappy. "It's impossible to glamor down for a role like that."

Reaper snorted. Sam's expression didn't change. "I know you can handle it."

Steel's eyebrows shot up, her full lips forming a tight line. "Fine, but next time, you owe me a center-stage role."

"Noted," Sam said and forced a neutral look on his face. "I've been acting as their wedding planner from the beginning, which brings us to Annie." All eyes in the room turned to stare at her. Annie squirmed under their scrutiny.

"We needed someone who could gain access to the upper rooms, someone who looks so innocent they wouldn't worry about her and would soon forget security around her. The dress shop that is providing all the wedding apparel has hired Annie to help their team with the clothes. The rehearsal apparel, wedding party clothing, and the reception party dresses all require pressing between events."

Annie's jaw slowly fell open. This is why Samuel and Jeremy got excited when they found out about her high school job. She assumed she'd hang out in the background while she hid from her hitmen. But actually joining the team meant she'd break the law. That was against her moral code. She'd escaped Dillan's illicit crew only to find herself trapped in another one.

Annie had no idea how they could assign her such a position. Her bridal shop experience gave her the skills to do the job, but she hadn't put out an application. "How could I have been hired? I didn't apply anywhere."

Jeremy swung around and popped his fingers. "That is my magic, Annie."

The Warden stood before she could ask any more questions. "As usual, I'll monitor the job and all comms. This is a one-shot situation, and we have to take it. Steel will get into the vault. The rest of you are there to make sure she does."

Jeremy handed him a stack of folders, and the Warden started passing them to everyone on the team. "You'll find everything you need for this job inside. Sneak, I want you to help . . ."

He paused, his eyes scanning Annie. She blushed. What was he doing? With a nod, he looked her directly in the eye. "Sneak, I'd like you to help *Nova* train." The Warden gave Annie a slight bow. "You can't work with us without a code name. It's my pleasure to gift you yours, Nova. From Kraken's intel and my observation this morning, I know this name fits you."

Annie's cheeks flamed bright red. A code name wasn't expected. She didn't know if she could remember yet another name. She rolled the code name over in her mind. *Nova*. It was beautiful. If she remembered the meaning, it had to do with a bright star. No one had ever called her something like that before.

"You got it," Sneak said, tossing her dark hair over her shoulder.

"Thank you," Annie said, a slight wobble to her voice. Now wasn't the time to become emotional, not unless she wanted the code name Bawl Baby or Sobbing Flower.

The Warden grinned before he turned to the rest of the group. "Nova is newer to the game. I expect you to share any hints you know with her to help us complete this job. Our Italian friends will not accept failure. Kraken will not accept failure. I will not accept failure. I expect perfection. I expect success."

"Promise me our cut didn't change?" Steel asked, her manicured eyebrows furrowed. Her gaze darted between Sam and the Warden. "I don't like it when things change at the last second."

Sam nodded at Jeremy, who put up a number on the screen with a lot of zeros. "Our clients have promised us $20,000 apiece for a simple snatch and grab."

Crank and Ink whistled. Steel rolled her eyes. Reaper and Sneak shrugged. Annie's jaw fell open. Who in their right mind would pay $140,000 to remove information? Crazy people, that's who—crazy people who were dangerous criminals.

Annie considered everyone in the room and wondered again how she'd gotten here. She'd refused Dillan because she didn't want to get involved in anything illegal, and now she sat in a room full of people who were talking about pulling off a heist. If it weren't for the tiny detail that they were taking down bad guys, Annie would have run straight out of the room.

"Payment is contingent on our success," Sam continued. "If we fail, we get nothing." He looked at everyone slowly as if making sure they felt the power of his gaze.

The Warden placed both hands on the table and pushed himself to his feet. "We will not fail. In three days, we will pull off one of the most dangerous heists of our careers, get paid, and relax on the beach. Feel free to use this space for training and prep work." He took up his cane again. "Don't disappoint me."

With a final nod, he turned and walked out of the light, disappearing into the dimness of the warehouse. The rest of the group picked up their folders and pushed back their chairs. They nodded to each other, and some said a quick word to Sam before they left the room.

Sam and Jeremy talked for a couple of minutes before Sam walked over to Annie. "Ready, Nova?" He wiggled his eyebrows.

Answers to his simple question jumped into her head. *No. Not at all. How could I feel remotely ready? Why am I staying with you all? Take me home.*

What if I don't want to break the law? So many thoughts twirled around in her mind, making her dizzy. How could she explain to Sam that she appreciated his desire to keep her safe, but she could not become one of America's most wanted?

"To go?" she asked, resisting the urge to spew all her confusing thoughts on him. After a meeting like that, all she wanted to do was lie down and figure out a way to explain her morals to a man who didn't know how her world worked. Because even if God ignored her, she still wanted to live by what she'd been taught.

He offered her his hand. When she hesitated, his gaze dipped to hers. "We'll start your training as Nova tomorrow." He reached out and tucked her hand around his arm again. Annie stood, but only because staying there with the lot of them was worse than going with Sam.

"See you later, Midnight?" Sam said while leading Annie to the edge of the circle of light.

Jeremy spun around in his chair. "I'll bring some Chinese. You like orange chicken, right, Nova?"

Annie cracked a smile. The code name felt less odd coming from Jeremy. "I love it."

Sam moved to the door but Ink stopped them. He grinned, a single dimple forming on his cheek, and handed her a folded piece of paper. It had a jagged edge; he must have torn it from his sketchbook. Whistling, he walked away. Annie looked up at Sam, perplexed. He shrugged. Annie studied the paper until they reached the door.

Sam let her go and slid back the locks. Once he pushed the door open and the daylight hit her, Annie unfolded the page. A perfect sketch of her new look stared back at her. It looked incredible, better than anything she'd seen. "Ink is an artist."

Sam inclined his head but took her arm to guide her to his car. "Yes, and let's leave it at that."

Didn't he understand? If Ink could whip something like this out in such a short time, he could have a real career—the kind where he didn't have to steal anything. Galleries would want his work. "No, he is amazing. Look at this." She shoved the paper under his nose.

Sam glanced at it, a gleam of mirth in his eye. "I know he's amazing. That's why he's on my team. But Ink isn't interested in art shows if that's what you're thinking. He's a forger. He told me himself that he always would be. He does things like this to keep his skills fresh." Sam opened the car door for her.

"He could change his mind," Annie insisted, refolding her sketch.

"I hate to say it, but not many of us do. This life finds us, and it's difficult to let go once it's sunk its claws into us." He nodded to the seat, but Annie couldn't move.

She felt an ache grow in her stomach. "Why would you bring me into it? Are you trying to change me? To catch me in some criminal web? Is that who you are? A recruiter?"

"No." Sam jerked his head back, his lips thinning into a straight line.

"Are you sure? I doubt any of you grew up as grifters and thieves." She gestured to the warehouse.

Sam stepped closer to her until they were only a few inches apart. "The last thing I'd want to do is change the real you. Most of us didn't have a choice, but you still do. Once this is over, I'm taking you home. I promise you that. You can go after your dreams and forget all this. You want to know who I am; I'm a man of my word. I will not change you, Annie. I won't force you to do something you're unwilling to do. I'll push your comfort zone with this job, but I won't make you work with us if you dig in your heels and refuse. I can always deliver you to Claw and walk away if you want." He inhaled sharply and stepped back, opening her door wide. A pang of hurt flashed through his eyes so quickly that Annie almost didn't see it. "Let's go."

Annie got in the car and chewed on her bottom lip. She hadn't meant to offend him, yet she had. He got in on the other side and quickly backed out of the ramshackle carport.

"I'm sorry, Sam," she whispered, unsure if she said it loud enough for him to hear.

CHAPTER 14

Sam drove her to the warehouse the next day. She still felt a lot of reservations about working with the team but hadn't found a way to explain it to Sam or Jeremy. After her failed attempt, she didn't want to risk hurting either of them or jeopardizing their fragile new friendship.

Sam kept his professional smile on his face, but deep in his eyes, Annie could see a new tightness there—a tightness she'd caused. "Sneak and Jeremy are going to work with you. I know it's confusing, but you'll go by your code name now. Do you remember it?"

Annie nodded. "Nova."

He threw the car into park under the dilapidated shelter again. "It's for your protection. Please don't forget it."

"They already know my real name," Annie pointed out, burying her worry.

Sam nodded slowly. "They know you as Annie Erickson, which they'll assume is an alias, so they'll discount it and remember you as Nova." With that, he opened his door and ran around the car to her side. Annie found little comfort in that statement.

She followed him inside, but there was no Reaper at the door to greet them this time. Crank checked them in at the door instead. His bald head gleamed in the sunlight as he stared down at them before admitting them inside. They returned to the circle of light. Jeremy sat at his computer, typing away. Sneak waited for them on the oversized couch, looking more like an Egyptian queen today. When she saw them, her face brightened, and she pulled her dark hair into a ponytail.

"What's up, Kraken," she said with a fake punch to his arm. "Nova, ready to get started?"

"Wait, I'm first," Jeremy said, tossing a cookie down his throat before twisting in his rolling chair. He slid over to the large table and pointed to the chair beside him.

Annie looked between Sam and Jeremy. Sam nodded to Jeremy, and Annie walked over to him. She glanced back to see Sneak and Sam talking. She hated the feeling that they were probably talking about her.

"Hey, Nova," Jeremy said, offering her a box of store-bought cookies. Annie shook her head, refusing the treat. He shrugged and downed another cookie. "For this job, you will work for the bridal dress company called White Lace Boutique. They're in charge of the wedding clothes for the bride's big day."

"You mean the job I didn't interview for?" Annie shot back.

Jeremy waved her comment away. "It's taken care of—no need to worry. What you need to know is that your new alias for your new employment is Annie Kendrick. I have a wallet for you." He handed her what looked like a brown, two-toned thrift-store wallet. Inside, she found a new driver's license with Annie Kendrick on it, some mixed cash, and a debit card.

Eyes bulging, she looked back at Jeremy. "This is getting out of hand," she said under her breath.

Jeremy laughed heartily.

"So, which wallet do I carry?" she asked in a quiet, clipped tone.

"Whichever suits your purpose," he said in his own lowered voice.

Annie groaned before she tucked the new wallet under her arm. "This keeps getting more complicated."

Jeremy waved her comment away. "You report to work tomorrow morning. Since they are understaffed, they needed to borrow you from another store. I'm positive they'll take you to the mansion tomorrow. It's vital that you make sure you're there tomorrow afternoon for the plan to work and that you gain access to the third floor. We'll talk you through the specifics if you make it in; it's not safe to give you the details now in case something goes sideways. If you're wondering how to gain access to the third floor, my advice is to show them that they can trust you."

There was that word again: trust. It was like Sam and Jeremy threw that word around and used it to wheedle their way into places or get people to do what they wanted. She had no idea how she'd pull this off. A feeling of dread began to twist in her gut.

He opened a small case in front of him. "Here is your set of earcoms." He pointed to what looked kind of like small skin-colored earbuds. "When on the job, they are always on and in. Do not take them out of your ears for any reason. Try them on, and let's make sure they're a good fit."

Annie liked this whole thing less and less, but she pulled one of the earbuds out of the case and put it into her ear. Jeremy watched her and nodded once she set it in place. He pointed back to the box, and she placed the comm inside.

He tapped the gold locket on her collarbone. "This is your tracker. It helps me find you if we get separated. Don't take it off, ever, okay?"

Annie looked down at the necklace that Sam had given her yesterday. She should have known it wasn't only a necklace. Apparently, nothing was what it seemed.

Jeremy stood up and popped a stick of cinnamon gum into his mouth. "Okay, Sneak, she's all yours."

Annie twirled around to see Sneak smiling brightly at her. Thank goodness she still looked like the kind of Egyptian queen who had the heart to pull a baby out of the Nile River. It made the idea of working with her feel a little bit less intimidating. *I can do this,* she thought over and over. She needed to do this.

"The first thing we're going to work on is how to walk," Sneak said, looping her arm through Annie's and dragging her to a large open spot.

Annie blinked. "What's wrong with how I walk?"

Sneak snorted. "Nothing, unless you want everyone to hear you. You've got to sneak when you're on a job." She started walking. No sound came from her thin black shoes. "Not walk." She changed how she moved, and this time regular footsteps sounded against the concrete. "Do you hear the difference?" Sneak demonstrated the two again to emphasize her point.

"Yes." Annie looked around to see if Sam or Jeremy agreed, but they'd moved off to the computer. She hadn't even heard them move. "Do you all walk around like that?"

Sneak giggled. "Of course. It's the most basic skill. Although I excel at it." She twirled her finger around her ponytail and tossed it over her shoulder. "Come on. It's easy once you get the hang of it."

Annie liked the idea of learning how to walk silently. Who knew when that skill could come in handy? Probably when she snuck out to work early in the morning and didn't want to wake Granny.

"There are four keys to sneaking. The first key is slow down—at least at the beginning. Key two, toes first. Key three is to use the ball of your foot. Key four, think light—dancelike and flowy." Super slowly, Sneak pointed her toes like a professional ballerina and placed them on the floor. "Walk on the ball of your foot, and ease down the heel. Think light thoughts, keep your core tight to support you and help you balance, then do the same with your other foot. Once you master going slow, you can use the same key steps to sneak quicker." She demonstrated a swift walk and then a run without making a sound.

Annie's eyes flew open wide. No wonder her code name was Sneak. She moved around like a graceful water skipper, floating on the ground instead of stepping on it.

"Ready to try?" Sneak asked, twirling around.

Annie nodded; it didn't look that hard. Perhaps she could do it. She attempted to copy Sneak's technique. Instead, she wobbled and had to sidestep to keep from falling over. *Never mind, this wasn't so easy.*

"Try again," Sneak encouraged with a calm Annie didn't feel at all. She tried again and again and again. Every time she wobbled or her feet made a sound.

With a groan befitting a child, Annie fell onto a chair. "What am I doing wrong? It's like I have no graceful cells in my body."

"Hmm." Sneak circled Annie, studying her every angle. Annie squirmed under her scrutiny. "Do you ever work out? You know, strengthen your core, run, do leg presses, leg lifts, yoga for balance, that kind of thing?"

Annie shook her head. She was probably the farthest thing from a gym rat. She got all her exercise from walking around ringing doorbells, and before California, she bussed tables at the diner. That's about it. She assumed all the walking kept her fit enough.

"Girl, we are starting in the *wrong* place. Kraken, why didn't you warn me your sister was soft?"

Sam looked up from where he and Jeremy were working, a confused look on his face.

Glamorous Steel rounded the corner, her hands full of darts. She scoffed. "Of course she's soft. Sneak, are you blind? Newbies always lack the finesse of us professionals. Start her out learning how to keep a straight face. She'll need that more than anything else."

Sneak stood up straight. "We don't have time for that. I need to make sure she's ready to help with *this* job. Do you want her clomping about when she's upstairs, drawing attention?"

Steel shrugged. "You could have a month and a newbie like her still wouldn't be ready for a mission of this complexity. She's a liability if you ask me." Steel threw a dart and hit the target dead center.

Annie's face flamed, but she had to agree with Steel. Annie wasn't cut out for this kind of thing. Everyone else knew that. Sneak and Steel continued to argue over what she should know for tomorrow's job. Annie's chest felt tight, her breath catching. Sam said the team had to trust her. He said they all were needed. He could have lied. He might have added her to his grift to make sure that he kept tabs on her. What if her role wasn't necessary?

She looked around for a quick escape, seeing nothing but large containers. She darted around the side of one and then another before she fell to her knees. Wrapping her arms around herself, she shivered. Her tears were on the edge of falling, but she didn't let them fall. She would not cry here. Not here with a room full of criminals, rule breakers, and thieves who already didn't think she was worthy of their trust.

Sam's fancy shoes stopped in front of her. Of course he came to find her. Couldn't he see she wasn't the right person for this? She wasn't an actor or a grifter. She wasn't a criminal. She was a good Christin girl who believed in Jesus, hoped that God didn't hate her for what she'd chosen to do, and she wanted to live. That's about it.

"Nova," he said, kicking at a stray rock. "You can't run away when things get hard. Our plans don't work like that. You're making me look bad."

She was making *him* look bad?

Something in Annie snapped, and with eyes narrowed, she glared at Sam. "You look bad? Excuse me, Mr. High and Mighty." She scrambled to her feet so that she was at least a little closer to his height. "My apologies for not coming perfectly wrapped and ready to do your every whim. Sorry if I don't understand how you all operate. Pardon me if I am soft. You know what? I'm done with all of this. It's not worth it. I'm leaving and taking my chances with Claw."

Annie turned to head toward the door, but Sam pulled her to a stop. "Nova."

Annie yanked her arm out of his grip. "Stop Nova-ing me, Samuel. We all know that isn't my name. I didn't earn it like the rest of you," she seethed through her teeth. Keeping her voice low, she stepped closer to him so he alone would hear her. "Thank you for your help, but I'm done skirting on the edge of danger. I'm done working with people planning to steal things, claim a treasure, and avoid the police. I can't hang around with people who willingly break the law and call themselves criminals."

"I don't allow that," he said quietly, his face hard to read.

"How can you not allow that? You're literally preparing to break the law, and Detective Claw lets you do it. Is Claw a dirty cop? Did she stop the police from coming to the hotel?" Maybe Annie couldn't even run to her for help. She hated to stand her ground with the one person who could grant her what she wanted—a ticket home and her life back. But she hadn't bent for Dillan, and she wouldn't bend for Samuel, no matter how much he claimed that he could help her. It wasn't worth her soul.

"Come on. Let's take a walk in the sand." Sam held out his hand, intensity in his blue eyes. He shot her a look that seemed to see right through her, and yet his eyes weren't harsh or angry. He curled his fingers inwards to encourage her. Annie sighed, her fire fading when his ire didn't rise to meet hers. Gathering her courage, she took his hand. He put her hand on his arm, as usual, and they walked out of the warehouse together past the sandy hill and onto the windy beach.

Sam didn't say anything at first, only led her down to where the waves crashed against the sand, but they stopped before the sand got wet enough to make their shoes dirty. Annie took a few deep breaths of the sea air, letting it calm her. It worked.

Sam let go of her arm and folded his arms behind his back. "I'm going to trust you with something top secret. No one can know about this conversation. What I'm going to tell you is something only myself, Jeremy and the Warden are privy to—and now you."

Annie licked her lips and looked down at the waves crashing near their feet. "Why?"

"Because unlike the people I work with most of the time, you have a moral conscience. You . . ." He dragged his fingers through his hair, and a smile tugged at his lips. "You ask questions they don't ask. You are a good person, Annie Grey, and the last thing I want to do is ruin that. I want you to know I won't turn you into a criminal. I'm not trying to change you. Honestly, this life didn't change me all that much, although I became a pretty good actor."

"I don't understand."

He nodded, reached down to scoop up a broken shell, and played with the sand inside it while they walked. Annie could see this wasn't easy for him. He didn't say so, but his face did and so did the way he fiddled with the shell. He never fiddled. Sam was poised and suave. Finally, he looked back at her, dropping the shell into the sand. "Yes, I bend the law, but I don't let anyone on my team steal anything. They talk about their cut or score, but it's their salary, although they don't know that. I let them believe it's their score. It's a lie, yes, but it keeps things closer to the law."

"So, you lie for the greater good?"

He nodded. "I fund these stings so that I can use the right people to take down the bad guy."

"Fund?" Annie blinked several times, thinking about all the zeros Jeremy put on the board yesterday.

Samuel looked away again toward the waves crashing against the rocks, farther out in the ocean. "Let's just say I have no problem forking out the money for these operations and leave it at that. Claw takes care of the law enforcement side, and I take care of my team. Jeremy even files everyone's taxes for them."

Annie nodded slowly, the clues finally coming together. "Okay, but what is a sting?"

His lips upturned. "Police run undercover operations called stings. They're deceptive in nature, and the whole point is to catch a criminal in the act. The truth is that I am a private consultant for the police, and I aid in these stings. Often, I help create the opportunity for a criminal to act, and then Claw and her partner, Finley Wright, or as we call him, Fang, swoop in for the arrests." He stopped walking, and Annie followed suit.

He waited until she looked him in the eye. "This is critical for you to understand. I work with criminals to take down worse criminals. But I keep *my* criminals from committing any crime. I pay them well for their time. The police seize the evidence they need. They can freeze accounts, arrest the criminals we target, and no one 'gets the score.' Everyone is happy."

He nudged the sand with his shiny shoe. "However, if Ink, Reaper, Steel, Sneak, Crank, or any of the others I occasionally work with found out about this, then no one would ever work for me again. I can keep tabs on them. I have records of their crimes. We talk about our past jobs. I could put all of them in jail for a very long time. Add the fact that I've taken away their biggest victory—the reason they play the game, which is their score—and I'm a walking dead man. I guess I'm what they'd call a double agent. For the criminals and thieves, I'm a fixer, which is why they hire me. For the police, I'm their favorite private consultant." He tossed a shell into the waves. A line of stress appeared between his eyebrows.

"Wow, Sam. I don't know how you keep that all straight."

A corner of his mouth moved up. "I made this my life. This is all I do besides my business investments." A faraway look entered his eyes. "It's all I can do."

Annie glanced at him and saw the tiredness behind his eyes for the first time. It was like he let a shield down so he could gift her his secrets. Honestly, she felt like she took on weight simply knowing the truth about him.

Annie kicked a stray rock into the water. "Let me make sure I understand this whole thing with this new perspective. The police want to take down Mr. Lichens, which is where we come in."

"That's correct."

"Right. So where do your Italian 'friends' fit in this whole thing? You know, the ones who freaked out that we were at the airport."

Sam scooped up another shell, breaking it into tiny pieces and dropping it back on the sand. "Remember how I said it was my job to create the opportunity for the bad guy to commit the crime?"

She nodded.

"I spent two months trying to find a way to do that with Roger Lichens, but he's too good. Everything I tried failed. Claw even bet me that we couldn't touch him. Thus, Jeremy and I started to think outside the box on this one. The Warden, Jeremy, and I then found Mr. Benicci, who wanted to take Lichens down and get his blackmail out of his vault. We struck a deal; the wedding came up, and the plan started to move along from there. Mr. Benicci thinks he's in charge, but he's not."

"You are." It wasn't a question. Annie could feel the I'm-the-one-in-charge vibe radiating off him.

He nodded slowly, again looking away from her. "If we can swing it, Claw will take down Mr. Benicci, his men, and Mr. Lichens all in one go."

Annie didn't know quite what to think. When he'd said that he did a lot of things, some good and some bad, she hadn't understood what he'd meant at the time. Now she had a much better idea.

Sam picked up another shell, but this time chucked it into the water straightaway. "I know this is hard for you. I know it tiptoes on your moral line. Just remember that this is actually a sting for the police, not a grift, and the police are working with me. Nothing will be stolen, no one will nab a score, and supremely horrible men will go to jail. Can you work with that?"

Annie breathed in nice and slow. Dillan had wanted her to help steal for his benefit. Dillan had wanted to skirt the police, collect the money, and do it on repeat. Dillan wanted a life of crime, but Sam didn't. This was different. Sam was different. Small jitters raced up Annie's spine at the very thought of continuing with their plan. If she followed through, what would that make her? The ski-masked face of the man who had shot at her with his scarred hand rushed to her mind, and she shuddered. Sam said he'd protect her and take care of her problem. Now it appeared he truly could make that happen. He had the right resources. He worked on the right side of the law.

"I'll do it, Sam. Thank you for explaining." She looked down and grasped his hand in what ended up more like an awkward lopsided handshake. Face heating, she let go.

"Not a word to anyone, okay?" he said, a finger to his lips. "I need you to swear to me that you won't reveal my secrets to anyone, not even if they act like your best friend or like they already know." He held out his hand for a proper handshake.

Annie gulped before she took it. "I swear I won't tell. You can trust me."

"I know I can." They shook and let their hands fall to their sides, turned around, and started back toward the warehouse.

It was only on the way back, with the sound of the waves pressing on her ears that she realized Sam had used the waves to block out their conversation. Annie smirked, amazed at this man. He was probably only a handful of years older than she was, but he ran more than one successful business. He was so much more than he seemed: braver, smarter, and more caring.

A seagull swooped down in front of them, going for an old french fry from someone's picnic. Annie jumped back. Sam put a calming hand on her shoulder. "He's not here for you."

Annie's face flamed. "I know. I guess I'm a little jumpy."

"If I were you, I'd feel jumpy too. You've been through a lot in a short amount of time."

Annie sighed and looked at her feet.

"Don't worry. Soon this will all end and you can return to your normal life. Perhaps go to culinary school?" He raised an eyebrow in question.

She nodded. "That's the dream. I've wanted to attend school and become a chef since I was fifteen. I used to iron prom dresses and pretend I was rolling out colorful fondant instead." He took her hand in his, this time lacing their fingers together, and a warm tingle wound its way up her arm.

"I'll make sure you get there," he promised.

Annie squeezed his hand, holding onto the sensation of warmth and comfort. She could trust him. Her head and heart both knew it now.

Annie sucked in a deep, fortifying breath of sea air. She could do this. It might take time to square with it in her mind, but she could do this. If Sam could balance this line and keep everything in check, so could she.

CHAPTER 15

After her walk with Sam, Sneak had pulled out weights and led Annie through an intense exercise routine, which she would now look forward to daily. When Annie protested, Sneak said she'd better get used to it if she was joining the life. To keep her cover, Annie couldn't tell her she wasn't really joining them, and so she had to do what Sneak told her. Then they worked on walking quieter instead of silently until well after dark. After that, they practiced with the comms so she didn't look like a total idiot. Feeling only slightly better about her role in this whole sting, Annie left with Sam to return to the hotel.

Sam talked with Mr. Benicci, or one of his men, in Italian the whole time. It was hard to tell precisely. Annie found the Italian words strangely soothing. Before long, her eyelids drooped, and she had to shake herself awake several times before they pulled into the hotel parking lot. Sam walked as jovial as ever, tossing his keys and catching them. Annie stumbled like her granny, whose right knee constantly ached when the weather worsened. He offered her his arm, and Annie took it, grateful for something to hold on to. Right now, all she wanted was her fluffy bed.

His phone beeped after they strolled into the elevator.

"Jeremy is tied up with a few things. We'll have to fend for ourselves tonight."

Annie blinked. "What do you mean by that?"

Sam smirked. "Food. We have to figure out our own food."

"Gotcha." Annie let a smile grace her lips. Jeremy was usually the one to make sure they ate. He had a way of producing food out of nowhere.

The elevator doors opened on their floor, and they walked into the empty hallway. Sam led her to their door and held a hand for her to wait. He used the card to unlock the door, slowly reached around the corner of the door frame, and flipped on the light. His eyes darted around the space, looking for anything out of place, before he opened the bathroom door and whipped the curtain aside. Used to this process by now, Annie waited until he moved into the main room before she entered and shut the door behind her. Sam checked under the beds and inside the closet before he gave her the all clear.

True to form, he also checked out the window for people watching them. Satisfied, he let the curtain fall back into place. "I'm going to get us some dinner. If you need anything, call me, okay?" He tapped her phone in her hand before heading out the door, leaving her with one of his brilliant, yet fake, smiles.

Annie trudged to her bed. Grabbing the remote, she fell onto the fluffy covers and stretched out. "Ouch. Sneak, this is all your fault." The idea of an Epsom salt bath sounded amazing, but with only Sam here and no idea when he would return, a bath wasn't an option. Instead, she flipped on the TV and turned on a cooking show. They were talking about cooking steaks at the right temperature. Annie's mouth watered. Thank goodness Sam had left to find food. A full belly and sleep sounded brilliant.

A knock pounded several times on the door. Heart hammering at supernova speed, Annie dove to the floor on instinct, landing like a cat on all fours. There wasn't a chance Samuel could have returned yet. He'd claimed Jeremy would be late, so it couldn't be him either. Annie looked at her phone; it had only been five minutes or less since Sam left.

She swallowed hard and looked for a place to hide. Someone knocked again. There was no space under the bed for her body. Only an arm would fit. The closet felt wrong, and the bathroom was too close to the door.

The handle jiggled. Her heartbeat jumped to her throat, her jugular veins throbbing. This felt wrong. It wasn't housekeeping outside her door, or they would have said so. It wasn't even someone from the team, or they would have used the secret knock. Trying to keep her breathing normal, she pulled up her contact list on her phone and found "Big Brother." She hit Call. The door handle jiggled again.

Sam answered, laughing. "Hey! It's going to be a little while. I ran into a friend in the lobby."

"Someone's trying to get in the room," she whispered frantically. She crawled around to the other side of Sam's bed. It was further from the door. "They keep jiggling the handle."

"Okay, no problem. I'll get it all straightened out. Girls . . ." he said as he hung up on her.

Annie stared at her phone in shock. *Sam!*

"No, Sam, please . . ." she said, hitting Big Brother on her phone again. She heard the click of the door opening. She scrunched back against the wall and curled into a ball between Sam's bed and the closet with only the fluffy bed coverings for protection.

"Lord God, please help me," she prayed. "Don't abandon me now."

This situation felt all too familiar. Annie began to shake. Her eyes were on her phone, and she tried to breathe silently like Sneak had taught her earlier that day. Sam didn't pick up his phone. Had he deserted her?

"Is this the right room?" a gruff voice said. A voice that sounded eerily familiar. "It looks like no one's here."

"The TV is on."

"A lot of people keep the TV on in hotels," the first voice said. "It keeps housekeeping from butting into their business."

"Shut it. You keep watch outside while I look around."

The door closed, and Annie pulled herself into a tighter ball. The sounds of a man moving slowly through the room reached her ears as if they were enhanced by a loudspeaker. Her heart pounded so hard it hurt. She couldn't believe he didn't hear it and use it like a game of Marco Polo. She stopped breathing altogether as she heard him brush up against the covers of Sam's bed. The barrel of a gun appeared in her line of sight, and then the hand holding it—a hand with a jagged scar right down the center.

All feeling went out of her limbs.

"Lloyd!" yelled the other man from the hall, just as the first dingy-looking shoe came into view.

The man turned. His footsteps raced to the door. The door flung open. There were sounds of a scuffle.

Annie heard a gun go off, and a second gunshot answered.

Sam!

She fell to her stomach on the floor, her head spun. Her vision came in and out of focus. This couldn't be happening again.

"Annie?! Please answer me. Annie!" Sam's breathless voice sounded as if it came from a kid's fuzzy walkie-talkie. "Annie!"

"I'm . . . here." She gasped, reaching a hand up to the edge of the bed. Her body wouldn't move.

Sam raced to her hiding spot, fell to his knees, and pulled her up by her shoulders. "Are you okay? Did they hurt you?" He rubbed his hands up and down her arms as he assessed her, sending a warm tremor through her to combat the icy feeling already to the depth of her bones.

"No," she finally wheezed.

Satisfied, he turned, slammed his gun into his holster, and pulled her into his arms. Annie shook against his chest, her hands grasping his shirt.

"I'm so sorry. If I had known, I never would have left . . . I'm sorry," he said, his arms holding her tightly.

"You hung up on me."

"I know. I had to." He gave her a quick squeeze and let her go, only enough to look into her eyes. "We have to move. I know you don't want to, but we must get out of here quickly."

Sam gave her arms one more squeeze, slid out of her grip, and rushed to the door. Annie glanced away as he dragged a body into the room. She watched, frozen in place, as he searched the man's pockets.

"The other man got away." He pulled out his phone and started talking, but Annie couldn't focus on his words. Annie remained where he'd left her. She felt numb. Horrified. This wasn't the kind of thing she wanted to live through once—let alone twice. She heard Sam say goodbye, but he didn't stop talking.

"Jeremy, we need to move. That's fine. We'll be there. I'll explain later. Yes, we're both breathing." Annie heard some shuffling, and then Sam came and took her hands in his. "Come on." He pulled her all the way up onto her feet. "Now is not the time to faint, Annie. Hold on a few more minutes. I need you to walk out of here, and then you can pass out in the car."

He put his arm around her waist and pulled her along next to him. Annie averted her eyes so she didn't see the dead man and buried her face in Sam's shoulder.

They rushed together to the elevator, avoiding all the curious faces in the hall. Sam pulled her close enough to whisper in her ear. "I figure we have about three minutes until the cops arrive. Claw and Fang should handle it, but we don't want to get caught in the mess. No one can know we were involved. I need you to take a deep breath and walk to the car."

Annie nodded shakily, focused on breathing in and out, and held tightly to the metal hand railings inside the elevator. Inside her head, she started to count slowly. One, two, three. The doors closed. Four through fifteen took them down to the ground floor.

Sixteen. Samuel wrapped his arm around her waist, taking on most of her weight. At seventeen, no one waited at the front desk. Eighteen, nineteen, and twenty.

They tore through the lobby and ran for the car. Thirty-six. Samuel threw open the door. Thirty-seven. He helped Annie fall onto the seat. Thirty-eight, thirty-nine. Samuel sat next to her and started the car. Forty-two. She clasped her hands tightly together to keep them from trembling. Fifty-five. She let out a long breath. She'd made it.

"They were my hitmen. How did they find me?" she finally managed to say as he pulled out into traffic. The image of the scarred hand holding the gun burned into the back of her eyes. She couldn't see anything else without that image marring it as well.

"It looks like they circled back to our hotel after checking around. I should have seen them . . . unless they rented a room nearby."

"How did they know?" She gestured to her disguise.

"I don't know. The disguise should have worked, but I swear I will find out." He drove fast and zipped in and out of traffic, making it difficult for anyone to follow them.

His phone rang a moment later, and he grumbled. Punching the phone button on his steering wheel, he answered the call. "*Ciao*?" He talked in Italian the whole time they drove. For Annie, the drive passed in a blur. An hour later, he pulled into a new hotel across town. Jeremy stood waiting outside. Samuel rolled down his window and pointed at her. "Help her."

Annie wanted to deny Jeremy's help. She could walk but felt shaky, so she let him escort her inside. Before she knew it, they were checked into a new hotel room, and she collapsed on one of the soft beds. Samuel and Jeremy paced the room, both on their phones. She couldn't follow either of their conversations. All she understood was that Claw and Fang were on it. That one piece of news gave her some comfort. If Claw and Fang looked into the men hunting her, maybe they could arrest them, and her nightmare could end before they pulled the heist.

She rolled into a ball in the center of her bed and hugged her knees to her chest. Her last thought before sleep claimed her was that maybe she would wake up at home in Idaho. This could still be a bad, detailed dream, right?

A few days ago, she would have believed her self-talk. She could have convinced herself to dismiss everything that had happened. She'd done so before. She'd pushed painful things away over and over, like when her parents died. Now she couldn't. Some things were too real to explain away. Too dangerous to ignore. Too deadly.

CHAPTER 16

THE MORNING SUN MADE THE filmy curtains glow. Annie stared at the thin crack of light between the thicker draperies and cringed. Why did the California sun have to incur overwhelming brightness? Couldn't today be a little more overcast with a hint of rain in the air? That would have suited her mood better.

Jeremy snored loudly from the couch, his laptop open on his lap. Annie glanced over to the other queen bed. She could barely see the top of Sam's head. Never in her craziest dreams would she have spent the night in the same hotel room with two guys who were basically strangers. Yet, she had done so more than once now.

She flipped onto her back. Running for your life did crazy things to a person, she supposed.

Recent memories flashed into her head like an old silent-movie film strip. Dillan's lifeless body on her living room floor, Sam interrogating her when they first met, the team she had to work with, last night's break-in, and the hand with the scar. She shuddered. She did not want to lay here and relive all her worst experiences on repeat until she went mad.

She hated that she didn't feel safe enough to leave. Yet, she didn't want to stay cooped up here. She needed a moment to think, to come to terms with . . . well, everything. She bit down on her lips to stop them from trembling, rolled over, and smacked her pillow repeatedly.

"It finally hit you?"

Annie looked up. Jeremy stretched and closed his laptop. "You don't have to take it out on your pillows."

Annie's lip trembled. "Yes, I do."

Jeremy's eyes flicked to Sam's sleeping form, and he lowered his voice. "I guess you can, but it won't do you much good."

Annie's eyes narrowed. "Thanks," she said dryly.

A bright smile broke across his face. "I'm not trying to sound mean. After you've been in this life for a while, you learn to deal with the stress in better ways."

"Like?" Annie asked, a flicker of hope igniting in her chest.

He peeked at Sam again. "Did he happen to buy you a swimsuit when you went shopping?"

Annie thought through the clothes Farica had picked out for her. "I think so . . . why?"

He threw off his covers. "Go change and meet me out here in five minutes."

It was Annie's turn to look over at Sam. "Are we going swimming?"

Jeremy nodded. "It's the best way to calm down. I swear by it."

Annie eyed the locked door; going out wasn't safe. Yet, if she stayed put in this room, she'd go insane. "Is there another way that isn't so dangerous?"

Jeremy shrugged while he rummaged in his bag. "Running works, pumping iron, I suppose . . . baking, but we can't do that, and the other two are less safe than the hotel pool. Trust me. Sam won't like it, but I think we're safe for now. He made sure no one tailed you here. I'll come too so I can watch your back. But we'd best not wake him." He nodded toward the bathroom and mouthed the word. "Go."

Shoving the covers off, Annie whisked her rolling suitcase that had somehow miraculously appeared last night into the bathroom. She dug around in her suitcase and came across a bright-red swimsuit with thin white and navy stripes.

Leaving the hotel wasn't an option, but if Jeremy offered something to keep her mind from reliving the last several days, she'd jump at the chance. Swimming had relaxed her in the past. It made sense that it would help now. This might be her only option to keep from falling apart. She looked to the ceiling, a silent prayer frozen on her lips. Prayer hadn't done much good of late. Shaking her head, she closed her case instead.

Quickly, she put the swimsuit on, wrapped a fluffy white towel around her shoulders, and snuck out of the bathroom. Samuel didn't move when she quietly opened the door. Good. She didn't want a Sam lecture right now. She needed a friend, and somehow Sam didn't quite fit that bill. Who he was to her, she hadn't figured out yet. She would deal with that later.

Jeremy was already in his swim trunks when she emerged. He grabbed a towel and carefully opened the door for her. They speed-walked to the elevator. A couple of people chatted about breakfast in the elevator when it stopped on their floor. The anxiousness she'd experienced yesterday rose higher inside her. It was similar to the adrenaline she felt intermittently for the last few days. Both feelings made her tense.

It took every ounce of her patience to wait for everyone else to exit the elevator before they moved. Once they had a clear shot, she and Jeremy raced directly to the pool. The pool had a unique design. Half of it was inside the spacious lobby guarded by a gate, and the other half was outside. The water ran to a glass wall raised a foot from the water, making it easy for people to duck down and swim under it to the outside half of the pool. The sun glinted invitingly off the water on the outer portion. A couple of girls in bikinis were outside sunbathing on lounge chairs. Annie had no interest in that. She needed the comfort of the water. She pushed on the gate to find it locked. The door required a key card.

"Allow me," Jeremy said, swiping a card.

He caught sight of the girls outside and lifted his chin, emphasizing his jawline. "This technique is pretty simple. Just float around and let the water do the rest." He flashed her a smile and dove right in, heading toward the sunbathing beauties. Annie rolled her eyes. So much for having a friend to help ease her burdens.

She'd never considered herself exceptionally beautiful. Never ugly or pretty, just average—normal. She was normal, unlike those girls. Feeling a different kind of frustration, she tossed her towel on a poolside chair.

With one look at Jeremy, who was now swimming slow laps, his eyes still on the sunbathing girls, she jumped off the edge and landed in the frigid water. Tucking her arms around her legs, she formed a little ball and kept herself under the surface, letting the water drown out all the sound. It was like putting the world on mute, and she needed that more than anything else. When she couldn't hold her breath anymore, she surfaced long enough to take a deep breath before pulling her head back under the water. When she emerged again, some of the crazy energy she'd felt in her limbs had disappeared.

Lying on her back like a star, she floated, keeping her face above the water but her ears below. Annie had never been one for meditation or mantras, so she simply breathed in and out, evenly watching the oxygen fill her belly. When her body was tired of floating, she swam a few laps, keeping to the inside portion of the pool before returning to her star position. She bet more kids would have taken over the pool if it hadn't been breakfast time. Only one couple sat on the steps outside in the sun with their baby, giving her free rein of the pool on the inside.

Every once in a while, Jeremy stood up and did a three-hundred-and-sixty-degree turn, scrutinizing everything. With a nod at her, he returned to his laps, mainly on the outside portion of the pool.

Was Annie safe? No.

Were her potential killers still on her trail? Yes.

Was she finally feeling a little calmer about it all? Amazingly, yes.

Did she know what to do now? No. Everything felt right and wrong at the same time. She wished the Lord would hint at what to do.

Annie flipped around at the squeak of the gate. Sam walked through. He looked disheveled for the first time. His hair stuck up at an odd angle instead of perfectly gelled. His navy-blue pajama pants and white T-shirt made him look like a regular guy instead of the super spy she'd first thought him to be. He dragged his hands down his face before sitting cross-legged on the side of the pool.

"You know you guys about gave me a heart attack. I woke up, and you were both missing. I thought—" He ran his hands through his hair. "I thought we lost you."

Annie bit her lip, guilt twisting in her gut. They should have left him a note. She searched for something to say, but nothing brilliant came to mind. "How did you find me?"

"I called the front desk and asked if anyone saw my sister leave this morning. He asked if I was referring to the woman in the pool." Sam got up and started pacing. A very normal thing for Sam, except he didn't have his fancy suit. Annie suddenly wondered if the perfectly suited Sam was an act. A grift. Was she seeing the real Sam for the first time?

"I'm sorry," she said lamely. "Jeremy said it would help me calm down."

"You're sorry? Great." His eyes shot daggers in Jeremy's direction. "I'm really glad to hear that. I'm having a crisis in the middle of a huge job, and you're both . . . swimming." He gestured to the pool.

Annie didn't like his tone. What did he think? That she came here for kicks and giggles? That she didn't take the situation seriously? She'd been nearly killed twice in a week. Of course she took this situation seriously. Jeremy suggested that she try something to calm down, and she needed the water to calm down. To find a way to deal with everything that's been going on. She wasn't just swimming. "I needed to find a way to relax. Jeremy suggested this."

"We relax after the job is done," he snapped, looking away from her to Jeremy, who was still attempting to show off to the women outside. "Come on. Let's go."

The tension Annie had worked so hard on draining snapped back into place. With a groan, she swam to the edge of the pool away from Sam and hoisted herself up and out. He grabbed a striped pool towel off the stack, skirted the pool's edge, and handed it to her. Annie took it and wrapped it around herself. "You know the difference between you and people like me is that you might have it in you to wait until a job is done to deal with all this stress, but I can't. I feel like I'm going to fall apart."

"I understand that this is different for you, but—"

"*Different* is the wrong word, Sam," Annie interrupted. "Difficult, crazy, challenging. Any of those words work better."

"That still doesn't give you an excuse to sneak out and swim." He turned and gave the pool a stern look.

"Is that what's bothering you?" Without considering it, she dropped the towel and, with both hands, shoved Sam hard. They stood close to the edge of the pool, and because of her angry momentum, they both fell in. The water slapped Annie's face hard across the cheek, stunning her momentarily.

It took Annie a second to find her footing. When she surfaced, Sam stood there, the water hitting him mid-chest. He shook the water out of his eyes. "Are you crazy?" he shouted, his teeth chattering. "It's freezing."

"It sounded like you were jealous," she snapped, rubbing her cheek.

"I'm not jealous. I'm angry." He wrapped his arms around himself, the water dripping from his brown hair.

He had no right to feel angrier than her right now. Her life had gotten all out of whack, not his. "Don't you dare. It's my life that's ruined. I can't even go home. I thought I was safe with you. I'm not. I thought you were somehow protecting me. Yet my assassins still found me." Annie straightened up to her full height, chest puffed out. "I thought it was worth staying with you and Jeremy."

Sam looked down at her, their faces only a few inches apart. His light-blue eyes found hers, and they both froze. Annie's heartbeat started thrumming wildly with how close he stood to her. She swallowed hard, suddenly hating the way she felt when she got close to him. His lips parted like he wanted to say something, but he didn't speak. His fingertips lightly brushed hers in the water, and a warm shiver rushed up her arms. She found it hard to breathe, hard to think as time froze around them, and all she could see was Sam. His gaze moved to her lips, and a different kind of shudder rushed through her.

Shouts of excitement from kids in swimsuits rushing toward the gate slapped some sense back into her. Shaking her head, she turned and dove into the water and swam toward the corner of the pool. What was she doing? She couldn't stand there and stare at Sam like that.

With gritted teeth, she climbed out of the pool, picked up her lightly used towel, and stomped over to the basket reserved for the used ones. She shoved it inside with more force than necessary and picked up the white one from her hotel room instead. Using her hair as a shield, she averted her eyes from Sam, wrapped the towel around herself, and stormed back to the gate.

"Hey, where are you going?" Jeremy called, swimming back into the inside half of the pool. "Sam . . . what happened to you?"

"What do you think?" Sam snarled.

Annie didn't want to face either of them, and she pushed the gate open. She kept her head down and rushed toward the elevator.

Sam caught up to her there. He had a pool towel wrapped around his shoulders, and his sodden pajamas dripped water onto the carpet.

Jeremy rushed into the elevator right before the doors closed. He took one look at the both of them and snorted. Sam kept his eyes on the elevator doors. Good. She didn't want to talk. She would have taken the stairs if she had any idea what their room number was, but she didn't. Instead, she had to follow Sam and Jeremy back to their room. Without a word, Sam pushed open the door and disappeared into the bathroom.

Annie sat on the edge of her bed and pulled her legs into the safety of her towel.

"I'm sorry he reacted that way," Jeremy said calmly, folding his towel in half and setting his computer and a bag of chips on his lap. "I knew he wouldn't like it, but . . ." He laughed. "I didn't expect him to dive in after you."

Annie buried her face in her arms. "He didn't dive after me. I pushed him in."

When Jeremy didn't answer, Annie peeked one eye at him. He gave her a full smile. "Epic," he said, tossing a few chips into his mouth. He chewed for a moment before leaning forward a bit. "Hey, Annie, I just want you to know that we care about you. Believe it or not, you're one of us, and that makes you family. He only reacted that way because he does care."

Her lips trembled, and she nodded before burying her head back in her arms. Family? For the past sixteen years, her only family had been Granny and Pa. Pa passed away four years ago, reducing her family to a total of two. Dillan and her other friends had never felt like family. She liked the idea that Sam and Jeremy thought of her like that. She might return the sentiment if she let her heart open up to them.

Jeremy cleared his throat. "You'll need to dress in all black today, okay?" he said as if nothing had happened before he popped another chip into his mouth.

"Whatever you say," she said, staying in her towel cocoon.

Ten minutes later, Sam emerged from the bathroom. His hair was perfectly gelled, and he had on a fancy suit, complete with shiny shoes that probably cost over a thousand dollars. He didn't say anything to her but gestured to the door.

Jeremy snorted again as she walked past him. The bathroom door clicked shut, and she locked it.

"Wow, Sam, what's with all the ice?" Jeremy asked just loud enough that Annie could hear his words through the bathroom door. Annie's eyes froze on the doorknob.

"Nothing you need to worry about," Sam said smoothly, his voice holding a professional edge.

Annie pushed away from the door and started the shower. This was one conversation she could live without overhearing. Once showered and dressed in black clothes, Annie felt a little better, or at least good enough to open the door.

Jeremy was the only one in the room when she emerged. "Sam had to leave already. The Lichens were expecting him. Claw should arrive here in a minute to drive you to work."

Good. Claw she could deal with. Claw was a police officer. Claw wasn't a grifter, con man, or thief. Claw didn't cause emotions Annie didn't understand to roll around in her chest. Annie slipped on some black sandals. Jeremy pulled out the box that held their equipment. A moment later, she had a comm in her ear, her golden locket around her neck, and a wristwatch to complete the look.

Jeremy pulled out another box. "I know you're worried about going out there after last night, but don't worry. You're going in disguise."

"I thought I already had a disguise," she said, gesturing to her brown hair.

He shrugged and pulled out a red wig. "Annie Kendrick is a redhead."

Of course she was. With a sigh, she let Jeremy help her put it on and attach it with pins to keep it in place. Annie found it odd that even though her relationship with Sam felt confusing, she still wished he was helping pin her hair. She shouldn't wish for him, but she did. She missed him, darn it. She wanted him there to wish her luck and tell her she could do it. She wanted to see some approval on his face after the fiasco yesterday.

Jeremy handed her a pair of thick black glasses, and Annie added them to her new look. Jeremy eyed her up and down before passing her Annie Kendrick's wallet and a weathered-looking purple purse. "You ready?"

Annie sighed and glanced at her new look in the mirror. "Not even close."

CHAPTER 17

Claw picked Annie up in an unmarked maroon police car and offered her a bright smile. She wore her long blonde hair in a tight braid and completed her look with a pantsuit and her badge attached to her belt. Annie got in the passenger side. She didn't want to feel like a criminal by sitting in the back.

"How are you doing?" Claw asked, easing onto the road.

"Um . . ." How did she answer that? She wasn't okay, ready, or excited. So, she shrugged.

Claw snickered. "I get it. I felt much the same way when I learned that crooks like Mr. Lichens and people like Kraken existed."

"You did?" Annie dared to hope someone would understand her mixed-up feelings.

"Yep. It threw me for a loop. I had a lot longer to get used to the idea, however. Kraken and I talked for a long time before I made him a private consultant. He even had to pass some of our tests. I thought I knew then what he did, but I had no idea. After I learned about his crew on that first job, I decided to stay out of it. He lets me know when my part comes, and it works better that way."

"Are you sure it's worth working with . . . Kraken?"

Claw full-on laughed. "Are you kidding me? I love working with Kraken. His ways are a little different, maybe, but his results don't lie. He knows what he's doing, and we capture sleazebags we haven't even gotten close to before. Honey, I know it's hard to wrap your mind around everything, so remember this: you're working for the good guys. Sure, Midnight might have gotten you a temporary job in a way I don't want to know about, but if we take down Lichens and Mr. Benicci, then I'm not going to complain about how he gets our foot in the door. Kraken does what he does so that me and Fang can do everything by the book."

Annie blinked. "If Kraken is in charge, how does the Warden fit into all of this?"

Claw shrugged her shoulders, her eyes still on the road. "The Warden is what they call the mastermind, the guy who calls the shots and assembles the best team. He monitors everyone's movements during a sting and makes sure things go off without a hitch, but without Kraken, they'd have to turn to crime. I'm all for having help on a sting as long as I'm not allowing a crew of people to gain a score along the way. We've had to create a ton of rules to make this work, and Kraken makes sure we stay within them, so in my mind, even though he claims he's the boss, the Warden is just part of Kraken's crew."

Annie nodded slowly, mentally adding a new layer of respect for Sam.

A few minutes later, Claw whipped the car into a parking lot. As she parked, a large window full of white and ivory dresses on black mannequins wearing sparkly, fake jewelry came into view. Claw turned in her seat and fixed Annie with a look that made her squirm. It was like Claw could see into her soul.

"Annie, it's up to you. It is. No one will make you stay and play along. I swear. You need to choose whether you're in or out and stick with that choice. If you want out, I'll free you from this burden right now. I'll turn around this moment and drive you to witness protection. But if the team needs you and you're willing to help, I'd rather take out the bad guys, because that's what I do. You need to make this choice for yourself, or this will always feel hard."

Annie swallowed with difficulty and looked over at the dresses in the window. She'd ironed and repaired dresses from the shop she'd worked for in high school. She'd dealt with bridezillas, sweet brides, picky brides, awful customers at the diner, and people who ignored her. This was something she could do. She looked in the mirror and saw her wig. This was honestly the last place her hitmen would look for her. Sam wanted to protect her, that she couldn't deny.

Annie looked down at her hands. "I'm scared out of my mind. I'm in danger, and now I'm working with dangerous people. But . . . Kraken says if he can finish this job with my help, he'll make sure I'm safe. He'll make sure I go home."

Claw stretched her arms out. "If you ask me, I'd say stay and help. Kraken has never broken a promise to me. Not ever. His word is something I can trust."

Annie took a deep breath. This was the moment of truth. She'd hate herself forever if she gave up on them and they failed because of her. She might not have known them long, but she liked Jeremy and Sam. Jeremy had said she was family. She blinked back the memory of her and Sam standing so close in the pool that morning and how his arms felt around her when he pulled her into his arms last night after making sure she was okay. She cared about them.

She cared about Sam.

Please don't let this be a wrong choice, she silently prayed. If she were going to live through this, she'd definitely need divine intervention. They were all trying to accomplish a good thing. Sam was keeping them from breaking laws. Claw was attempting to apprehend horrible men. God blessed good things. If He saw she wanted to follow a good path, maybe He'd bless her side. With the team and God's help, she could do this. "Okay, Claw, I'm in."

Claw nodded once. "Good girl. Turn your comm on."

Annie pulled the earpiece out and pushed the button on the end. "Ah, there she is," the Warden said in her ear.

"You didn't think we'd let you do this alone, did you?" Jeremy said.

Annie brightened. They hadn't thrown her to the wolves. A sudden warmth grew in her chest, one only found through friendship.

"Are they on?" Claw asked, turning in her seat to look behind them.

"Yes."

Claw turned to face forward in her seat. "Ignore or listen to them. It's up to you. Kraken is at the house, and Midnight and the Warden are in the van across the street." She poked her thumb in the direction of a white van. "You'll do great."

Annie took a deep breath and opened the car door.

"We got you, Nova," the Warden said in her ear. "We're with you every step of the way." It was comforting to hear the Warden in her ear. However, she wished it was Sam's voice, no matter how awkward they'd acted toward each other that morning.

Annie walked into the bustling bridal shop. All the consultants were dressed in black. A couple of consultants helped brides on a pedestal near a wall of mirrors, and the rest rushed about. A woman with big curly brown hair dashed up to her.

"Annie." She pulled her into a crushing hug. "We are so glad you could transfer over to help us with this wedding. I'm Nadia, the owner of White Lace Boutique."

"I'm glad to help," Annie said, pushing back from the unexpected hug. Fixing her fake glasses, she pasted on a smile.

Nadia whirled around and clapped her hands. Every employee in the room froze except the consultants currently with brides. "All right, you all, team meeting in ten."

Annie shuffled her feet, her gaze darting all over the posh store. Nadia put a hand on her arm. "I have a few papers for you to sign and a mums-the-word contract for the Lichenses' wedding." Nadia nodded toward a door leading to the back of the store. Annie turned and followed Nadia into a small office.

"Nova, sign everything and act excited," the Warden said. "Midnight set you up well." Annie listened to Nadia gab on and on as she filled out the paperwork while Jeremy fed her the details. About fifteen minutes later, they emerged to find everyone waiting for them in a small break room.

"Okay, team," Nadia said, squishing her way to the front. "This is the weekend we've all been dreading for months. We have the Windover wedding, the Kallsen wedding, and the Lichens wedding all on the same weekend. Julia will keep her crew here running the shop and ensuring we hit our sales goals. Raziel and her group are taking on the Windover wedding. Fantino is taking the Kallsen wedding, and I will take on our biggest wedding of the year, the Lichens wedding." She sighed dramatically and fanned her face.

"It's a good thing I trust you all with my life or, better yet, my business reputation. We will make this work. Our good friends from Sunset Bridal loaned us one of their best press girls. Thank you for joining our team this weekend, Annie, even if it is for a short time."

Annie smiled and offered a slight wave to the group.

Nadia clapped her hands sharply. "Let's get to work."

Most of the consultants broke off, but Nadia and a couple others stayed where they were. "We don't have time to waste. We are all heading to the Lichens mansion in twenty."

Nadia helped Annie put a kit together like everyone else's. It included needles, thread with the wedding colors, satin-covered buttons, ribbons, scissors, fray check, extra sequins, and more. She also gave Annie a second case with her iron, sprays, and cleaning supplies. Once they were packed, they loaded up into a large van together. Annie listened as everyone swapped stories about their experiences with the Lichenses so far. The Warden and Jeremy were probably lapping this all up. McKay, the bride, wasn't described as a bridezilla, but her parents sounded like a nightmare to work with.

They began a slow, twisting ascent up a hill toward a lone mansion on top. Large iron gates blocked the way, and the driver seemed like he had to pass some kind of test to get inside. Annie bit her lip while the driver and the guard talked. Finally, he must have passed because the gates swung slowly open. Once through the gates, the driveway turned to cobblestone and widened around a large ornate fountain. Beautiful green grass and expertly landscaped lawns stretched in all directions, adding to the house's grandeur. The stone building stood three stories tall. Annie thought it looked like the perfect mesh of a modern home and a castle.

They followed Nadia to the front door, where a big burly man waited. He gazed at the van, then at them. "I need to check every case." He held up a metal detector wand like one used at the airport.

They slowly moved through while the man looked inside each case, assumedly searching for weapons. Annie held her breath while they looked through hers. Technically an iron was a decent weapon, but the guard let her through. Inside the hall stood Sam, looking as suave as ever, with a bright smile on his face—one of his better fake ones. Annie jittered and looked down at her black sandals.

"Welcome to the mansion, everyone," he said, sweeping his hands out as if gesturing to the whole of the house. "I'm glad you're here, because then I don't have to do everything for this wedding."

The group chuckled. Nadia stepped forward and looped her arm around Sam's shoulder. "This is Mr. Samuel Erickson. He's the wedding planner and hired us to help with all the clothing." Nadia squeezed him tighter. His smile tensed slightly, but Annie doubted anyone else noticed. Sam wiggled out of her grip and took her hand instead, quickly kissing it. Nadia giggled and turned pink.

"Nice to see you again, Nadia," Sam said. "I see your team finally arrived. McKay has been pacing all morning. She can hardly wait to see all your amazing work."

Nadia waved his comment away. "Brides."

Sam led them further into the entrance hall.

Nadia turned to a man standing by a door at the end of the hallway. "Don't worry about the bodyguards; they don't bite usually. Right, Lloyd?"

Lloyd grunted and kept his position.

Annie's eyes shot open wide when she saw the man. His hands clenched into fists, and she saw the thick, jagged scar running directly down the center of one of them. The scar that haunted her dreams. The scar on the man who had shot at her.

Lloyd's face didn't move an inch as he stood stoically at his post by the door, but she knew for a fact that he was the same guy. She'd seen his face briefly in the hotel before she'd turned back to the elevator that first morning. The scar itself would have identified him. Annie saw a massive flaw in their plan. Her assassin worked here. Dillan had tried to rob the place, and now she was helping

Sam do almost the same thing. If they saw through her disguise, she wouldn't make it out of here alive. Annie's chest constricted.

Sam's eyes found hers, and he gave a subtle shake of his head.

"Let's get to work," Nadia clapped her hands.

Annie felt faint but clenched her teeth and let Nadia lead them upstairs. She dropped each team member off in a different room with an assignment. Finally, she opened a door for Annie.

Rows of purple dresses lined the room. Nadia gestured to them. "Rachel is in charge of our alterations. She's already altered these, but they need to be pressed properly. The bride had a few last-minute changes to her dress." Nadia rolled her eyes. "So, I'll work on that one tomorrow." She turned to leave but paused by the door. "When I say they have to be perfect, I mean perfect—got it? We got the parents', groomsmen's and groom's clothes covered by everyone else. Can you handle this?"

"Absolutely," Annie squeaked, forcing a smile.

Nadia nodded once. "Good. I'll check back in an hour or so." She left Annie alone. The moment the door closed, Annie dropped to the floor and started breathing hard, hyperventilating, actually. What in the world had Sam signed her up for? Annie's head hurt, and she wanted to crumple into a ball under the table and hide for the rest of the day.

"Nova? What's wrong? Nova?" the Warden asked.

"She's okay," Sam's voice joined the conversation. "Don't worry. She's got this."

Annie took her earpiece out and squished it in her armpit to keep her loud breathing from transferring through the earpiece. She covered her mouth with both hands as if that would help somehow. Sam didn't want their team to know about her situation. That was clear, or else he would have explained right then and there. Her hitman was her secret. But what was Sam thinking bringing her here of all places? Lloyd had a chance to recognize her. Without meaning to, she could inadvertently ruin the whole sting. If Sam had told her, she never would have come.

A shiver rushed through her, and she realized precisely why he hadn't told her Lloyd was one of the guards. He needed her here. He needed her to come even though it was dangerous because he didn't want to fail Claw. He needed to capture Benicci and Lichens and do whatever it took to ensure he got it done.

"Sam," she whispered into the big empty room. "How dare you."

CHAPTER 18

A DOOR OPENED ON THE other side of the room. Annie flinched, fully expecting to see her gunman pulling a concealed weapon out of his coat. Instead, Sam came through the door. He didn't rush toward her. Instead, his eyes darted all over the room as if looking for something. Annie knelt frozen in place. She didn't know how to react to his presence, especially if this was a setup.

A tug-of-war started in her heart. On the one hand, she wanted to do nothing but bury her face in his chest and let him hold her until she felt strong enough to stand on her own. On the other hand, she wanted to yell at him and slap him across his smoothly-shaven face. She shouldn't have told Claw she was ready to stay and do her part. Sam claimed he would push her but not make her do something she didn't want to do.

With a nod to himself, Sam took out his earpiece and pressed the button on the back to turn it off. She had forgotten about that nifty feature. "There, we're clear to talk. I already swept this room for bugs." He put his comm in his jacket pocket and turned to her. "Are you okay?"

Annie managed a nod. She felt far from okay, but she was intact, and that had to count for something. "You knew about him?"

He nodded. "Need a hand?" he asked with his brilliant smile. The fake one. He extended his palm to her, and Annie had to decide which side of the tug-of-war should win.

"Did you know he worked here?" She glared up at him.

Sam's jaw tightened, but he nodded again. "Let me explain."

She stared at his hand but didn't move. "How could you do this to me? That man wants me dead, and you had me walk right in here like a lobster with no idea she was about to be boiled to death and served with butter. You tricked me."

Sam let his hand drop. “It’s not like that. I know it’s risky bringing you here, but it’s also not a place they’d look for you. Lloyd chased Dillan away from here, and I secretly chased him. I had to find out who was attempting to destroy my operation. Then we both found you.” He turned away from her and took a deep breath. “You want the truth. I didn’t want you here, remember? I wanted to send you home, but I made a mistake and had to switch gears. Then you had a skill I desperately needed. If I told you that you’d have to face him, you never would have come.”

“You should have told me,” she snapped. “I ought to have known what I was getting into.”

“Would you have stepped foot here if I did?” he asked.

“No.” Annie turned away. “No, you’re asking me to risk my life for a cause I hardly believe in. I thought you wanted to protect me, not use me.”

“I’m not using you.” Sam rubbed the spot between his eyes.

“Are you sure? Because that’s what it feels like.”

“Listen. You don’t look like you at all, and he wasn’t paying attention to the lot of you. There is no way he recognized you. I kept an eye on him the whole time.”

Annie gasped, a sudden horrible thought popping into her head, and she whirled around. “Didn’t he recognize you?”

Sam slowly shrugged as if he had to think about his response. “I don’t think so. I took great pains to ensure he didn’t know I followed him to your apartment. I opened fire in a dark corner, so he couldn’t have seen me. Yesterday he was the one in the hotel room with you. He ran out that door and passed me like a bull after a red-capped matador. Lloyd dove over me without a glance at his ‘friend’ who I’d wrestled to the ground. So far, he’s shown no sign of recognition, and I made sure to talk to him directly today. If he had made any indication that he knew me, I would have pulled the plug already.”

“And if he recognizes me?”

“I’ll pull the plug. I made you a promise. I will keep you safe. Yes, you’re risking your life today, but I also took care of every precaution.” His hand twitched like he wanted to reach for her but didn’t. “I’m sorry; perhaps I should have warned you that he worked here. I’m not used to working with . . . civilians.”

Annie let out a slow breath and tried to force some calm back into her body. That last statement was true. She could feel it. Jeremy and Sam rushed about planning and scheming like what they did was normal. They probably didn’t know what it felt like anymore to have a regular day.

Annie fell into an oversized wingback chair, some of her anger dissipating. "I don't appreciate this curve ball. You can't assume things for me. I'm a regular person who deserves to have a choice. Especially after I promised Claw I wouldn't back out."

Sam's lips twitched, one of his eyebrows quirked, and he took a step closer to her. "You made a promise to Claw?"

Annie rubbed her arms in an attempt to fight off the twisting emotions she felt. She'd learned the hard way what standing too close to him did to her heart. Right now, she didn't want to feel any of that. "Of course I did. She said, 'You must choose whether you're in or out.' Isn't that why you asked her to pick me up in the first place? To guarantee your plan would play out?"

"No," he said. The word was drawn out a little. "I mean, I did ask her to take you to work, not solidify your allegiance to the team." He shook his head, his fingers tapping against each other. "Did she want you to say no?"

Annie had no idea what Claw wanted her to say. "I don't think so. I think she wants me here. If you both want me here—and Dillan wanted me here, ironically—I'm supposed to be here. Although I'm not sure why."

Sam leaned against the chair. "You're here, Annie, because we need you, no matter the risks. Will you forgive me for not telling you everything?"

Annie thought about that. Sam and Claw had both given her the option to leave. He might not have told her she'd have to work near the man who wanted to kill her, but he hadn't forced this. "I will give you only one second chance, Sam. I learned the hard way that additional second chances are not worth it."

Sam smiled his real smile this time and offered her a hand. "I'll not waste it. I swear to you that I won't hide anything from you. I promise you that this plan is going to work. And Lloyd will not get you."

Annie let out a long breath, and it took every brave cell in her body to say, "Okay."

He reached out both hands, cupping hers in his. "Something else you should know; you underestimate your control. I know plenty of people who would have fainted or run away when faced with a man who tried to kill them. Instead, you held it together long enough to break down when you were alone. I think you controlled your fears better than any regular civilian I know."

He pulled her up but didn't drop his hands from hers. Tug-of-war over. This is what she wanted. She needed comfort. She needed the safety of his hands wrapped around hers. It was strange that he somehow held the power to stop her from falling apart with a simple hand grasp.

He extracted a small, black case from his coat pocket along with his comm. "We'd better turn ours back on or the Warden will flip out and assume we've been murdered. You okay now?"

Annie nodded, burying the rest of her concerns, and extracted her comm from her armpit to put it back in her ear. Jeremy's voice came through. "There isn't any reason to freak out. I'm sure they are both fine," he said.

"Who's fine?' Sam asked, winking at Annie.

"Problem with the com, Kraken?" Jeremy asked, a bit of a laugh to his tone. "You didn't answer us."

Sam rolled his eyes. "Isn't electronic failures your department?"

"Are you saying I need to upgrade all my equipment? Because if that is the case, I have a long list of upgrades I'd love to order. In fact, I'll email you a list right now."

Sam snorted, and Annie's lips twitched, more of her worry fading. They were professionals. The cops had their backs. They could do this. She could do this.

"We can discuss that later. I need to explain the details of Nova's mission." He turned to her. "When I'm here, I usually spend all my time with the bride, McKay, Mrs. Lichens, and occasionally Mr. Lichens, but I don't get invited to the top floor. Midnight told you that it's your goal to gain access to the top floor, and this is why." He leaned closer and lowered his voice. "We think Mr. Lichens has a quick access point to the room we want somewhere on the third floor. We haven't been able to find it. If we had this secret entry point, we might skip many hurdles and finish quicker. This is where you come in." He handed her the case. Annie wrapped her hands around the cold metal box, and a shiver rushed through her. "You're going to plant some cameras on the third floor."

Annie opened her mouth to argue, but Sam put his finger against her lips, effectively shushing her.

"After ironing each rehearsal dinner dress for the bridesmaids, you'll need to deliver it to the rooms where each bridesmaid is staying. This gives you full access to . . . pretty much everywhere that the rest of us don't." He flipped the latch on the case she held and revealed hundreds of tiny black dots. "All you have to do is stick these mini cameras around the house. This will give a video feed to Midnight and Claw."

"Try to think strategically about it," the Warden cut in on her comm. "Make sure we have a clear line of sight and aren't blocked by a lamp or a vase full of flowers. You're the only one we've been able to get access to the upper floor. We're counting on you."

"So, no pressure." Annie had seen things like this in movies. She had no idea that people planted cameras for real. Sam gave her a quick shoulder squeeze. A reassuring gesture she sorely needed.

"Nova, there's also a button on your glasses." Jeremy's voice came through in her ear. "If you push it, I can see what you see. Now I know ironing may seem like a ton of fun to you, but I'd rather you only push it when you leave the room unless you think you'll forget. This will help us as well."

Annie took off her glasses and looked them over. They looked normal. Sam took a step closer to her and pointed to a small circle just inside the frames by the nosepiece. Annie hit it and put the glasses back on. Nothing changed in her view. "Can you see what I see?"

"Only Kraken's ugly mug." Jeremy laughed through the comm.

"Very funny. I'd better get back before I'm missed." Sam offered her his fake smile, lightly brushing her arm before leaving her alone in the big room, holding a box full of tiny cameras and glasses that showed her every movement.

"Better get to work, Nova," the Warden said. "We can't risk you getting fired before you've started."

Annie let out a long breath. The calm of that morning's swim had long since lost its effect. She'd simply have to go again if she lived through the day.

With that thought in mind, she rolled up her long black sleeves and pulled out her iron. It took a few minutes to set up. Every once in a while, someone said something through the comms, but never to her. She assumed Jeremy muted Sam's comm for everyone else while he talked with the bride. That at least made sense since she didn't often hear Ink, Sneak, Steel, Reaper, or Crank either. Jeremy must have a way to mute and unmute people so that not everyone heard everyone else's conversations all day.

The bridesmaid rehearsal dinner dresses were all tea length and purple with matching sashes. The chiffon fabric had a light sparkle to it. McKay must have spent a fortune on them, because they looked attractive and these were only one of three dresses her bridesmaids would wear.

Annie pulled one out of its rose-gold dress bag and got started. Picking a discrete corner of the hem, she tested her water and iron before pressing the dress. Thankfully, all seven rehearsal dinner bridesmaid dresses were the same, so she didn't have to repeat the test. Annie ironed meticulously as she'd been taught, and thankfully, her prior habit made this skill come back quickly.

Nadia came in to check on her right after she finished the first one. She looked the dress over with a practiced eye, nodded, and handed her a map of the house. "Fix the sash on the ends. I want them perfectly pointed. Each dress needs to be hung in the girl's closet. The bridesmaids are taking bridal photos with the bride in their other dresses this afternoon. We'll spot clean and press them tomorrow so they're ready for the wedding in a few days. It's an exciting time." With a laugh, she clapped Annie on the shoulder and rushed out of the room.

"You're doing great, Nova," the Warden said. "You've officially gotten yourself in place for tomorrow's heist."

Annie shivered. She hadn't done anything. She'd pressed a dress and followed directions. Directions she assumed Sam had a lot to do with as the wedding planner. "You'll need me here tomorrow too?" Annie honestly thought her part of the job was over after today. She couldn't risk coming again with Lloyd, her hitman, here too.

"We'll need all hands at the ready," the Warden replied.

Annie reached for the next dress. "Can you deliver that first one?" Jeremy asked. "I need you to start placing those cameras.

"Of course." Zipping the first dress back up in its rose-gold bag, Annie checked the label pinned to it: *Isabelle, purple lily room.* She pulled out the map. Hopefully, this wouldn't prove too complex. According to the map, the room was on the third floor.

Annie opened the door and followed her map. She looked left and right. No one stood in the hallway on the second floor. Good. The last thing she wanted was a run-in with Lloyd. Her hand trembled while holding the hanger above her head to keep the dress bag from touching the floor. Taking a deep breath, she moved to the staircase and up to the third floor.

I can do this. I can do this, she thought repeatedly.

A large guard with dark, shaggy hair stood at the top of the stairs, but he was not her shooter. Annie held her breath as she offered him a weak smile and raised the dress bag.

"What room?" he asked in a deep base voice.

She swallowed hard and held up her map. "Purple lily?"

He nodded once and stuck his thumb toward the left. "Go that way, and don't touch anything."

"Thanks."

Annie walked slowly, glad a plaque with the room name was next to each door. She pulled out a couple of cameras from her pocket under the guise of studying each nameplate. She peeled off the backing of the cameras and stuck them in place. The guard on the stairs didn't look over, so she continued the practice on her way down the hall.

I'm okay. I'm doing okay.

Once she found the purple lily room, she knocked. When no one answered, she walked inside. It was a huge room.

"Nova?" Jeremy asked through the comm.

"Yep," she said, resisting the urge to touch her comm in her ear.

"I need you to look slowly around each room so I can get a good visual."

Annie adjusted her special glasses. "What are we looking for?"

"Technically everything. Escape routes, places to hide, if need be. Secret passages, security measures . . . stuff like that."

A king-size bed sat against one wall covered in a purple comforter. A window seat with white fluffy pillows, a big TV, a walk-in closet, and a bathroom took up the other walls. White lily wallpaper tastefully accented two walls. It looked stunning.

Annie walked to one of the tall windows. From this vantage point, she spied the wedding party. The bridesmaids were laughing by the side of the pool. As one, the bride and her bridesmaids blew a kiss at the groom and his groomsmen before they tore off their fancy dresses, revealing their swimwear underneath. The groom and his men looked on with envy as the bride and her friends jumped into the pool. Those dresses might need more than a spot clean and press tomorrow.

"Are you seeing what you need?" she asked as she walked to the closet to hang up the pressed dress.

"Yep. Look at the south window frame for me. I need to check something," Jeremy said.

"What are we looking for?" Annie asked, moving to the window.

"I disabled the security on that window several weeks ago. I need to know if it's reconnected." Annie had no idea what to look for, so she slowly moved her head in a square, tracing the shape of the window.

"Okay, I'm good. You'd better head out before the guard gets curious."

Annie glanced at the dress on the hook on the back of the closet door before she made her way to the bedroom door. She paused with her hand on the knob. "Do I put any cameras in here?"

"I'd place one by the door that'll face the window," the Warden said. "Just in case."

Annie took care with how she stuck it up. Now she only needed to repeat this process six more times without running into Lloyd.

The stair guard checked in with her for the following two dresses, but after that, he ignored her when she walked up the stairs with a dress bag in hand. She'd either passed a test, or they'd decided she wasn't worth their time. Either way, Sam was right. She could move around the house without anyone paying attention to her. At least she finally got something right.

After delivering her last dress, a door that looked tucked into the corner drew her attention. A large, potted bush covered part of the door as if trying to mask its presence. Annie stuck a camera in the hallway facing the partially hidden door. She turned to leave, but something inside her wouldn't let her turn away. With a glance down the empty halls, she moved in for a closer look.

"Uh, Nova? What are you doing?" Jeremy asked through the comm.

Annie jumped. She'd forgotten that the glasses granted Jeremy access to everything she saw. "There's something about this door . . . that makes me wonder."

Annie stepped carefully, using all the skills Sneak had taught her, and darted to the door. Holding her breath, she pressed her ear against the shiny wood. No sounds came from inside.

"Be careful," Jeremy warned.

Annie turned the knob. "It's locked." Annie peeled a sticker off a camera and placed it on the potted bush so that the camera looked directly at the door. "Just in case." Annie moved to dart away from the door when something else caught her eye. The large plant had a lining with leather-tied bows every couple of inches. One of the bows closest to the door was partially untied. With another look at the empty hallway, she reached her hand into the lining under the untied bow. She felt something cold. A key.

"Score!" Jeremy said through the comm.

"Try the door," the Warden chimed in, excitement lacing his words.

Annie snatched up the key and shoved it into the lock. She doubted she had a ton of time. Guards patrolled these halls every once in a while. The door unlocked, and Annie pushed it open enough to peek inside. It appeared empty. She slid in and closed the door.

It was the least fancy room in the house. An old brick fireplace stood cold and empty on one side of the room. Long maroon drapes hung limp and dusty on either side of the window. A large, wooly, brown-and-gray-striped rug lay on the floor, with two gray chairs facing the fireplace. Leather pillows sat on the chairs and showed a thin layer of dust. A bookshelf full of worn novels stood against one wall. Opposite the fireplace was a sizeable ornate wood wardrobe.

"Don't dawdle. This looks like an unused room, Nova," the Warden said.

Annie pulled another tiny camera from her pocket. "I'm going to place a camera."

"I wouldn't waste many in this room," Jeremy yawned. "Just cover the basics."

Annie understood this room didn't look like much, but her gut said otherwise. She couldn't help but wonder if it was bland on purpose . . . Quickly, she darted forward and stuck a camera to the fireplace where it wasn't visible. She raced across the room and stuck one on the wardrobe between two twists of wood decoration.

Returning to the door, she eased it open and twisted the lock. Voices came from the hall.

"Midnight, how does the hall look?" She'd placed enough cameras for him to answer this question accurately.

"I'd say you have seconds. Get out."

Rushing out the door, she pulled it closed behind her. With quivering hands, she dropped the key back in place, pulled the map out of her pocket, and walked down the hall, pretending to study it.

"Well done, Nova," the Warden said. "You're getting the hang of this. Kraken wasn't wrong about you."

Annie honestly didn't know if that was a good thing or a bad thing. A group of girls in bathing suits came up the stairs laughing and completely ignored her.

Her sigh of relief jammed in her throat when Lloyd darted up the stairs. Flashbacks of him hanging out the window and aiming a gun at her assaulted her mind. Unbidden, her gaze dropped to the scar on his hand. Annie couldn't help the tremble of her hands holding the map. She raised it a little higher in an attempt to hide her face.

"It's okay, Nova," Jeremy said. "Keep walking. They're only changing guards."

Lloyd hardly glanced her way as they passed on the stairs. "If this is the view you've been getting all day, then I'm happy to trade places."

"I think they're done with the swimsuit show," the other guard replied.

Lloyd harrumphed. Annie reached the bottom step and rounded the corner, barely out of sight.

"Did you take care of your little problem?"

Annie froze. *Problem*? She hit the button to turn off her recording glasses. This probably wasn't a conversation for the team. Annie bet the entirety of her small savings account that they were talking about her. She turned to look up the stairs through the dark wood railing.

Lloyd leaned against the railing at the top of the stairs, stretching his arms. "No."

"Seriously?" The other guard laughed.

"I thought she was alone. I was wrong. Someone's helping her." Lloyd sounded distressed about it. "Someone with training."

"Or you shot the wrong guy in the beginning."

Lloyd's face grew tense. "I shot them all. Everyone in that pitiful crew is six feet under right now, even that scrawny kid, Dillian, who thought he got away. Tyson will have to reward me for that."

Annie bit the insides of her lips to keep from gasping out loud. They talked about taking people's lives with no remorse at all.

"Except for her," the other guard scoffed.

Lloyd's face turned bright tomato red. "What are you inferring?"

"That if you don't take care of her, you're fired. Tyson isn't happy you left a loose end. He prides himself on how effectively we do our job."

"I'll get her. I swear. It's only a matter of time."

"You'd better."

Annie jumped at the sound of footsteps coming down the stairs. She rushed to her room with her ironing supplies, closed the door, and leaned against it. She could hardly breathe. All her insides felt like they'd stopped working. She'd done her part today. They didn't need her tomorrow. She'd placed all the cameras, and that had to count for something. She could call in sick or lock herself in the hotel bathroom. It was far too risky to return with her hitman there. Sam would back her up, or Jeremy would, right? They understood the danger.

Annie slowly started packing up her supplies. Her trust for her protectors wavered. She knew Sam promised to safeguard her, but she also got the feeling that if it came down to saving her or saving this job, he'd choose the latter. Something he'd proven today.

CHAPTER 19

Although Annie waited for him, Sam didn't show up until after she fell asleep, and he left before she woke up. She should have shaken him awake at 3:00 a.m. when she roused long enough to check the time. The only clue that he'd shown up was the mussing of the covers on his queen bed. Was he avoiding her? She didn't have a moment to ask him if she could stay out of the heist.

Jeremy wandered up from the hotel breakfast just after seven in the morning with a yogurt cup in hand. He was her only hope.

"Jeremy, if my part in this plan was to plant the cameras, can I sit out today?"

He paused, the spoon halfway to his mouth. "You want to sit out on a day like today? Annie, today's the whole reason Sam and I have spent so much time in this part of LA. Today's the peak, the high moment. The literal day we've been waiting for . . . you want to miss that?" His eyes were wide, and he looked at her with a baffled expression. These guys truly had forgotten how the real world worked for most people.

His life must have revolved around crime for a long time if he had forgotten what it was like to be in her shoes. "Jeremy, you and Sam know more than anyone that I am no—" She gestured to him, completely unsure what to call them. Was it wrong to call them thieves, grifters, vigilantes, and con men when they helped the police?

Jeremy tossed his empty yogurt cup into the trash. "We might need you. We have a solid plan, but things don't always go smoothly. Sam is going to get the last passcode we need this morning. Sneak and Steel are going to crack the safe. Ink acquired the last fingerprint yesterday. Reaper is ready to remove Tyson, the Lichenses' head of security, to grant us access to ground zero. Thanks to you, we now have cameras on almost every inch of the place except ground zero. Crank is more than ready to drive us out of there when we're finished. Claw informed me this morning that she's readied her team. Everything is in place, but that doesn't mean things will go smoothly."

He looked at her with an expression like a puppy wanting a treat. "At least come in your Annie Kendrick disguise and sit in the van with the Warden and me in case we need you."

Annie squirmed under his gaze. Should she tell him about Lloyd? Jeremy knew she was in danger, but how much had Sam told him? She bit her lip, indecision warring in her chest. Staying in the van wasn't a pass, but it kept her from entering the house.

"It's fun watching from the van," Jeremy added, a hopeful plea to his tone. "It's like watching an action movie from a bunch of different angles. I've also got a ton of snacks."

Annie's shoulders fell. If she didn't go inside the house, she wouldn't have to worry about Lloyd. Swallowing her fear, she nodded. "When do we leave?"

He held out a hand for a high five. Annie smiled despite her situation and slapped his hand with hers. Jeremy plopped down on the couch and pulled his laptop onto his lap. "We'll leave in about thirty minutes to start monitoring everyone else."

"What about Sam?"

Jeremy shrugged, hitting a few keys. "Sam's already there."

"With no one monitoring him? What if he needs help?" Annie might not have liked how things went yesterday, but what if something went wrong? Sam was in as much danger as her if Lloyd remembered him.

Jeremy smiled and tapped his temple. "I got an ear on him. Besides, Reaper is also there. They'll watch each other's backs."

Not ready for this kind of stress, Annie dragged herself out of bed and into the bathroom to transform into Miss Annie Kendrick, red wig and all. When she exited, Jeremy stood waiting by the door, his bag packed while he tapped on his phone.

"Ready or not?" Jeremy said.

She smirked. "Here we come." Annie grabbed her two cases with her ironing equipment and followed him out the door, down the elevator, through the lobby—where she snagged an apple off the counter—and to a waiting white van. "You can sit up front," Jeremy said.

Crank gave her a small wave from the driver's seat, but Jeremy opened the back. With a bright smile, he disappeared. Annie went to the passenger side of the van. "Hey," she said, setting her cases on her seat. Crank grabbed them and placed them behind her chair so she could climb inside.

Annie buckled her seatbelt and turned to see what looked like a high-tech computer lab in the back. "Wow."

"Yeah, Midnight gets all the cool stuff," Crank said, pulling away from the curb. Annie split her time trying to listen to the Warden and Jeremy in the back while Crank kept commenting on the traffic. He pulled the van into a space between two trees at the bottom of the hill leading up to the Lichenses' mansion. A large black limo waited in a clearing behind them with a few other cars. "This is as close as I could get you without drawing attention," Crank said.

"It will do," the Warden replied, snapping on a pair of headphones.

"I can't believe I agreed to wear a monkey suit for the rehearsal dinner." With a loud groan, Crank went into the back and pulled off his T-shirt. Annie abruptly turned forward, her face flaming.

"I'll have the limo parked by the front door if you need me for anything." A couple minutes later, Crank hopped out of the van.

"Come on back, Annie," Jeremy invited.

Annie crawled through and found several monitors showing different parts of the Lichenses' mansion house switching on rotation. One screen had everyone's code names and what looked like a sound bar. The Warden, Kraken, Midnight, and Reaper were active. The rest seemed to be on standby. The Warden had one keyboard, but Jeremy had three different ones. True to form, Jeremy popped open a bag and grabbed a handful of chips. They all watched the monitors for several minutes before a knock sounded on the door.

The Warden let Ink inside. Ink gave Annie a wink and took an ear comm from Jeremy. The Warden did a sound check to make sure it worked. Ink cracked his fingers. "Time to finish my masterpiece. Play nice, cats."

Sneak and Steal showed up a little while later for their comms. They were dressed in black, although Steel still looked like a model with her black accessories glinting in the sunlight. Sneak spared Annie a bright smile before putting in her comm. They both nodded professionally and left with their photography equipment. Annie breathed out. Everyone was in place. How did they handle the stress?

The Warden didn't say anything about Annie not going up to the house, and she didn't want to risk bringing it up. Jeremy might have said something; she'd rather hang out in the background and be forgotten. Every once in a while, she caught sight of Sam helping organize things for the dinner or Ink, Sneak, or Steel.

The bride, McKay, bounced around excitedly or yelled depending on whom she talked to. Annie felt a little guilty about them ruining her rehearsal dinner. Here she was preparing for the most important day of her life, and if the sting succeeded, she would lose her painter, photographer, wedding planner, and father a couple days before her wedding. It was worth it if they could take down both horrible men, but she still felt bad for the girl.

Annie scooted closer to Jeremy and lowered her voice. "What about McKay? Are you sure this is the best time to grab her father?"

The Warden jumped. He must have forgotten she was there. Jeremy shrugged like he didn't see any problem with it.

The Warden turned his chair around and fixed her with a stern look. "There's no other time. Kraken spent two months trying to find another way in, then six months setting this whole thing up. This is it. We'll send her a card or something. It's not our fault that her father is unsavory." He shook his head as if she'd asked something mental. Without another word, he turned to the monitors.

Jeremy kept to his task at hand. Annie pushed off her worry. It was too late to look for a different way. She'd make sure they sent McKay a card; it wasn't much but at least it was something.

"Warden." Reaper's voice came through the comm. "I think we might have a problem."

"What do you mean?"

"I saw—" His voice garbled, and a loud, high-pitched sound came through all the equipment.

Annie, the Warden, and Jeremy all covered their ears. Jeremy reached out and hit a button, cutting off the sound. The monitors in front of Jeremy and the Warden blinked before they distorted, and gray lines appeared. They fluttered again, then blacked out completely.

"Midnight, if you spilled your soda on the wires again, so help me, I'll—"

"It wasn't me. I swear." Jeremy held up his hands.

The Warden started punching buttons on his keyboard. "Reaper? Reaper? Can you hear me? Kraken? Claw? Ink? Steel? Crank? Reaper? Sneak? Can anyone hear me? Hello? Kraken?" The Warden turned wide eyes on Jeremy. "No one's answering. We've lost communication with the team. Get them back. Now!"

Jeremy dove under the counter and fiddled with the wires. He unplugged and plugged things back in, opened his laptop, tapped buttons, and twirled knobs. His face was getting paler by the second.

"Midnight, I need them back." The Warden tapped his feet impatiently. "Reaper tried to tell us something important."

"I can't. I've lost everything. There's no connection." He looked up at the Warden, his eyes wide. "Do you think we're burned?"

The Warden grabbed Jeremy by his shoulders and shook him. "We can't do this job blind. Get them back now!" He let go of Jeremy and pointed to the black monitors. "They. Need. Us."

Jeremy straightened his shoulders and spoke calmly. "There's nothing I can do from here. I need to get inside to fix this. I planted my access weeks ago on the roof. Something must have happened to it."

"Midnight, you have to do something about this right now," the Warden said, his voice deadly calm. "We cannot fail. You might think Lichens is bad, but you've never met Mr. Benicci, and you don't want to."

Jeremy turned to her, his eyes wide. "Annie, you're getting me in."

"What?! How? I . . . can't." Her eyes darted around for some kind of ally, but the Warden and Jeremy were stuffing things into a small case.

Jeremy tossed her a black wrist brace. "Put that on your left wrist."

"Why?"

"I can't act like your brother helping you carry your supplies if you're not injured somehow. But you must be able to work, or they won't let either of us in. We need you now." He nodded to the brace he'd tossed her.

Annie bit her lip, her eyes darting to the Warden. "I can't. It's not safe for me."

"It's not safe for anyone," the Warden growled.

"No, you don't understand." She looked at Jeremy, pleading with him to read her mind, to clue into the danger. He only shot her a sympathetic look. Annie grabbed his arm, towed him a few feet from the Warden, and lowered her voice to a hiss. "The man who tried to kill me is in there."

Jeremy's eyes widened. "What? Does Sam know?"

"Yes. He's known all along. I can't risk going back in there."

Jeremy tapped his teeth together. "When did you find this out?

"Yesterday. He's one of the guards, the one named Lloyd."

Jeremy pushed his bright-blue glasses up his nose. "Sam should have told me. I suppose he didn't want to get us all involved." He glanced at the Warden, who was hitting keys on his keyboard again. "Did he recognize you yesterday?"

"No."

Jeremy shook his head slowly. "I'm sorry, Annie. My friends—our friends—are in there alone, flying blind in the middle of a heist. Danger or not, we have to go in. You wouldn't abandon Sam, would you? Sam needs you, Annie."

Annie turned away and swallowed hard. A tremor rushed through her. He was right; she couldn't abandon Sam. Something dangerous was happening, and the last thing she wanted was to see Sam dead.

Annie stared at the wrist brace, then glanced at the blank screens. She hated the idea of going inside that house. But she'd promised them she'd help. Claw must have known that Annie was no good at breaking promises. With a heavy sigh, she wrapped the wrist brace around her left wrist. Everyone in that house would be extra busy today, and that included her hitman. Most people ignored her yesterday; maybe they'd ignore her today.

"That's our girl," Jeremy said.

Jeremy opened a cabinet and pulled out a baby-blue dinner jacket. He slipped it over his T-shirt and picked up both of her cases, including his newly packed one.

The Warden put a hand on Jeremy's shoulder. "Your first goal is to reestablish communication. We need the comms up right away. From there, you can fix everything else." He swung open the door. "We have no time to waste. Every second could lead to their doom. Go. Go."

Jeremy jumped out of the van with Annie scrambling after him. "Annie, we're going to keep this simple. You're a little later than the rest of the consultants from the shop because you got hurt last night. I'm here to help you keep your job. That's it. Simple. We both have to appear calm. No matter what happens inside, we must pretend nothing is wrong."

She nodded and silenced all the warning bells going off in her head. She could do this for Sam and Jeremy. Sam had saved her; it was her turn to return the favor.

A few minutes later, they reached the guard house. Annie waved and pointed to her case. "Sorry I'm late," Annie said. She pulled her fake ID out of her case. "Annie Kendrick from White Lace Boutique."

The guard checked his list, gave her one nod, and then looked at Jeremy. "Oh, I'm her good Samaritan brother. She couldn't carry these up the hill to the house by herself." He shrugged, holding up the cases, before nodding to the brace on her wrist.

Annie winced at the lie. The guard looked them both up and down before he hit the button to open the gate. "Nadia said that her consultants would trickle in all morning. You're okay to go up, but you . . ." He eyed Jeremy. "Drop off her things and report to the guards at the front door."

"Will do," Jeremy said, hefting the cases. Together they walked through the gates.

Annie eyed the guards at the front door. "You know they're going to dig through the cases."

He nodded once, pulled his phone out, and typed away on the tiny screen. "I've got it covered."

They reached the front doors where two macho-looking men stood. They glared at both of them. One of the guards pointed to a table. "Your cases."

Jeremy set up Annie's first before his own.

Annie's heart beat hard in her throat. Jeremy's case did not contain any sort of dress-care supplies. The guard opened her cases and moved things around before he pushed hers aside and reached for Jeremy's.

"There you are," a voice she knew yelled, but for the first time, it sounded angry.

Everyone, including the guards, jumped. Sam strode down the hall, a look of fury on his face that she'd never seen before. "You're late. I'm not paying Nadia's consultants to show up whenever they please. I pay for punctual, professional people." He rushed forward, slammed her cases closed, grabbed Jeremy's, and shoved all of them into Jeremy's gut. He winced. "Get going before I have you fired. Don't you know what day it is? Don't you know whom you're working for?"

Annie and Jeremy both scurried down the hall.

"Don't think I won't report you," Sam called after them. "I expect you to finish on time." He pointed to the stairs. "McKay deserves the best."

Annie and Jeremy rushed toward the large staircase that led up to the second floor.

Sam turned around, straightened his jacket, and looked at the door guard. "You can't find good help these days, even from the most respected businesses."

The guard grunted in reply. Annie turned her focus back on the staircase as she and Jeremy raced to the same room she'd worked from yesterday. Annie pushed the door closed and leaned against it. She clasped her hands together on her chest, feeling her heartbeat ram hard against her ribs. They were all inside. No going back now.

Jeremy laughed. "Sam went all out for that one. Let's find out what's wrong." With his usual casual air, Jeremy walked calmly to a chair in the corner of the room and pulled out his laptop. "You'd better gather the bridesmaid dresses before Sam's forced to yell at us again."

Annie breathed out slowly, still feeling a little stunned by Sam's performance. Picking up her cases, she staggered to her ironing board. She set her cases down and looked at the note pinned to the board.

Annie K.

Your focus is the bridesmaids' dresses. Make sure they are perfect. Iron them all and then deliver them at the end of the day. I'm happy with how the rehearsal dinner dresses turned out. Keep up the excellent work, and we might steal you away instead of borrowing you. The rehearsal dinner will be going on around 4:00. Make sure you stay out of sight as much as possible. We don't want to get in the way. I'm two doors down if you need me.

Ta ta,
Nadia

Annie grabbed her list from last night and walked to the door. *Please, Lord, protect us and don't let Lloyd see me. If you care what happens to me at all, keep us safe*, she prayed before she opened the door. A prayer felt like such a small thing when faced with this danger, but it was all she had. "Need anything while I'm out there?" Annie asked, trying to mimic Jeremy's calm.

"I wouldn't say no to some gummy worms."

Annie blinked in surprise.

"I'm kidding." Jeremy laughed. "I'm trying to establish a connection. It's not working. I might need to check out where I placed my access." Jeremy stood up and nodded to her brace. "You need help gathering dresses because of that wrist, right?"

"Sure, but I'm going to the third floor."

"Perfect." Jeremy pointed to the purple lily room on her map. "That's where I need to go."

They left the room together and approached the guard at the top of the stairs. It was a different man from yesterday and, thankfully, not her shooter. "Where do you think you're going?" he snapped.

Annie pressed her "hurt" wrist against her stomach and held up the list. "I'm gathering the bridesmaid dresses. I need to press them; my brother is assisting me." She raised her wrist brace. "I can't lift them on my own. The other guard said it was okay for him to help me."

The guard grunted and swiped the list out of her hand. He eyed the rooms circled in purple pen. "We'll start with the sunset room." He waved for them to follow.

Jeremy paled slightly as they followed the guard. Annie had the feeling that they needed to break away from the guard, but she had no idea how to give Jeremy that.

The guard opened a door not far from the stairs. "Go on." He nodded for them to enter first.

Annie and Jeremy rushed inside. The guard waited at the door, his eyes following their every step. Annie went straight to the closet. A floor-length light purple dress with a sage-green sash lay in a heap on the floor. It took them a second to find the hanger and dress bag. Once put together, Jeremy held it up.

"Now to the orange room," the guard stated, looking back at the list and then his post on the stairs.

Jeremy leaned close to Annie. "Go slow, and maybe he'll give up escorting us to each room."

In the orange room, they didn't find the dress right away. After spending much longer than she would have to search the closet, Annie found the dress hanging in the bathroom on the back of the door. They located the dress bag in the tub after she and Jeremy "searched" for several more minutes.

"We'd better take these two down and come back up for the rest," Jeremy said, watching the guard's eyes bulge. "They're heavy."

"Good idea," Annie said, closing the door to the room.

They left the guard at his station at the top of the stairs. Walking at a slower-than-usual pace, they made it down the stairs and hung the dresses by her ironing board. Jeremy had them wait and count to one hundred three times before they left and made their way back up. Annie leaned over to look at her map in the guard's hands. "We can take it from here if you want. I can hold the map."

Jeremy smiled pleasantly. The guard looked from her to the map. Annie didn't know if it was his annoyance at waiting for them or her innocent request, but the guard handed her the map. "Don't touch anything you don't have to. I'll check the bags when you come back down to make sure you don't steal anything."

They nodded. Jeremy led her to the purple lily room. He knocked and then opened the door. "Find the dress. I have to reestablish communication," he said, running to the window.

Annie darted to the closet. This bridesmaid had some respect for her things, and her dress was hung and bagged with hardly a wrinkle. Annie rushed back into the room to find Jeremy slipping out the window. She scurried to it. Jeremy held onto the decorative ledge and made his way slowly across the stone wall.

With a wink, he pulled himself onto the roof and out of sight. Jeremy was stronger than he looked. Annie held her breath until his legs appeared a minute or two later, and he swung down to make his way to the window. "I got it."

"How did you plant that in the first place?" Annie knew from the briefing that doing so would have been nearly impossible.

He smirked. "A rock through the window and a repairman's uniform." He pulled his phone out and tapped a few buttons. "This should do it." Yelling came through her comm from multiple people, and it didn't sound good.

"I can hear you."

"What's going on?"

"Calm down, everyone, for two seconds. Reaper, are you there? What did you need to tell us?" the Warden's voice cut through the noise. "What's . . . Kraken? Midnight, the video feed is coming back up now."

Annie froze, listening, holding the dress above her head.

"Hold on," the Warden requested. "Everything is back up. Kraken, Reaper is fighting Tyson downstairs. It's early, but it's do or die. Sneak, Ink, and Steal, you are a go. Kraken, get them what they need. It's go time. Midnight, some of our feeds are still crippled. We need to bring them all up."

Jeremy grabbed the dress bag and waved for Annie to follow him. With a huff, he slowed his steps when they approached the stairs and turned to her with a strained smile. "You sure you want to start with the first three?"

"Yes," she said, clueing in and fighting hard to keep the tremor out of her voice. "I don't want to mix them all up."

Jeremy held up the dress bag for the guard. "We'll get started with these three."

The guard felt the bottom of the bag and nodded. "Fine."

They started down the stairs.

"Warden, we have a problem," Sam said through the comm. "Tyson isn't down. I repeat, Tyson isn't down. Reaper is on the ground. It's not safe to approach ground zero."

"Is he dead?" the Warden asked.

"I don't know," Sam replied.

Jeremy and Annie closed the door in her room, and he tossed the dress on the ironing board before opening his laptop. "Where are Sneak and Steal?"

"I don't know," Sam said. "Something's gone wrong."

"What's happened?" the Warden shouted. "Everyone report in. What's going on right now?"

No one answered right away. Annie raced over to Jeremy, her eyes on the ever-moving camera angles on his screen.

"I can't," Sam finally said, "because I don't know." The worry in his voice was the last thing any of them wanted to hear.

CHAPTER 20

Jeremy typed so fast that his fingers were a blur. Annie stood there, staring at his computer screen. She needed to do something to help, but she had no experience in this kind of situation. "What can I do?" she asked.

Jeremy shook his head. "I don't know yet." He clicked through several screens showing various parts of the house.

"I've lost a bunch of my cameras. I don't see Sneak, Steel, or Ink," Jeremy said. He got up, snatched her map, and pulled a pen out of his pocket.

"Crank is waiting outside," the Warden said. "I've lost visual on Reaper. Kraken, give me an update."

Sam didn't answer. Was he hurt or keeping his cover? Annie didn't like either option. Her gut clenched as horrible images of him suffering or worse flashed through her head. She couldn't wait here, with her stomach in knots. "Midnight, I can help. Please give me a job."

Jeremy thrust the map into Annie's hands. "Go check your cameras on the third floor. I'll check the main floor," he said. "Just tell Big-and-Scary at the top of the stairs that you're missing a sash from one of the dresses. Go."

Annie rushed to the door, the map rolled in her hand. She slowed her steps once the guard could see her and made every effort to stay calm. The guard sneered at her as she approached the top of the stairs.

"The dress from the purple lily room is missing a sash," she said, her voice wobbling.

He grunted. Before she reached the top of the stairs, his hand flew to his ear. He must have an earpiece. With wide eyes, he rushed past her without a second glance. Annie's eyes followed him. He didn't pause long on the landing before rushing down the next flight of steps. They must have caught someone. "Jeremy, the guard up here just bolted downstairs."

"They're chasing Ink," Jeremy said in a monotone as if his concentration was elsewhere. "Hurry, Nova. We're running out of time."

She unrolled the map, and her muscles tensed while she ran. Jeremy had marked where she'd placed the cameras. She found the first dot. The camera was still there. She tapped it. "Midnight," she asked under her breath.

"You got it, Nova. It's back on. These cameras turned on when you stuck them to the wall. Someone must have walked around and turned them all off."

"Who?" she breathed, walking to the next one. She pressed it.

"I don't know, and I don't like it. Keep turning them on while I figure this out."

"Is she safe up there?" Sam asked. A warmth grew in her chest at his question. He was alive. Thank the Lord! She couldn't stomach the idea of Sam hurt.

"I think so, Kraken."

"Make sure," Sam said. Annie's heart lifted. Even when everything was on the line, Sam thought about her.

"Kraken, Ink's hiding in the living room. Can you help?" Jeremy asked.

"I'm on it," Sam said.

Annie pressed each camera button until she reached the hidden door. It was slightly ajar. She looked at her map. The two cameras she'd placed there were not marked. Had Jeremy forgotten about them, or had they never turned on? Remembering her glasses that recorded everything, she pushed the button on them. "Midnight, you missed two of my cameras."

"It's possible." He sounded winded, like he was running a marathon. More was going on than she knew.

Taking a deep breath, she pushed the door open. The room looked exactly like it had the day before. She stepped into the room and pushed the door to its original position. A bunch of questions popped into her mind. The most important was who had unlocked this room and left the door open?

A creak behind her made her whirl around. Annie imagined Lloyd cornering her, with his silver gun pointed at her heart or the stair guard rushing her. Instead, Steel stood behind her with her hands up. "It's me. It's okay. I came to help." Annie let out a long breath. It wasn't her shooter or one of the Lichenses' other guards.

"Steel, I put cameras in this room yesterday. I know I did." She gestured to the fireplace.

Steel tossed her long blonde hair over her shoulder and came inside. She closed the door, looked left and right, her lips curled in thought. "That's strange," she said. "I doubt a couple of cameras matter too much. Midnight usually places far too many for my taste."

"No, you don't understand." Annie stormed across the room and pointed to the fireplace. "I put one right here." She pointed to the empty spot. Annie strode over to the wardrobe where she'd put the other one, rather cleverly, she thought, in the bend of the woodwork decorations. "And here. Someone found them and took them down."

"Okay, calm down, Nova." Steel went to the window and looked outside.

Everything was falling apart on this job; Annie could feel it. Shouting sounded on their comms, followed by a high-pitched tone, and Annie and Steel ripped their comms out.

"What is that all about?" Annie asked, rubbing her ear.

Steel peered out the window. "Police cars are coming up the drive. Time's up."

Annie rushed over and looked out the window. Sure enough, the cops were on their way. "But they're early. Everything's early."

Steel clapped a hand on her back. "Sometimes, not everything goes to plan. I'm going to check on the situation. You wait here." Steel rushed to the door.

Annie nodded, her eyes on the police cars. Their perfect plan had somehow failed. They failed the moment they'd lost all communications. Sam was so particular about every detail. Didn't he have a contingency plan?

Another squeak sounded behind her. Annie whirled but only made it halfway before something hard crashed into her skull. Bright pinpricks of light flashed in her eyes; the searing pain registered before she fell limply to the floor. She couldn't see. She couldn't think. She fought it, but in the end, she blacked out.

Throbbing pain registered in her head first. With a loud groan, Annie tried to push herself up. A sharp burst of pain zipped across the side of her head, and she slumped to the floor. She blinked several times to clear her eyes. Brown-and-gray carpet came into view. Tenderly, she reached up and touched her head. Her fingers came away red and sticky with blood.

Tears rushed to her eyes as she pushed to her knees, the pain banging in her head harder.

"Nova," a gruff voice said. Annie looked up to see Reaper filling the doorway. "Come on. We have to get out."

"What's going on?"

"The job is a bust." He darted forward, wrapped his arms around her, and pulled her to her feet. She clutched her searing head.

Reaper started towing her toward the door. Annie's head throbbed incessantly in protest. "We'll figure out what happened later. Right now, we have to get out. I found a secret passageway to this floor. We can escape downstairs that way."

Reaper half carried her out of the room. "Kraken, I found Nova," Reaper said while pulling her down the hall. Shouts and screams sounded downstairs.

Annie's head whirled, and she felt she needed to say something important but couldn't find the words. She felt for her ear. Her comm was missing. She'd left the glasses on the floor in the room. What else was she missing? Her head hurt too much to figure it out.

Reaper shifted her to one arm and pulled on a decorative pillar. The wall cracked, and Reaper pushed it open. He waved to her to follow him down a tight tunnel. "Hold on to me. We don't have time to waste."

She prayed at this moment that she could trust him to get her out of there. Together, they rushed into the tunnel. Annie hissed as her head seared with sharper pain.

"Your head is spinning, right?" he asked.

"Yeah."

"I have a similar injury." He pointed to his head, which indeed featured a large spot with dried blood. A metal spiral staircase appeared at the end of the tight hall. He let go of her and stationed himself in front of her. "Hold on to my shoulders."

Annie obeyed, and the throbbing increased with every step she took. They burst out into a side hallway near the kitchen.

A guard rushed them. Reaper shoved Annie out of the way, and she hit the wall hard. The breath knocked out of her. She slid to the ground, gasping. Reaper and the guard started punching each other in a fight worthy of an action movie. Annie crawled to the side door a few feet away. With a crack and a groan, the sound of punching ended.

"We're coming out," Reaper said, picking Annie up and setting her on her feet. He kicked the door open, and they ran outside to the side yard toward a waiting limo.

Sam threw open the car door. Annie didn't wait for instructions before diving over Sam's lap into the limo. Reaper followed her and slammed the door closed. He climbed over the seats and sat next to Jeremy, who was typing like mad on his laptop. With a loud squeal, the limo tore down the side yard, rocks spewing behind them.

"I found a back service entrance, part of my prep work," Crank yelled from the front seat. "I don't think the police have blocked it off yet.

"I think you're right," Jeremy replied, adjusting his computer on his lap.

Sam gently pulled Annie to a sitting position and looked her over. With light fingers, he brushed the injury on the side of her head. He pulled a handkerchief out of his pocket and pressed it against her wound. "Are you hurt anywhere else?"

She shrugged. "I don't think so. What happened?"

Sam hung his head, a look of defeat filling his eyes. "We were betrayed."

"By who?" Reaper asked. "All I heard was Midnight yelling 'abort, abort!' I ran to the passageway I'd found as an easy escape just in case. Then I saw Nova on the ground in a side room upstairs. I think someone stole her comm."

Jeremy sighed and pulled out a water bottle. He filled a crystal glass with it and tossed his earpiece in it. Sam and Reaper followed suit. Crank handed his back from the front seat, and they added it to the water.

"Who was it, Midnight?" Reaper asked. "Who turned on us?"

All eyes focused on Jeremy. He paused his erratic typing long enough to look at them all in the eye. "It was Steel. Steel betrayed us." Jeremy's eyes moved directly to Sam's, and a pained expression filled his eyes. "Steel turned on you."

CHAPTER 21

THE INFORMATION THAT HAD ELUDED her clicked into place. Steel had been in the room the moment before Annie got knocked out. Steel must have hit her. "She hit Reaper and me," Annie said under her breath, and she felt Sam stiffen.

"Are you sure?" he asked.

"No, but no one else was in the study with me," Annie said.

Jeremy nodded from across the limo, his eyes on his laptop. "The cameras confirm it. Nova went into the room, Steel followed, then Steel left. No one else entered until Reaper found Nova."

Sam sighed. "We'll deal with this after we escape."

Every bump on the side road made Annie hiss with pain. Reaper gave her a sympathetic look. He must have felt the same way.

"Hold on tight," Crank said, taking a sharp turn.

Sam wrapped his arms around Annie to soften the turn for her. Annie leaned into his embrace, needing him more than she'd admit out loud. They found a paved road and sped down it.

A few minutes later, they grabbed the Warden, who was walking down the street, working his cane like a man ten years his senior. Annie expected him to rant and rave about their failure. Instead, he sat stoically in the front seat with Crank.

The silence in the limo felt thicker than a dense cake. Annie hadn't known Steel very long and still felt betrayed. Everyone else in the car must have felt fifty times worse. From Jeremy's comment, Annie assumed that Sam would feel her betrayal worst of all, although she didn't want to know why. What if they used to be a real couple? The idea squirmed uncomfortably in her belly.

She had no right to feel any jealousy toward Sam and Steel's relationship, yet she did. It rolled around inside her chest, green and ugly. She leaned away from Sam and stared out the window in an attempt to fight the ugly fang-ridden monster. The last thing Sam needed was her acting snippy at him for having a life. She wasn't Sam's, and he wasn't hers, so she shouldn't feel this way anyway.

Crank drove the limo into the middle of town and parked at a busy mall. "Wait here," he said. "We have to switch cars. Steel might have a tracker on this one."

Annie did not doubt that he'd take a car from some unsuspecting person. She thought Sam would keep them from any actual crime, but everything was such a mess. Sam leaned forward, his elbows on his knees, his face in his hands. He didn't look distraught but seemed more distracted, like he was thinking hard.

Annie moved Sam's hanky off her wound. Red blood scarred the white square of fabric.

"You should keep it on there," Sam said, guiding her hand back to her head. Annie swallowed hard at the tingly feeling that rushed down her arm at his touch.

"Does she need stitches?" Reaper asked, feeling his similar wound. "I think I might."

Annie attempted to feel her wound through the cloth, but stopped when Sam nodded beside her. Jeremy perked up and started typing on his laptop. "There's an urgent care five miles away and another twenty-five miles away." He looked up at them for some instruction.

"Better make it the twenty-five," Sam said.

The side door flung open. Everyone jumped.

"Good grief, Crank," Jeremy said. "Way to give us all heart attacks."

Crank's face appeared in the opening. "Come on, quick."

Annie followed everyone out, her head throbbing again with the movement. Sam wrapped his arm around her and guided her to the red minivan Crank had secured them. Sam's arm didn't feel nearly as bulky as Reaper's and was so much more comforting. She couldn't help but note how nicely she fit by his side.

"It was the only one close by without car seats," Crank said. They climbed in. Jeremy jumped in the front. Reaper and the Warden took the captain chairs in the middle, leaving the back for Sam and Annie. What an odd grouping of people. If anyone watched, they'd feel so confused. Jeremy looked like a messy college student; Reaper looked like a bodyguard no one wanted to mess with; an old man; Sam in his tux suit jacket; Annie dressed in black and bleeding; and Crank, who had shed his formal shirt and jacket for a T-shirt.

"We need a safe house that Steel doesn't know about," the Warden said once they closed the doors.

"Working on it," Jeremy said, his fingers flying on his keyboard.

Crank pulled onto the road. "I'll drop off Reaper and Nova at the urgent care, then the rest of us can go off the grid."

"Drop me off with them too," Sam said, squeezing Annie's hand.

The Warden turned around in his seat. "Reaper can take care of Nova. We need you right now, Kraken."

Sam's jaw tightened. "She is my responsibility."

A little bit of warmth grew in her heart. Sam wanted to stay with her. He did care what happened to her. She didn't necessarily need him in the urgent care. However, she did like that he chose her over the job.

The Warden shook his head. "We don't have a lot of time to cover our tracks. And we need to find a place where Claw can meet and bring us up to speed."

Sam shook his head. "Claw will need a couple hours before she can meet."

"We need you, Kraken. Everything blew up in our face," the Warden growled.

Sam's eyes narrowed. "I'll fix it. You know I will. It's what I do best."

"I found us a safe house," Jeremy cut through what had quickly become an argument. "I'll text you the address, Kraken."

Jeremy to the rescue.

The Warden grumbled and turned to face forward again. The thick silence grew but somehow felt even thicker, like a pound cake gone wrong. About twenty minutes later, Crank pulled up to the curb of the urgent care. "Want me to collect you?" he asked as Reaper climbed out.

Sam shook his head. "I'll take care of it. You have things to do."

Sam helped Annie out of the car, and they shuffled into the doctor's office together. The entryway had two signs. The one to the left led to an orthodontist while the right led to the urgent care.

The three of them stepped into the small reception area that smelled strongly of antiseptic. Sam pointed to a seat near the fish tank, and Annie sunk into it while Crank and Sam walked over to the front desk. Annie didn't want to know what kind of lie they'd create to explain their injuries, so she tried to tune out their voices and watched the TV playing the news. At least there wasn't a breaking headline with their failure playing on there.

"Annie?"

Her head jerked up to see a nurse in bright-pink scrubs. She smiled brightly at Annie and nodded toward the door. Annie took a deep breath and followed the nurse. What she didn't expect was Sam to follow her. After she passed the nurse, he looped his arm through hers. Annie turned to him, wide-eyed, but all he offered her was a tight smile. She could see the stress of what had happened in his eyes. He probably wanted to rant and rave about the whole job becoming a colossal fiasco. Yet he held his cool. How much longer could he hold out before he cracked?

"You don't have to come with me," she whispered in an attempt to release him if that's what he needed.

He fixed her with a gaze full of emotions she couldn't decipher. "Yeah, I do." He squeezed her arm. Annie's heart fluttered in her chest, but she squashed the fluttering. Those feelings were not allowed. She could feel grateful that he wanted to come with her. She could allow warmth in her heart from his actions. What she couldn't do is allow any real feelings toward Sam. She couldn't. Shouldn't. They were from entirely different worlds, and soon he'd send her home, and she'd never see him again.

The nurse weighed her and took her blood pressure before depositing them in a room. Sam's phone beeped. He led her to a chair before he pulled his phone out. "Jeremy texted me the address of the safe house."

Annie nodded. She didn't like the look on his face. "Sam, are you okay?"

He turned toward her, a new emotion on his face—one she didn't recognize and could hardly puzzle out. Whatever it was, the emotion that held firm on the edges swirled and changed with every moment, as if too many were fighting to push through and take over his face. "Physically, yes." His gaze dropped to the ground. "Otherwise, no." Annie pointed to the chair beside her, and he fell into it, dragging his hands down his face.

Before she could respond, the door flew open, and a bright, happy doctor with a laugh in his voice walked in. "I'm Dr. Byrd, and it sounds like someone in here had an accident."

Annie watched Sam quickly gather his swirling emotions and store them away. He somehow forced a mask, clearly proving he had the grifter talent. He smiled pleasantly at the doctor. "She's ready for you." Sam stood and gave him room to look at Annie's head, but Sam's eyes never strayed from her.

The doctor checked her pulse and her eyes first. "No sign of a concussion, thankfully." He examined her laceration with practiced fingers, moving her hair out of the way. "We're going to need a couple of stitches," he said, moving to open a drawer.

Annie took a deep breath; she never had to endure stitches before. Without missing a beat, Sam came over and wrapped his warm hand around hers.

Numbing cream was followed by lidocaine and, thankfully, a small-gauge needle. The doctor cleaned the wound and then gave her six stitches. Annie clenched her teeth and tried not to twitch the whole time.

Dr. Byrd patted her shoulder. "You're going to feel tender." He handed her two pills and a small cup of water. "Take these painkillers now. You're welcome to take some more pain medication in about six hours. Keep the wound clean, okay? The stitches will dissolve on their own but let me know if you spike a fever or have any other problems."

Annie swallowed the pills. The doctor gave her another bright smile, slapped Sam on the back, and left.

"Thanks for coming with me. I'm used to doing things like this on my own." Tears rushed to her eyes, but Annie blinked them back. Now wasn't the time to cry.

"Why is that?" Sam asked, his grifter mask still in place.

Annie sighed, looking out the tinted windows. "My parents died in a car crash when I was six years old. Don't get me wrong; I adored my granny and my pa, but if I ever got hurt or sick enough to go to a doctor, they couldn't always take me. So I went alone." She looked down at her crumpled tissues in her hand. "When Pa died a few years ago, Granny and I got used to caring for ourselves."

Sam didn't say anything. Instead, he laced his fingers with hers and squeezed. That small action alone made her tears slip. She wasn't alone this time. Sam had made sure of it. Annie wiped at the unbidden tears with her fingers. He handed her the tissue box. Annie pulled several out and blotted at her eyes.

"What are we going to do now?" she asked, her face flushed.

"We're going to find a way to fix everything." He stood, his face impassive, and pulled her to her feet.

"Because that's what you do? You're a fixer?" she asked, her eyes searching his for what she knew he'd hidden inside.

He nodded and turned to go, but she held him back.

"You know this isn't your fault, right?" Annie said.

His mask fell. "When you're the one in the middle of holding together a heist and a sting and it falls apart, it is your fault. Annie, I should have seen the signs. I should have stopped her. Steel acted grumpier than usual, but I never thought . . ." He paced away to the sink, his fingers gripping the counter. "The Warden only knows the breakdown and danger of things on this side, but what about Claw's side? A sting falling to pieces could do serious harm to her career." He swung around to face her. "They trust me to hold it all together, and I didn't. We had one shot at this, and we failed."

Annie still didn't think that made this whole fiasco his fault. Steel had made her own choices. He couldn't hold himself accountable for that. Yet the look in his eyes gave off the whole vibe of the captain going down with the ship. Sam might have the code name Kraken, and he might sink ships, but that was only one part of this complex man. He also steered his ships to victory.

"So, how do we fix it?" Annie asked, thinking about the mess they were in. "Is that even possible?"

Sam shrugged. "We'll find a way." He opened the door, reached for her hand, and they walked back into the lobby. Reaper stood when they entered and held the door open for the parking lot. Annie spotted his stitches when she walked past him. A bright-orange car waited for them at the curb. Orange was a far too cheerful color for their moods today. A dark-hued car would have been more fitting.

The three of them climbed in the back, with Annie in the middle. Sam gave the driver an address, and they all rode in silence. Annie felt like Reaper and Sam had a lot to say but had to wait until they were in a secure place to start shouting.

Sam's phone beeped, and he pulled it out. This time he leaned over to show them the text.

It said, *Claw is coming. Hurry up.*

"Is that a good thing or a bad thing?" Annie whispered. Claw was a cop, after all. She could arrest them for the heist/sting gone wrong or for stealing that minivan. She'd sworn to uphold the law. Sam helped her team so they could go by the book while he didn't. It's possible she'd drag them in to cover her behind because things went sour. A shiver of worry raced up Annie's arms.

Reaper shrugged. "That all depends on how things went down after we left."

"And her mood," Sam added.

CHAPTER 22

Annie expected their hired car to drive them to some secluded, dark place in the middle of LA. One of those neighborhoods she was warned to keep at a distance while knocking on doors for her summer sales. No one would find them in one of those places. Instead, the driver dropped them off on a corner of what looked like a regular, friendly neighborhood. The kind where houses all had cute painted shutters, flower beds, and bikes on the lawn.

Looping his arm through hers, Sam led her down the street with Reaper following behind. Sam leaned close and whispered, "Sorry, we have to walk. There's no point in having a safe house if we let others know about it." Annie couldn't argue with his logic.

At the end of the street, they found a cul-de-sac. Behind three large palm trees was an older house, probably built in the seventies. Annie bet it was the first house built in the neighborhood. Set back a little farther from the road than the rest, it had more privacy. It appeared far from dilapidated, but the yard showed some neglect.

Reaper bounded up the steps and knocked on the door. It opened a crack before Crank threw it open for them. The house had light furnishings with a beach theme. A large, framed print on the wall directly across from the front door said, *Our home is your home, so treat it as such. Thanks for staying.*

Annie's lips twitched on their own accord. Jeremy must have rented the house. Sam let go of her and immediately crossed to Jeremy and started whispering. Jeremy sat cross-legged on a seafoam-green couch with his laptop on his lap and a box of fresh pizza on the table in front of him. A thin smile spread across Annie's face. At least some things never changed.

Annie rounded the corner to find two cops dressed in full uniform standing by the dining room doors. She recognized Detective Price, aka Claw, right away. Her partner wasn't quite what she expected. He stood taller than everyone else and seemed entirely made up of lean muscle. However, he had what appeared to be a kind smile behind his tailored mustache.

Claw smiled at her. "This is my partner, Detective Wright."

"Or Fang," Jeremy said from over the top of his laptop.

Detective Wright smirked at the comment. Apparently, he liked his code name.

Annie nodded to the cop, a slight tremor racing up her arms. No one wore handcuffs, at least not yet. Maybe they hadn't come to arrest them. The Warden sat on a chair in the dining room, his head in his hands. Crank stood at the window, his fingers on the curtains in what Annie thought was a pose only Sam took up. Reaper fell into a salmon-colored wingback chair by a white brick fireplace. Unsure of where to go, she fell into a seat beside Jeremy. He felt like her safest choice. *Lord, help us,* she thought.

Sam walked into the dining room, and after a short exchange of words, the Warden returned to the living room with Sam. "We're all here now. We can start," Sam said, standing behind the Warden.

Claw let out a long sigh and tucked her hands into her pant pockets. "I wish I had better news."

The Warden stepped toward Claw, his eyes narrowing. "How bad is it?"

Claw glanced between Sam and the Warden before her head drooped. "I'm sorry. We caught Ink and Sneak when they attempted to escape. I couldn't save them. I'll do what I can to get them out soon, but I can't promise anything."

"Are they okay?" Sam asked.

Claw nodded. "We have them in a holding cell. So far, they're sticking to the story that they were hired for the wedding and freaked when the police showed up. Both claim that their fight-or-flight leaned heavily on the flight aspect. As you know, Steel has a different story, and she's blabbing like a bird on a Saturday morning. Her 'friend' on the force isn't helping our cause." She looked at Sam. "You're right. We have a double agent playing on the other side, but we don't have proof. If we did, maybe we could stop Steel."

Jeremy looked up from his laptop. "Is there a way to complete the job?"

Claw and Fang exchanged glances. Annie could understand why. This wasn't only a job among thieves who thought they were doing good, taking out the competition, and gaining a score. This was a sting for the police that had failed.

"I don't think so," Fang said, fingering his gun in its holster. "I think the window of opportunity has closed. Catching Lichens was a tall order."

Sam stepped past the Warden. "Not necessarily. We might have to wait, but I don't think this is over. We'll find a way."

The Warden shook his head slowly. "It's over, Kraken. Our covers are blown. Our plan was ruined. All we have is a failure, some of our team in jail, and an angry client. A client who will kill us given the chance."

Sam ignored him and stepped closer to the two cops. "I can figure out a way to fix it. Maybe in a few months—"

The Warden strode to Sam and straightened up to his full height. "Stop trying to save something that's already dead. We're going on the run, and neither you nor I can do anything about it. It's over. My whole enterprise is compromised. There is no redo button for a situation like this." He started pacing while he ran his hands through his gray hair. "It's all over. There's no trust among thieves. Not even ones I personally vetted."

The Warden whirled around and pointed his finger right at Sam. "You convinced me that killing two birds with one stone was worth it. Mr. Benicci is not the kind of man we want to cross. And now we've failed. Epically failed."

Everyone erupted into shouts. Reaper said something along the lines of working too hard and too long not to receive any compensation while Sam kept fighting to stay. Crank demanded his cut, and the Warden kept spouting words of failure. All their opinions mingled together in a chaotic mess.

The Warden would hear no more of it. He put his fingers in his mouth and whistled, stopping every voice in the room. "I know what I'm talking about. I've been in this game for thirty years. I can see when something is hopeless. Can't you all understand that? All you can do at this point is create new identities, grab your go bags, start a new life, and pray Mr. Benicci doesn't find you."

This time Crank stepped forward. "I need my money . . . there has to be another—"

The Warden stuck his face inches from Crank's as if challenging him. "I said, *go home.*" His gaze burned into each of them before he strode into the other room as if he'd finally settled everything. Only he hadn't.

Claw stepped to Jeremy, her voice low. Annie noticed Fang's attention was still on the other three arguing men. Annie had the distinct impression that Claw didn't want Fang to know what she wanted to say. "How long will it take for you to set everyone up with what they need to escape?"

Jeremy shrugged, shoving the last bit of pizza into his mouth. "Probably twenty-four hours."

Claw pursed her lips. Her eyes narrowed in thought. "Make it fifteen."

Fang turned to look at them, and Claw grinned at him before nodding toward Annie. It looked like Claw didn't tell Fang everything about this band of grifters and thieves. If she didn't, what did that say about her? Annie shook off the thought. Now wasn't the time to start distrusting the police.

Claw and Fang squatted beside her, their voices lowered. "Annie . . ."

Claw glanced around the room quickly, but no one was paying attention to them. Reaper and Crank were arguing with Jeremy about their aliases. Sam had assumed his usual position at the window.

Fang leaned a little closer. "I'm sorry. With the way things ended up, witness protection is your only choice. These guys will split up and spread out all over the planet."

Claw patted Annie's knee, but it was far from comforting. "They cannot protect you anymore, and I probably shouldn't have allowed them to do so in the first place. We'll collect you in the morning after we make all the arrangements."

Annie didn't know what to say. Should she feel glad? Sad? She had no idea. If she left with Claw, everything would change. Until they figured out a way to nail Lloyd with the attempt on her life, she'd never see Granny or go home. She'd also lose Sam. A thought that made her gut hurt.

He was the first person other than Granny and Pa that she'd felt any real connection to. He had taken her under his wing and showed her that she could do things she never thought she could do before. With a simple look or touch, he made her heart hammer in her chest. Something she swore only existed in fairytales. Going with Claw meant he would disappear and become a phantom to haunt her memories. She glanced over to see him looking as super-spy as ever with the fading light coming in through the window, and her breath caught in her throat.

Claw squeezed her shoulder. "It's going to turn out fine." With a final nod, Claw and Fang made their way to the door. Claw leaned over and whispered something to Sam. His eyes widened, but he nodded to whatever she said. Annie wished with all her might that Claw had spoken louder. Had that surprised look been because of her impending departure? Her heart and head both hoped so.

His gaze found hers after the door closed. Sam reached down and straightened his jacket before he walked over to the couch, where Annie sat next to Jeremy. "It's been a long day. Let's find you a room so you can rest and start healing." He held out his hand as if he were a gentleman attempting to help a lady out of a carriage.

Annie's pulse quickened when she placed her hand in his. He pulled her up and led her to the staircase.

"Claw told me she's coming to take you tomorrow," he said, a sigh in his tone.

So that look of surprise *had* been about her. Upstairs he opened the first door on the right. It was a small bedroom decorated with anchors and seagulls. "I think it's a good idea. You'll be safe. I'll do everything I can to get you home soon. I promise." He looked down at his shoes. "I should have warned you about Lloyd. I should have sent you with Claw from the start and not pushed you to participate in the sting. I hope you can forgive me."

Annie's hand dropped from his as if it had suddenly gained one hundred pounds. He regretted taking her under his wing. He regretted not handing her off to the police from the start. Not trusting her voice from the surprising hurt that rushed through her, tornado style, Annie walked into the room. She blinked several times as if that would keep the tears at bay.

"I'm sorry things ended up like this. I'm sorry you got hurt. Please know that I only wanted to protect you." He huffed as if there was more he wanted to say but forced the words down instead.

Annie could guess that most of those words had to do with how he'd lost his sister, Hazel, which was why he desired to save her.

His hand twitched at his side as if he had to stop himself from reaching out for her. "Goodnight, Annie."

Annie swallowed hard. "Goodnight, Sam."

He quietly closed the door to her room, cutting off the light from the hallway. Blinking back her tears, she turned on the bedside lamp. She refused to cry. What did she expect from Sam anyway? He wouldn't fight for her to stay with the crew. He couldn't argue with Claw about taking her away. She understood who he was when this whole thing started. He wasn't about to risk giving up his entire life ambition for her, especially after only a couple of days. A couple tingles from his touch didn't mean enough, particularly if he didn't feel them in return.

Without any luggage, she didn't have to do anything to prepare for bed. Still dressed in her black clothes, she slid into the cold sheets and stared out at the sky with the tiniest bit of orange hue left in it. This wasn't how things were supposed to end. She knew it, but what could she do? Witness protection and losing Sam were going to happen. The sooner she accepted that, the better. Granny would worry, but if Claw could pass her a message or ensure her safety, Annie could do this. She could accept the police's protection instead of Sam's.

"This is my choice," she said to herself. Feeling more empowered about the situation, she pulled the blankets over her shoulders.

Annie lay in the bed alone in her small room, staring out the window long after things quieted below. It's strange that she felt more vulnerable now than when she'd slept in a hotel room with Sam and Jeremy. She pulled the nautical blanket up under her chin. Forcing her eyes closed, she prayed for sleep, pleading with God to remember who she was and asking Him to care about her. She prayed for a long time until she must have fallen asleep.

The following day Annie woke with a start, her head aching from her laceration. She fought with her blankets until she pulled her legs out. Making her way down the hall, she looked in the bathroom for any pain pills. All the drawers were empty.

She made her way downstairs. Jeremy was asleep on the couch with his arms wrapped around his laptop. No one else was in the room. Annie found the kitchen through a pocket door. The Warden sat at a small round table. Annie froze. She'd never spent any time alone with the man and didn't want to.

He gave her a tired smile. "Good morning."

"Morning. I'm looking for some pain pills," she said, pointing to her head. Awkwardly she started pulling open drawers.

"I don't think there are any in the house."

He set down his mug and pushed up from his chair. "Come on. There's a small gas station down the block. They'll have something we can purchase."

Annie had no idea how to respond. They were in a safe house for a reason. She doubted they were supposed to leave. She trusted Sam and Jeremy with her life but she wasn't sure she could do the same with the Warden. He grumped and yelled, and she had a feeling he partly blamed her for their failure. She backed away a couple steps. "It's okay. I can cope."

The Warden snorted. "Nonsense. Do an old man a favor and help me stretch my legs before I have to face the rest of the day. There's no need for you to suffer through the pain."

At that moment, he looked so much like an old grandpa that Annie couldn't resist accepting his offer. She touched the locket that Sam gave her. It had a tracker in case something happened. "Okay, thanks."

Jeremy stirred when they walked through the living room. Annie wanted to ask him to come with them just in case, but he hardly looked capable of thought, let alone the ability to defend them. "We're running to the gas station down the street. Need anything?"

Jeremy rubbed his eyes before adjusting to a more comfortable position on the couch. "I wouldn't say no to some powdered donuts or cinnamon rolls." He opened one eye, looked at Annie and the Warden standing by the door, and then sat up. "Or if they're on the ball, a hot dog with relish, ketchup, tabasco sauce, and mustard. No, wait. A radish sauce instead of tabasco."

Annie stared in disbelief. Who'd want to eat something like that at seven in the morning? The Warden pointed to the door. "We are not a delivery service. You want something, you have to walk for it like the rest of us."

Jeremy shrugged and pulled on his shoes. Annie snickered and followed the Warden through the open front door. Thank goodness Jeremy wanted to go with them.

Together they walked out into the already warmed air. The toasty morning air was probably the only thing she'd miss about California. The Warden stuck his hands in his checkered pants and said nothing to her. Jeremy hummed lightly to himself. At least with Jeremy, this didn't feel awkward.

She moved ahead a couple paces and whispered to Jeremy, "Any idea where Sam is?"

He bit the side of his cheeks and chanced a glance back at the Warden. "Dealing with stuff."

Annie raised an eyebrow, but Jeremy shook his head, clearly showing he'd not answer any more of her questions. She glanced back at the Warden. Maybe Jeremy couldn't speak in front of him. Sam and the Warden had shared a lot of angry words yesterday. If Sam needed to do something the Warden would disagree with, Jeremy was wise not to say anything about it.

A couple minutes later, Annie caught sight of the small four-pump gas station. The Warden nudged her elbow and held out a fifty-dollar bill. "Don't let Midnight buy out the store. I'll wait outside and breathe the fresh air. It's hard to say goodbye to all this nice weather. I'm going someplace cold." He took a deep breath and settled on a bench outside the door.

Jeremy opened the gas station door for her, and they found shelves filled with junk food but no hot dogs. Groaning, Jeremy grabbed a bag of donuts and started scanning the racks for something more. Annie rounded the shelves, searching for any kind of pain medicine. At that moment, she didn't care what type or what brand.

On the farthest side, next to the refrigerators holding drinks, was a small section with Band-Aids and medicine. After grabbing the first small container of pain meds, she turned, snatched a water bottle, and rushed to the counter to pay. After paying, she handed Jeremy the rest of the bills and moved to a space by the restrooms. Annie popped open the medicine and took out two pills. With the help of the water, she swallowed them down, then pocketed the medicine.

Finished, she glanced at Jeremy, who had picked up a basket and was in the process of filling it up. "I think I'll wait out in the sun," she said. Missing the beautiful weather was one thing she and the Warden agreed on. Jeremy nodded, concentrating on two different kinds of chips. Smiling, she walked outside.

She looked left and right but couldn't see the Warden anywhere. She thought he'd taken a seat on the bench. She stepped away from the doors to see if he was around the edge of the building, but he wasn't. It felt strange to yell, "Warden, Warden, where are you?" Rushing toward the sidewalk, she hoped he might have taken to pacing along the sidewalk while waiting for them. The street and the sidewalk were empty.

A sound behind her made her arm hair rise. Whirling around, she found herself face-to-face with two enormous men. They said something in what sounded like Italian. She turned to run, but one clapped his large hand over her mouth while the other grabbed her, roughly crushing her against his chest.

Annie struggled, kicked, and elbowed but couldn't shake the big man. He held her tight, keeping her feet just off the ground. His partner ripped the locket off her neck and tossed it in the gutter. The man removed his hand briefly, and Annie tried to scream, but a weird smell filled her nose. Before she uttered a single sound, her eyes rolled back into her head, and all she remembered was everything fading to black.

CHAPTER 23

Before she opened her eyes, Annie's head radiated pain. The pounding felt like the climax of a migraine. Easing one eyelid open, she hissed at the bright light that hit her right in the eye. This only made her head hurt worse.

"Ah, she's coming around," a man said in a thick Italian accent.

"Go get the *capo*," another man said. The two exchanged what sounded like harsh Italian before a door opened and closed. Annie kept her eyelids smashed together while the pounding slowly subsided to a dull ache.

The door opened again a few minutes later. Annie clenched her teeth. Why did this keep happening to her? Honestly, it made no sense to her whatsoever. She would have prayed for help, but considering her luck, it seemed the heavens were closed to her.

"*Salve*, Annie," a deep voice said, followed by the sound of a chair scraping against the floor. Annie hated the idea of not seeing what was going on, so she slowly lifted her eyelids. This time the light didn't directly blind her. Someone must have moved it. Blinking several times, she eased her eyes open to find herself not in a cell or a prison but sitting in a state-of-the-art kitchen on a wooden chair.

A few feet away, the Warden sat tied up and gagged. He wiggled and fought against his bonds. Annie looked down to see her hands were tied, but she wasn't nearly as restrained.

The Warden looked at her wide-eyed, his white gag obscuring whatever he fought to say. She couldn't read his eyes or muffled speech. Finally, she let her gaze wander back to the kitchen. An older man in a suit Sam would have appreciated sat in a chair across from her. Two large men in black stood on either side of the older man, guarding him. Annie recognized them. They were the same goons that had chased her and Sam out of the airport.

Another younger guy, closer to Sam's age if she had to guess, with dark hair and a nice suit, leaned against the counter. The older man glanced back to where she looked. "Ah yes, that's my *figlio*, my son, Antonio. Ignore him. We have a business to discuss, *donna*."

He let out a long, exaggerated sigh. "*Fidati di me.* Trust me, Annie, we did not want to resort to this." He brought both of his hands up and pointed to his chest. "I am Signor Benicci. I know you know my name. I know that you know your Samuel made me some big *promesse*." He brought his pointer finger up and wiggled it in front of his face. "I do not accept failure."

"But—" she tried to cut in.

"No speak, *donna*. I have brought you here to make sure I get what I bargained for."

Annie's eyes widened. Was he joking? No one would try for that job again, not even to save her, and even if they did, it was impossible. The Warden had said so himself. Antonio strode forward, yanked her arm up, and clicked a thick black metal bracelet around her wrist. It clicked tightly with no room to slide it off her hand, measuring about an inch wide. It felt cold, bulky, and ominous. Two metal points the size of rock salt dug into the soft skin of her wrist.

"I will make this simple. *Fai quello che diciamo*. Do what we say, and you will not die."

Annie's tongue must have instantly swollen because of how hard her breathing became. Mr. Benicci wasn't done with her, however. He tapped the table with two of his thick fingers.

"This bracelet cannot be taken off except with our one-of-a-kind key. You will tell your *fidanzato* that I expect him to keep his deal." He laughed. "Yes, I know he is not your brother. There is too much *amore* between you. This is why we picked you." His eyes narrowed at the black metal on her wrist. "That band is fitted with an ingenious deadly taser with remote access. So strong it will stop your heart. Your Samuel will deliver what I need within a week or else we will trigger it."

Annie forced herself to swallow so she didn't pass out. Her eyes lingered on the deadly trap on her arm. She did not speak Italian, but even she knew that *amore* meant love. Sam didn't love her. He couldn't do this. Benicci had this all wrong.

The Warden started yelling something indiscernible.

"Your *amico* doesn't think your Samuel can do this. I know he can. I know his reputation. I am counting on his victory, and I must have it done. He must fix this. You see, you and I, *siamo della stessa parte*, we are on the same side, and you will guarantee it. *Capisci*?"

Annie assumed he asked her if she understood. She understood all right.

He leaned closer. "You will deliver this message for me, *capisci*?"

Annie nodded, her eyes on the black death sentence on her wrist. This was the epitome of how something could go from bad to worse. "W-what if he can't? W-what if he tries but—" She couldn't finish.

Mr. Benicci shook his head. "He cannot fail, *donna*. Do you understand? Not if we all want to get out of this alive. Tell me you can help encourage him. We know he cares what happens to you."

Annie felt faint for more than one reason. The Warden continued to yell indiscernibly through his gag. Annie noted that his wrist did not have a death contraption like hers. Apparently, they assumed Sam's *amore* was all they needed to motivate him. "I'll try," she squeaked.

"Ah, see *sono tuo amico.* We are all friends. You pull this off as promised, and everyone wins." He stood up and addressed his men. "Drop them off. Mr. Erickson is expecting them." He turned to her again. "One more tiny detail. That bracelet has GPS, is waterproof, and is hammer resistant. You cannot break it. However, if you and your clever friends try anything to destroy it, zap." A wicked smile spread across his face. "I'll be watching."

Shivers raced up her arms. She wanted to beg, to plead her case. Explain that Sam might not care enough about her to attempt the impossible. She sensed that they wouldn't care. Her life meant nothing to them. Her only hope to survive this was Sam.

Before she could process what was happening, the two burly bodyguards wrenched her up from her chair. Antonio grabbed the Warden. They dragged them to a navy-blue sedan and stuffed them into the back seat. Annie did everything in her power not to hyperventilate in the back of the car. Only yesterday, she'd chosen to accept her fate, and her fate was throwing everything into a tailspin. *Lord,* she prayed, *please help Sam know what to do. Please don't forget me.*

The Warden turned away from her and peered out the window, ignoring her completely. Had she done something wrong? Honestly, what else did he expect her to do in that situation? She had no choice but to agree to Mr. Benicci's terms.

Annie expected they'd take them back to the gas station where they abducted them. Instead, they pulled up behind a wind-chapped building a block or two from the beach. Sam, Reaper, and Crank stood beside a regular black car.

"Take the *vecchio uomo* first," the driver said.

The other man opened the door on the Warden's side and yanked him out. Annie watched as they slowly approached Sam and his crew. She had no idea what was said, but Crank ripped out the Warden's gag a moment later and started on his ropes. The guard walked to her side this time and opened the door.

Mr. Benicci leaned toward her from the front seat. "Don't forget your promise, *donna*. We'll know if you do. You have seven days."

The guard yanked her out of the car. She tripped over her feet but thankfully didn't fall. Reaper and Crank talked with the Warden in whispers, but Sam stood front and center, waiting for her. His face was hard as granite.

"If you hurt her, so help me—"

"We did not harm your *amore*," the guard said, pushing Annie forward.

She stumbled a few steps before Sam caught her. He wrapped his arms around her, holding her tight. Annie melted into him, taking strength from the comfort his arms provided. He'd come to get her.

"At least not this time," the guard added.

Annie pressed her face into Sam's starched shirt. She didn't need to see the man to know that he sneered. She could hear it in his voice. Sam slid Annie out of his arms enough to wrap one arm around her and lead her away. She expected them to climb into the black car, but he led her around the building where his Ferrari waited.

"Are you hurt?" he asked, opening the door of his car.

Annie shook her head and raised her wrist. "No, but . . ."

Sam froze, his eyes on the black bracelet. Recognition shone in his eyes. He knew exactly what it was. He swore under his breath and put a finger to his lips. Slowly he mouthed, "Don't say anything."

Annie nodded her understanding. If Mr. Benicci said he'd be watching, he'd probably listen too, waiting with bated breath to hear what Sam thought of this. Annie slid onto the seat, and Sam bounded to the other side. His jaw tightened. He put the car in gear and gunned it.

Once they were in the flow of traffic on the highway, he withdrew one hand off the steering wheel and laced his fingers through hers. Annie loved the way his hand felt in hers. The warmth of his hand made her skin tingle, taking the edge off some of her worries.

They drove in silence out of necessity, but Annie didn't mind. She was still trying to puzzle out what to do. Sam didn't take his hand away from hers except to turn, and even then, he returned his hand the moment he could.

Sam gave her hand a slight squeeze and let go when they pulled into a new hotel parking lot. He put his fingers to his lips, his eyes glancing down to her wrist, and nodded toward the building. They got out. He pulled a duffel bag out of the back seat, and they quickly made their way to the hotel's side door to get to the elevators.

Inside, Samuel retook her hand, but the gesture wasn't what she thought. He twisted her wrist, looking the bracelet over. On the bottom of her wrist above the two metal taser pinpricks, shown a bright-green light the size of the tip of a pencil. He shook his head. They went up to the fifth floor to room 508. She expected the room to be empty, but Jeremy was there, already spread out on the couch. Several black cases waited on the desk.

Jeremy shot to his feet, his mouth open, but Sam held a finger to his lips. Jeremy nodded and didn't say a word, but his eyes held an apology. He didn't have to apologize. It wasn't his fault she got abducted.

Sam pointed to Annie's wrist, and Jeremy's eyebrows shot up. He rushed forward and grabbed her arm. After twisting and turning her wrist like Sam had in the elevator, he let go of her arm with a grimace.

"I'm going to take a shower and get cleaned up for tonight, then we can talk," Samuel shouted, turning on the water in the bathroom, but he came out instead, darted past them, and peeked out the curtains, per usual.

Jeremy began waving his hands wildly at the TV. Taking the hint, Annie raised her voice as well. "Okay, I'll turn on one of my cooking shows." Jeremy gave her a thumbs-up before turning on the TV himself. He flipped through the channels until he found a cake-decorating show. He turned it up a little higher than she usually would.

"Thank goodness I don't have to listen to that," Samuel said, leaving the window. He raised an eyebrow at her.

"You're funny, Sam," she said. Both men nodded encouragingly at her.

"Hey, I like it," Jeremy said. "It's not too girly," he said, flipping open a black case and grabbing a notebook.

He tossed it to Sam. "Whatever. I'm hitting the showers." Samuel slammed the bathroom door closed and waved them over.

Jeremy and Annie both leaned in. Sam scrawled. *Dark-blue van. Benicci's men are keeping a very close watch.*

Jeremy grabbed the notebook and wrote, *What did they tell you about the bracelet?*

He handed it to Annie. She wrote, *I can't take it off or else. It's fitted with a GPS.*

Wired? Jeremy wrote.

Sam took the pen. *I have no doubt. He's guaranteeing that we finish the job.* Sam's gaze met hers. That was precisely Mr. Benicci's intention.

Annie took the pen, her hands shaking. *It's a taser*, she wrote. *One he claims will stop my heart.*

Jeremy puffed up his cheeks with air, a perfect impression of a puffer fish, and started pacing. Annie walked toward the window. She knew taking pity on her had added stress to their already impossible job. She didn't want to know how much this new curveball would cost them. Annie peeked out the window like Samuel. A dark-blue sedan pulled up behind the van, and a man exited each of the vehicles. They stood off to the side, where she could barely see them, and talked. Were they going to storm the place because she hadn't told Sam the message?

Annie turned and waved at the boys, but they weren't looking at her. She jumped up and down and waved, but they were too focused on what they were writing in the notebook. Annie turned to look outside and saw the men shouting at each other. Annie took off her shoe and threw it at them. She hit Samuel right in the back. He whirled around, his hand on his gun. She pointed at the window, and they both raced over.

Ripping the notebook out of Jeremy's hand, she wrote, *More men joined the van. I think they are waiting for me to give you Mr. Benicci's message. Do I say it out loud?*

They exchanged looks again before nodding. Another set of guys got out of the van. *Remember, I'm in the shower,* Sam wrote.

Annie nodded. She knew what she needed to say. She cleared her throat and spoke clearly. "Jeremy, I need your help."

They watched as the men pressed their fingers to their ears.

"With what, Annie?" Jeremy asked, walking back across the room to grab his laptop.

She let out a long low breath. "Mr. Benicci—"

Jeremy rushed back, typing one-handed. "Annie, we don't need to talk about this right now."

"No, we do." She looked right at Sam. His eyes were soft, and a corner of his mouth lifted in a half smile. "Mr. Benicci demands Sam finishes the job. He needs his information out of Lichens's vault, and this"—she lifted her wrist—"is his way of making sure Sam's successful."

"Do you mean to say you're strapped? Annie, that's serious."

"How do I tell him?"

A wave of emotion hit her hard, and she turned away from them both. This wasn't a part to play or something happening to someone else or a con. This was real. A deadly taser was on her wrist. She wrapped her arms around herself to try to keep the emotion inside. The last thing she expected was two sets of arms wrapping around her. Sam and then Jeremy pulled her into a three-way hug.

"I'll help you think of something," Jeremy said. "There's no way I'm letting a friend die. If Benicci wants this, I'll talk to Sam."

At that, Annie broke down. The fear and emotions that had built all day erupted. She'd felt close to death ever since Dillan was shot in her living room, but now she felt like that gap had closed even more. She was seconds away from death if Mr. Benicci deemed it. Only this time, she couldn't escape. Yet she had friends—real friends who cared what happened to her. That was something she'd never had before. Jeremy gave her a final squeeze and let go, but Sam didn't. He stayed right there and let her cry into his shoulder.

"What do I do?" she asked through her tears.

Jeremy looked up from his computer. "You take a break and learn how to properly roll fondant. Leave the rest to us. We'll meet Mr. Benicci's demands and get that abominable thing off your wrist."

Sam pulled her away from the window. She climbed onto her bed. "Don't worry. We can fix this," Sam whispered in her ear, his lips lightly brushing her skin. He and Jeremy sat back down, notebook in hand. Annie balled the blankets on her chest and tried to focus on the TV show. But if asked to repeat anything she saw, she wouldn't have been able to.

CHAPTER 24

The next morning, Annie woke to the TV playing in the background. Sam looked asleep in his bed, but Jeremy was missing. By the bit of sunlight coming through the curtains, she assumed he had gone down to find breakfast.

Crawling out of her bed, she found her way into the bathroom. She looked like a complete wreck. There was still some dried blood in her hair, which had turned into what looked like a sagebrush. Groaning, she turned to close the bathroom door.

The hotel room door opened. Annie jumped, expecting a gunman. Instead, Jeremy walked in laden with food. He gave her a nod and a smile before setting out his smorgasbord all over the desk. Annie fought down a laugh before she shut and locked the door. She turned on the shower and spent the next twenty minutes gently washing her hair and letting as many of her worries fall down the drain as she could.

Feeling better, she wrapped herself in a towel and frowned at the black clothes she'd worn now for two days and nights. They were dirty and stained with blood in several spots, although it was hard to tell because of the color.

A soft knock sounded on the door. Annie looked at herself in the mirror. She wasn't exactly decent, but at least the towel was on the larger size. "Annie, it's me. I have some new clothes for you." Sam's voice came through the door. "Jeremy recovered our suitcases."

Thank goodness! She eased the door open a small crack. "How?"

Sam smiled at her and pushed her white suitcase to the door. "He has his ways." His gaze darted to her taser accessory. Right, Benicci's men were probably listening in.

"Thank you."

He nodded once before he walked away, leaving her in privacy to pull the door open enough to wheel the suitcase inside. She'd never felt so grateful for clothes. A few minutes later, feeling like a new human, she emerged with her hair combed, a tiny bit of makeup on, white capris, and a flowy light-green top.

Sam's eyes widened, and Annie felt her cheeks warm in response. He looked pretty good himself, more casual but still debonair. His light-blue button-down shirt's sleeves were rolled up to his elbows, adding to his easygoing look. Jeremy raised the notebook he and Sam had kept using, even while she was in the bathroom. How good was the listening device in this thing, anyway?

The TV was also on for interference. She dropped onto the end of her bed, and Jeremy handed her a plate piled high with scrambled eggs. She nodded her thanks and dug in. Jeremy and Sam kept their quiet conversation going on paper. Annie focused on the cooking show. She found it easier to follow today.

Into her second episode, Jeremy packed up his things. "I'm heading out for a bit." He stuffed a few snacks in his pockets. "You two should get out too," he added with a wiggle of his eyebrows.

Sam rolled his eyes and swatted at Jeremy. Annie loved watching these two friends—her friends. In many ways, they acted like brothers. Jeremy dodged Sam's attempts and saluted before he shut the door. Sam looked around the room, his gaze settling on her. "You know, he has a point. It's been a rough couple of days. Fancy a walk on the beach?"

Annie didn't need a second to consider that question. "Absolutely."

Annie rushed to put on her sandals, and a few minutes later, they were in the Ferrari on the way to the coast. Unfortunately, their hotel was about an hour from the sand, and the car wasn't noisy enough to talk without eavesdroppers. Halfway through their drive, Sam reached for her hand. Annie laced her fingers with his, and warmth shot up her arm right to her heart.

Sam took his time parking. He zigzagged through the beach town. Annie only thought it odd until she remembered they probably had a tail. Finally, he parked between a twelve-passenger van and a dumpster. With a last squeeze, he let go of her fingers, and they both jumped out. A strong beach wind blew her hair, but she didn't care; the wind felt like freedom, and she needed a taste of that. He met her at the front of the car and took her hand in his. He mouthed, *Let's run*.

She nodded, and together they darted through the hot sand toward the waves. They didn't stop until their feet sank into the wet sand, and the crash of the waves drowned out all other noise. "I think it's safe to talk now." He wrapped an arm around her waist, pulling her close.

Annie giggled at the waves washing over their feet and the wind tossing her hair wildly. She so needed this. A moment where the world felt normal. Where no bad guys were chasing her. No crime bosses who threatened to stop her heart if they didn't deliver. Just her, the waves, the sea breeze, the sand, and Sam.

Sam looked less relaxed.

"Are you okay?" she asked, glancing up at him.

He shrugged. "I'm fine. It's hard to recover when someone you trusted for so long betrayed you. Steel and I worked plenty of jobs together. I thought I could trust her. Then she does this. It makes me wonder if I can trust anyone at all."

Annie bit her bottom lip and felt that familiar worry wiggle its way to the surface. "Did you and her have a relationship?"

Sam shook his head and directed their steps toward the pier. "No. I don't date people I work with, especially if they're criminals. At least not for real. I've fake dated if the sting requires it." He fiddled with his fingers, rolling the sand between his thumb and forefinger of his left hand. "Honestly, I haven't had a real relationship since my sister died."

Annie looked down at their clasped hands. She wasn't a criminal, and she wasn't exactly working with them. Did she dare hope that all this hand-holding wasn't only for show? Could he care for her for real, even the tiniest bit?

She swallowed hard. "No time for yourself with all your vigilante work?" she asked in an attempt to lighten the mood.

He snickered. "It's like you know me."

"I know you have several smiles, and all of them are fake, except one."

His eyebrow shot up. "You noticed that?"

She nodded. "I know you put your whole heart into your work and do none of it for money. It's all for her, for Hazel's sake." They slowed their steps as they approached the pier. Annie hoped he didn't mind her describing how she saw him, but she wanted him to know. "I can see how much you care for your friends, the stings, and how much you don't want to disappoint anyone. You're respectful, and I know you'd never physically hurt me. I know that for a fact. You're not violent unless you have to be. You're a respectable person, Sam."

They stopped underneath the pier. The waves were a bit softer, with the supports breaking the whitecaps. He took her other hand in his and held both of their hands up between them. "You're only describing the good things. When we met, I told you I did bad things too. I've had to break the law a few times. I've even killed people when forced. I work with thieves, forgers, and grifters. To do what I must, I have to walk a gray line."

Annie tipped her head up to make sure she looked him directly in the eye. She needed him to hear her. Their faces were mere inches apart, which made her heartbeat race, but she held his gaze. "I know you'd never kill anyone because you wanted to. I know you'd never do unnecessary harm. I know you work within the law as much as you are able. I see the good in you, and those are the things I care about, because that's who you are inside. You're a good person, Sam. A person who deserves happiness. Who deserves to know that you are worth it."

On impulse, Annie pushed up on her tiptoes and pressed her lips to his. She meant to keep it a short, soft kiss, one to prove her point, but his hands immediately came up and cupped her face. Pulling her closer, his lips fully captured hers. He returned her kiss with earnestness, almost like he'd needed to kiss her too. Annie's heart pounded out of sync with the rhythm of the waves, and she let her hands slide around his back. Dillan had kissed her a couple times, and it had felt like kissing cardboard compared to this absolute bliss.

Sam eased back from her, their breath heaving in unison. "Wow," was all she could say. Not a romantic statement in any way.

He stared at her, his eyes searching her face before he jerked away as if stung. He stepped back from her. His head shook back and forth while the wind played with his hair. "I'm sorry, Annie. I shouldn't have done that."

"What?" She reached for him, but he took another step back. "Sam?"

"No, don't tell me it's okay. You're vulnerable. I'm vulnerable." He started pacing in the sand. "I feel like my whole life, and all my plans, have fallen completely apart. Then here you are telling me how good a person I am . . . I cannot kiss you like that again, okay? I'm sorry. I stepped over the line."

"I'm not mad. Besides, I started it," Annie said, trying to gather words to explain what she felt.

He dragged his hands through his gelled hair. "I still shouldn't have kissed you back. You ought to have slapped me across the jaw."

"Why?"

"I'm a fixer, a grifter, Annie, a liar and a thief. Sure, I might take down evil men, but that is who I am. I walked away from a normal life when I chose this path. I associate with dangerous people. My life is hazardous. I am the last thing you need in your life." He looked down at the bracelet on her arm. "Exhibit A."

"Shouldn't I have a say?" Annie snapped.

"In normal circumstances, yes, but this time, no." He reached toward her like he wanted to caress her face but checked his hand before he touched her.

"I swore I would get you home safely—that I would protect you. And that includes protecting you from me and the life I live. I should have never gotten you involved."

"Sam?"

"No, Annie. I'm right about this." He turned and started across the sand, striding away from her with his phone already to his ear. Annie rushed after him and could discern only enough through the wind to tell that he was calling a car. By the time they reached the road, a little red car pulled up with an "I'm your ride" sticker on the back window. Sam walked right up to it, and the driver rolled down the window.

"Take her to 456 Elm, the Carraway bed-and-breakfast." He straightened and motioned her toward the door.

Annie let her eyes bore into him. "You're not coming with me?"

His jaw tightened, and he looked down at his feet. "I have things I need to fix—dangerous things." His gaze shifted for a second to her wrist before he looked away. "Please get in the car."

"Without you?"

"Yes." His hand twitched, making her think he wanted to reach for her again. Instead, he shoved his hand into his pocket. "Annie, please, I need you to go. I can't do what I need to do if you're not safe." An emotion entered his eyes that she did not understand. Yet she sensed he wouldn't explain it, and she had more important things to worry about right now anyway.

"Sam, don't. Please don't send me away. Not after all we've been through," she begged. He couldn't kiss her like that and then abandon her. "I'm sorry I kissed you. Blame me, not yourself."

He shook his head and directed her to the car. "If Mr. Benicci expects results, I will meet with him and make a deal. That green light on your bracelet will turn off, and I swear to you that you won't have to worry about people chasing you or threatening your life. I will fix it. Watch for that light to disappear, and then you'll know you're safe."

She looked down at the black bracelet on her wrist and the green light glowing like an iridescent alarm clock. "You can't, not without backup."

He reached around her and opened the back door of the car. Jeremy smiled at her from the back seat, a hand full of pretzels. "Hey, Annie."

Sam put a gentle but firm hand on her shoulder and directed her into the car. She stumbled onto the seat, but she turned to Sam. He had already stepped back. "Sam."

He shook his head, closed the door, and banged the top of the car with his hand. The driver pulled away from the curb. Annie turned to look out the back window to find Sam walking away from her.

"Should I ask?" Jeremy said.

Annie blinked back tears and turned away. "I . . . I . . . kissed him."

Jeremy choked on his pretzels. "You what? Annie, nobody kisses Sam."

Annie wrapped her arms around herself in an attempt to keep herself together. "I find that hard to believe."

Jeremy shook his head. "I know he cares about you, but you have to understand he doesn't let anyone get *that* close to him. Sure, he's kissed someone for the job. Steel a couple times when the con required it, and even Sneak had her chance, but it wasn't ever real."

"He kissed me back," she said quietly, her face in her hands.

Jeremy didn't respond, and after a minute, Annie peeked up at him. He stared off into the distance, his hand scratching his chin. Was it so hard to believe Sam could like her, that she could pick him? Had she read everything wrong? She shivered suddenly, feeling small and embarrassed. Who was she kidding? These guys were all con men, grifters, and thieves. The last thing Sam wanted was her.

CHAPTER 25

Annie stood on the threshold of the small bed-and-breakfast with an amazing view of the beach. It looked like a quaint cottage with a green roof. The sea breeze blew gently across her face. All in all, it looked like the kind of place someone would go to relax and escape the hardships of the world.

But there was no way she could relax. Not only had Sam shared a world-altering kiss with her, but he'd also sent her away with the feeling that he was about to take on the world alone.

Behind her, their ride drove away after Jeremy handed him a wad of cash.

"Wait here," Jeremy said, walking into the building. Annie crossed her arms and watched him approach the front desk. The sound of waves crashing against the beach drowned out all other noise. Even the traffic on the road behind her sounded dim.

With nothing else to do, her eyes focused on the green light of her unique jewelry. Could Sam do it alone? Not from the impression Mr. Benicci left with her. If he took on this challenge without help, it would likely cost him his life. A minute later, Jeremy waved to her. Without a bag or any of her things, Annie threw up her hands and walked directly to the front desk.

"Your turn." Jeremy pulled out his phone and walked into the hall. The woman behind the desk smiled at her. Annie glanced between Jeremy and the woman. Great.

"Hi. I'm Annie—" She hesitated. If Sam made a reservation, what name had he used—Grey, Erickson, Kendrick, or something new?

The front-desk agent's smile grew. "Yes, your assistant called and took care of everything, and he also checked you in. Here is a pamphlet about the facility and the restaurants nearby."

Annie did everything she could not to let the surprise register on her face. Assistant? Sam had told the woman he was Annie's assistant. What kind of story was she expected to play now? The woman at the desk busied herself with paperwork and making keys.

"Here you go, Ms. Erickson. Room 24, straight down that hall."

Erickson. Good to know. "Thanks."

Annie turned to see that Jeremy had disappeared. Were her friends a package deal? If she lost Sam, did she have to lose Jeremy too? They'd abandoned her here . . . hadn't they? She'd assumed Jeremy had checked in, but he could have left. Feeling more than a little awkward and so alone for the first time in over a week, she walked down the carpeted hall. With trembling fingers, she placed the key on the reader and waited for the light to flash green. She'd done this for a while now, and it was the first time it felt weird.

Annie opened the door to find a beautiful room that was modern in style with plush furnishings. There was a tiny, black metal table, a fluffy king-size bed, a balcony, and a floral chair ideally situated to look out the large windows. The bathroom had a jetted tub and a shower with a smoothed pebble-style floor. The grays, browns, sage greens, and whites made the whole place feel cozy. With a deep breath, she stepped inside, locked the door, and promptly latched the chain to give herself what little security she could.

Annie fell on the bed and massaged her temples. Her mind jumped back to Sam's arms around her. At that moment, everything had felt so perfect, and then in the next moment, everything shattered. He'd pushed her away as if she had some kind of contagious disease. She'd drive herself mad reliving that moment over and over again. Rolling onto her stomach, she reached for the remote.

Seconds from turning on the TV for a cooking show, a knock sounded on her door. Annie blinked at the door. No one knocked again or tried the handle, but that didn't stop every nerve in her body from standing at attention. No one knew she was here. She looked down at the "present" on her wrist from Mr. Benicci and let out a long breath. He probably knew where she was.

So much for safe, Sam!

She tried to ignore that she'd heard the knock but couldn't get it out of her head. If Jeremy had returned, he would have done the secret knock. Slowly, she scooted along the wall toward the door. Surely if some villainous shooter stood on the other side, they'd expect her to stand dead center. She was done taking chances. Annie bent at an awkward angle and looked through the eyehole. No one stood out there.

"Hello?" she called.

No response. Gosh darn it. Why would someone knock and then hide? Only someone with nefarious ideas would do that. Sam had warned her about making it on two hit lists, and now that's exactly where she found herself, on Mr. Benicci's and Lloyd's. She looked around for any kind of weapon. All she could see were a handful of wire hangers with wooden bottoms. Holding a fist full of them above her head, she looked out the eyehole again.

"I'm warning you; I'm . . . armed."

Infuriated by the silence that met her ears, Annie unlocked the door and eased it open a crack, ready to slam it shut. Still no one. Had someone knocked on a neighbor's door instead? Had she imagined the knock? Her eyes fell to the floor, and she caught sight of her familiar white suitcase. An envelope waited on top. With a glance down the hallway, she also found it empty. She eased her door open enough to pull the suitcase inside, then wheeled the bag into the room.

After securing the door again, she ripped open the envelope.

Annie,

It's still unsafe to talk with Benicci listening in, but look—you get your own room. This is where Sam and I were planning to take you so that Claw didn't put you in witness protection. We hope you like it. Sam wanted me to tell you that he'll take care of things. I'll also monitor the situation; I'm nearby if you need me. If Sam's attitude today persists, you won't have to stay here long.

We decided not to tell Claw about your new jewelry from Benicci. Besides, she's livid that she couldn't pick you up and put you in witness protection as planned. Please don't contact her. Last I heard, she's not her precinct's favorite person, and the chief has her on a short leash.

Fang did bring Lloyd in for questioning this morning and issued a search warrant for a gun. If they find one and ballistics can match it to Dillan's killer, he'll go down for one count of murder and another for attempted murder. I told Fang he should throw in a breaking-and-entering and trespassing charge. We're also hunting for cameras that will show his face. This is almost over, so relax.

We'll be in touch. Sam made me take your phone out of your suitcase. Sorry about that. He wouldn't explain why.

Jeremy

Annie knew why he'd taken her phone. Without it, she couldn't call him. Annie stared at the note, mixed feelings rushing through her like a hot water geyser. Anger, resentment, joy, fear, and sadness all combined into an odd mix swirling around inside. She hated them for pushing her away, and yet she knew they were doing it to protect her. At least Jeremy was "nearby".

Tossing the note aside, she returned to her bed and drowned out the odd swirl of feelings with her favorite cooking shows. But the feelings didn't fade away as she had hoped. They swirled with a vengeance.

The need for some normalcy pumped through her veins, and she threw open her suitcase and started digging through it. She hoped to find her pink shorts and the oversize T-shirt—the only clothing that was actually her own—but they weren't there. Farica must have destroyed them. Instead, she pulled on some soft pink PJs, hoping they'd provide some comfort. She paced the small room, her eyes darting between the TV and the sun that moved far too slowly toward the horizon.

Frustration built in her like a pot about to boil over, and she slid the door open to the small porch connected to her room and leaned against the railing. The hot metal seared her skin, but she didn't care. She held it. "Lord," she said into the wind. "Can you even hear me?" Annie looked up at the wispy clouds, but the only reply was the crash of the waves. She sank to the floor.

"Don't let Dillan be right. I need a God who cares about me, no matter where I am or what I do." A tear slipped out and rolled down her cheek. She didn't expect a vision or a miracle like Moses, but could it hurt to have a feeling in her gut that things would work out? She only wanted something that said her God still cared about her. "You do answer prayers, don't you?"

Granny believed He did. If God couldn't answer her, maybe Granny could or at least give her a way to stop the tumult of emotions churning in her chest.

With a groan, she picked up the phone in the room and followed the instructions taped to the desk to make a call out. She dialed the one number she had memorized but stopped before she hit the last digit. Her gaze fell on the black bracelet. Benicci could listen in. She needed to talk to someone or go mad, but she wasn't willing to include the man in her private conversation. With limited options, she turned the volume up on the TV, shoved her arm into a pillowcase, and arranged the pillow to the front of her arm. She placed a pillow on her chest and squished her arm against it, hoping to muffle her voice.

With a deep breath, she started over and dialed her home number.

"Hello?"

"Granny?"

"Honeybee, I thought I would have heard from you before now."

"I know. Things have been . . ." What could she say that wouldn't worry Granny but was still the truth? ". . . busy." Annie walked onto her small balcony and let the sea breeze comb through her hair. "And complicated."

"Let me guess; you didn't call me to simply say hello." There was no question in her tone. Granny knew her well.

Annie dragged her hand through her hair, adding to the beach-wind tousle. "I hardly know how to explain it."

"Start slow."

Annie doubted that would help, but if she wanted to figure this whole thing out, she needed help. "I met some . . . friends. They're terrific friends. I was helping them with something, and . . . we botched the whole thing badly. I mean, we really failed. I owe them a lot, and I want to make it better, but I don't know how." Annie placed her shaky hands on the railing. "I've prayed. I tried my best. I've racked my brain. I . . . I just feel like God's abandoned me."

"Annie," Granny cut her off, "I can hear that you're upset. My question is, are you ready to listen?"

It was a statement she'd heard a lot during her life. Granny always said it when she wanted to stop Annie's moaning monologues and give her the help Annie needed. Annie smiled at the familiar words. She was ready to listen. She wanted answers. She was prepared to end the swirling emotions.

Annie walked inside and shut the door, cutting off the sound of the waves and wind. "I'm ready."

"Honeybee, first things first. God never abandons us. It's us who doubt Him. Secondly, sometimes you need to do the opposite of what you've been doing. For example, if all you've done is pray, then get up and start fighting for what you need. There are times when God desires you to start acting before He can bless you. He's always there, but He can't change your own choices or actions. Faith and works go together. We've got to do our part. And sometimes, we are the answer to our own prayers and can only see it later on. Does that make sense, honeybee? You can't leave it all up to Him. He'll help and guide you, but it's your own feet sometimes that get the job done."

Annie fell back into the floral chair in the corner of the room. It did make sense. It made a lot of sense. "He's there, always. Do the opposite," she said, repeating Granny's words. Words that felt so much better than Dillan's ever had.

"Yep. Sometimes doing the opposite is just the thing. Remember when I thought I could grow corn in this climate, and I did what I'd always done? I chose a spot of ground and tossed in the seeds. Did my corn grow? Yes, but only about a foot tall. I tried that same spot over and over again, never paying attention to the shade tree that made it so the corn never got enough sun. Remember the year I moved it to the other side of the garden?"

Annie smirked. "It only grew four feet tall, if that." East Idaho weather wasn't always the best for corn.

"I know those stalks were not award-winning, but we grew some tiny corn that year. The opposite side of the garden was my answer. So, what have you not tried? I bet if you think about it a little more, you'll solve the mystery. God's on your side."

Annie nodded, even though Granny couldn't see her. Tears pricked at the corners of her eyes. The swirling emotions halted and gathered in her chest, creating a heavy weight. "Did you ever wish you hadn't made . . . a certain choice in your life?"

"Sure have, but I also wouldn't be me if I took all those times out of my life. Just because something didn't turn out the way you wanted doesn't mean your path is bad or that the Lord has abandoned you. It's the times that don't go well that grow your character."

One short bark of laughter escaped Annie's mouth. She certainly had learned a lot about who she was and what she could handle. If someone had asked her if she would jump out of a second-story window, she would have said no. Yet, she had done that. If someone asked her if she could live through getting kidnapped, she would have said no, but she had. She wouldn't have wished this whole mess on her worst enemy, but then she never would have met Sam or Jeremy, people she cared a lot about and who she knew cared about her.

She'd hung out with Dillan and his friends all through school because he was the only person who'd give her the time of day, but what if she'd tried to make other friends? What if she tried to fight for a life she thought an orphaned girl, who had to shop at secondhand stores, could never have? One full of love and adventure. What if she pushed herself to try things that scared her? What if she'd leaped forward instead of fell backward?

Do the opposite.

"Granny, I think you're right." An idea slowly formed in her mind. It was time she tried to help instead of feeling tugged along for the ride. If she thought about it, maybe she could devise a plan to save them all. She looked down at the deadly bracelet. Sam would do anything to get it off her, but what was she willing to do to free herself? "I think you helped answer my prayer."

And at that moment, Annie knew God hadn't abandoned her. It was she who'd questioned Him instead. She could have died multiple times in the last week, yet she hadn't. She'd been thrown into an impossible situation but wasn't going through it alone.

Granny laughed. "What are grannies for?"

Annie smiled, her heart warming up at the long list of what her granny was good for. She might have lost her parents, but at least God provided her with grandparents. "For so many things. You've helped me my whole life. I'm sorry I didn't listen to you. I'm sorry we fought about me coming out here."

"Oh, sweetie, it's okay. Finish what needs finishing so you can come home."

Annie bit her lip, her eyes on the note from Jeremy on the bed. With a deep breath, she nodded. "I'll get right on that."

"Now that's what I wanted to hear. However, I hoped to hear it with more enthusiasm."

"I'll work on that too."

Granny snickered. "Love you."

Annie gripped her phone tighter. "Love you too."

Annie hung up, removed the pillows, and sat staring at the big, flatscreen TV while thinking over her granny's words. It was time to do the opposite. Trust in the Lord, not question Him, and do her part. She wanted things to turn out differently, so it was time she helped the outcome.

"Lord," she prayed, shoving away the doubt, "I need to find a way to help. If you help me, I'll try to trust you."

Slowly, she rose from her chair, logged onto the hotel's streaming service, and looked up the action movies. If she wanted to attempt to create a plan, she needed to do some research. She had little patience for the real thing, but action movies, she could handle. They were bound to spark an idea.

She read the titles of several movies she'd watched in the past, remembering how the characters had made it through the danger to the happily ever after. With a complimentary notepad and pen in hand, she turned on a few movies and fast-forwarded to the ending. Yes, most of the things in those movies were impossible, but so was her task. Maybe this time, she needed something that sounded impossible to fix this whole thing.

Annie stared at her list and circled a few ideas that seemed like they'd work. Then one of the last ideas on her list sparked a whole stream of ideas that could work together. She flipped over her notepad page and began to write. Once finished, she held up the page, feeling both unsure and excited. She had no idea if this was a good plan or not. Jeremy was nearby. She bet he could tell her if this was the kind of plan that would stop Sam from doing something stupid alone. She ripped out her list of ideas and slipped on her sandals.

With a deep breath, Annie opened her door and trudged to the lobby. The evening sun cast colors in the sky and on the water, proving how long she'd spent gathering her ideas, but she didn't know what to do next. For that, she needed a friend.

Annie pushed open the heavy glass door and approached the desk. "Hi, my friend who checked in just before me forgot to tell me his room number. Can you tell me?"

The woman eyed her sternly even though she'd seen her a few hours before. "What's his name?" she said, turning to her computer.

Annie prayed he went by Jeremy. "Jeremy."

It took a moment, but the woman looked up. "He's directly across the hall from you." The woman looked at Annie like she was a time waster, and maybe she was right. Jeremy said nearby, not across the hall. But Annie knew the last thing they'd do is leave her without protection.

"Thanks." Annie rushed down the hall, skidded to a halt at her door, then turned to the one directly across the hall and knocked the secret knock.

CHAPTER 26

A moment later, Jeremy poked his head around the edge of the door. "Annie? What's wrong?" he asked, his gaze darting up and down the hallway.

Annie chose to ignore his question. "Jeremy, order us a pizza. We have work to do." She tried to push the door open, but he held it firmly in place.

"Annie, we're laying low, not working," he whispered.

Annie narrowed her eyes. When had Jeremy ever been less than welcoming? She expected him to not only like the idea of ordering a pizza but invite her in with a flourish and an offer of some obscure snack food. Then it hit her.

"Sam is in there, isn't he?" She folded her arms and offered him her best impression of Granny's glare.

"Sam's busy," Jeremy said just as quietly. He gave her a weak smile as if apologizing for his behavior.

A flare of warmth lit in her chest. Sam hadn't abandoned her after all. Neither had Jeremy or God. Annie straightened up to her full height. This might feel a little awkward, but she'd deal with that better than feeling useless. "You guys didn't go far, it seems."

A corner of Jeremy's mouth lifted. "Of course not."

Annie should have known. Sam freaked out about their moment on the beach, but that didn't mean he'd stop watching out for her. "Open the door."

Jeremy shook his head. "I don't think that's—"

Annie raised her voice. "Sam, tell Jeremy to move. I caught you both here, and there is no reason to pretend otherwise."

Jeremy smirked and opened the door. Annie pushed through it and found a room that looked like hers, except it had a regular bathroom and two queen beds. Sam sat on the edge of the bed closest to the window. He kept his eyes averted from her, and he wore a neutral expression that edged on stony. Reaper sat in a chair by the window with a tablet in hand.

Jeremy closed the door, picked up the remote, and turned on the TV. Interference was necessary with her bracelet in the room. This planning meeting wouldn't go as smoothly as she had hoped.

Jeremy moved past her and set down a bag of mixed candy on the second bed, which was full of folders, papers, and his computer equipment.

"I'm here because I want to help create a new plan." Annie shuffled her feet, suddenly nervous. She hadn't expected Sam or Reaper to be there when she came over. Tentatively, she raised her paper. "I have an idea."

Sam's eyebrows rose as Annie walked to the front of the room to stand closer to them. She stood tall, even though her insides trembled.

"We're willing to listen," Jeremy insisted, unwrapping a chocolate bar.

Reaper put his tablet on his lap and folded his arms, his expression doubtful. Sam kept his eyes on his hands.

Annie bit her lip and prayed they would listen. "We know we failed on this job, and we all have reasons to try again. And when I say 'all', I mean the whole team."

"True," Jeremy said. "But we've been considering options all day, and nothing looks good."

Annie nodded. It was time to work together, not try to solve things alone. "For this second attempt, I suggest that we use what we have already in place, but we do what Steel and Lichens won't expect. If Steel knows it takes you four to six months to pull off a heist of this magnitude, then she'll never anticipate us to do it in a day."

"That's because it can't be done in a day," Sam said calmly, looking at her for the first time. "Jeremy's right; things don't look good. I spent the day at Lichens's trying to smooth things over, but they tightened security and released me from my obligations. Benicci won't take my calls. I can't prove to him I know how to finish our deal. We're being shut out."

Annie tried not to let his expression stop her. This was her moment—she could feel it.

She began again. "We all have our reasons to try. Maybe it's revenge." Annie glanced at Reaper, who looked away from her gaze. "For the Warden, it might be to keep a perfect resume." Annie clasped her hands together. "Perhaps you hated how things ended and want a second chance." She let her gaze land on Jeremy. "As for myself"—she held up her hand with her special bracelet—"I'd prefer not to get tased to death."

Reaper gasped. "What?" He turned accusing eyes on Sam and Jeremy. "You didn't tell us about that."

Sam winced, because they both knew he left her with that thing on while he tried to figure things out. Jeremy tossed more candy in his mouth.

"We didn't want—" Sam began.

"To what? Bother the team with your problems?" Reaper stood and stormed over to Annie to examine the bracelet. He shook his head and swore under his breath. "You should have told us about this. Nova is part of our team, and none of us want her death on our hands." He folded his arms across his chest and leaned against the dresser under the TV.

Sam cleared his throat and then stood up. "I made a judgment call to let you and the rest of the team escape the consequences of our failure."

"I didn't go anywhere," Reaper said darkly.

Sam straightened. "I know you want to salvage this job just as much as we do." He gestured to Jeremy and Annie. "But as we explained, it can't be done. Claw can't help us. We can't even help ourselves. All that's left is to make some kind of deal with Mr. Benicci to save Annie."

"No, you're wrong," Annie said.

Sam turned to her. "Annie, things like this are complex. We can't wing a heist. Especially not with your life on the line."

"But you could go in alone and risk your neck?" she snapped. She knew that's exactly what he'd planned on doing.

His jaw clenched, confirming her thoughts.

Reaper turned to him. "You were going to risk going in alone? Without protection? What, do you have a death wish? If you died, how would that help us gain our score?" Reaper asked. "I trusted you when I signed up for this job. I've heard tales of your jobs and I thought I'd finally landed a gig that would change my life."

Sam stuck his hands in his pockets. "I'd ensure you got paid, but we can't pull it off. I've tried to think of a new way in for twenty-four hours, and there isn't a clean option. Steel burned us." Sam started pacing the small room. "We only know part of what she could have told Lichens's guards. It can't be done. Not in a way that won't land the lot of us in jail or killed. I can't accept those options."

Annie needed to end the argument right now. "We *can* do it. I have an idea that will work."

Jeremy dropped his candy bar, and Reaper straightened, but Sam shook his head as if he didn't believe her. Jeremy gestured for her to continue. Annie had no idea if they thought her wholly crazy or if they were considering listening to her. Best to keep talking while she could.

"Lichens and his men think they're covered because Steel is their inside woman."

Sam turned to look at her, his arms still folded.

Annie's breath lodged in her throat. *Please listen, Sam,* she begged. "Steel knows all of us, your plans, and your MO. Therefore, we have to do exactly the opposite of what she expects. If, for example, she says the safe is uncrackable without her, let's take it with us and crack it later. If she says we can't get past their security, let's bypass them. If she says the only way in is the road, then let's come by the sky."

"Yes, hang gliders. I said we'd use them one day," Jeremy said, causing Reaper to snort.

"Hang gliders are too flashy," Sam said. "They'd spot us circling. The same goes for parachutes, in case that's your next suggestion."

Jeremy snapped his fingers. "Hang gliders might not work, but we could climb in through the sewer?" He looked around the room as if an entrance to the sewers lay waiting in the corner.

"As creative as those ideas are, I have a different plan." Annie grasped her wrists behind her back. This was the moment of truth. They either would agree with her plan or she had nothing. "We will gather up the team and then zipline in. There is a tree-covered hill that will hide the equipment all the way to the house."

All jaws dropped.

"Our job is impossible because we've done everything they expect. It's time for the unexpected. Tomorrow is the wedding. As we know, their security is weakened, even though it's tightened. You taught us that, Sam."

Reaper nodded in agreement. Sam looked thoughtful. Annie took a deep breath and continued. "Our task is to get to the safe. I know we understand the kind of security that protects it, but what if we found a quicker way to the basement?"

All eyes were on her, including Sam's, although his face held no expression.

Annie took a deep breath, not letting his coldness unnerve her. "When you sent me in, Midnight asked me to keep an eye out for a secret way to ground zero. That study on the third floor, the one in the corner with the fireplace and wardrobe, is the right room to find this secret entrance. Reaper found top-secret passages, so we know they exist. I think one exists in that room and will lead us directly to the safe. Why else would they lock that room and leave it to look abandoned? Why else would Steel have snooped around in there?"

Reaper shifted, interest entering his eyes. "I don't think she liked finding you in there. That's probably why she hit you."

Annie bobbed her head. That was true, and one thing she hadn't even considered. "I know someone removed the cameras I placed in that room. I doubt Lichens wants to go through all his security measures each time he visits ground zero. What if he made himself a shortcut? Midnight, did you ever see Mr. Lichens go into that room and come out a long time later?"

Jeremy perked up, his eyes wide. "Yes. I've continued to monitor the few cameras we have active. There is one in the hallway pointed toward that door."

Annie felt a bit of hope bubble up in her chest. "I thought you might have. The dust is too thick in that room for me to believe he hangs out there for fun. My plan is simple. I propose that since their house is on a mountain, but not at the top, we zipline to the roof through the cover of the trees during the commotion of the wedding reception tomorrow evening, then we climb in through the purple lily room window that Jeremy has already disabled from their security."

Jeremy smirked. "Awesome."

"After we're inside, we will go down the secret passageway in the study and get to the safe without anyone the wiser. Steel would expect us to fan out and blend in, doing separate jobs like the first plan. We won't; we're all on this one task. We go in and find our way to the safe together.

"Reaper and, if he comes, Crank can take care of anyone in our way. Sam and Jeremy will handle the safe. If we can convince the Warden to join, then he and I will act as lookouts. We can call Claw and Fang and have them on standby to make the arrest the moment we give them the go. Mr. Benicci will receive his evidence, and I'll get this thing off my arm."

Annie breathed heavily, her eyes darting to each of them. Their faces were blank. Had she somehow sprouted an extra nose? She knew she wasn't suddenly speaking a different language. She swallowed hard.

"You know, I think this could work," Jeremy said, giving her slow applause.

"What do you think?" she asked Reaper and Sam, wringing her fingers together.

Reaper stood up and faced her directly. "I'm in. It's a decent plan, and I'd like my score. I know a friend who could get us the zipline stuff. I'll gather it up and have it ready by tomorrow evening." He checked his watch. "I think I can convince Crank to join if I can catch him before his flight leaves." He looked at Jeremy. "Text me the coordinates of where we should meet."

Jeremy nodded, already pulling his computer onto his lap.

Without another word, Reaper left the room, his phone out, presumably trying to contact Crank. Annie bit her lip and looked at the other two men.

Jeremy slowly stretched. "You know I'm all for it. I'll contact the Warden and see if I can convince him to come."

Sam ran his hands through his hair. "We can't do this without Claw. She isn't talking to me either. I burned too many bridges on this one. She said they'd try to take care of Lloyd for us and then asked me to leave her and Fang alone while they patched up their careers. They stuck their necks out for us and nearly had to turn in their guns and badges."

"Then I'll talk to her," Annie said.

Two sets of eyes turned to her; both held surprise.

"You know that means you'll have to hunt her down possibly at the police station . . . right?" Jeremy asked.

Annie laughed. "I think you're both more afraid of that than I am."

"She could drag you off to witness protection or, worse, put you in a holding cell and make you talk," Jeremy shot back.

Annie held up her wrist with the thick black bracelet on it. "You might not have wanted to tell her about this, but I think she'll find it just as motivating as we do. Let me talk to her. I can convince her to help."

Sam and Jeremy exchanged looks. "Okay," Sam said. "But if she refuses to help, then we have to call it right then and there, and you'll have to let me handle our issue with Benicci my way. Deal?"

Annie nodded. She understood that for their plan to work, they needed to have some arrests at the end, and to do that, they required Claw. She prayed Claw would agree and that they wouldn't have to resort to Sam making some ludicrous deal with Benicci to free her from the bracelet.

Jeremy looped his computer bag over his head. "I have a few items of equipment that might help. I'll run out, gather them, and return with that pizza." He looked at his watch. "Give me about an hour and fifteen minutes." With a smile and a wink, he scurried out the door.

Annie found herself alone with Sam. She stared at him, her heartbeat thrashing unsteadily. He sat on the edge of the bed with his arms folded, but his eyes were focused on her. Annie fought the urge to step closer to him. She wished she knew what he thought. She couldn't tell. After a minute, she cleared her throat. "I couldn't let you do it alone."

"I can see that," he said, his jaw still tight.

"Come on, Sam. I know my plan isn't as elaborate and fancy as yours. Given the time, I know you could've devised something better. But I'm done for if we don't try again right now." She took a few cautious steps toward him. "Are you with me?"

Sam's hand clenched and unclenched, and he looked away toward the door. "We'd better all come out of this alive."

"That's the plan."

"Yeah, but plans don't always work out, do they?" he said, a sharp edge to his words.

Annie's hands flew to her hips. "Don't you trust me?"

A slight uplift of his lips gave her a small bit of hope, but then his smile faded. "I don't trust most people; it must be a side effect of my job." He gestured to the door. "We will try it your way, but if it feels too risky. I'll pull the plug and we'll try something else."

Annie nodded; that seemed reasonable. Some of the weight on her shoulders lifted. He might not have drawn her into a hug and apologized for what happened at the beach, but he had agreed to try her plan, and that meant a lot to her.

"I'll escort you back to your room." He stood and walked toward the door.

Annie took a deep breath as he walked past her. She'd expected their meeting to feel a bit awkward, but not so cold. Did he regret their kiss that much? Perhaps he hadn't felt the same sparks she had when he'd pulled her into his arms.

She had to know one thing to make it through the night. Annie put her hand on his to stop him from opening the door. "Why are you so angry with me, Sam?"

His gaze jumped to her fingers on his. He cleared his throat and moved his hand. "I'm not angry at you. I'm mad at myself."

"Is that why you sent me away?" Annie asked as calmly as she could.

Sam turned to look at her. "Yes. I needed time alone to deal with everything that happened in the last two days. You don't understand that most of my plans don't go astray. Sure, we deal with an issue here or there, but never a complete failure."

Annie could feel the frustration and disappointment radiating off him and tentatively stretched her hand out and placed it on his arm. She prayed he'd see it for what it was—an attempt to comfort him. Sam took a deep breath before he wrapped his opposite hand around hers on his arm. "I'm not used to making mistakes or losing focus. All I've had since my sister's death is the cause, the fight to take out as many deplorable men as possible. Anyone who could have done the deed."

He squeezed her hand. "I thought I could do it all. Save you and take down my targets. I failed." He let go of her and stepped away, putting space between them. "I don't let anyone get close to me, Annie. It's too dangerous, and what I do is far too important to stop. There isn't room for anything else in my life." His eyes turned to look at the bracelet. "I shouldn't have shown any attachment to you. That's what made Benicci target you. I was weak, and I'm sorry."

Annie didn't want him to say anything more. She knew she shouldn't have let any feelings grow between them. He was trying to distance them before either of them got hurt. She should thank him and walk away. "I understand, Sam." Her stomach ached, and she suddenly couldn't stay near him anymore. She reached for the door herself and pulled it open. "I'll wait in my room until I can see Claw tomorrow."

"Annie."

She slowly turned around.

He offered her a weak smile. "Thanks for the plan. You're giving us a second chance. Something I thought was impossible."

Annie nodded once before opening her hotel room door. She slipped inside, closed it, locked it, and slid to the floor. She wouldn't cry. The headache she'd have in the morning wasn't worth it. She needed her head on straight, because tomorrow, she was determined to save them all.

CHAPTER 27

The next day, Sam and Jeremy dropped her off a block away from the police station. She wasn't sure how else to find Claw. Jeremy offered her an earpiece, but she needed to do this alone without their interference.

"We'll only be half a block away," Sam said, opening the door for her.

Annie nodded. She didn't want to say anything and risk them changing their minds.

Sam helped her out of the car. A familiar zing raced up her arms, but she chose to ignore it. Perhaps if she ignored it enough, it would go away. "I can go instead," Sam said, tucking his hands into his pockets.

She shook her head. "No, we can't risk Claw not listening to you. I've got this." With a deep breath, she started down the sidewalk.

"Be careful," Sam called.

Annie couldn't stop the smile that blossomed on her face. He might not want her, but he still cared what happened to her. That was enough for now.

Annie crossed the street, keeping to the side across from the police station. The odds were not in her favor if she got too close. If Mr. Benicci misunderstood her intentions, he'd trigger her jewelry. Annie considered her options. A little boutique shop, a few busy restaurants, and an empty bus stop. Annie walked to the bus stop. It was the least suspicious. She eyed the police station further down the block.

With one last breath, she sat on the covered bus stop bench and pulled out her phone. She pulled the sleeves of her white jean jacket straight to make sure it hid her bracelet. The last thing she needed was for someone to ask questions about it.

Annie smiled at the amount of noise on the busy street serving as interference for Mr. Benicci. She dialed the number Jeremy had written on a piece of paper. It was the non-emergency line for the police. It rang several times before someone picked up.

"Hello. LAPD."

This was it. The wind blew harder today, and with everything going on outside, Annie hoped Benicci's men would have difficulty figuring out what they were saying. "I'm looking for Detective Price."

"Our detectives are very busy. What is this call concerning?"

Annie didn't have time for this. The longer she sat here, the higher her chances of getting tased to death. "I have important information for the detective about one of her investigations. May I please talk to her?"

"One minute. I'll see if she is available."

Annie looked around at the cars zooming past her. Her blood raced in her veins. A dark-blue car drove slowly down the street, and Annie broke out into a sweat. It didn't stop in front of her but continued down the block where it parked. Oh no, they followed her here.

"This is Detective Price." Annie jumped. She'd nearly forgotten about her phone call.

Annie squished the bracelet between her legs. "It's Annie. Please, I need to talk to you, and I'm being followed."

"Wow. You are the last person I thought I'd hear from. I thought you were under house arrest or something. Where are you?"

Annie lowered her voice. "Across the street at the bus stop. Please come out and meet me, and if there is anything you can do to not look like a cop, please do it."

There was silence on the other line for a moment, long enough for Annie to check that she hadn't been disconnected. "Honey, how much danger are you in? Five being highest, one being lowest?"

Annie blew out a breath, her eyes on the car. "Probably a 5."

"I'm transferring this call to my cell. Don't move. There, can you hear me?"

"Yes." Annie shifted on the hard plastic bench.

"Alright, I'm coming around the building so whoever is following you doesn't see me exiting the police station. Are they threatening you now or watching?"

Annie swallowed hard. "Watching."

"Are you running from Kraken or someone else?"

"Someone else."

"I'm on the street. I can see you. Stay where you are. Act casual."

Out of the corner of her eye, Annie watched Claw pocket her phone in her slacks. She wore a suit jacket but could have passed for a businesswoman rather than a cop. Annie placed her phone on her lap.

Claw stepped into the small bus stop and leaned casually against the glass wall. "Where are your friends?" She asked without looking up.

"Down the block. Blue car." Annie said, barely loud enough for her to hear. Claw's eyebrows shot up before they narrowed slightly, and she used her hand to shield her eyes from the sun. Annie turned to look in the same direction—at a dark-blue sedan waiting on the corner. Now that Annie had her here, a flood of nerves rushed through her, and she hardly knew how to start. A car honked, and she jumped. "Where is—"

"Detective Wright?" Claw finished for her, her eyes on the busy traffic in front of them.

"Yeah."

"He's booking someone we picked up this morning. I have one better: Where is Kraken?" She eyed Annie with an intense look.

Annie let her gaze drop to her toes. "I told them to stay back. I wanted to talk to you alone." Claw's gaze darted to her ear, and Annie moved her hair. "No earpiece. I swear. I'm here of my own choosing, and every word from my mouth is my own."

"They cut off communication? Kraken? He's so unpredictable lately." She hung her head. "What are you doing here, Annie? I thought *he* wanted to protect you."

"He *is* trying to protect me." Annie shuffled and prayed there was enough interference that Benicci couldn't hear what she was saying.

Claw sunk onto the bench, leaving a few feet between them. "Fine, but I get the last say on how this encounter ends. Do you hear me? If I decide to toss you in a car and take you into protection, you can't argue with me. Got it?"

Annie nodded. She'd accepted that as a possibility when she'd chosen to talk to Claw. "I need to show you something, and then I think you'll understand." With a glance around to ensure no one watched, Annie placed her arm on her knee and pushed up her sleeve enough to reveal the bracelet Mr. Benicci gave her. Claw's jaw fell open.

"I've only seen one of those once before, and it was on a dead man's arm." Claw picked up Annie's arm while she looked it over.

"It's a little gift to motivate Kraken. Yes, I'm sure we are being overheard and recorded, which is why a busy street helps with interference. Yes, they can and will trigger the deadly taser mechanism if Kraken doesn't fulfill his contract."

"Would you care for a corn dog, Annie?" Claw said, shooting to her feet. She walked quickly down the block. Annie got up and scampered after her. This seemed like an odd time for a snack, right after Annie showed her the bracelet of death on her arm.

The corn dog shack appeared packed with a crowd for lunch, all laughing and talking over each other. Annie could hardly hear herself think in the room.

Claw pushed her way into the center of the crowd and then turned to her. "Okay, give it to me quickly."

Annie barely heard her over the noise. Suddenly it dawned on Annie why they were in there. Interference. Her respect for Claw shot up a notch.

"Kraken, the team, and I are going to try the job again tonight. We have a plan."

Claw shook her head and pointed to the bracelet.

"Oh, right. If we don't pull this off, Mr. Benicci will trigger the device. If I try to take it off, he'll trigger it. If I run, he'll trigger it."

Claw rubbed her forehead with her hand. "So, what you're telling me is that this will happen no matter what I say?"

Annie shook her head. "No, we can't do it without you. The most important part of any sting is when the cops come in with handcuffs. I'm here to ask for your help—no, beg for it. I know you don't want anything to do with Kraken or his crew after that fiasco, but I need your help more than ever."

Claw looked thoughtful, her eyes glancing at the bracelet and then back to Annie. "Will your plan help us all?" she asked, her thumb pointing at herself.

Annie could see that Claw cared a lot about her job, and their failure might have made her look bad. Annie glanced out the window. The blue sedan now waited across the street opposite the corn dog shop. Benicci's men had come closer. Annie shivered and looked further down the road to the car Sam and Jeremy hid in. If she ignored them both, maybe she could get through this.

Annie put her arm with the bracelet behind her back and leaned closer to Claw so she could lower her voice. "Detective Price, if we pull this off, then it should solve all our problems. Even if my plan is flawed, I expect some of our friends will know how to make it work. I need your help."

Claw rolled back and forth on her feet as if thinking Annie's words over. "What exactly do you need from me?"

A bit of hope lit in her chest. "I need you to reassemble your team. I know with the way things went down, that's easier said than done, but Kraken says you're the best, so I know you can do it."

Claw rolled her eyes. "How long do we have?"

Annie breathed a sigh of relief. Claw hadn't straight up refused to help. "I need them this evening or else I don't have a plan that will work."

Claw stared at her as if trying to figure her out. Annie knew she looked like an average homespun girl entirely out of her element. But her heart was in the right place, and that had to count for something.

Finally, Claw nodded one short bob of her head. "Order me a footlong corn dog with honey, mustard, a coke, and whatever you want." She pressed a fifty-dollar bill into Annie's hand. "Give me a minute. I need to make a call."

Claw disappeared into a corner of the room, away from the crowd, next to the trash cans. Annie stepped in line and tried not to freak out. All her cards were on Claw helping her. She had to come through.

The line moved quickly, but Claw kept talking in the corner of the room. Annie ordered herself the same thing as Claw. She doubted she'd eat it with the way her stomach churned like an industrial mixer turned on turbo speed.

Once she had the food, Annie sat at a table close to Claw and sipped her soda. Claw offered her a quick smile before turning away so Annie couldn't see her face. Did she do that on purpose? Could she have decided to call the marshals instead of helping her? Annie gripped the side of her chair, her eyes wandering to the exit sign. She wasn't exactly against the witness protection program, but she had more important things to do today.

Claw spun around and slipped her phone into her pocket before she sat across from Annie. "Fang didn't want to talk to me at first. We both nearly lost our jobs over this sting, but once I explained the situation and your particular issue . . ." She glanced down at the bracelet. "Thankfully, he agreed to help. I'll meet with him after this, and we'll talk to the captain. Our men won't refuse a direct order from him."

"You're coming then?"

Claw snickered and picked up her corn dog. "Can't get rid of me now. I'm in. We all need this win. It's time for all hands on deck."

Annie sighed a long sigh of relief, her gut unclenching slightly. One tiny detail still wiggled in her chest. Annie bit her lip and picked up her steaming corn dog. The thought haunted her, and she couldn't take a bite. She had to know.

"Did you arrest Lloyd by chance?"

Claw set her corn dog down and wiped her mouth with a napkin. "No. We couldn't find the right weapon and didn't have enough evidence to make the charges stick. I'm sorry—but we'll keep trying."

Annie played with the end of her corn dog, rolling the opposite side in a pile of honey. "What about Ink and Sneak?"

Claw took another bite of the crunchy corn-battered hot dog. She chewed and swallowed before answering. "If this ends well, Kraken won't forget them once this is all over. Right now, they are safer where they are. If we can pull off this plan of yours, they'll get out. Kraken promised, and he doesn't *often* break his promises." She emphasized the word *often*, and Annie knew their failure still bothered Claw. It bothered them all.

Don't worry, Annie thought. *We are going to make this right.*

Annie's agitated stomach churned a little less violently. She hadn't entirely fixed anything yet, but the possibility of success hung in the air as an option ready for them to grab. Annie picked up the corn dog. Unlike the frozen corn dogs in the grocery store's freezer section, it looked good. She let the excess honey drip onto her plate before she took a bite. Her teeth crunched through the warm, crispy outside. The saltiness of the hot dog combined with the sweetness of the corn batter crust and the honey made her mouth instantly water for a second bite.

"Wow." Annie blinked at the corn dog. How could something like this taste so good? *This is why I need to go to culinary school*, she thought.

"I had more than one reason for choosing this place," Claw said, swirling her corn dog in a mustard-and-honey mixture. "I have a feeling that we have a long day ahead of us. Might as well eat something amazing before we dive in."

Annie laughed and took another bite. Choosing to trust Claw worked out in her favor after all. She took another crunchy bite, savoring the sweet and salty mix of flavor that danced on her tongue. Claw was right. They had a very long day ahead of them, so she might as well enjoy this moment.

CHAPTER 28

Jeremy, Annie, and Sam wound their way up to the Lichenses' man-made forest. They traveled on a much less traversed road that required a "borrowed" four-wheel-drive car rather than Sam's Ferrari. The sun inched closer to the horizon. It was nearly time. Annie looked down at her wrist with the taser bracelet and breathed slowly. If they failed this time, it would all be on her. She rotated the bracelet so she could see the green light. They could not fail.

In a copse of trees near the peak, Reaper, the Warden, and Crank were hooking themselves into harnesses when they arrived. Each of them gave her a nod in greeting. Annie's eyes followed the black cable to where it was attached to sturdy trees down the mountain, where the Lichenses' house waited, all lit up. Party music floated up from the yard on the other side of the large L-shaped stone house. Their distraction was in full swing. She swallowed hard. Ziplining was the only way in on a night like tonight, and she knew it even if the idea made her stomach churn.

"Did you have difficulty setting the zipline up on the house?" Jeremy asked, picking up a harness from the pile on the ground.

Reaper shrugged, tightening his straps. "I knew the timing of the guards, and my friend and I ensured the cable was hidden by the trees. We might eat some leaves, but we got it done. Thankfully, the window we wanted is on the opposite side of the festivities and nowhere near the front door."

Sam pulled a harness out of the stack and handed it to her before pulling on his own. Annie jittered. She'd never dreamed of ziplining. It was the kind of thing that only thrill seekers did. She was no thrill seeker. The men tightened their harnesses in a jiffy, but Annie struggled with the straps. No one noticed except Sam, who took pity on her. Without looking her in the eye, he yanked the straps around her waist to help secure her in tight. He gave her a short nod and walked over to the line.

She knew things would feel tense between her and Sam, but she hadn't expected Sam to act cold. Annie's gaze found Jeremy's. He gave her a half smile and mouthed, "Sorry." Annie nodded in response.

They put on extra-thick gloves, but no one wore helmets. Annie gulped. Wouldn't a fall from this height kill them? What if the line failed? Annie shifted her weight from foot to foot, trying to calm the blood that rushed through her veins at hyper speed. She yanked a hair tie off her wrist and pulled her hair into a messy bun. She supposed it didn't matter. If the line broke and they failed, she'd get tased by Benicci anyway.

How had her life come to this?

Jeremy walked over and hooked his carabiners to the line, each one going in opposite directions before he adjusted the bag on his back. Crank followed suit, and Sam did the same. Then all three men glanced at her. Annie stumbled to her spot in line and looked up at the thick wire. She stretched up with her carabiner, but the zipline was a tad out of reach. Without a word, Sam took her clips and secured them for her.

"Thanks," she said quietly.

"No problem," he said, his voice quiet. A pang of hurt hit her in the gut, but she shook it off. Now wasn't the time to worry about her and Sam. This job couldn't afford those kinds of distractions.

Reaper clipped his carabiners to the line behind her, and the Warden followed him, mumbling about getting too old for this kind of thing.

"Wait fifteen seconds before the next person goes," Reaper said behind her. "Don't scream. We have to act like ghosts. Nova, use both of your gloves on the line and squeeze hard to slow down. They are specially made to handle intense friction. It's that easy, got it?"

"Okay," she said, her voice a little breathy. All her nerves tingled in her fingers. *Don't think about it*, she told herself. *You're safe, completely safe*. Annie looked toward the sunset on the other side of the house. It was the perfect moment. No one would look toward the boring old mountain with the brilliant colors filling the sky on the opposite side. The time had come.

"On my mark," Reaper said behind her. "Midnight, go."

Jeremy pushed hard with his feet and disappeared down the line. Annie trembled a little more.

"Crank, go." Shouldn't they make sure Jeremy made it first?

In a second, Crank was gone. Nerves rushed up Annie's veins, making them feel like someone had pumped fire into them. She'd chosen this option.

"Kraken, go."

Sam disappeared without a moment of hesitation.

Her turn was next. Annie slid to the cliff's edge, her gloved hands gripping the line. Her mouth went dry. Every fiber of her being told her this was not something she was capable of doing. She should have found a different way. "I—I—don't—"

"You don't have a choice," Reaper said. With a shove, he pushed Annie off the edge. Annie bit down on her lips so hard that she tasted blood. She soared through the sky, leaves hitting her in the face, a mix of regret and exhilaration warred in her chest.

The wind whipped past her so fast that tears sprang to her eyes. She gripped the line tighter with her double-thick gloves but hardly slowed. The house got closer and closer. She squeezed tighter and prayed with all her might that she didn't smack into someone or the stone house itself. The image of her flattened against the house made her squeeze with everything she had, and she started to slow right before she caught sight of Sam. He swung around in time to catch her. She felt him bump against the other two, but no one complained.

All she could do was shudder in his arms. "Hey, you made it," he whispered in her ear. "You're okay." His voice was friendlier than before, and she appreciated that. Reaper came down and barely bumped into her. He had a lot more control over his ziplining experience.

The Warden knocked hard into Reaper, and only then did Sam let go of her. He took his hand off the line and pushed her back a couple inches to help with the spacing situation, but she slid right back against him. The angle of the zipline didn't want to grant them any breathing room. He gave her a fleeting smile, but it was a real one before it twisted into one of his fake smiles as he tapped into whatever persona he'd created for this job.

"Oh no." Jeremy turned wide eyes back at them. "It's locked."

"What do you mean locked?" Reaper said from behind Annie, his face smashed against her back.

"I mean, someone noticed I'd disabled it before and fixed it. I need some space." He pushed Crank back, who attempted to slide up the thick cable. His movements only made them all side closer. Crank grasped the zipline and braced his feet against the wall. He pushed his back against Sam with all his might to keep everyone away so Jeremy had at least some room to move. Annie's cheek smashed in between Sam's shoulder blades. Jeremy reached into his pocket and pulled out a black box with a cable that he attached to something on the window.

"You got them, Crank?" Jeremy asked, hooking everything up.

Numbers began spinning on the screen of the box, and Annie realized it was a device to crack the code.

"For a bit," came Crank's strained reply.

This was the oddest situation she'd ever found herself in. All five of them were suspended on a thick cable three stories above the cobblestone. Sam was smashed against Crank. Annie was crushed against Sam. It would have felt intimate if Reaper wasn't pressed against her and the Warden behind him.

"Almost there," Jeremy said.

"Good," Crank replied through gritted teeth. "My arms are going numb."

This is okay, Annie thought. No plan ever went smoothly. One little bump didn't mean the whole plan would fail. She clenched her teeth and prayed Jeremy's device would work. With a light beep, the machine registered some numbers, and Jeremy unhooked the device. Sliding his fingernails under the windowsill, he pushed the window open to the purple lily room. Like a spider, Jeremy crawled on the ledge and unhooked his carabiners before he dove into the room. Crank and Sam followed suit.

Sam and Jeremy reached an arm out the window for her and pulled her onto the sill. Sam reached up and unhooked her while Jeremy kept hold of her. "All right, Nova," Jeremy said, pulling her inside. "I say we zipline more often."

Annie jumped into the room and stepped out of the way. She bent, doubled over, holding her knees and sucking in several long breaths. If she was going to get through the rest of the night, she needed to stop the trembling right then and there.

Reaper and the Warden followed. Everyone unhooked their harnesses and dropped them in a pile on the floor. Reaper took a rope off his shoulder and tied the end through a carabiner. He hooked it to the zipline, letting the rope dangle down the building.

Annie blinked and glanced at Reaper. "Are you sure it's a good idea to leave the harnesses here?"

"Don't worry about it," he said, tossing his own on the pile. "Claw has my back."

Jeremy opened the bedroom door a crack. "Reaper, we'll need you to act as a guard. There are some guests in the hall."

Reaper straightened up and strode out the door, full of confidence. Jeremy swung his bag onto his back and peered out. Crank and the Warden flanked him, ready to move at his signal. Sam stood behind, face impassive, arms folded. Annie pushed back her emotions and strode forward to wait beside Sam. She didn't care if he wanted to keep space between them. She felt safest close to him.

Jeremy opened the door a little wider and held up his hand. "Wait . . . wait . . . go." He flung open the door, and they started down the hall. Annie did her best to imitate Sneak's technique of walking quietly. Reaper stood on the stairs instead of the guard that usually stood there and gave them a wink.

Jeremy rushed to the door half hidden in the corner. The men crowded into the tight space to get out of the main hall. Annie dove for the plant, where she knew the key was hidden. She dug around, rotated it, and even untightened the strings, but the key wasn't there.

"It's not here," she said, her gaze darting around the group.

"I could break down the door," Crank suggested.

"That would make too much noise," the Warden and Annie said simultaneously.

Sam pushed his way through the group and pulled out a small case from a pocket of his suit jacket. He took out two thin pieces of metal and stuck them in the keyhole. Annie had to blink to keep her eyes from bugging out. Sam could pick locks.

"Where are you heading?" Reaper's voice raised enough to reach them as he spoke to some guests out of sight.

Annie turned to Sam, who was struggling with the door. "Sam?" Annie said under her breath.

"Give me a minute. There's an unexpected pin." Sam's face looked scrunched in concentration. Annie bit her lip and looked around at her group, who did not fit in the tight space.

"You'd better hurry," Reaper said down the hall, his voice raised. "I think the bride and groom are going to cut the cake soon."

"Got it." Sam pushed the door open, and they fell into the room. Jeremy, Sam, and the Warden clicked on flashlights. Crank handed her one before he turned his own on.

The room looked the same, like the study from Clue, her favorite board game. Feeling like Mrs. Peacock who needed to solve a murder, Annie peered around the room, looking for clues.

"Hunt for a secret passageway," Annie said. They obeyed and spread out around the room.

Annie shone her flashlight at a canvas above the fireplace. She hadn't noticed it last time. A dark sunset took up most of the picture, capturing the moment before the light faded behind the mountains. The white lettering printed across the middle stuck out to her. It was a C. S. Lewis quote: "*You can't go back and change the beginning, but you can start where you are and change the ending.*"

She stood in the middle of the room while everyone else knocked on the walls or moved various pieces of furniture. Annie turned on the spot and looked around the room. Her eyes settled on the wardrobe. She shook her head. The bookcase on the opposite wall of the door caught her eye, and she spotted a fancy leather-bound set of C. S. Lewis's books. Her eyes darted back to the quote and then to the wardrobe again. Could it be? She walked slowly to the wardrobe and pulled on the knob. It was locked.

Sam appeared by her side. "Annie, we can't find anything. We might have to think of something else."

"Can you unlock this?" she pointed to the wardrobe door.

"Easily, but why?"

"I have a feeling." She turned to look up at him.

He scrutinized her but pulled out his lockpick set. Within a moment, the wardrobe door's lock clicked. Sam stepped back, and Annie threw open the door. Old, out-of-fashion jackets hung in a straight line on the rod. There were two sets of shoes on the bottom, one on the left side and one on the right, but none in the middle.

"Sorry, Nova," Sam said, putting a hand on her shoulder, causing a warm zip to rush through her. "It was a good thought."

Annie shook her head. She looked at the shoes perfectly centered on each side of the wardrobe. This was it; she could feel it. Lichens had created his personal entrance to his fantasy world based on his favorite author. Ignoring Sam, she pushed the jackets aside and shoved the back wall of the wardrobe. Nothing budged.

Sam reached for her hand. "We are going to run out of time. You got us this far but we need to look for another option while we can."

Annie shook her head and looked around the tiny space. No. This had to be it. She knew it. She slid her hands over the back wall.

"Another failure." The Warden snorted. "I hope you have a good escape plan, Kraken."

Reaper burst into the room. "Lichens's men are on their rounds."

"How much time do we have?" the Warden asked, a tremble to his voice.

Annie touched a notch on the wood that felt like a small handle, only big enough for three fingers, or four in her case. She curled her fingernails around the notch and pulled hard. The back of the wardrobe slid open. The men behind her gasped when a small, lit hallway appeared behind the fake door she'd discovered. Annie turned around with a bright smile on her face. "I found it."

"Way to go, Nova," Jeremy said, jumping in the wardrobe beside her. He hopped down on the other side and held out his hand. Annie bit her lip and let him help her into the passage. The Warden, Sam, Crank, and Reaper followed behind. Reaper slid the wardrobe door closed behind him.

"I wouldn't have guessed that," Crank said, slapping her back as he walked past her. "Not too shabby for a newbie. I'm impressed."

Annie grinned as she followed Jeremy and Crank down the narrow hallway. After several feet, a winding black metal staircase led downward. They followed it as it twisted down two floors. Another small hallway followed, and then another regular staircase led them underground to floor zero. A large, silver metal door stood at the end of the hallway. Annie felt excitement bubble up in her chest. This was it. It's what they'd worked so hard to find.

Jeremy paused at the front, and Sam pushed past her to examine the door. It looked like any door, except it was made out of steel. Beside the vault attached to the wall was a black box.

"It's a fingerprint scanner," Sam told the rest of the group. Sam stared at the fingerprint scanner from more than one angle. "I'd guess that we need Mr. Lichens's fingerprint since this is his private access."

Reaper groaned. "I didn't grab Ink's portfolio of fingerprints."

"Can't you use putty or tape?" Annie asked, thinking about all the action movies she'd watched.

Sam leaned down and breathed on the scanner. "I think he's wiped it. Probably out of habit. We can't get in this way."

"We're not giving up now," Reaper growled. "We're too close. I'll go up and get the print."

"You can't," the Warden said.

"You'll get caught," Crank said at the same time.

"I'm not going to the party. I'll go to his room. There must be something in there that has a clean print. All I need is a shiny surface. Besides, I was hired as security. They may ignore me because of my familiar face with all the other chaos today. I stand a chance."

All eyes turned to Sam and then to Annie.

"Why are you all looking at me?" Annie asked, her gaze darting between them.

"Because you came up with this plan," Jeremy said, nudging her with his elbow.

Annie squirmed a bit while looking at all these men who were much more intelligent than she felt. She let her gaze fall on Sam, who gave her a slight nod. Annie could hardly believe they were putting all their trust in her.

"I think Reaper can go if someone goes with him as a lookout." She let her gaze fall on the Warden.

He shrugged, looking a little put out. "Fine. I signed up to act as a lookout anyway."

Reaper slapped the Warden on the back. "Great. We'll return in a jiffy." Reaper and the Warden rushed down the hallway and up the stairs.

Crank started pacing the hallway. Jeremy set down his bag but kept his eyes on the box like he was analyzing it. Annie glanced over at Sam. He seemed less bothered by her now, but he still wouldn't look at her like he had. That kiss never should have happened. The last thing she wanted was to lose him and Jeremy. They'd become her best friends. She opened her mouth to say something of that nature to him when a creak sounded above them. Everyone's gaze shot up to the ceiling.

More noise emanated from the stairs, like feet pounding at a fast pace. Crank's eyes narrowed, and he walked down the slender hall to where the stairs came down.

"It's not Reaper or the Warden," Crank said, popping his knuckles. "They're onto us. Midnight, it's time you did something brilliant." With that, he darted up the stairs, and what sounded like a fistfight started above them.

Jeremy dropped his bag on the ground and started digging around inside. Sam moved in front of Annie and pulled his gun out of his holster. His stance was firm, as if he were preparing for battle.

"Midnight, can you get in without the fingerprint?" Sam asked.

Jeremy looked up, and his eyes were unsure for the first time. "Maybe, but not cleanly. They'll know we're here."

"They already know," Sam said, cocking his gun as a grunt of pain came from above them. "Do what you must to get us inside."

CHAPTER 29

Annie's head moved back and forth to keep an eye on Jeremy and the staircase. Shouts and sounds of fighting continued to grow closer. Annie's blood rushed faster in her veins, and it took everything she had to stay still instead of pace the hall. The last thing she wanted was to get in the way. However, at any moment, she expected a horde of gunmen to rush the stairs and end them.

"One more second," Jeremy said, typing like mad on his laptop. He hooked some wires to the fingerprint scanner and continued punching keys.

"Jeremy?" Sam snapped, releasing the safety on his gun.

"I know, Sam," Jeremy said through gritted teeth.

Sam turned to look at her. "Annie, get behind Jeremy, please."

She nodded once. This wasn't the time to argue that standing behind both of them would make little difference in the timing of her demise. They'd only kill her a second after them. A shout and a moan sounded, and Reaper crashed to the bottom of the stairs. An ugly lump was visible on the side of his face, and his fists were bloody. He groaned but struggled to his feet.

"Jeremy!" Sam shouted.

"I'm trying," Jeremy said through gritted teeth. A moment later, Jeremy's eyes widened, and he glanced at her. "Annie, I need you to put your thumb on the scanner."

"Mine?"

He nodded. "In three . . ." Annie pushed aside the torrent of questions that flooded her brain and turned toward him. "Two . . ."

This is crazy. This is more than crazy, Annie thought.

"One." Jeremy's eyes snapped to hers.

Annie mashed her thumb to the fingerprint scanner. It blinked red three times before it blinked green, and the door clicked. Jeremy shot his fist into the air like he had crossed the finish line after running a marathon. Sam didn't wait. He pushed the door open. In one fluid movement, he reached for Annie and pulled her inside. Jeremy unhooked his wires and slipped in before the door slammed shut and relocked. They were plunged into complete darkness. All Annie could hear was the three of them breathing hard.

A warm, masculine hand wrapped around hers and squeezed. "We made it in." Sam gripped her fingers like he wanted to make sure she was still there with him.

"Will they kill our guys?" Annie asked, thinking of Reaper's bloodied face. She'd hate herself forever if a single one of her team members died. They'd all come here because of her.

Sam let out a long sigh. "I don't know."

Jeremy opened his laptop and started tapping on his computer, the screen's light brightening his face. "Hold on, you two . . . one more second . . . there." The lights flickered and then turned on in the room.

Annie blinked against the bright lights. Sam gave her fingers one more squeeze before he let go. The back wall was taken up by a large table, a comfortable leather chair, and what looked like a stack of logbooks. Large paintings hung around the room, and Annie bet they were worth a ton of money to be squirreled away down here instead of displayed upstairs. The safe they were after stood in the middle of the room. It looked enormous, daunting, and heavy.

"I hoped we could simply pick it up and take it with us," Annie murmured.

Sam and Jeremy laughed out loud. Sam's face brightened. "Oh, Annie, this safe would have been put here with a crane after the foundation was poured. We have to crack it."

Annie's eyes bulged. "Can you do that?"

Sam shrugged. "I'm a fixer, not a thief. Without Steel, this will be tricky, but since we're not trying to hide the break-in, we might have a better chance." Sam pitched his gloves into the corner of the room and set his jacket aside. Jeremy tossed Sam a heavy-duty-looking drill and pulled a wedge and chisel out of the bag for himself.

Annie's head jerked. "You're going to drill it?"

"We'll do whatever we have to," Jeremy said, flipping the wedge in the air and catching it again, his other hand on his computer.

"Steel is the real expert for something like this. My skills are limited," Sam said, testing the drill to make sure he had a battery charge. "We'll have to make this work and fast. She's taught me enough about the borescope that I think

I can get in." Sam walked around the safe as if trying to decide where to drill. He shook his head. "The door is the thickest, so if I can, I'd rather go in from the side." He looked at the drill, then at Jeremy. "Any chance you have a blow torch in your bag of tricks?"

Jeremy looked up from where he sat cross-legged on the floor with his laptop and rolled his eyes. "If I did, I'd have another bag the same size as me. I do have this." He turned his computer around to show Sam what looked like information on the safe. "Steel and I did our research. This safe has a cobalt plate, so we can't drill it straight through the face. It also has glass that will trigger the locks if we aren't spot-on."

Sam lowered the drill, his face grim. "You're positive about not having that blow torch?"

Jeremy laughed and zoomed the photo in on his computer. "Lucky for us, Steel marked the exact spot."

Annie squinted her eyes to see a little red X on the screen.

A bang sounded outside on the large metal door like someone fell against it. A few things Annie knew for certain; they didn't have a lot of time, they couldn't mess up, and they couldn't fail.

Jeremy waved Annie over to him. "I need to help Sam. Can you hold the spacebar on my laptop down?"

"The spacebar?" Annie had no idea why that would be important at a time like this.

"Yeah, I wrote a program to jam the doors, but it's not working so well down here. Hold that one key down or else my program will fail, and anyone could walk in this room."

Gotcha. That made a lot of sense. "Sure."

Jeremy waited until she pressed her fingers down on the spacebar before he removed his fingers. With a quick squeeze on her shoulder, Jeremy rushed off to help Sam break into the safe. This was not on the list of things she thought she'd ever do. Her gaze darted back and forth between the computer, Jeremy, and Sam. The banging on the door grew more insistent, like someone was trying to break it down.

Sweat drops gathered on Sam's head as he angled the drill. "Here we go."

The whir of the drill grew louder as he pushed it into the thick safe. Shards of metal fell to the ground all around him. Sam's teeth clenched, and the muscles on his arms bulged with the effort to drill the safe correctly. Annie couldn't tear her eyes away from him. He looked so opposite from the man who'd pulled her from the dumpster. Not in a bad way. He looked stronger, vibrant, and real.

It wasn't the right time to focus on her uncertain feelings for him. It took effort, but she forced herself to look away and focus on the spacebar and the sound of the drill working through the metal. Jeremy darted from one side of Sam to the other, commenting on the drill and the speed.

"I'm through," Sam said.

"Knew you had it in you, Sam," Jeremy said, rubbing his hands together. He dove back into the bag for a tiny camera on a thin wire. "This is a borescope," he said over his shoulder as he rushed back to Sam. "It will allow us to see where to turn the dial to line up all the notches inside the lock."

Sam took it and threaded it into the hole he'd drilled. With a deep breath, he leaned against the safe and spun the dial, his eyes on the tiny screen connected to the borescope. They were getting close to unlocking the safe. Anticipation gathered in Annie's gut.

Annie jumped at another loud bang on the door. She let go of the spacebar for a fraction of a second. She slammed her fingers back on the spacebar, but it was too late. The door to Mr. Lichens's secret entrance burst open, and Lloyd, Annie's hitman, rushed into the room. He brandished his gun in front of him, pointing it at Sam.

"That's enough. Step away from the safe, Samuel," he shouted.

Jeremy dove for his laptop.

"Don't move," Lloyd barked, his eyes dark.

Annie froze her eyes on the familiar thick scar on Lloyd's hand. Sam stayed flat against the safe, but his fingers slowly spun the silent dial.

"I said move away from the safe."

"You also said not to move at all." Sam countered his hand, now spinning the dial the other way. "Which command would you rather we obeyed?"

Lloyd rolled his eyes. "Move away."

Sam spun the dial quickly and let go. He turned, his hands also raised.

Lloyd shook his head, a deadly look in his eyes. "You thought you were so smart sneaking in here tonight. Margot said you'd take half a year to try again."

Margot? That must have been Steel's real name or another alias. Annie doubted that she'd told this brute her real name.

Lloyd ground his teeth. "I trusted her information. She proved correct before." He rubbed his chin. "Unless she double-crossed me? No matter, our security team is on its way. The cops have already been called. You've lost." His eyes narrowed at Jeremy. "Quit typing. It won't do you any good."

Jeremy sat quietly, but his fingers still flew across his keyboard. Annie had no idea what he was doing, but it had better involve a plan to save them.

"I said quit it." Lloyd aimed his gun at Jeremy. The door behind them slammed shut, and the distinct locking sound alerted them to the fact that they were now sealed in the vault.

Lloyd's face turned a purple-red color, and he shifted his feet as if they'd somehow thrown off his groove. His steely eyes turned to Jeremy. "Reverse it."

Jeremy shrugged. "It's not that easy."

"Get started," Lloyd spat. "You're all going down for this, and I'm getting a big fat raise." His eyes slowly turned to look at Annie, and his mouth split into a broad smile. Annie shivered.

He waved his gun around. "That's right. I hold all the cards. All the power." He laughed and took a step closer to her. "I've been trying to kill you for over a week. Have you any idea what that does to my record?" He shook his head as if such a thing was the worst thing that could have transpired.

"Here is what's going to happen. Samuel will walk over to the wall slowly with his hands on his head." Lloyd waved his gun at Sam, who gritted his teeth and raised his hands, placing them on his head. Lloyd nodded, satisfied. "You"—his gaze sliced to Jeremy—"are going to open the door."

Lloyd took another step toward her. The room wasn't large, and Annie doubted that, if she tried to run, his gun would miss its mark. "And you . . ." Lloyd dove at her, his rough hands yanking her toward him. Annie slammed hard against his chest.

He pushed the gun against the skin of her neck. The cold tip felt like an icy branding, as if the spot that touched her skin would always bear the mark. Annie froze, her breath shuddering in her throat, and her body trembled uncontrollably. Sam stared at him wide-eyed, his fists clenched on top of his head, but he didn't move toward the wall. Lloyd squeezed her tighter against his chest.

"I know you don't want me to shoot her," he scoffed, the corners of his lips curling wickedly. "I know you'll do anything I say while the barrel of my gun is right here." He flicked the safety off before pressing the gun deeper into her neck, forcing her to gasp.

Annie's head started to pound, and she sucked in a quick breath. *Please, Lord,* she prayed, hoping this wasn't her last moment to breathe or her final second to live. Her gaze went to Sam. There were so many things she wanted to say. So many things she felt swirling in her heart. She did not want to die this way. But only one word squeezed out of her lips, and she could barely hear it herself.

"Help."

CHAPTER 30

Sam uncurled his fists. Lloyd grinned, his gun pressed against her juggler. Annie looked at her bracelet. Would Benicci realize they failed and trigger it? Or would Lloyd get to her first? Lloyd twisted his gun against her skin. She winced. Sam's jaw tightened.

"Move to the wall, Samuel," Lloyd said again through gritted teeth. Lloyd wasn't about to let her go, and they all knew it.

Sam obeyed this time. Lloyd twisted her around so that she faced Sam directly. It was as if he wanted Sam to remember he literally held her within an inch of her life.

Sam's eyes focused on a spot behind them as if he couldn't bear to look at her. *Don't abandon me, Sam,* she thought. He'd never claimed hero status. Even if he'd saved her more than once, it didn't mean he could somehow do it again. Those instances hadn't included a gun to her throat. *Lord, help us,* she prayed.

Lloyd wrenched her head back, cracking her neck. His chin rested against her face. Annie inhaled in pain. "Your boyfriend, Dillan, and his crew were all fools." His spittle dripped onto her face as he spoke. "Why they thought they could rob this place, I have no idea. They made me look incompetent and failed at their task. Their brains must have been made of mush. But you could have led them to victory with the resources you had. I should have known you were no ordinary girl from the moment you jumped out that window. It's too bad you have to die like your pesky friends."

Lloyd bent her wrist back until she screamed. Agony rushed to the joint. Annie fought and cried but was pinned against him. She couldn't prevent him from bending it. Something popped under her skin. Annie choked on her scream as a sharper pain burst through her wrist.

"Stop it. Stop it. You don't have to torture her," Sam shouted, his eyes wild. "She wasn't part of their schemes. Dillan was an old irritating friend. She's innocent. She knew nothing about it."

Lloyd let go of her wrist, but the pain remained. She cradled it against her stomach. He'd broken it. Annie sobbed, her neck throbbing from the way he held her with his gun to her throat, but the pain felt dull in comparison to her wrist.

"Unlikely. Even so, my reputation is on the line. She'll die the moment I make sure you can't do anything about it." He laughed as if he'd already won.

Sam's eyes narrowed. "If that's how you see things, so be it." He nodded, but not to Lloyd or Annie.

Out of nowhere, a loud crack rent the air. Lloyd's head snapped back, his gun hand flung upward, and a shot fired into the ceiling. He stumbled back. Annie fell forward. Sam caught her, and before she got her bearings, he dragged her backward to the big metal door. The bolts unlocked, and Sam towed her out. Annie looked back to see Lloyd on the ground, Jeremy's broken laptop next to him. Jeremy dashed to the open safe. Sam had cracked it after all.

Sam tucked her under his arm. "We have to run!"

She held her broken wrist against her chest, and Sam led her up the hall and to the winding staircase. A few unconscious bodies lay on the ground, but Annie couldn't see Reaper, Crank, or the Warden among them. Jeremy hurried to catch up. "He's already stirring. Run!" he yelled.

Sam pulled out his silver phone as they rushed up the stairs. "Claw, you're on," is all he said before he hung up. Jeremy shoved the next door open, his hands trembling as much as she felt hers were.

"Do you believe in prayer, Annie?" Sam asked, taking her good hand in his.

"I think so," she said, staring at his hand wrapped around hers. She was trying to believe God cared.

"Now might be a good time to rekindle that belief. We'll need Him to get out of here alive." They heard a gasp of pain and feet running their way. Jeremy looked around the corner, and his eyes widened. "I'll open the door." He squeezed past them and started down the hallway that led to the secret wardrobe entrance.

Vile language sounded behind them, and Annie knew Lloyd wouldn't give up easily. Sam reached out to Jeremy, pulling him to a stop. "Get her out. He won't hesitate to shoot her this time."

Jeremy's jaw worked as if trying to figure out what to say, but he looped his arm around hers and kept running instead of saying anything. Annie glanced back to see Sam remove the small gun he kept hidden on his leg before he followed after them. Jeremy turned the corner, and Annie looked back, a lump of fear settling in her stomach like a cold stone when she lost sight of Sam.

"What about Sam?" she asked, slowing her steps.

Jeremy tightened his grip on her arm. "He can take care of himself."

Annie didn't want to risk that. Sam mattered too much.

Jeremy stumbled to a stop when they reached the wardrobe door. It was slightly ajar. Jeremy let out a quick breath, his fingers stretching before he pulled the door open. Rough hands yanked Jeremy through the opening. Annie screamed and turned to run. A hand reached out and grabbed her good arm. She fought and tried to push it off.

"Nova, shush. It's me."

She turned to see Crank. She stopped fighting, and he pulled her through the wardrobe door.

"Where is Kraken?" Reaper asked, standing next to Jeremy. He had blood smears on his hands and face.

Jeremy nodded back toward the passage. "He's got someone on his heels."

Reaper nodded once before he rushed back through the passage to help Sam. Annie released a pent-up breath. At least Sam had backup.

The Warden glanced at them from the doorway. They'd used the chairs and other bits of furniture to block the entrance. Bullet holes marked the door, making it look more like Swiss cheese than a door. Annie's jaw dropped.

The Warden paced the room. "The cops showed up a minute or two ago. All the commotion is going on below. I think it's our moment to slip out."

"They won't forget that we're here," Crank said.

"No, but I think they will assume we'll stay put. I have no intention of getting caught, not even by Claw or Fang." He moved to the door and started shoving furniture. The faint sounds of a fight started in the secret passageway, and Jeremy rushed to help the Warden. With indecision written all over his face, Crank looked between the passageway and the blocked door. With a loud groan, he rushed to help shove things out of the way.

Annie bit her lip before helping with her one useable hand. In only a couple of minutes, they had the door clear. Crank opened it slightly, only enough to spy out. "They left one guy." He rolled his shoulders and popped his knuckles. "Wish me luck."

With that, he rushed out the door, his fist already raised. Annie, Jeremy, and the Warden all watched Crank take out the one guard left to watch the room. Crank barreled over him, knocking them both to the ground. Crank kicked the guard's gun across the hallway and slammed his fist into the guy's jaw, claiming victory.

Annie jumped as the sound of a gunshot reverberated in her ears. It came from the secret passage. Annie whirled around. "Sam?" she screamed. "Sam!"

Jeremy wrapped his hand around her good arm and yanked. "We're going."

"I can't leave. Not without knowing if—"

"Kraken told me to get you out. That's what I'm doing." He pulled her with him. Annie didn't want to go. What if Sam or Reaper had gotten shot? What if they were stuck there in the hallway, praying for help?

"We have to go back," she said, fighting tears and Jeremy.

Crank strode over to them, picked Annie up, and threw her over his shoulder like a sack of potatoes. Annie tried to wiggle off him, but he held her firm as they raced to the purple lily room.

Jeremy followed close behind. "Kraken would kill us if we let you run back there. You didn't see him when you were kidnapped. He'd want you safe first."

"But they could die—" Annie started.

"Kraken and Reaper can take care of themselves," the Warden cut in, an edge of ice to his tone.

Lights flashed, and sounds of commotion wafted up the hallway. "We have seconds," the Warden claimed, throwing open the door. He rushed to the window and yanked on the rope Reaper had connected to the zipline. "We're sliding down. We don't have time for harnesses." Without another word, he placed his hands around the rope and jumped out the window.

Annie gasped. She couldn't believe the Warden did that so easily. Crank set her down by the window. Jeremy gave her a wink before he held onto the rope, weaved the rope over his feet, and slid down. His feet acted like a break, and his hands guided him down the rope.

Annie stepped back. "I can't do that. I'll fall to my death."

Crank put her hand on the rope. "It's easy. Keep the rope to your right side, step on it with your right foot, then let the rope loop between your feet and over your left foot. Hold on tight."

"I can't do that." Annie jumped back from the window. "My wrist is broken, and even if it wasn't, I still couldn't do it."

Crank jabbed his finger toward the window. "Nova, now isn't the time to break under the pressure. If you want to be in this business, you must have these skills, hurt or not."

Annie groaned. "I don't want any part of this business. I never did."

Crank moved around her and put his hands on the window frame. "Look, I can't wait around for you to decide. I'm not getting caught." Without another word, he slid down the rope.

At that moment, the door burst open. Reaper and Sam barreled into the room, looking a little banged up. Sam slammed the door shut and turned the lock. Reaper didn't wait for anything and rushed out the window and down the rope.

"That won't hold them," Sam said, turning toward her. He had purple bruises forming under his eye, his shirt was ripped, and his knuckles were bloody, but he appeared whole.

Annie stood there, frozen in place. "I thought he killed you. I thought you were dead."

"I'm a lot harder to kill than that, Annie. Believe me. I handed Lloyd to Fang. You're safe from him."

"We both are," Annie said, amazed they'd gotten through.

"We can celebrate that we're both breathing later. Right now, we need to get out. The police's SWAT team is already on this floor."

Sam climbed onto the windowsill, but he reached back for her. "Hold on to me tight."

Annie nodded and wrapped her good arm around his shoulder and under his other arm. She couldn't clasp her fingers together, so she gripped her arm above her broken wrist across his heart. Sam wrapped his feet like Crank had explained, and Annie prayed that she wouldn't fall. She gripped her arm tighter and winced in pain.

"Don't let go." Sam pushed off, and they started to slide down the rope. Inches from the ground, her hands gave way, and she tumbled into the shrubbery. Her wrist throbbed, and she gritted her teeth to keep from crying. Loose rocks bit into her arm from the flower bed she'd landed in. Sam landed firmly next to her, a smile on his face. *How could he smile at a time like this?* She brushed off the rocks, and he helped her to her feet.

"Come on. We're not out of the woods yet." Wrapping his hand around her good one, they took off into the man-made forest behind the house. While they ran through the scraggly trees, Sam pulled an earbud out of his pocket and put it into his ear. "Claw, we're all out. Take your team through the study on the third floor to get to ground zero and the evidence. Midnight set the usual code."

They kept a fast pace until they reached the top of the hill where they had ziplined. The Warden and Crank were nowhere to be seen. They must have driven off already. Reaper and Jeremy laughed about something while they dismantled their makeshift zipline. Annie held her heaving chest, her eyebrows scrunched in confusion. Why were they cheerful? They'd lost again, but this time right at the finish line.

"We failed again, Sam. Why is everyone so happy?"

Sam opened the passenger door of the car they'd driven up the mountain and nodded to the inside. With a huff, she slid onto the seat. Sam walked around and climbed in. A moment later, Jeremy got in the back. Without a word, they started down the bumpy pathway. It looked like they didn't want to talk about it. They had trusted her to get the job done; instead, they had to run for their lives again. Annie gingerly tested her wrist; it seared with pain. She held it against her chest in an attempt to lessen the throb.

"Got my spare laptop?" Jeremy asked casually as if nothing untoward had happened at all.

"In the back seat," Sam answered in the same tone, pulling out onto the regular paved road.

Annie looked away from their cheerful faces.

Sam snickered at her. "Annie, we didn't fail."

"What do you mean we didn't fail? We didn't have time to find Benicci's information. We didn't accomplish our goal. We didn't stop Benicci from—" She swallowed hard. All eyes darted to her bracelet containing the deadly taser.

"That's where you're wrong. We got it all," Sam said, giving her a sideways glance. "Hear that, Mr. Benicci?" He raised his voice. "We got it, and if you want it, you'll meet us at Dockweiler State Beach with the key for Annie's infernal bracelet. We are heading there now."

"How?" Annie snapped, her emotions feeling like they were on a teeter-totter.

Sam pulled onto the highway. "Remember when Lloyd had you and me by the door?"

Annie nodded.

"I'd already cracked the safe. What you didn't see is Jeremy when he opened it, slipped inside, and found Benicci's information before he knocked Lloyd over the head with his laptop. Thankfully, Mr. Lichens is extremely organized."

Annie whirled and stared at Jeremy. He winked at her while taking photos of a large stack of papers in the back seat. He held up a finger and shook his head. She took that to mean he didn't want her to talk about what he was doing while Benicci was listening. Annie turned forward and watched as they drove through the traffic toward the dark space that signaled the ocean.

They hadn't failed. She hadn't failed them. A tingle raced up her arms and warmed her heart. She blinked back a few tears. Her plan had worked. They'd done it. She'd helped them successfully pull off the sting or heist—whatever they wanted to name it.

"I can't believe it," she said under her breath.

Sam drove right to the beach and pulled into one of the long rectangular parking lots with a picnic area. He parked under a light, ensuring they didn't meet Benicci in the darkness. "Jeremy, I think it's best for you to stay in the car."

Jeremy nodded. "I'm not arguing with that." He stuffed all the paperwork back into its folder and handed it to Annie. "Don't give it to them until Sam says." He then laid down on the back seat with his laptop open and continued typing.

A couple minutes later, two blue sedans drove up and parked next to them.

Sam looked at her. "We're on, Annie. Let's get that darn thing off your wrist. We're almost done." Sam squeezed her good hand before opening his door. Annie took several long breaths. She held the folder against her chest next to her wounded wrist. She could do this. "One . . . two . . ."

"Three," Jeremy said from the back seat.

Annie's lips twitched, and Sam opened the door.

CHAPTER 31

Sam pulled her door open wide. He took hold of her elbow and helped her out. His eyes were on her curled hand. "After this is over, we'll either go for ice cream or to the ER, your choice."

Annie cracked a smile despite her aching wrist. "ER, please."

He nodded. "Stay behind me."

Together they walked to the front of one of the blue cars. Sam stood with his back straight, so Annie followed suit. Her insides squirmed like they'd suddenly come alive and wanted out.

Mr. Benicci's bodyguards and his son, Antonio, exited the car before Benicci stepped out. He eyed the folder in Annie's hands before he started to clap. "I knew all you needed was some motivation, *donna*. My contraption seems to have worked on both you and your *fidanzato*."

Sam stepped forward, keeping Annie a little behind him. "We have fulfilled our end of the deal, Mr. Benicci. It is your turn."

Mr. Benicci laughed. "Of course, once I ensure that folder isn't full of blank paper." He held out his hand, his fingers curled to indicate that Annie should give him the folder.

Sam shook his head. "I need your guarantee that this atrocious thing will come off her wrist before you trigger her death." Sam pointed to her left arm.

Mr. Benicci's men shuffled their feet, their stance indicating they were ready for a fight. Annie sucked both of her lips in and prayed with all her might that it wouldn't come to that. They were no match for Benicci's men.

"*Fidati di me*, Samuel. I am a man of my word. I never wanted to kill your *amore* unless pressed. My information, if you will." He held out his hand again.

Sam took the slightest step back and nodded at her. "Hand it over."

Annie held out the folder, and Mr. Benicci took hold of it. He flipped through it quickly before handing it back to his son, Antonio.

Mr. Benicci eyed them both before producing a small key from his pocket that looked like it would fit in the lock of the bracelet. "I have half a mind to leave this on . . ." He shrugged. "But a deal is a deal. You captured Lichens and destroyed his blackmailing empire. I am no longer tethered to Mr. Lichens. As I said, I am a man of my word."

He eyed Sam, and Annie could feel the heaviness of those words. Sam stiffened as if he understood the weight behind them. Annie doubted that she wanted to know. Whatever it was, it wasn't good. Mr. Benicci took her arm in his hand. He eyed her opposite swollen wrist. "Looks like it wasn't easy, *donna,*" he said. Annie sucked in a sharp breath as he lightly touched the wrist. "You'd better have that looked at."

Mr. Benicci twisted the key, and with a slight pinch, the heavy black bracelet fell into his hand. Annie retracted her freed arm. "It's too bad, Miss Annie. I enjoyed listening in on your conversations." Annie took a step backward, an uneasiness settling on her.

"Annie, go back to the car, please," Sam said, his eyes still on Mr. Benicci. His tone was severe. Annie didn't need telling twice. She'd count herself lucky if this was the last moment she had to spend in the presence of a man like Mr. Benicci. She rushed back to the car. Jeremy gave her a tiny air fist bump from the back seat after she closed the door.

Sam and Mr. Benicci talked for a few more minutes before they shook hands.

"Wait for it, Annie," Jeremy said.

Wait for what? Annie looked around, half expecting to see Claw or Fang descending on them with a whole team of cops, but no one came. Wasn't the plan to arrest Mr. Benicci as well as Mr. Lichens? Not a single cop car appeared before Sam walked away. Mr. Benicci raised his finger and waved at her, a gleeful look on his face before he turned to his car. Annie's gut churned and twisted until Sam got to the safety of their vehicle.

"Sam?" she asked. He shook his head, and they drove away. Annie looked between him and Jeremy. They acted so calm.

"What just happened?" she snapped a couple of minutes later. "I thought we were going to bring everyone down."

A crooked, real smile spread across Sam's face. "One nice thing about having a hacker in your car and a detective on standby is that the police could hear every bit of our conversation. Jeremy has downloaded all the audio that Benicci recorded from your bracelet. This means we have audio of when he threatened you right after he put it on your wrist and evidence of what he did to you, the fact that he consorted with thieves, his dealings with us, proof of Lichens's blackmailing business, and that he had something more to hide. Unbeknownst to him, he confirmed that what we took from the Lichenses' safe was his. Jeremy spent the last half hour uploading everything in that folder and has already sent it to our police friends. We got him. We got them both."

They passed a police car, and Sam flashed his lights three times. The cop car returned the flash and started toward the beach. "Claw and Fang are a little busy tonight at the Lichenses', but we've sent in a handful of black and whites to scoop up Mr. Benicci tonight." He nodded toward the police car that had turned on its lights. Another police car joined it as they raced toward the beach they'd just vacated.

"There are more cop cars on the other side of the beach parking lot. Mr. Benicci is surrounded. It's over. We won." He laughed. "I can't believe it. I thought for sure this was a lost cause." He turned to her. "You saved us, Annie."

"Woot!" Jeremy shouted from the back seat. "Go, Annie."

They'd won, but somehow, it felt like a loss. She didn't want to hang out the window and scream into the wind that they were free. Her gut still felt knotted up. "Are you sure?"

Sam nodded. "The Warden excels at the wrap-up. I'm sure he and Crank have already gotten started. Right, Jeremy?"

"Yep, they are on the system."

Annie smiled tentatively, still afraid to let the joy sink in. Thank goodness it was all over. "So, what happens now?"

Sam glanced at her quickly before returning his gaze to the road. "That's easy. You get to go home. The target on your back has been eliminated, and Mr. Benicci removed the bracelet. I'm sure your granny can hardly wait for you to return. You get what you wanted all along."

Her gut unclenched a little. She could go home. Annie closed her eyes, imagining the red brick house with the white wraparound porch, the tall evergreen trees around the yard, and Granny's warm hugs. They'd done it. She was free.

"I'm already booking your flight," Jeremy said behind her. "If Claw needs you to testify or anything, she'll let you know."

"You want to get rid of me already?" she teased.

"I could delay it a week or two if you want," Jeremy said, pausing his typing, his gaze darting from her to Sam.

Annie shook her head. As much as she loved Jeremy and Sam, this wasn't her world. This wasn't the kind of life she wanted. "No, it's okay. As you said, Granny's waiting for me."

He clapped a hand on her shoulder and continued working. Annie glanced at Sam to see his jaw tight.

"Is everything okay?" she asked. "Did Mr. Benicci escape or something?"

He gave her one short laugh. "No," he adjusted his earpiece. "They've got him."

"Then what is it?"

He looked at her, a sudden seriousness entering his eyes. "We're going to miss you."

Annie felt her chest contract before a warmth grew inside it. She was going to miss him too, all of them. She never knew people like them existed in real life. "I'll miss you all too."

Sam drove them to the ER. Once inside, Annie tuned out his excuses about their appearance, preferring not to know. After an X-ray, Annie's wrist was set and placed in a temporary cast. Sam had a few cuts stitched up before they were released.

Jeremy found her a flight that left at 8 a.m. It flew from LAX into Salt Lake City with a slight layover until she flew to Idaho Falls, Idaho, where she'd get a rental car to drive the rest of the way home. Exhausted, they decided to stay in Annie's bed-and-breakfast room until she had to leave for the airport.

It took everything she had not to hug them both and cry her thanks. The last thing she wanted right then was to be alone. Annie got the bed, Sam piled pillows on the floor, and Jeremy tucked the ottoman up to the floral chair before he promptly fell asleep with his laptop on his lap.

Sam got some ice from the ice machine and put it in a bag for Annie's wrist, making sure she was settled before he laid down on the floor. Annie doubted she'd fall asleep after a day like today, but with Sam and Jeremy's familiar, steady breathing in the room, she zonked out before she knew it.

Sam shook her awake a couple hours later. "Come on. It's time to go." He had her white suitcase waiting next to the door.

"That isn't mine, remember? It was all for the disguise."

Sam's smile softened. "What are we going to do with clothes that only fit you? Please, take them as a gift."

Annie swallowed hard. She knew they cost a small fortune. "Are you sure? I bet Farica would let you return them if you sweet-talked her a little."

He snorted, shook his head, and pulled her to her feet. "I'd rather you take them. Please?"

Annie nodded, her cheeks warm. "Okay."

Jeremy snored in the chair.

Annie shook her head. He always slept in the oddest positions. "Are you sure we should leave him like that?"

Sam laughed. "He's fine. Come on. We don't want to miss the flight."

Sam drove his Ferrari to LAX. He parked in the visitor parking lot, then pulled a duffle bag out with her suitcase. "It looks better if I have some kind of luggage too."

"Are you coming with me?" Annie asked, barely daring to hope.

"What kind of gentleman would I be if I didn't ensure you made it home safely?" he said, taking the handle of her suitcase from her. "Last time I thought you were safe, a gunman knocked on your door. I want to guarantee all is well for you and your granny."

Annie hardly knew what to say. No one had cared that much about her, ever. "Thank you, but don't you have to report or debrief with Claw or something?"

"Jeremy is tying up the loose ends. I'll meet them later. Right now, you are my priority." He reached forward and tucked a stray strand of her brown hair behind her ear. His fingers slowly caressed her jawline as he dropped his hand. Annie shivered at the warm tingles that rushed through her at his touch. Her breath caught in her throat and her lips upturned at the feeling that simple action ignited in her heart.

Annie couldn't contain her smile, especially when Sam reached for her good hand and wrapped his fingers around hers. Annie breathed what she hoped was a silent sigh of relief. He had no idea how suddenly worried she felt to be alone. Or maybe he did. Who knew? There were a lot of things she didn't know about Sam, but one thing she did know: she trusted him with her life, and if he'd wanted to love her, she would have let him wholeheartedly.

They worked their way through security, Sam only letting go of her fingers if required. Every time he retook her hand, a new thrill rushed through her. Once in their seats on the airplane, Annie again thought he'd let go of her hand. Instead, he only adjusted their hands, lacing his fingers with hers. He didn't complain when she squeezed his hand extra tight at takeoff. She didn't hate planes, but takeoff always caused some worry.

"Thanks for going through all this trouble," Annie said after they were in the air and she didn't have a death grip on his hand anymore.

Sam's smile grew, his real smile, and he let his thumb softly rub the back of her hand. "I knew you were trouble the moment I met you."

Annie faked horror. "What gave you that idea?"

"I don't know. It might have been the garbage-stained clothes, the fact that you were already running for your life, or that you agreed to stay with us . . . with me."

Annie blushed and turned to stare out the window at the ground moving underneath them. She liked very little of her time spent in California. Honestly, she'd probably never return. California might be warm, and palm trees were amazing, but to her, it would always remind her of Dillan, blood, guns, and danger.

The flight was uneventful, unless she counted the odd stares they kept getting. Sam's face had become a bit of a black-and-blue mess. Then there was her wrapped wrist. Who knew what people thought of them?

Sam rented an average Ford car once they reached the Idaho Falls airport. "Much less flashy," Annie said as he held the door for her.

"You know that the Ferrari wasn't mine, right?" he asked once they were on the highway.

"Oh, no." Annie knew he could afford it if he wanted since he funded all his "jobs."

He sighed, "Sadly, I will miss it. I was undercover for six months as Samuel Erickson, the wedding planner. A cover I would happily play again any time."

She laughed. "So, tell me. If your name isn't Samuel Erickson, what is it?"

He looked over at her as if debating whether or not he wanted to answer her. "That would be telling you classified information, Annie. I'm not a secret agent, but I'd also rather you not Google me either."

"Oh." A deep sense of disappointment nestled in her chest. Knowing that Samuel Erickson was a fake name made her feel disconnected from him. It made her question what else was fake.

"What about your first name?" she pressed.

He sighed. "I see no harm in that—since you already know."

She looked at him and frowned. He raised his eyebrows and smiled. "Wait, is it Samuel?"

He smirked. "Yes, Annie."

"So, Erickson was your cover name? Unless we count Kraken."

"I hate to say it, but more people know me as Kraken than Sam. So, you should count yourself one of the blessed few."

"Okay, I can live with that." Annie looked out her window and watched the flat land around her with mountains in the distance, so familiar, yet not as comforting as she thought it would be. Each new landmark made two emotions swirl inside her like a striped straw. Joy at returning home and worry she'd never see Sam again. God wouldn't have put him in her path only to take him away . . . would He?

"Do me one favor, Annie," Sam said after pulling off the highway at her exit. "Okay?"

He wrapped his arm around her shoulder instead of taking her hand. They stopped at a red light, and he turned toward her. "Call me at the first sign of trouble. You shouldn't have any. We removed all your threats, but . . . if anything happens, call me first, okay?"

The rawness of his voice made a warm shiver race up her arms. "You sure you want me to?" she asked, hoping he'd hear her jesting tone. "That will probably mean there's a gunman in my room."

"Then you'd better hope I'm only around the corner." His teasing tone sounded a bit forced, but she was grateful that he tried to lighten the mood like she had. The light turned green.

"Yeah right. Your next job is probably in Tahiti."

He laughed and removed his arm from her shoulders to navigate the small town. A couple minutes later, he pulled onto her street. Annie leaned forward to take it all in. Most of the houses on her street were older, with well-established yards. Few kids lived on her surrounding blocks. Most had grown up and moved away from their little town. She smiled at the green grass and evergreen trees. Even though she technically lived in a dry place, everything looked so bright compared to the yellows and browns of LA.

Her heartbeat pounded harder when he pulled to the curb across the street from her granny's house. It looked the same, but she felt completely different. Hopefully, she would still fit in here.

Sam drummed his fingers against the wheel. "I have a confession to make."

"What kind of confession?" Annie's heart raced at super speed.

"When we succeed at a job, everyone gets paid. So Jeremy will probably hack your bank account." He gave her a tense smile.

Annie's head jerked up. "He will? I mean, you don't have to. I mean, I don't have to get a paycheck. He doesn't have to hack anything."

Sam held up his hands. "There's nothing I can do about it. Jeremy doesn't listen to arguments regarding money and getting it to our team members. He does it his way, and not everyone is paid the in same style, depending on who they are."

"What, don't you trust a check in the mail?" Annie nodded to her granny's bright-yellow mailbox.

"We don't." He unbuckled his seatbelt.

Annie snickered. She'd miss Jeremy almost as much as Sam. "Okay, but you don't have to give me anything."

"I know, but we would have failed without you. I think you deserve some compensation." He reached for his door handle.

"Can you stay for a bit?" she asked, unbuckling her seatbelt.

"I wish. I have a few things to finish with Claw before I can walk away from this sting." He gave her a halfhearted smile before getting out of the car.

Annie let out a slow breath. This was it. Pushing back all her whirling emotions, she got out to see him holding her suitcase. He nodded toward the house, and Annie followed him across the street and up her front walk. "Claw said they'll return Dillan to his family now that the investigation is closing. I thought you'd like to know."

"I'm glad." And she was. She could say a proper goodbye at the funeral.

Sam set her suitcase on the porch and pulled her into a hug. "You are the bravest person I've ever met, Annie Grey. Don't forget that. Take care of yourself and use that money for culinary school or something."

Annie hugged him back, loving the way she felt in his arms, all warm and protected. If only they could freeze time and stay that way.

"Will do," she said, keeping her eyes on the porch steps. She didn't want him to see how bent out of shape she felt at having to say goodbye. He let her go and gave her good hand a quick squeeze before he turned slowly and walked down the porch steps.

A cold shiver rushed through her as a new pain grew in her chest. She rubbed her sternum, but it did nothing to alleviate the growing throbbing that felt worse than heartburn. Only then did she realize this aching wasn't the kind of hurt that could be cured with a rub or even pain meds. This was a more profound soreness, a hurt caused by Sam leaving. This couldn't be the end. Sam couldn't simply walk away and out of her life forever. He would, however, unless she did something about it.

Spinning around, she jumped over her bag on the porch and bounded down the steps. "Sam!"

He turned, and a grin blossomed on his mouth. His real smile. He opened his arms in time to catch her. Without missing a beat, he tipped her chin up. She didn't need any more permission than that. Their lips met in a kiss of equal wanting. His arms held her as tightly as she clung to him. His lips caressed hers in a way that sent a warm shiver through her, chasing out the cold feeling of before. Every cell in her body cheered at the warmth that rushed through her.

If only she could bottle this feeling up and spray it on herself every morning like perfume. His hands moved up her back to tangle in her hair. His kiss said what he could not. He cared about her. She could feel it.

Slowly, he eased back. His hand gently caressed her cheek. Annie jittered and opened her eyes.

"Stay safe and call me if you can?" she said, pushing her hair back behind her ear.

"I will . . . I promise."

Annie smiled at those words. She could always count on a promise from Sam. With one final soft kiss against her lips, he let go of her. Annie watched him walk across the street and get in his less flashy rental car. He waved and drove away without turning to look back.

Annie straightened her stance and strode much more confidently than she felt to the steps of her home. It took everything in her to walk away from the man who held her heart while he disappeared down the street. But as she put her hand on the knob and took one final look behind herself, she noticed something.

A dark-blue sedan with tinted windows started moving from where it had sat a few houses down. It drove slowly past her home in the same direction Sam had driven off, and Annie swore whoever was driving the car looked directly at her.

ABOUT THE AUTHOR

Cassie M. Shiels is a multi-genre author. She was born in Idaho but loves living in southern Utah, where it is warm. As a kid, she was often found reading on the school bus, before she did her homework, and late into the night. (Wait, she still does that!) In middle school, she determined that she loved creating her own stories as much as she enjoyed reading them and decided she'd become an author. Besides writing, she loves crafting, chasing her five kids, and using random things as bookmarks or listening to audiobooks while cleaning the house, as she balances being an avid reader and a mom. She loves writing clean contemporary romance, romantic suspense, and young adult speculative fiction.